THE LUCY GHOSTS

Also by Eddie Shah
RING OF RED ROSES

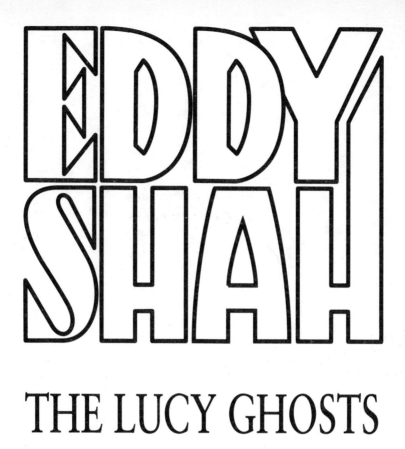

THE LUCY GHOSTS

Doubleday

LONDON · NEW YORK · TORONTO · SYDNEY · AUCKLAND

TRANSWORLD PUBLISHERS LTD
61-63 Uxbridge Road, London W5 5SA

TRANSWORLD PUBLISHERS (AUSTRALIA) PTY LTD
15-23 Helles Avenue, Moorebank, NSW 2170

TRANSWORLD PUBLISHERS (NZ) LTD
3 William Pickering Drive, Albany,
Auckland

Published 1992 by Doubleday
a division of Transworld Publishers Ltd

A catalogue record for this book is available from the British Library.

ISBN 0 385 403003

Typeset in 12/14pt Garamond by
Chippendale Type Ltd, Otley, West Yorkshire.
Printed in Great Britain by
Mackays of Chatham, Plc, Chatham, Kent.

To

Brian Nicholson
who skips the sexy bits

Brian MacArthur
who doesn't

John Harris

and all the people at Messenger who I had
the privilege to stand next to when
our backs were against the wall

Preface

Tegel Airport
West Berlin
12 January 1990

THE PEOPLE OF Germany, driven by the eternal need to be a
united nation once again, had only just torn out the first few
slabs in the Berlin Wall when I flew into Tegel Airport.

The reason for my visit was simple. I had never been to
Berlin and I wanted to see this great concrete barrier, the
definitive symbol of the Cold War.

It was a time of life when I had decided to see the world
for myself instead of through the safe eyes of the television
news camera.

I stayed in East Berlin, drove through the infamous Checkpoint Charlie before it was insignificantly hoisted upwards by
a giant crane and delivered to the oblivion of a museum where
it resides today. It was a time of learning and wonder, I saw
the expectancy of a new era in the faces of those who passed
me, and I was touched by the mushrooming hopes of a new
Europe that seemed to promise peace and prosperity.

Yet there was a brittleness that went beyond the cold of the
January air. I knew the promised land was a long way off, that
the road to freedom would be tortuous and painful, that the
destination we all wanted might never be reached.

But I was privileged and pleased to be there, to be brushed
in those few fleeting moments of my life by history in the
making.

Two instances stood out above the many I experienced.

The first symbolized youth and the relentless drive of enterprise that we take for granted in the West, that is only slowly
being grasped by those in the East.

Like all the tourists who came, I wanted to take back a
small piece of the Wall that was now being torn down. I

have to admit that, even though I had a small hammer and chisel, I actually cheated and bought my concrete chunk of history from a young man who was peddling his wares near Checkpoint Charlie.

Following my capitalistic instincts, I started to negotiate with the young man, not a German, but an Englishman. He was from Manchester (the same town I come from) and was working his way across Europe. Selling sections of the Wall to tourists helped pay for his adventurous sojourn.

It was an odd moment, with Russian soldiers driving past in their Lada cars, the overshadowing watch-towers and barbed wire that had claimed hundreds of lives, and two Englishmen bargaining for a piece of painted concrete that had divided a nation and would now adorn my mantelpiece.

The second instance was more important and gave me the idea that led to this book.

I had flown my own plane, a Citation jet, into Berlin. After my short stay, I returned to the airport and waited for the plane to be refuelled. The refueller was an old German, near to retirement age. As he pumped fuel into my wings, we spoke of Berlin and of the way things were. He told me that, although he was a Berliner, he had never visited East Berlin since the Wall was put up. In that time he had visited America, Africa and Australia. As soon as the Wall came down he had crossed into the East, and now spent most of his weekends driving across East Germany with his wife. In his small Mercedes car, with a picnic hamper in the trunk, he had visited all the major cities, and regaled me with stories of the beauty of Dresden and Leipzig.

'They have not changed,' he said in impeccable English. 'To go there is like going into the past. There are few modern buildings, the Russians never had the money to build, only to waste on defence. Little in the East has changed, it is like it was before the war.'

'I didn't realize that,' I said, eager to share the old man's emotions.

'Oh, yes,' he replied before uttering the words that made the hairs on the back of my neck stand up. 'For them, the 1939 war has only just finished.'

It was the closest I had come to seeing the world through the eyes of a German. The tearing down of the Wall wasn't a step towards world peace, towards a safe future, as the rest of us saw it.

To many Germans, it was simply the end of a fifty-year war.

BOOK ONE

Before Today

Peenemünde
Northern Germany
1945

THEY WERE STILL at Peenemünde, burning the pile of papers, during that last act of attrition, when a V1 doodle-bug rocket was hurled at London, launched from the belly of a Heinkel bomber over the North Sea.

The seven scientists left at Peenemünde knew nothing of this. Nor did they appreciate that for all their efforts to turn the tide of the war back in Germany's favour, no more rockets could be launched because there was no more fuel; the supply had simply dried up.

In truth, their attention was elsewhere. It was directed towards the sounds of gunfire from the Polish border only a few miles to the east. When they saw the first flashes of exploding shells spark across the sky no more than twenty miles from their position, many of them decided to leave the testing site and make their way to Berlin, to the safety of the capital.

They knew the war was over.

If they were to surrender, then it was the Americans to whom they must turn. The Russians were to be avoided at all costs, they were barbarians who would exact a most cruel revenge.

The sky flash visions and nightmare sounds of battle from the east meant the Red Army was getting closer. Peenemünde must be abandoned to its own fate, the rocket test pads and launch structures weren't important any longer.

Before they departed in the last truck, they piled up the secret files they had taken from General Walter Dornberger's offices, doused the paper stack in petrol and set fire to it. Dornberger, the head of the rocket section, had long since left the site and was already surrendering to the Americans with his brightest aide, the twenty-one-year-old Werner Von Braun.

The papers this young group of scientists were burning

13

were not the secret technical data that they had meticulously prepared and worked on these past few years. That had already been taken by the senior officers as insurance for their safety in the hands of the Americans. These documents actually related to the foreign workers imported into Peenemünde. The Poles, the Czechs, the other Slavs . . . and the Jews. It was a slave force, transported in its thousands to this god-forsaken northern peninsula. This place, which was a technical triumph for the Germans, became a death-curse for its workers.

'Get the truck started!' said the senior administrator, a man in his early twenties called Grob Mitzer.

One of the others, the most junior of the scientists, rushed over to the truck and started the engine. He watched the remainder of the group through the side window. They all stood around the blazing fire, some still throwing piles of documents on the pyre, others mesmerized by the leaping flames that were the final reminder of their failure.

'Damn the politicians!' said Mitzer.

'Damn Hitler!' said the scientist next to him, Heinrich Trimmler-Spiedal.

'No. It wasn't him, Heinrich. He did what was right for Germany. It was the others. Those who were not equal to him who let him down. The politicians and the generals. The clever arses. That fat pig Goering and his kind. Those bastards let him down.'

'He's right, Heinrich. They let him down.' Albert Goodenache now joined the discussion. 'Christ, they're all running for cover now. Did you hear that Martin Bormann was seen just over the border with Russian soldiers?'

'When?' asked Trimmler-Spiedal.

'The other day. You remember that group of nurses that came through on their way to Rostock?'

Trimmler-Spiedal nodded.

'One of them saw him. Some general's daughter. She'd met him before.'

'She said it was Bormann?'

'So she said. And he wasn't even under guard. Just sat in the back of some staff car on his way east.'

'I don't believe it.'

14

'I'm just telling you what she said.'

'The big wigs are OK. All looking after themselves. But what do *we* do now?'

'Start again,' said the administrator. That was Grob Mitzer's duty and his strength. At twenty-one he was the architect of order amongst the unbridled enthusiasm of the young rocket scientists. His nature was to close one file and immediately open another. 'As we did after the Great War. Like the Führer said, this is a thousand-year war, that's all. Never forget.'

A sudden burst of gunfire in the distance brought them back to reality.

'Time to go,' said Mitzer. He turned and shouted at the others. 'Come on, everybody. Into the truck. Before it's too late. Albert, Heinrich, get in the front with me.'

The group, startled by the ferocity of the latest explosions, moved towards the truck, their faces lit up by the blazing fire and the redness of the erupting sky.

'That's near Swinoujście,' shouted one of the group to no-one in particular. 'They must have crossed the border.'

'Come on, come on,' urged Mitzer. 'Let's get going.'

He followed the group of hurrying scientists and stood behind them as they climbed into the back of the truck, an unmarked grey army vehicle which had been used for transporting the work force to the site from their huts on the other side of the sand dunes. There were no seats, only a slatted wooden floor. The scientists held themselves upright on the bowed metal crossbars that had supported a canvas tarpaulin long since lost.

When the last of the group had climbed aboard, Mitzer swung the tailgate up and locked it into position with a metal latch.

'Hang on tight,' he shouted. 'It's going to be a bumpy ride.' He ran round to the front and opened the driver's door, surprising the young scientist he had sent on ahead to start the engine. Albert Goodenache and Heinrich Trimmler-Spiedal sat jammed together on the passenger side of the short wooden bench seat that stretched across the cab. 'In the back,' he shouted at the driver. 'Join the others. I'll drive. I know the way.'

The man tried to protest, but Mitzer reached up and pulled him out of the cab. He sprawled in the wet mud. As he began to pick himself up there was a piercing, shrilling sound followed by a booming explosion from what seemed only a few hundred metres away.

'Hurry up, or you'll get us all killed,' yelled Mitzer, putting his hand out to help the fallen scientist. 'Come on, come on.'

The scientist scrambled through the mud to the rear of the truck as Mitzer climbed into the cab and slammed the door. The engine screamed as he poured on the power, but nothing happened.

'Damn and shit!' cried Mitzer.

'What's wrong?' asked a frightened Albert Goodenache.

'We're too heavy. Too much mud. Too much bloody mud.'

Mitzer took his foot off the accelerator, swung the door open and climbed out into the mud. He rushed round to the rear of the truck.

'Everybody out,' he shouted as he unlatched the tailgate and swung it down. 'It's too heavy in the mud. You'll have to push.' The scientists stood there; they were men of reason and considered logic, not an instinctive breed by nature. 'Come on, get out. Do you want us all killed?' He climbed up on to the back and started to push them out; most fell into the mud. Then he leapt down among them and helped them to their feet. 'Push, damn you. Get behind and push. Come on, we only need to get out of this mud, then we'll be on our way. Hurry, hurry!'

He rushed back to the cab and jumped in, put the truck back into gear and gently fed power to the engine.

'Shall we help?' shouted Trimmler-Spiedal.

'No, stay where you are,' replied Mitzer.

'But . . .'

'Do as you're bloody told,' he ordered, then leant out of the cab and shouted back at the group. 'Push, damn you, push. Push for everything you're worth.'

The shrilling distant sound came again, low to start with, then building in its intensity until it exploded on the sand dunes near the experimental rocket launch tracks. As the shell deafened them, so the truck, having been rocked backwards and forwards by the small group, finally broke loose of its

16

slippery hold and shot forward. The pushers collapsed as they lost their grip.

Another shell exploded near by.

'Stop!' shouted Trimmler-Spiedal. 'Wait for the others.'

Mitzer kept his foot rammed to the floor, not wanting to lose momentum, not wanting to be clawed back into the wet soft earth under the vehicle.

Thirty metres farther on he drove on to the road and safety.

He stopped the truck to wait for the others.

At that moment Albert Goodenache saw the silhouette of a Russian soldier rise into view across the sand dunes. Before he could shout a warning, the soldier opened fire on the small group.

Mitzer heard the scientists calling, screaming for him to wait as they scrambled out of the mud. He also heard a bullet ricochet off one of the metal crossbars at the rear. He put his foot down and drove away. The shouts of those left behind disappeared as the sounds of war enveloped them.

The three of them never looked back at Peenemünde, the place that was to have been their shrine. The two scientists said nothing. Like Mitzer, they had not been prepared to help their comrades. They had nothing to say. They couldn't face their own cowardice.

After five minutes, Mitzer stopped to check the petrol cans tied to the back of the cab. There were four of them, containing nearly one hundred and twenty litres in total, enough to get them to Berlin. He looked back at where the explosions were, knew he could outrun the Russians as long as the truck kept going. He hoped the others were safe, not gunned down by some ill-educated, ferocious Russian soldier. He climbed back into the truck and, without a single glance or comment to his two companions, drove off towards Wolgast and the road to Berlin.

'We should go west, not south,' said Albert Goodenache after they had been travelling for nearly half an hour.

'Why?' asked Mitzer.

'Because Berlin will be lost to the Russians. If not today, then tomorrow. Peenemünde is directly north of Berlin. All their effort will be directed there. Go west, towards the Americans and the British. They're not the barbarians, the Russians are.'

'All right. We'll follow the country roads towards Hamburg. Do you agree, Heinrich?'

The young scientist nodded. He wanted only to get back to his bride of four months, Trudi, who waited for him in Düsseldorf; to hide with her and avoid the questions that would be asked of him, of his Nazi Party membership, of his treatment of the workers he had controlled at Nordhausen and Peenemünde, of what he saw as expediency and others would see as evil.

They drove on, through the villages of Jarmen and Demmin and the town of Güstrow. They saw few people, mostly straggling refugees who, like them, were escaping the oncoming Russian army. One group tried to stop them but Mitzer kept his foot down and almost ran them over. They skirted Güstrow and followed the road to Schwerin.

The sounds of war were far behind them now, but visions of defeat became clear as dawn broke. The isolated groups of refugees they had passed in the dark swelled as the morning light flooded the countryside. These people had slept in the hedges and ditches for protection against the night's cold and were now striking out for the last leg towards the safety of the Western Allies. The country roads were filled with an army of homeless people, a sad pitiful line of Germans moving west. Many pulled handcarts piled high with their belongings, but most carried whatever they felt was worthwhile on their backs. It was a pathetic sight, a people beaten into submission, now trying to salvage whatever they could from the days when they had arrogantly set out to conquer the world. There were children everywhere, many struggling to keep up with their parents, many crying for food. A shabby, shuffling line stretching to the horizon.

The truck had slowed to a crawl. Mitzer kept his hand on the horn, but it had little effect on the fleeing mass. He edged the vehicle forward, making slow progress through the crowds.

Those farms and houses along the route which had been abandoned were now being looted by small gangs of armed soldiers who had deserted their units to escape to the West.

18

Others, who had decided to remain behind and take their chances with the Russians, had boarded up their homes as a defence against the looters. Some had even taken their livestock into their houses and now guarded their properties with guns and pitchforks. There were occasional flurries of shooting between these groups, but no serious attempts were made on the fortified dwellings as the main concern of all the deserters was to escape the oncoming Red Army.

A few individuals tried to jump on the back of the truck, and some succeeded. As they progressed along the route over twenty people climbed on to the rear. It caused Mitzer little concern as they were on a hard asphalt road and the vehicle could cope with the extra load. What he didn't want to do was open the doors and invite an attack on them. In this case discretion was definitely the better part of valour.

The sights they witnessed were a constant reminder of their own vulnerability. Images of greed and despair, of fear and degradation: the man with his middle fingers sliced off by a fellow traveller who had wanted his gold rings; the old woman, who had died in the cold of night bundled up against the hedge, naked after she had been stripped of all her clothing by others intent on keeping warm; the children, crying and hungry; the parents who could do nothing about it; two men fighting over the carcass of a dead pet dog, hardly able to lift their arms and strike each other in their weakness; the eighteen-year-old mother by the side of the road trying to feed her baby from breasts in which the milk had long dried up, her baby who had already been dead for hours, had surrendered to the cold of the night. They saw the eyes of a lost nation; and in their fear they saw themselves, and realized how lost they had all become.

This was Germany turning on herself, cutting her own throat in the face of oncoming defeat.

They were on the outskirts of the village of Crivitz, some fifty kilometres from what was to become the border between a divided East and West Germany, when things started to go horribly wrong.

The sixteen-year-old girl had already been raped when they came upon her. She was crawling into the hedgerow, trying to hide her shame from the passers-by, most of whom weren't interested in her plight. The thorns and thick branches of the hedge cut into her flesh, but she felt nothing except the need to go to ground and lock herself into her own privacy. Her clothes had been torn from her body and now lay scattered between the road and the hedge. A woman had already picked up her coat and run away, another was now darting in to grab her shoes before the girl could recover.

The men, five foot-soldiers wearing *Wehrmacht* uniforms, were sitting near by, the effort of their exertions taking its toll on their strength. They were unshaven, unwashed, desperate men. Life had become cheap on the Russian front and, hardened veterans that they were, they had decided to take whatever they wanted in their anger and frustration against those who had led them to war.

The girl, beautiful and fulsome in her youth, had simply been something that stood in their way, something they decided they wanted. They had just walked up to her, dragged her away from her father and pulled her to the ground by the side of the road in front of everyone. It was their way of showing they didn't care.

The eldest soldier, a sergeant, had knocked the father to the ground with his rifle-butt when he tried to stop them attacking his daughter. When he rose to his feet again and stumbled forward to help her as she screamed, the sergeant pulled back his rifle and bayoneted him through his stomach.

The girl stopped screaming as she watched her father fall, saw the bayonet slip out of his flesh as easily as a knife out of butter. She shut her eyes and let the men claw at her, one by one. When they had finished, and only when she felt they had finally lost interest in her, did she pull herself up on her elbows and drag herself backwards into the protection of the hedge.

That was the moment the truck came down the road.

'For God's sake!' shouted Albert Goodenache. 'That poor girl. I just don't believe it.'

'There's nothing we can do,' replied Mitzer. 'Nothing.'

'You've got to stop!'

'No.'

'We can't just ignore what's going on around us. Stop, for God's sake!'

'No. We're only three. We can't save the whole of Germany.

Shit, we're having enough trouble saving ourselves.'

'Fuck you, Grob. You must stop. Tell him, Heinrich.'

The other scientist said nothing, kept his head lowered. He just wanted to get home.

'Grob, for Christ's sake. Stop and help. Just give her a lift.' Albert Goodenache turned back to Mitzer.

'Shit, Albert,' shouted Mitzer, slamming his foot on the brake and pulling the truck up sharply. 'Shit, man, you're always trying to save the fucking world.'

'Well?' asked Albert Goodenache. 'Well?'

'Get her in here. Quick. Hurry up.'

Goodenache unlocked his door, swung it open and jumped out.

'Close that door!' Mitzer shouted at Trimmler-Spiedal. 'We don't want anyone else getting in.'

Heinrich leant over and pulled the door shut as Goodenache reached the girl. They watched him talk to the girl and try to bring her out from the hedge. The girl, in too great a state of shock to understand Goodenache's good intentions, fought against him and started to scream. The harder he pulled her, the louder she screamed.

One of the soldiers, attracted by the commotion, shouted at Goodenache, 'Leave her, bastard. Find your own tarts.'

'Come on, Albert,' yelled Mitzer. 'Leave her.'

But Goodenache persevered. He shouted back at the soldier, but his words were lost in the loudness of her screams. The soldier stood up, pointed his rifle at Goodenache and shot him in the left knee.

'Shit, shit!' cursed Mitzer, as he watched Goodenache roll away from the girl, clutching his shattered knee and screaming in pain. He put the truck into gear.

'No!' shouted Heinrich Trimmler-Spiedal.

'They'll kill us. They'll kill us all. It's too late.'

The other soldiers had now come to their feet. Before the truck could gather momentum, the sergeant had run across the road and jumped on the running board, his rifle pointing through the closed window at Mitzer.

Mitzer stamped on the brake once again and stopped the truck.

'Get out,' ordered the sergeant. 'Get out now.'

21

'Do as he says,' said a defeated Mitzer to Trimmler-Spiedal. 'Easy. These men have itchy fingers.'

The two men climbed out of the truck as the sergeant called to the others.

'Come on. Get in. Come on, hurry. And get that rabble off the back.'

One of the men grabbed the girl and tried to pull her out of the hedgerow.

'Leave her!' ordered the sergeant. 'Unless you want to stay behind and fight the fucking Russians on your own.'

The soldier cursed, gave her one last hefty kick with his boot and rushed towards the truck as the others cleared the other passengers off the rear. The sergeant and one of the soldiers climbed in the cab, the others on to the back.

As they drove off, the sergeant waved cheekily at Mitzer and Trimmler-Spiedal. The administrator turned away and walked towards Goodenache who was still clutching his knee and screaming with pain.

'Let me see,' said Mitzer, kneeling down and examining Goodenache's knee. 'Jesus Christ, what a mess.'

Heinrich Trimmler-Spiedal stayed at a distance, watching Goodenache take control of himself while Mitzer nursed him. The bullet had passed right through his leg, but shattered the knee. It was a pulpy, fleshy mess, and Mitzer set about bandaging it with the remnants of Goodenache's trouser leg and sleeves off his own coat.

'We need a doctor,' said Mitzer. 'Someone who can stop this bleeding.'

Trimmler-Spiedal took off the scarf that was wrapped round his neck and gave it to Mitzer. 'Use that for a tourniquet,' he said.

Mitzer applied it to Goodenache's thigh and, with a broken branch, turned it tight until the bleeding eased off.

'You're going to have to walk with us,' said Mitzer. 'Lean on us. Between us. Can you manage that?'

'I'm sorry,' replied Goodenache. 'I was only trying . . . '

'I know. To help.' Mitzer looked up to where the girl had been, but she had scrambled away by now, had run down the road, her dead father and the terrible ordeal behind her. In her

22

panic she was running east, back from where she had come and straight towards the Russian troops. He shook his head. God knows what they would do when they stumbled on the half-naked girl. Shit, what a mess. 'Forget it. Can you walk?'

'I don't know.'

'Come on. We'll give you a hand.'

They helped Goodenache to his feet, supporting him between them, while he held on to the tourniquet. In this slow and painful fashion they continued their journey to safety.

Just before night fell, when they had only managed to complete another six agonizing kilometres, they heard gunfire to the south. It was the Russians, having entered Berlin, sending their troops north to mop up any resistance in that area.

'You'll have to leave me,' said Goodenache, voicing what they all knew to be the only course of action.

'No,' said Mitzer. 'We've come this far together. We've been friends too long to split up now.' He wondered if they believed him. He knew he was lying.

'At this rate it'll take us three weeks to get to the Americans or the British. And we don't know if they're any better than the Russians. Look, I caused this. If I hadn't tried to . . . we'd have been there by now.'

'We can make it,' said Trimmler-Spiedal. 'If we go through the night.'

'Stop dreaming. He's right,' interjected Mitzer. 'And he'll bleed to death if we keep walking. He needs medical attention.'

'Go on. I'll be all right. I will,' said Goodenache. 'Put me down and get going. Before it's too late for all of us.'

They helped him down, let him sit with his back against a cedar tree.

There was so much to say, but little that could be said. They had known each other for more than six years and had worked closely as a team on the rockets and other weaponry projects. They hadn't seen war through the eyes of the soldier, death was something you read about. War to them was a state of being, somewhere they practised their arts without seeing the fruits of their results. War was no more than a laboratory, where success wasn't a nation's victory, but a scientist's achievement. They knew they had failed, their rockets had been too late and too futile to change the final destiny of the war.

The whole thing was so bloody useless now.

'If the Russians get to you first,' said Mitzer, 'tell them that you're a scientist.'

'Why?' asked Albert Goodenache.

'Because they'll want your experience.'

'I can't work for them.'

'We'll all be working for someone else now.'

'But the Russians . . . ?'

'Wait and see. It might even be the Americans first,' lied Mitzer. 'Look, when someone finds you, then you must ask for an officer. Say it's important, a matter of life and death. When you speak to the officer, tell him who you are, that you worked on the rockets. Tell him you must speak to his superiors. You must tell them that, Albert.'

There was no answer from Goodenache as the awful realization of his predicament sank in. He leant against the tree, twisting the tourniquet above the shattered knee. None of them asked each other what his chances were. It was a slim thread that kept him alive, he might either bleed to death or be killed by a passing looter or invading Russian.

'Whatever happens,' Mitzer attempted to raise his friend's spirit, 'we must never forget we are comrades. Let's not forget the past, especially the failures. We must be one. Let us not forget that. They will destroy our Germany. Just like they've tried to do before. But we must wait, and believe, and work towards becoming one again. Don't lose the dream. Believe in that, believe it with all your heart, always remember it, and one day . . . all this . . . shambles . . . will be just a bad memory.'

Mitzer held out his hand to Goodenache, who reached up and took it.

'To the day we meet again,' he said.

'And if we want to communicate? If we are to be friends at a distance? If we are found on opposite sides? Then how do we talk?'

'*Die Lucie Geister*. That must be our password,' said Mitzer after a long pause. And then he told them of the Lucy Ghosts, what they had been and what they would become. When he

24

had finished, the others nodded. The Lucy Ghosts would be the password to their future.

Two days later Mitzer and Trimmler-Spiedal stumbled on an American unit at the town of Marienstadt and were taken to a senior officer who arranged to transport them in an army Jeep some fifty kilometres to Hamburg.

After a series of interrogations and interviews, it was decided that Heinrich Trimmler-Spiedal would join the eighty-nine other Peenemünde rocket scientists who went to America under the leadership of Werner Von Braun. This same team, the most experienced and integrated of rocket scientists in the world, were to spearhead the drive that would result in America putting the first man on the moon twenty-four years later.

Grob Mitzer, the administrator, was to remain in Europe and use his exceptional organizational skills to build one of the most successful electronics corporations in the new West Germany, a cornerstone of the economic miracle that would revitalize that country.

It would be a long time before they found out what had become of the scientist Albert Goodenache.

Two days after Trimmler-Spiedal and Mitzer were driven to Hamburg, the Russians rolled into the eastern outskirts of Marienstadt. The border they established was to split Germany for the next forty-five years.

BOOK TWO

Today and Tomorrow

Riumen
Finland
The Present

SANTA CLAUS LEANT against the sled and took a last deep draw on his cigarette before dropping it in the snow and stamping on it with his boot.

Next to him, the old reindeer waited patiently, trapped by the harness that was attached to the heavy sled that it would soon be urged to pull out from its crystal-flaked hiding-place in the trees.

The man in the red suit and padded stomach looked at his watch; it was time for another show. The snow was starting to fall again and he was impatient to get things done. He stood up, took the white flowing beard from the sled and put it over his chin, hooking the wire strands behind his ears to hold it in place.

In the distance he heard the excited shrieks of the children, now waiting on the balcony of the wooden-structured restaurant for him to make his appearance.

He sighed, already bored with the show that was to follow, dreading the rush of the shrieking youngsters towards the sled as soon as he appeared. It was his twentieth performance in ten days, part of an annual ritual for more than forty years that helped keep the Spirit of Christmas alive in that far northern area known as Lapland, the home of Santa Claus.

'And now, the moment we have all been waiting for . . . ' a woman's voice boomed, metallic in its resonance over the loudspeakers hanging from the trees.

Santa moved alongside the reindeer, took the leather reins in his right hand as he held the animal by its wide antlers to keep it from moving forward and spoiling their staged entrance. He could sense the excitement and anticipation, knew the children would be straining over the balcony for the first glimpse of Santa.

The reindeer was also an old hand at the game. Patient, as the breed are, he waited for his handler to push him forward and into the path of the bright lights that had snapped on, illuminating the area as if it were day.

'. . . the moment that Santa and his elves work all the year round for, to bring toys and gifts to the children of the world.'

The reindeer felt Santa's hand slip from his antlers, felt the reins relax and fall free around his neck.

'Yes, the real reason you have all come here, all the way to Lapland, to Father Christmas's home . . .'

There was a thud as something fell heavily into the sled, but the reindeer ignored it, knew it was almost time to go.

'. . . from faraway places, here is Father Christmas, just to see you.'

The animal leant forward, strained to start moving, knew they must go forward in the silence that always followed the loud voice that came from nowhere.

But the reins were slack, the hand that always prodded the antlers missing.

The old reindeer stepped forward – it was an instinctive reaction – out into the brightness of the floodlights and away from the protection of the spruce trees.

A sharp-eyed, six-year-old boy from Ayr in Scotland saw the reindeer first. It stepped from behind the trees and into the brightly lit opening in front of the restaurant chalet.

'Mum. Mum, there's Santa! Look, look, it's Santa,' he cried excitedly, pulling at his mother's arm as she stood protectively behind him.

'I can see, I can see,' she replied.

By now the rest of the group had seen the reindeer pulling the sled across the snow with the red and rounded Santa Claus sitting in the back, a sack of toys across his knees.

The children were shouting loudly, waving at Santa, calling for him to wave back.

Snow began to fall, glistening across the floodlights.

The reindeer reached the centre of the clearing, stopped instinctively without waiting for the tug on the reins that always came at this point. He and his master had done this short journey many times over the years.

'Children,' came the voice over the loudspeaker. 'You can go down in the snow and meet Father Christmas. Go on, children, go and help Father Christmas come up to the restaurant.'

Some of the children broke from the group and ran down the gentle incline towards the sled. Others, nervous in their excitement, urged their parents to accompany them.

The six-year-old boy from Ayr was the first to reach it, his mother not far behind. He climbed up with outstretched arms to hug the red-coated figure who sat there, the sack of toys now fallen open across his knees. The child's sharp and sudden movement sent Father Christmas sprawling sideways over the edge of the sled. As his head twisted backwards, the white beard fell to the snow. The boy's mother, realizing that Santa was dead, screamed.

Before she could grab the boy, the reindeer, frightened by her shrill cry, jerked forward and galloped through the crowd that now surrounded him. Behind him, the child held on, still not knowing what was wrong, still eager to be with Santa Claus.

As the reindeer rushed forward, the mother screamed even louder and longer, panicking the reindeer even further.

No-one was hurt by the animal as it pushed through the small group, its swinging antlers well above the height of most of the children.

One of the men raced behind the sled and took hold of the reins that were sliding through the snow. He pulled the animal to a halt some twenty yards further on. When the Christmas tableau had finally come to rest he turned and lifted the boy out of the sled.

'I saw Santa, I saw Santa,' said the excited boy to his mother. 'He took me for a ride.'

The officials from the Christmas party had now reached the group and were marshalling them, hurrying them back to the restaurant. One of them, an elderly man who was the car-park attendant, stood in front of the reindeer and stroked its muzzle to calm it. As he did so, he looked over the animal's head into the sled, at the slumped figure of Father Christmas.

He saw the red coat had fallen open.

He saw the spread of blood and turned away, sickened.

When the police came half an hour later there was nothing for them. The deep footsteps that led away from the small wooded patch where the man and his reindeer had first waited had been covered by falling snow.

The only clue was the deep knife wound that had sliced through Father Christmas's heart.

CIA HQ
Langley
Virginia
USA

AT MIDNIGHT, THE phone that never rang suddenly shrilled across the European communications room.

The clerk on duty, startled by the unfamiliar alarm, leapt back from the computer terminal where he was indexing yesterday's Wall Street prices and hurried across the big room.

In the far corner sat a myriad of telephones linked directly to various towns, cities and embassies in Western and Eastern Europe.

They were the emergency lines in the old days of the Cold War. Since then, even years before the Cold War had finally thawed and been overtaken by the Gulf Crisis and all the other troubles, communication by phone had been superseded by satellites, micro systems, faxes and more modern systems. But Intelligence Services were hoarders by instinct. The phones had only remained because the CIA had a jackdaw-like appetite for keeping all lines of communication open.

And when one rang, it meant someone was in trouble.

The clerk, an underpaid, computer-systems man who spent most of his time researching the secret information that the CIA collected on Wall Street companies so that he could play the markets with the few dollars he managed to save from his salary, searched the phones to see which one was ringing.

It took time, over a minute, before he identified the correct one.

'Yes?' he said breathlessly into the receiver. He didn't know what else to say. Answering these phones was not part of his training.

'Washington?' came the hushed reply, a woman's voice, sing-songy and foreign.

'Yes.' He had no idea where the call came from.

'America?'

'Of course . . . ' He tried not to show his irritation. 'Yes.'

'CIA?'

'Yes.' Who the hell was ringing if they didn't know they were connected to Langley. 'Who is this?'

'I was told to ring if anything happened,' the woman said. 'He gave me an envelope, to be opened if anything happened.'

'Where are you ringing from?'

'Rovaniemi.'

'Where?'

'From Rovaniemi. In the letter, it says if anything happens I am to ring this telephone number and say, "Reindeer is dead".'

' "Reindeer is dead?" '

'Yes. "Reindeer is dead".' That's all she knew, her husband's life had been his own. She paused before she went on. 'Will I still get the money?'

His instinct was to hang up, but he knew these phones were connected to the past. It was time to pass the buck upstairs.

'Wait,' he said. 'I will get someone more senior to talk to you. Don't hang up. Don't go away.'

He put the receiver down and hurried back to his terminal. He switched the programme out of the Wall Street file before he dialled the senior night officer. There was no way he wanted to be fired from the service for insider dealing. The pay wasn't great, but it was steady.

'Phil Tucker,' came the immediate response from upstairs.

'Phil, it's Greg in the European room. I've got a call on one of those direct lines.'

'What direct lines?'

'The old ones. The ones we keep for back-up.'

33

There was a pause. 'You're *kidding*? Who?'

'I don't know. A woman. Foreign.'

'What does she want?'

'Says she's been told to report in.'

'Who by?'

'Don't know. Just says, "Reindeer is dead".'

'Reindeer?'

'That's it.'

'Is that an open code?'

'Haven't checked the book yet.' He didn't add he didn't know which cypher manual to check.

'Fuck it, I'm coming down. Who the hell's Reindeer?'

Before the clerk could answer, the phone went dead in his hand. As he waited, he remembered it had been Kuwait's invasion by the Iraqis that had been triggered off by these phones. He hoped this wasn't going to be the start of another such crisis. Only this time it was Europe. It had to be the Russians. 'Damn it,' he thought, 'the Cold War's over.' Then he grinned. Crisis meant falling stocks. He decided to ring his broker first thing in the morning and sell before this leaked out and prices started to tumble.

Across the room, at the other end of the phone, Mrs Santa Claus waited patiently to find out if the death of her husband a few hours earlier also meant the death of her housekeeping money. Times were hard and she hoped those nice Americans would go on sending the dollars that her husband used to pick up in a plain envelope once a month at the local Post Office. She had no-one left now. No-one except the nice Americans who had looked after her husband and, she was sure, would now look after her.

As she waited, she also wondered who Reindeer was.

The Royal Bistro
Goose Bay
Canada

HANS PUTILOFF SIPPED his decaf and wondered how he was going to get into Room 17 before its occupant, a senior officer in the German *Luftwaffe*, returned from the Goose Bay air base.

Ever since the Germans had built a new hangar for their NATO exercise aircraft at Goose Bay, the Royal Inn Hotel had become the centre for their off-duty pleasures. Visiting aircrews tended to stay there before they were billeted on the base. It was an ideal situation for someone who wanted to pick up loose talk among servicemen.

Goose Bay, a small township on the inhospitable east coast of Labrador, is one of the West's most strategic air bases. With two long runways, it is the centre for NATO exercises and houses large British, German and other NATO contingencies in addition to the Royal Canadian Air Force. Under snow for nearly five months of the year, it is also a safe haven and staging post for the many small private aircraft that are ferried across the North Atlantic on their way to and from Europe.

The town's economy is based on the airport and its three hotels are usually fully booked. Two of them, the Labrador Inn and the Royal Inn, are wooden structures with blockboard partitions between the rooms. Privacy is not one of the luxuries afforded guests in these three-star outback hotels.

But, as Hans Putiloff often said, one man's misery was another's reward. Now approaching his sixty-ninth birthday, he had, to all intents and purposes, come to Canada as an immigrant from East Germany in 1956. Of German origin, he had adopted the identity of a dead Polish sailor called Lalek Widowski, and had thus, with the appropriate forged documents, escaped from East Germany and into Western Europe. In those days, before the Berlin Wall split the continent, it was an easy escape route for those who were prepared to take it. It hadn't taken him long to work his passage across to Canada, where he eventually applied for an immigrant's permit. Five years later, he swore allegiance to the Canadian flag and became a citizen. He changed his name to Lou Widders and began work as a refueller for Shell Aviation Services at the civil terminal at Goose Bay Airport. In time, when his foreign accent had been replaced by Canadian clip talk, people forgot about his Polish background and his European ancestry.

To them Lou Widders was a Canadian. Which would have pleased his Russian masters in what had been the GRU (the Fourth Department of the General Staff of the Red Army formed by Trotsky after the Russian Revolution) and become in more recent years, the KGB. It had been there, in Moscow, at the KGB Headquarters in 2 Dzerzhinsky Square, that the young Hans had been scrupulously trained to prepare for his future role as a Canadian citizen. Hans Putiloff, who became Lalek Widowski, now residing as Lou Widders, was one of the great sea of unknown spies planted across the Western world as 'sleepers', those who integrated into local communities and waited to be called one day to exercise their duties by Moscow.

It had been a long wait. And now, in this time of *perestroika*, it was unlikely that the call would ever be made.

But that didn't worry Lou Widders. He was one of a rare breed, a conscientious, workaholic spy. He did it because he loved it. Even the thought of returning to a unified Germany had not excited him after all these years. But then, there was always that other past which had been wiped clean by his Russian masters all those years ago. Dachau. The little town near Munich. A place of death where birds still never sang. It had been Hans Putiloff's playing fields, a playground where he had exercised his pleasure on those unfortunate inmates who were placed under his care. When he saw the war coming to an end, he escaped to the East. His instincts told him that the Russians would appreciate his talent for cruelty; what he hadn't expected was to be sent out to Canada and simply cease to exist.

36

He was over-zealous in his duties. Rather than wait for his orders, commands he knew might never be made, he had, over the years, set about building up a most comprehensive file on Goose Bay, its airport, visiting aircraft and crews and improving weapons systems. These files, handwritten for the first thirty years, were now totally inscribed on two 180 megabyte hard discs that were linked to his Apple Mac 11 personal computer. It was a record that his control in 2 Dzerzhinsky Square would dearly have loved to have seen, if only they had contacted him.

But the only contact was a member of the Russian diplomatic staff whose annual holiday always coincided with Hans' in Niagara Falls. The meetings were brief, the contact simply checked that Hans was well and out of trouble. The next was scheduled for the following Tuesday.

With this in mind, and eager for more information, Hans waited for the moment when he could go into Room 17 and see if the German officer had left anything that would be a valuable addition to his data base. He smiled as he sipped his decaf. The thin walls at the Royal Inn and the Labrador Inn were to his advantage. He had often slid into an empty room next to someone he was spying on and listened through the blockboard to secret conversations. There had been surprises over the years. The happily married station commander with a penchant for young men, the visiting diplomat who had waited to be beaten in his room by a black French airman, the cypher clerk who dealt in narcotics. These, and many more, were the daily paraphernalia that filled his computer file.

'Everything all right, Lou?' said the plump young girl behind the counter, her bulk shapeless under the large knitted sweater that would have kept two lumberjacks warm on a snowdriven night.

'Fine,' he said, nodding warmly back at her.

'Another coffee?'

'No. Time to go.'

He stood up, took out a paper dollar from his pocket and left it on the table, wrapped his thick anorak with the Shell logo emblazoned on the back around himself and prepared to leave the warmth of the small restaurant that fronted the hotel.

'See ya, Lou.'

'See ya.'

He opened the door and stepped out into the night, the air bitter and cold, a minus 20° chill factor.

He looked towards Room 17, motel-style with its door opening on to the wooden board-walk. There was no light on inside, nor in the room next door. When he was satisfied that he wasn't being watched, he drew out the master key he had stolen many years earlier and walked towards the door.

On reaching Room 17, he listened, heard nothing. He knocked softly, waited until he was sure that no-one answered, that he had given ample time for a sleeping man to awaken, then put the master key in the lock and pushed the door open.

He was about to slide into the room when the stranger spoke.

'Excuse me?' said the man's voice.

Hans swung round, surprised to see a tall man in an overcoat standing next to him, on the step of the now-open door of Room 16.

'What d'ya want?' Hans asked, impatient, yet hushed so as not to attract any passing attention.

The man said nothing, simply held out a rolled-up newspaper towards Hans.

'What d'ya want?' repeated Hans, made nervous by the man's unexpected action.

'Have you read the news today?' came the muffled reply, East European in its dialect.

'What news?'

'You made the headlines, comrade. Hans Putiloff has passed away.'

Before Hans could react, the stranger pushed the rolled-up newspaper towards him, to within one foot of his nose, and jerked it sharply. There was a soft pop followed by the sound of tinkling, breaking glass.

Hans Putiloff, the conscientious spy, inhaled the deadly vapour of the Stashinsky gun and fell dead to the snow-covered board-walk. Sharp and swift. No time to scream, no blood, no tell-tale mark of death.

His assassin, within a matter of seconds, had picked up his victim's now-lifeless body and rolled it into Room 17. He closed the door and went to catch the airport bus at Royal Avenue in time for the Air Nova flight which would return him to Halifax, Nova Scotia. He threw the gun away. Who would concern themselves with a rolled-up newspaper and a metal tube nine inches long? It was just part of the everyday junk that filled the lives of the citizens of Happy Valley, Goose Bay.

Unaware of what had happened, some five thousand miles to the east, in Moscow, the Director of the KGB relaxed in the back of the Zil limousine that took him from his offices in Dzerzhinsky Square to his small home on the outskirts of Moscow.

The days when all top Communist officials had country dachas were long gone, now that the Russian Republic and its Commonwealth Nations were starving and their leaderships struggling.

He looked forward to getting home. A few friends, old and trusted comrades, were coming to drink tea and vodka and play a game of vint. They met once a week, had done regularly for the last fifteen years; it was the highlight of their joint friendship and shared lives.

He watched the slow line of Moscow traffic edge its way out of the city.

Times are good, he thought. Even if the enemy is now our friend – and still mistrusted. He recalled his earlier meeting when he had been summoned to the Central Committee Security Plenary. It was a regular meeting and he was expected to say little, just listen to the committee members rambling on about how Russians must learn to work with the Americans, yet be watchful at all times. His American counterparts probably went through the same scenario.

The business of spying had crossed the borders into diplomacy. It made life difficult. Suddenly there were no obvious enemies, no loyal and trusted friends.

'Ah!' he sighed. 'Such is the way of the modern world.'

Little did he know, as he leant back and closed his eyes, that the death of Hans Putiloff, all that distance away, was about to test the new spirit of co-operation between the Intelligence Services of the Russian Commonwealth and America.

Someone was trying to rock the boat, and there was little the KGB would be able to do about it in the coming days.

London
England

THE PROBLEMS OF the KGB and CIA were of no concern to Adam Nicholson.

What did anger him was the ineptitude of his superiors.

Twenty minutes after his face was splashed across the front page of *The Times*, they pulled Adam Nicholson out of Northern Ireland.

The picture wasn't of Adam himself, but of a colleague and his family who had been the unintentional victims of a Belfast bombing. Adam, in military uniform and showing his rank as captain, was clearly identifiable in the background. Which was the last thing an undercover member of the SAS 14th Intelligence Unit in Northern Ireland wanted.

After a short de-briefing, he was sent home to London on four weeks' leave to start immediately.

'We want you to stay out of sight.'

'I thought I was to take some leave.'

'We don't want you recognized. They'll be looking for you. Just because you're in London doesn't mean you're safe.'

'I wasn't intending walking up and down Kilburn High Street.' Kilburn was a haven for IRA members and supporters. 'London's a big place.'

'That's the way it is. Otherwise we'll transfer you to a safe house. A sealed safe house. I don't think you want that.'

Adam shrugged and got up to leave.

'I haven't finished yet!' barked the de-briefer.

Adam walked to the door before turning round. 'What else did you want to discuss?' he asked insolently.

The officer sighed. 'Understand one thing. Stay out of sight at all times.'

As Adam left the barracks in an armoured personnel carrier, the de-briefing officer heaved a sigh of relief. Even though Adam was one of the best covert operators the Army had, his attitude made him the most hated. The last thing his superiors wanted was that arrogant bastard wandering round the barracks with nothing to do, upsetting his colleagues, disregarding the officers, contemptuous of their tradition and discipline.

Lifted out by army helicopter, a small brown Maxfli sports holdall as his only luggage, Adam was back in his London apartment by three o'clock that same afternoon.

He was pleased to be home, although regretful because he knew he could never go back to Belfast again. He had been there for nearly two years, had enjoyed his tour of duty. The danger had always appealed to him and Northern Ireland had given him the best years of his life. Before that, there'd been the Gulf War, where his sojourn behind enemy lines had taught him that he could only rely on his own ability. It had been a lesson he learnt well, a lesson that was to save his life many times. Those had been good days, out there, on the edge of danger in the sands of the desert. Then there'd been a spell in Germany, undercover as a building-site labourer, on the look-out for IRA terrorists who were attacking servicemen and their families, indiscriminately killing them with their guns and booby traps. It had not been a happy time; failure to root out a terrorist cell had left him frustrated and feeling useless. But he'd learnt to speak German, although that was of little use in the Irish provinces. It had been his introduction to army life.

At thirty-two, he now faced a future in uniform and behind some desk. He knew it wouldn't last, that his service career was probably over. Adventure, his constant mistress, would have to be found in some other form.

Adam had recognized the dislike in the de-briefer's eyes during their short meeting. He had relished that. He knew everybody hated him. It was the way he preferred it. Through his arrogance and disdain of others, something he had consciously cultivated since his earliest school days, he was left alone to plough his own course. It suited him, he owed no-one any debts, lived his life the way he wanted.

Over the years the image and the reality had become inseparable. In his own misguided way, Adam now saw himself as the perpetual outsider, the ultimate loner. He had simply become, in one colleague's terms, 'not a nice person, not a regular chap'.

Being rich helped. His parents had been killed in a motor-car accident while on holiday in Spain when he was only nine. A successful property developer, his father had set up a trust fund for his two sons that had accumulated over the years to give Adam the sort of unearned income some considered obscene. Adam's identical twin, Marcus, the second to be born, had also died in the car. Adam had been left at home to keep his ailing grandmother company, something on which his father had insisted. His father knew it would help the old lady, his own mother, and the children's only living grandparent. Indeed, she had been the family's only living relative.

She died three weeks later, after the funeral that she wasn't well enough to attend. Adam had never forgotten standing between his father's lawyer and his accountant, both of whom were now trustees to the boy's future. Even at that age he knew they didn't really care about him; only when he was much older would he discover how large a fee they had charged to administer his inheritance and his upbringing.

He missed Marcus most of all. He often remembered the desolation as he watched the last coffin, the smallest, being lowered into the ground in a Woking cemetery. He'd stood there, refusing to cry because his father wouldn't have expected it of him, and watched the earth being scattered over the wooden coffins. The lawyer, the one he disliked most, had grabbed his hand and half dragged him away. The funeral was over and he probably had another meeting to get to. Adam remembered the other mourners staring at him, saw the pity in their eyes. 'Poor little boy. Fancy losing his parents at such a young age.' None of them had been close friends, mostly business associates. But it paid to go to the funeral. You never knew who you might run into. Adam had straightened up, held his head high and walked out of the cemetery. He was his father's son.

He wanted to stay in the flat that night, to sleep in the bed next to where Marcus should have been. But he went to his grandmother's. He stayed there until she died. He was never allowed back to his parents' flat. After they had died, it was sold and Adam lived in a mixture of boarding-schools and trustees' homes until he was eighteen. With a handsome income at that young age, he had to wait until he was twenty-five before his parents' flat came up for sale. He didn't mind paying over the asking price, it was the only home he had ever wanted, the only place he felt he belonged. He was close to Marcus again; his twin had never died in his own mind. He had shared his school-days, his whole growing up with him. With Marcus so close, he knew he wasn't on his own.

He hated the emptiness of the flat when he had been away. To him, this home, where he had lived with his family, was a living being. As all homes should be. Although regularly maintained by a live-out housekeeper, it needed the daily wear and tear of life to generate its character.

Lily, his elderly housekeeper, had not expected him, so the fire was unlit, the services off. He decided to let her rest at home, there was no need to call her over. He smiled, knew she would chide him for not contacting her. She could organize his life from tomorrow morning.

He dropped the brown holdall on the sofa and crossed the lounge to the big Georgian window on the far side. He un-latched the security lock and swung it open, letting in the cold December chill and the sounds of London street-life below.

The noise and the vitality of the street pumped him up, swirled through the room and made him feel at home im-mediately. It was always good when the apartment came to life again.

He picked up his bag and entered the bedroom. He threw it on to the bed and unzipped it, took out his shaving gear and toothbrush. He was a dapper and meticulous man, always perfectly turned out, always looking his best. He went into the bathroom to freshen up. He took off his dirty workman's shirt, part of his undercover disguise, and stepped out of his torn blue jeans.

His hair was still straggly, unwashed and partly matted. He would have to wait for the water to get hot before he could wash it. He pulled the hair gel and apple shampoo out of the wall cabinet and put them beside the shower, ready for use.

With time to spare, he returned to the bedroom and opened his wardrobe. The suits waited like empty soldiers, racked in parade formation on their hangers, the ties and shirts in the shelves alongside. He ran his hands over the clothes, felt their expensive softness, looked forward to wearing what he felt most comfortable in.

Half an hour later, the badger-hair shaving-brush was being soaked under the tap and then whisked in the Geoffrey Trumper, cream shaving-mug. LUXURIANT SHAVING-CREAM FROM HIS CELEBRATED ESTABLISHMENT IN CURZON STREET, MAYFAIR – BY ROYAL APPOINTMENT read the lettering on the side. When he had lathered his face he picked up the sharpened, cut-throat razor and carefully shaved off the stubble that had been a necessary part of his appearance for the last few months.

The shaving complete, the face washed clean, he examined his features. He was annoyed at the white outline on his lower face where the stubble had been, so markedly different from his upper face which was weather worn. An hour under the sun lamp would soon sort that out. The eyes, dark brown in colour, were clearer and brighter now, more dominant than they had been with his stubbled face. The face was no longer that of a workman, but of a young, alert and intelligent man. He smiled, enjoyed the sophistication of his features. It was good to be back.

When Adam stepped out of the lift into the underground garage that evening, there was no comparison to the stubbled workman who had entered the flat earlier.

This was urban man.

The suit he wore was brown with a faint stripe woven through it, the shirt pastel blue, the tie hand-painted. The trousers were held up by a slim, black-leather belt, the monogram AN shaped into the buckle. The clean-shaven face was

44

crowned with gelled black hair, short, slick and swept back at the top, long in a Pharaoh style down his neck. It was wavy as it ran back, sharp ridged and glossy. The end of the Pharaoh cut fell over his upturned coat collar, the lapels folded forward as was expected in the high fashion of the day. Black, highly polished, soft-leather slip-on shoes completed the outfit.

He crossed the shared garage to his car bays and switched on the light. Seeing his cars after a tour of duty always gave him a burst of pleasure. Emma and Steed, named after his favourite characters in the TV series *The Avengers*.

Emma was a red 1955 Mercedes Gullwing 300 SLC sports car with a white interior. Capable of over one hundred and fifty-five miles per hour, it was probably the finest sports car ever produced. Adam loved its shape, its sexuality, its sense of speed even when it was standing still. The Gullwing's sensuality simply gave him the horn.

Steed, the more masculine of the two, was a 1990 Ferrari F40, with a top speed of over two hundred miles per hour with 0-60 in 2.4 seconds. Just as the Mercedes had been during its time, it was a racing car with a road-going body.

These were Adam's children. These, and the apartment upstairs, the only things he considered of value to himself.

He decided to take the Ferrari.

Whatever his orders, Adam Nicholson wanted people to know he was back.

La Jolla
Southern California

NEARLY SEVEN THOUSAND miles away, in the early California morning, Billie Wood looked out from her La Jolla condominium at the mist that rolled in from the sea. Behind her, Christmas decorations spanned the big living room, the fairy lights still flickering on and off in unison.

It had been a hot night and the air-conditioning had rattled incessantly, not quite coping with the temperature. But it wasn't the heat that kept her awake, rather her restlessness. She wondered where Peter was, her husband of nearly seventeen years, now separated from her as he frantically chased his dream of a disappearing youth – probably curled round some bimbo he had acquired in a disco the night before.

At forty-one, after four years apart, she still missed him. She resented his womanizing, his wasting of money on his latest flame, his fight to keep middle age at bay. For all that, she missed his companionship, his humour, his ability to lift her when she was down.

From the dark of the bedroom, she heard Gary move in his sleep. Her latest live-in companion, Gary was a health freak in his late twenties, the sort of exciting lover that most older women imagined they wanted. So different from Peter, with his flabby gut running to waste and his soft skin loose as he tried to shed weight.

So why did she still miss him?

Damn you, Peter. I deserved better.

It soon would be time to get ready for work. Another of life's disappointments. The daughter of a local doctor in Long Beach, California, she had worked hard as a student, all those years ago, and finally left Berkeley with a degree in law that awed the most judicious and prudent of employers. Any law firm or major corporation would have employed Billie without a moment's hesitation. Add to that her fluency in French, German and Spanish, she seemed destined for a life of achievement and reward.

But nothing turns out the way we plan it.

Although a child of the sixties and a strong proponent of flower-power, she was suitably impressed when the CIA approached her, covertly through her tutor. With her exceptional qualifications in law and languages, she was an ideal candidate for the Agency.

The CIA, primarily responsible for the clandestine collection of foreign Intelligence, co-ordination of national Intelligence and for conducting Counter-Intelligence abroad, gains many of its employees from the college campuses of America. Whereas the FBI, responsible for national security and operating like a police force, is far more open in its selection of candidates, the CIA can only operate in a secret and underground manner.

The recruitment of Billie Knutsford, as she was before her marriage, was conducted in such a way. Before she had completed her final day at Berkeley she was interviewed and accepted into the Agency. She was assigned to the Office of Collection and Dissemination and was based on the West Coast where she continued to keep in touch with the college fraternity, seen as a breeding ground for insurgents and agitators. She went to work each day at the Mayfair Cab and Taxi Company and became assistant to the Vice-President of Scheduling. The network of cabs that covered Southern California was ideal for gathering information since some drivers worked as operatives for the Agency. Then the department, responsible directly to the Executive Director of the 'Company', was restructured into the Office of Management, Planning and Services (Domestic). Overnight, Billie found herself at the bottom of the tree, now under the control of the Deputy Director for Administration. They'd sent her on a computer course; they now had software programmes that collected and disseminated information for her; used its vast data base not to help her make decisions, but to make decisions for her. She regretted her decision to join the CIA, the perpetual snooping on people she considered no more than young rebels depressed her. Nevertheless, she decided to stick it out and work her way to the top.

Love soon blunted her ambition.

Peter Wood, five years her senior and the son of the richest and most successful mortician in San Diego, met and married Billie Knutsford. Life changed and she got used to the wealth; she settled for comfort and a social life that was the dream and envy of all those who aspired to the life they read about in the glossies. She decided to keep working and retain her independence and individuality until she had children.

But she never did. Tests finally showed that Peter simply didn't have it in him. Her parents died and her marriage broke up after twelve years. It had been no-one's fault; it simply

47

went sour. He turned to younger women and the life of an ageing playboy, she to the career that had never been. So she kept working, kept her head down, kept collecting and disseminating the information on the kids at college.

For all her promise, for all that bright glow of a future, Billie Wood was no more than a well-paid clerk in a cab company. Just another faceless number in the tide of civil servants who worked for the faceless bureaucrats of Langley.

She suddenly remembered the memo on her desk. It had been addressed to her, had come from Langley. She was asked to prepare a report on her section. In truth, they wanted her to justify her existence. She'd seen it before. It was the first step in closing down the section, the latest in a long line of cost-cutting exercises.

So much for a job for life.

The fear of failure and impotence, of a wasted life, reared itself again, a choking feeling, a depression. She wanted to do something important. Achieve something. Make an impact.

The clock on the mantelpiece chimed seven.

Time to stop thinking.

Time to go to work.

The phone rang in the sitting room and startled her. She hurried over to it and snatched it up, not wanting the ringing to wake Gary.

'Hallo,' she whispered into the receiver.

'Billie Wood?' a woman's voice asked crisply.

'Yes.'

'I have a call for you.'

There were clicks on the line as she was transferred. She listened for any movement from the bedroom, but Gary remained asleep. She was relieved. He was like a bear with a migraine if he was woken from a deep sleep.

'Billie?' asked a voice that she had never heard before.

'Yes,' she said cautiously. It sounded official, probably Langley.

'This is the DDA.' It was the Deputy Director of Administration himself. She'd only met him once before, many years previously, just after his appointment when he'd visited California to see their operation for himself.

'Yes, sir.' She immediately hated her subservience.

'Whatever we say now goes no further. Is that clear?'

'Yes, sir.'

'Good. Phil Tucker, from our European Communications Sector is on his way to San Diego. He'll be bringing some computer tapes with him. I want you to give him all the help you can. Do exactly as he asks.'

'Yes, sir.' She cursed herself as she said those words again. Pretty original, Billie. You're really impressing the guy.

'This is important to us. On a need-to-know basis. Make sure you give it your best. My secretary will ring you with Tucker's flight times.'

'I'll make sure I . . . ' Too late. The phone had gone dead. 'Yes, sir,' she snapped and slammed the phone down.

In the bedroom she heard Gary stir.

Damn. She knew it was going to be one of those days.

Shepherd's Bush
London

'SAR'N'VINGER?'

'Please.'

'OK.'

Adam watched the old Chinaman behind the counter sprinkle the salt shaker over his chips, then follow it with vinegar. When he had completely doused the chips, he handed them, wrapped in newspaper, to Adam. Having spent the last few days treating himself to meals in some of the best eating houses in London, nothing gave him more satisfaction than simple fish and chips.

'Great. Thanks.'

The old Chinaman in his white overall turned to his next customer as Adam left the fish and chip take-away.

'Sorry. I'm on my way,' he shouted to the traffic warden

who was inspecting Emma, who was parked on a double yellow line.

'Never booked an old car like this before.'

Adam swung the door upwards. He turned to the warden and offered him a hot chip from his newspaper packet. 'I wouldn't call this bribery,' he joked.

The warden laughed and took one of the chips. 'They're not going to carpet me for this,' he replied. 'Some car!'

'A 1955 Mercedes Gullwing 300 SLC. Fourteen hundred made, about three hundred left.'

'Horny shape. For a car that old. How fast?'

'About a hundred and fifty.'

'Good brakes?'

'No. Drums, not discs. Which is why there are only about three hundred left.'

'Expensive, is it?'

'Yes.'

'How much?'

'A lot.'

'Go on. How much?'

'About a quarter of a million.'

'Pounds?'

'Pounds. But this car's not about money.'

'When you've got a quarter of a million in a car, you can afford to say that. Here, give us another chip.'

He leant towards Adam and helped himself. 'You're being watched, you know.'

'Watched?'

'Yeah. Don't look, but that grey Rover across the street. I saw it pull up just after you. When you went in the chippie, the passenger got out and came over, watched you through the window. Scarpered back just before you came out.'

'Thank you.'

'No sweat. You're not bent, are you?'

'No,' Adam laughed. 'And this isn't a stolen car.'

'Never thought it was. Anyway, they're not police. I know all the unmarked cars.'

'So why tell me?'

'Why not? Fellow shares his lunch with me, he deserves

a favour. Even if he does drive a car that could pay my wages for the rest of my life.'

The warden moved off as Adam swung himself into the car. Climbing into a Gullwing was an acquired knack and he made it look easy. As he pulled the door down, he examined the Rover in his rear-view mirror.

It was Army.

He knew what they wanted, knew they'd been trailing him ever since he got back. Suddenly he was irritated by them.

He switched on the ignition, the roar of the three-litre engine exploding as it always did.

Emma was a car born on the racetrack. The strange method of entry, with the doors opening up instead of out, was necessary because of the side members of its, for then, advanced multi-tube frame. The engine, a 2996 cc straight six cylinder, with Bosch fuel injection, pulled 240 b.h.p. The four-speed, fully synchromeshed gearbox was positive in its movement, unlike many other squashy boxes of the era, and powered the car from a standing start to sixty miles per hour in just over seven seconds. The most remarkable feature was the engine, tilted at sixty degrees to its left, which allowed the hood to be lower than any other sports or racing car of its time.

Adam slipped the thin, upright gear stick into first and pulled out from the kerb.

The Rover hastily swung into the line of traffic behind him and caused an elderly driver to brake her Renault sharply.

'Bloody amateurs,' he chuckled as he heard the woman blare her horn at the Rover.

He half-saluted the traffic warden who winked his acknowledgement as he ticketed another car farther down the street.

The Mercedes worked its way through Shepherd's Bush and on to Bayswater Road, towards Central London. It was early in the afternoon and the traffic was light. The Rover kept its distance, not wanting to be noticed in the near-empty road, an impossible task at the best of times. Five minutes later Adam passed Marble Arch and swung right into Park Lane. He kept the speed steady at twenty miles an hour, grinned when he saw the Rover being honked at by faster-moving traffic. Staying in the bus lane, he passed Grosvenor House and the Dorchester before turning into the set-back road at the front of the Hilton. He drove past the commissionaires at the entrance, the small crowd waiting for taxis gawking at the bright red sports car, and into the rear entrance where he pulled up under the canopy and parked.

Although it was a NO PARKING zone, he knew the car was safe. Wardens and policemen were usually reluctant to ticket or clamp it. The advantages of being a legend.

Adam walked into the Hilton lobby and round to the lifts in the centre of the foyer. He took his time, knew they would be following him. The lobby was crowded, the lifts busy. It wasn't difficult to waste time, he was just one of the crowd.

One of his followers came around the corner and towards the lifts. He stopped sharply, surprised at seeing Adam still there. He was an earnest young man, probably a pen-pusher.

Adam stepped towards the lifts and spoke to the man next to him.

'Hope these lifts don't stop on every floor.'

'*Que?*' asked the man, an Hispanic foreigner.

'Lifts. Very slow. You like London?'

'*Si. Si.* Very nice.'

'First time here?'

'*Que?*'

'Good. Very nice.'

'*Si.* Is very good.'

'You enjoy. Is a great city.'

Adam laughed and slapped the man gently on the back. He knew Pen-pusher would be confused, would think Adam knew the stranger well.

They both entered the lift, the follower also slipping in behind.

The foreigner pushed the button for Floor 16, Adam selected 17. Pen-pusher, having elbowed himself to the back of the crowded lift, did nothing.

The Otis lift stopped on Floors 2, 7, 11 and 12 before reaching the sixteenth.

As the doors slid open, Adam once again patted the foreigner's shoulder.

'Well, have a good time.'

'*Si.* Thank you,' replied the surprised man, stepping out into the corridor.

'See you later. Won't be long,' shouted Adam through the closing door, waving a final farewell.

The stranger, now totally mystified and not comprehending, waved back as the door finally closed in his face.

There were only three people left in the lift, Adam, Pen-pusher and a grey-haired man in a Burberry raincoat – always the giveaway of the American tourist.

The lift stopped on the seventeenth floor and Adam stepped out. Pen-pusher didn't have the nerve to follow him, which is what Adam expected. He saw him lurch forward as the doors started to close, probably to push the button for the eighteenth floor. Adam walked quickly to the housekeeper's closet by the emergency steps and went in, pulling the door to, but not shut, behind him.

A few moments later Pen-pusher appeared out of the emergency exit door, having climbed down from the floor above. Adam gave him five for resourcefulness.

Pen-pusher disappeared down the corridor and turned left at the end.

Adam slipped out from the closet and went through the emergency exit. The concrete, uncarpeted stairs dropped away endlessly. Without hesitation he started to run down the stairs, two at a time.

Two hundred feet below, in the foyer, Pen-pusher's colleague had come in search of his partner. After a fruitless quest he went to the concierge's desk to ask if there were any restaurants or coffee shops on other floors, just as Adam came out of the stairwell doorway and left by the front entrance. Neither saw each other in the throng of the lobby crowd.

Adam walked round the building to the back entrance where he saw the Rover parked. The Gullwing had drawn a small crowd of admirers, two boys in jeans and their mother. Adam crossed the street quickly.

'Excuse me,' he said, putting the key in the lock and turning it to release the slim door handle.

'Your car, mister?' asked the elder of the two boys.

'Yes.'

'It's beautiful.'

'Thank you,' replied Adam, swinging the door up.

'Cor!' blurted the younger brother. 'It opens up.'

'Would you like to sit inside?'

'Could they?' said the mother.

'Of course.' Adam knew he should be moving, but also enjoyed sharing the car with these two young boys. He reached out and lifted up the younger brother, who was no more than seven years old, and lowered him into the car.

'The steering-wheel's broke,' said the elder of the two.

'No, it's not,' answered Adam, leaning in and pulling the tilted wheel upright, locking it into place. 'It's meant to be like that. To make it easy to get in. Remember, this was a racing car. Not many would be able to get in, let alone drive it.'

He watched the young boy twist the wheel and pretend to drive the car.

'Careful, Alex,' said his mother.

'He's OK.'

'Let your brother have a go now.'

The disappointed boy, disgruntled and vocal with it, climbed out and his brother lowered himself in. After Adam had answered his questions about what this knob did and what that switch was for, the grateful mother and her two excited sons disappeared into the hotel.

Adam slipped into the Mercedes, switched on the engine and pulled away from the kerb. Then he noticed the packet on the passenger seat. He grinned and stopped the car.

He climbed out, went over to the Rover and left the packet jammed under its windscreen wiper.

Ten minutes later the pen-pusher and his partner came out of the rear entrance and saw that the Gullwing was gone.

'Fuck it!' shouted Pen-pusher, dreading the report that he would have to file highlighting his failure. 'Fuck it!'

They opened up the Rover and climbed in.

'What's that?' asked Pen-pusher's colleague.

'Where?'

'Under the bloody wiper.'

54

There, as a final taunt to their dismal failure, was the remains of a bag of chips wrapped in grease and the newsprint of yesterday's paper.

'Very clever,' said the official voice on the telephone. 'And very childish.'

'Why was I being followed?' asked Adam, the receiver resting on his shoulder as he looked out of the apartment window to the street below. The blonde he fancied in the jewellers would soon be going home, her day's work complete. He still hadn't angled out how he was going to introduce himself to her. Probably the F40. She was definitely a Ferrari type, the Gullwing being too noisy and too basic. He decided then that he would browse in the jeweller's tomorrow, leave the red-coloured sports car at the kerb where she could definitely see it. Maybe he'd ask her to show him something in the window.

'You were told to keep out of sight.'

'Nobody's going to recognize me.'

'As a soldier you're expected to obey orders.'

'I was told I was to go on leave. That didn't mean being trapped in my flat.'

'No, you were told to lie low, not to draw attention to yourself. Those were your orders. In the three days since you've been back, you've done everything except stay at home. Nightclubs, casinos, trips to restaurants for lunch. Usually with companions who are, let's say, more than noticeable' – the puerile envy in the voice made Adam smile – 'not exactly keeping a low profile, are we?'

Adam snorted. He was more than capable of looking after his own security, more capable than Pen-pusher and his pal.

'What?' demanded the official voice.

'I don't need nursemaids.'

'What makes you so . . . The trouble with you, Nicholson, if your records are anything to go by, is that you don't give a damn. That you've got a bloody death-wish. Now, some people say that makes you an exceptional soldier. I say that makes you a liability. I don't mind you getting killed. But I don't want half a dozen innocent bystanders gunned down

55

with you in your blaze of glory. You're to stay in. That's an order.'

'For how long?'

'Until we tell you you can go out.'

Adam heard the phone go dead. He returned the receiver to its base and went back to his vigil. In the background, from the kitchen, he heard Lily preparing his evening meal.

'What's for supper?' he shouted.

'Just you wait and see,' came her muffled reply.

It was a game they played, she never telling him what she was cooking, he always asking. In the six years she had been with him, he had never been disappointed. It was simple English cooking, so different from the *haute cuisine* he lived on in restaurants, but it was the best food he knew.

He decided not to stay in. Even if he was recognized because of that picture, he would far prefer to be out in the open, in the freedom of his own space where he could defend himself without hindrance. He hated being under the control of the office wallahs, missed the companionship and shared respect of the field units.

He dreaded whatever they had in store for him. He couldn't return to Northern Ireland; he had become an outsider.

The depression would come soon, it always did when things were out of his control. It was his dark half, the part of his soul that plunged him into despair and solitude, that ignored his strength and his fortitude. He thought of Marcus, of his other spirit, that shared soul that was always in his body.

In silence, as he waited for the girl across the road, he cursed the unknown security officer who hadn't clipped the photo that had been sent to be splashed across the front page of *The Times*.

Lindbergh Airport
San Diego
California

SHE'D BEEN WAITING for him at the airport; had grown frustrated as the tannoy had barked out that the United Airlines' flight from Washington would be late.

The frustration had remained bottled up, turning to anger as a second announcement informed her that there would be a further delay due to traffic problems over Denver.

'It's always Denver,' Billie thought. 'What's so special about Denver?'

Phil Tucker came through the gate thirty minutes later, more than ninety minutes late.

'Billie Wood?' he asked, approaching her cautiously.

'Yes.' Damn it, she nearly said, 'Sir,' again.

'Hi.' He smiled, offering his hand. 'Phil Tucker. Say, I've got a flight out of here in another fifty minutes. We aren't going to have time to get to the office.' There was no way he was going to stay overnight; not if he wanted a peaceful weekend at home with Jean, his wife. She always hated him going out of Washington. 'Can we find somewhere here?'

'Sure. How about my car?'

'Great.'

She led him out into the car-park, towards a bright yellow-and-red 1989 Jeep Renegade. Billie unlocked the central locking system and they both climbed in.

'These discs're for you.' Tucker took out a case of floppy discs from his briefcase and passed them over. 'They're just slices from our data base in Langley. From our main computer. I need you to run some checks on them for me.'

'What am I looking for?'

'You understand this is top secret? I mean, no-one.'

'Yes.'

'Good. OK if I smoke?'

She nodded. She hated cigarettes and it would take days to get the smell out of the car. She watched him take out a Camel from the soft pack and light it with a Zippo. Then he told her about Reindeer. As he spoke, she opened a window. There was more smog in here than San Fran, she thought.

'But who was he?' she asked when Tucker had finished.

'A nobody. Someone we'd forgotten about.'

'Important enough for someone else to remember. Lapland's in Finland, isn't it?'

Tucker nodded. 'Reindeer was over sixty. Been drawing a pension for more than ten years. Through our usual channels. I mean, why knock off a pensioner?'

'Could've been for another reason. Nothing to do with us.'

'It sure as hell wasn't one of his elves. It was a professional hit. Clean, right on the button. Anyway, he left an envelope for his wife, to be opened if anything happened to him. She rang the number he'd left.'

'How many of these assets have we got out there?'

'A few. Not as many as we had. Not since we turned to satellite surveillance under the Carter Administration. But enough, in case we ever needed them. Anyway, a lot of them were just stuck out there in the field, they'd integrated into their communities, there was no way we could get them out.'

'One old guy gets killed. Doesn't mean the Russians, or anyone else, took him out. Could just be a local murder, an accident that we're taking the wrong way.'

'No. Too professional.'

'Was "Reindeer is dead" an open code?' asked Billie. This was CIA jargon for a code concealed within an innocuous message. The Japanese had established this technique successfully during the Second World War, just after their attack on Pearl Harbor. 'East wind rain' had been the sentence, a grim warning to their embassy staff in Washington to destroy sensitive documents as the two countries were about to enter into war. Such codes were being used regularly by the activist groups on the Californian campus.

'No.' Tucker wound his window down and flicked out his spent cigarette.

'What's the computer say?'

'Nothing.'

Billie sensed they had come to the heart of the problem. 'If he was an asset, he must've been in the computer. I remember when we transferred from paper to tape. I spent three boring years inputting some of that information.'

'Which is why this thing is so damned sensitive.' He lit another cigarette and didn't see her scowl. 'When we checked the computer, we found all the information relating to sleeper networks before 1958.' Tucker paused. 'I know this is crazy, but there's a virus in the system that's knocked out all that information on our European networks.'

'You're kidding?'

'I haven't flown all the way here for a joke. No. The virus was activated yesterday.'

'How?'

'As soon as we punched in a question on Gunnar Yokob—'

'Who?'

'Reindeer. That was his name. Anyway, as soon as we input his name, this virus just upped and knocked out the file. The words just disappeared on the screen, one by one. First the As, then the Bs, right through to Z. Just fucking destroyed the file. When we called up the rest of the European network, exactly the same happened. Within fifteen minutes it had wiped out 10 per cent of the information we had on the agents in Europe right up until 1958.'

'That's impossible.'

'So impossible it happened. We've sealed off the computer room, switched off the whole system. When we powered up again, it just continued where it left off. We tried to dump the information on to floppy discs, but they wouldn't transfer. Just got a message up saying, NO COPIES OF THIS CLASSIFIED INFORMATION CAN BE MADE. So we've isolated the pre-1958 section until we can get some answers.'

'Only on info before 1958?'

'That's right.'

'What're these?' She held up the discs he had given her.

'A few files hadn't been corrupted. Expenses, simple memos, that sort of thing. Just thought there may be an answer in there. If you chase the binary. Also what we know about Reindeer and a breakdown on our asset base. To help you disseminate this thing. You could just come up with something we can't see.'

'How long's that virus been there?'

Tucker shrugged. 'We've only just found the damn thing. And it ain't difficult to introduce it into the system, as long as you've got access to a terminal, or to any new programme. Hell, it could even have originated from California.'

'Is that why . . . ?' She was suddenly alarmed.

'No. I'm just telling you. There's a million ways to get into it. Maybe not now, but in the early days. No sweat.'

'Don't you check for viral infection?'

'Regularly.' The question irritated Tucker. It hadn't been his idea to involve the girl. 'As long as you know what you're look-ing for. Trouble is, these files are never opened. No need for it. The virus could've been introduced years ago. Even before we knew about viruses. It was just waiting for us to go into those old archives, waiting to be triggered off. It was Reindeer, and not knowing who he was, that made us backtrack into the files. Nobody's needed them for nearly fifteen years.'

'My terminal's still operating. It's linked to Langley.'

'Shut down the main computer and the Company grinds to a halt. It deals with everything from your expenses to who really killed John Kennedy. Let this out and our enemies will have a field day. You close it down and people will soon work out why. How long do you think we can keep it a secret then? The last thing we want is the Soviets finding out about this fuck-up. Even though they may have started it in the first place. With all these latest peace and trade negotiations, the last thing we need is to find the KGB are still up to their old tricks. And we have to protect our assets. Even if they are all sixty and senile.'

'That it?'

'Yes.' Tucker flicked his second cigarette out of the window. 'Gotta quit these soon. They're killing me.'

'I'll need an index. A list of everything that's been con-taminated.'

'OK. Anything else?'

'Why me? I mean, you have the best collection and dissemination team in the world sitting in Langley.'

'Because we don't know who's introduced this thing. We want it out of there. You're trained to come up with ideas. Now's the time to show us how good you really are.' Tucker turned the door handle and climbed out of the car. 'You get off. I'll wait for my connection inside.' He closed the door, then leant in through the window as she started the engine. 'I forgot. Before the computer went down, it came up with one fact on Reindeer. We recruited him after the war. He was German. We think he could've been SS. The VT regiment.'

'What's that?'

'Special purpose troops. They were the guys who were really mean.'

'What were we using them for?'

'I don't know. Trained men, I guess. Ready for the OSS to plant in Europe. I don't know if it means anything. Except it's all we got out of the computer.' He stood back and smiled at her. 'See you, Billie Wood.'

'Bye, Phil.' She watched him walk towards the terminal.

Then she shifted into gear and drove out of the parking lot.

This was her big chance. Her crack at the major league.

The Croisette
Cannes
South of France

THE CARLTON HOTEL is the Queen of all the great hotels that span the Croisette in Cannes. It is where everyone who is anyone must be seen, where the rich and famous can be rich and famous and not be embarrassed by their excesses. Nobody asks if the jewels are real, it doesn't matter at the Carlton. To be there, to be seen, is all that counts.

The building, set back in its majesty and overlooking the blue azure of the Mediterranean, even this late in December, is crowned at each corner with two cupolas shaped like enormous, skyward-pointing breasts, nipple perfect in their form. For that is what they are. They were designed by an amorous architect to represent La Belle Otero, the most beautiful and most famous of French courtesans at the turn of the century. The left cupola is slightly larger than the right one, a further tribute to the architect's search for detail and historical accuracy.

It was the witching hour before lunch, the time when the experienced Canne'ites stroll out to the beach from their hotels, knowing the morning beach-restaurant tables will be vacated by the families who have tired of their early morning sojourn and are heading for the shops and amusements that will keep their children occupied. The whores, and there is a plentiful supply of them in Cannes all the year round, from housewives and students paying for their holidays to hardened Parisienne professionals on the look-out for Christmas money, emerge from their small bedroomed work places to pick up the early trade, to prepare themselves for their daily diet of wine, dirty intentioned glances and sex with strangers whom they love for a few brief minutes. There are the hustlers, the pimps, the fancy boys, the workers, the retired, the taxi drivers, the beach workers, the restaurant waiters, the hopefuls, all filling the streets, all swelling the crowd that makes the Croisette one of the busiest and most interesting thoroughfares in Europe.

And then there were the watchers, the army of ordinary people who wanted to touch fame by seeing it pass by, as if viewing this extraordinary procession of life somehow made them a part of it. The crowds were building, the mass saturating the Croisette.

Heinrich Trimmler came out into this thronging world from the comparative sanity of the Carlton Hotel. An American by naturalization, a German by birth, the sixty-nine-year-old, large-framed Trimmler spent each Christmas period in Cannes, a month's holiday away from the 'cultural wasteland', as he described it, of America. He had lived in California for over forty years, yet his instincts were still European, the American lifestyle never blunting his attitudes. His wife Trudi, only a few months younger, walked beside him, an elegant blond woman. They made a chic couple, he with his blue, vertical-striped matelot top over white cotton trousers, her in a multi-coloured wrap round her dark blue, one-piece play suit. With two weeks left to run of their holiday, their tans looked expensive and established. You could tell they weren't part of the gawking trade, but players in the rich world of the Côte d'Azur.

Trimmler took his wife by the arm and led her under the great entrance archway and down the shallow steps to the Croisette. He pointed across the bay, to an American aircraft carrier that had berthed overnight.

'Looks like the fleet's in town,' he said, his accent American, yet still heavy with Germanic traces.

'I hope they behave themselves,' Trudi replied. By and large the American sailors behaved themselves during their shore leave, although there were the occasional fights usually caused through heavy drinking and women.

'I'm sure they will,' he replied. He led her on to the thin strip of sandy beach that was the exclusive preserve of the Carlton Hotel and its guests.

The restaurant area was set back, partly under cover but most of it on the open board-walk that ran along to the wooden jetty.

'A beautiful day. The way it should always be,' said the expansive *maître d'* as he recognized the Trimmlers and came forward to greet them.

'Very good, very good,' replied a patronizing Trimmler.

'Your guests have arrived,' the *maître d'* informed them, holding his arm up to show them the way as he led them to the far table nearest the water. 'Did you visit the casino last night?'

'We did.'

'A profitable evening, I hope.'

'Profitable enough,' Trimmler lied. He looked at Trudi and smiled. The baccarat table had, in fact, cheated him of over three thousand dollars the night before. It was not something he was prepared to share with her.

Their friends, a couple similar in age and appearance, waited for them. They were a West German couple, Marta and Grob Mitzer. He was an industrialist, the main shareholder in one of Europe's largest aerospace suppliers. They had all been friends since the last days of Hitler's war; Trimmler, the young brilliant scientist, whilst Mitzer had helped organize the work forces at the rocket centres of Peenemünde and Nordhausen. They had escaped to the Allies together and had never broken their friendship. They had met every year since 1957 for this Christmas vacation on the Côte d'Azur.

With them sat a young man, in his early forties, a native of East Germany before Reunification. Willi Kushmann was now one of the country's leading corporate lawyers. The three of them were staying at the Martinez Hotel, further down the Croisette.

The two men stood up as the Trimmlers reached their table, Mitzer taking Trudi's hand and kissing it.

They welcomed each other in German, the *maître d'* holding out a chair for Trudi. When they had all sat down, the *maître d'* signalled over a waiter to take their order and left to lead another group to their table.

'Give us five minutes,' said Mitzer. Then, as the waiter started to lift the champagne out of the bucket, he snapped, 'Leave us! We will do it!'

Kushmann leant over and took the bottle from the waiter who, confused and apologetic, bowed and walked away.

'Bloody poodles,' Mitzer swore in German as Kushmann poured two extra glasses of champagne. When he had finished, he put the bottle back in the bucket and sat down.

'Where's Gloria?' Trimmler asked.

'Probably still in bed,' replied Trudi. Gloria was their nineteen-year-old daughter, an unexpected mistake that had been added to their three other children.

'To the future,' said Trimmler, raising his glass, changing the subject from his daughter who had not returned to her hotel room until five in the morning. God knows what she got up to.

'To the *new* future,' added Kushmann.

The five of them held their drinks aloft and shared the toast.

'Did you see the latest pictures of the Reichstag in Berlin? Did you see how it's looking on the inside? They're recreating it like it was before the fire in 1933.'

'Which pictures?' asked Trudi.

'In *Frankfurter Allgemeine*. This morning's edition. And they're going to rebuild the dome as it was.'

'What dome?' Marta asked as she sipped her champagne.

'Don't you girls know anything?' Mitzer joked. 'The one on top of the Reichstag. It was destroyed in the fire by the Communists. When Hitler had it rebuilt, he left off the dome. Big bloody thing. Almost covered the whole roof.'

'Anyway, they're going to rebuild it,' said Kushmann.

'But they're already using it. For the Government,' interrupted Trudi.

'No problem. They'll build it round them. That's how they do it these days. But what a great centre for the Government, eh? I tell you, Germany is becoming great once again. And to have such a grand building as its Parliament' – he held up his glass – 'to the new Reichstag and to our new Germany. It's been a long time waiting, but our hour is finally near.'

They all toasted with Kushmann again, the tinkle of their glasses sharp in its resonance across the wooden board-walk.

'And to the *Heide*. For what it has become,' said Mitzer. The *Heide* was a large expanse of land that he had started to develop in Dresden.

'A symbol to our future,' replied Kushmann. 'It is exhilarating to see so many members of the Stasi coming forward to join us there.' They were all Germans; there was no need to explain that the Stasi was the name commonly used to describe the previous German Democratic Republic's Ministry of State Security. 'Lost souls. Made to feel guilty about what they were trained to do.' He held up his glass. 'To them, and to other lost souls in Germany.'

'And one more toast,' jumped in Mitzer, when they had drunk. 'To one Germany and the end of the bad jokes about the GDR.'

They all laughed and joined in with him, once more clashing their glasses.

'But I have to tell you one. Just one,' Mitzer went on,

ignoring the howl of good-humoured protests that engulfed him. 'How do you double the value of a Trabant motor car?'

'How?' shouted Kushmann.

'I've already heard this,' said Marta, winking at Trudi.

'Tell us how,' squealed Trudi.

'By filling the tank full of petrol,' finished Mitzer.

They all joined in the laughter, except for Trimmler, who brought his glass down sharply on the table, the loud dull sound surprising the others.

'You didn't like my small joke, Heinrich?' asked a smiling Mitzer.

'When is it to happen?' asked Trimmler. 'When?'

Kushmann leant forward confidentially. 'Be patient. Soon.'

Further along the thin strip of beach, eastwards towards the Martinez Hotel, an ebony-black Senegalese pedlar shuffled through the sand, as he headed towards the Carlton jetty.

The Senegalese work the beaches with their wares, straw and leather hats, cheap sunglasses, wraps, thongs, leatherware. It is tourist trade that produces a good revenue for these once-proud warriors. Although a nuisance for most visitors, the pedlars, in their brightly coloured native dress, are part of the culture that is Cannes beach.

But that is in the high season. Most of them return to their homes in Africa during the winter months.

The pedlar who worked his way along the beach in December was out of place, a lone black figure bedecked with his wares. His dress was also unusual; instead of the usual robe, he wore a green combat jacket over black jeans. The sunglasses he wore were as black as his skin, pock-marked and scaly in its texture. His head was covered by a tartan beret. A man easily noticed. As he progressed towards the Carlton, he passed two young women sitting on a shared deck-chair near the water's edge.

One of the women, a plump blonde, called to him, waved him over.

He paused, reluctant in his attitude, then crossed over to them.

'Show us what you've got,' the woman said in French.

He smiled, then took a six-inch-high rubber toy gorilla out of his pocket and held it towards the women.

They giggled, not knowing what to expect.

He grinned and squeezed the gaudy toy. A long rubber penis, bright red in colour with a black-topped head, popped out of the gorilla. The toy's erection pointed straight at the women, who burst into surprised and embarrassed laughter. The pedlar's grin grew bigger.

'That's not very big,' the second woman, a petite brunette, teased him. 'I'm used to bigger.'

He pushed the gorilla down and pressed the erection against her left breast. She jumped backwards and fell off the deck-chair. Before the other woman could react, he rubbed the plastic gorilla on the inside of her leg, then stroked her thigh with his large coarse hand.

The girls, made fearful by his blatant sexuality, jumped up, collected their belongings and ran towards the Croisette.

He taunted them as they ran. 'I've something bigger if you want. Big, big,' he shouted.

Then he turned back to his task, to watch the German group at the last table before the jetty. He could hear them laughing, enjoying their champagne.

With some hundred metres to go, he pulled the thin steel tube, some seven inches long and no thicker than a finger, from the bag he was carrying round his waist. He connected the firing pin which would ignite a small charge, inserted a glass ampoule in the mouth of the tube, then wrapped the assembly into a copy of yesterday's *Nice Matin*. To an onlooker, the Stashinsky gun was only a newspaper, crumpled and harmless.

He slowed as he approached them; it was not in his interest to arrive too early. He walked towards the beach restaurant, under the sign over the jetty that read: CARLTON HOTEL INTERCONTINENTAL.

The pedlar was now only a few metres from the Germans, their laughter accompanied by the soft music that drifted out from the shelter of the inner restaurant. Above the building, on the wide Boulevard Croisette, the crowds mingled and watched in the December sun.

Very few people bothered about the small group at the end of the jetty.

The Senegalese, after a quick look to ensure that he was not about to be discovered, pulled the newspaper from under his arm and moved rapidly towards them.

The laughter stopped, frozen suddenly in the realization that danger was upon the group.

Trudi screamed as she saw the pedlar rushing towards them, a metal tube held out from under his newspaper, pointing directly at her.

'He's got a gun!' shouted Mitzer, trying to get to his feet.

The pedlar turned to Kushmann and held the Stashinsky tube towards him. He pulled the trigger, released the deadly vapour from the prussic acid capsule.

'*Attention!*'

The pedlar swung round and was surprised to see a young gendarme advancing towards him from the restaurant. Realizing he was trapped, he reached under his jacket and brought out a sawn-off shotgun. The gendarme, seeing it was not a simple case of robbery, fumbled, panic-stricken, with the clip on his holster, tugged desperately at his gun which refused to come out of its leather pouch.

The German group scattered, Trudi Trimmler screaming, as the black pedlar bore down on them in his panic, the shotgun aimed directly at her.

The crowds on the Croisette, the other occupants of the restaurant, attracted by the screams, craned to watch the drama that was exploding in front of them.

The pedlar turned to Trimmler and pulled the trigger. Nothing happened. The safety catch was still on and he clawed at it with his thumb, attempting to release it.

At that moment, the gendarme, his hand-gun finally free, fired. He missed, but deflected the assassin from his target. The pedlar turned and ran towards the gendarme. But it was an old shotgun, not maintained as well as it should have been, with sand trapped under the safety catch. The pedlar frantically pulled at the trigger as he ran.

The second shot from the gendarme's pistol caught the pedlar in his left eye, more by accident than design, and killed him instantly. The spasm of death jerked the black man's thumb and its force kicked the safety catch free. The same spasm tightened his finger and triggered off the shotgun. As he fell, the full blast of the released twelve-bore cartridge, all 330 pieces of shot rammed out by twenty-six grains of gun powder, shattered Willi Kushmann's chest and sent him spinning backwards across the wooden floor and on to the sand.

What no-one realized was that the young lawyer was dead before the pellets tore into him, the deadly cyanide already having done its work.

Church of the Resurrection in Kadashakh
Zamoskvorechie
Moscow

ALEXEI ROSTOV WAS a devoutly religious man who also happened to be the Deputy Director of the KGB.

To him there was no conflict in this situation. He did what was right by his Christian God, but never allowed himself to forget that he was a Russian who had been blessed with certain responsibilities. Since the early days of *perestroika* and *glasnost*, the spread of religion had, at first, been tolerated, then encouraged. Political leaders soon understood that religion was a source of comfort to many, and, at a time of dramatic social change, they needed all the help they could get.

Rostov had always believed in a divine power beyond man himself. As a member of the Communist Party in his youth, he appreciated that the Party was created by man in man's image. If you believed in God, as he had been secretly brought up to do by his parents, then God was bigger than the Communist Party. With that belief, Rostov had worked his way up through the Party and KGB ranks to the very top. Apart from a three-year sojourn as a military attaché in Washington, where he both enjoyed the freedom to worship every day in a church and to control one of the most efficient letter-box networks in the United States, he spent his entire career in

Moscow where his exceptional organizational abilities were quickly recognized. Moving up the promotion ladder was easier than he thought. He was never frightened of tackling the toughest assignments, of resolving the most complicated tasks, however distasteful they appeared. He saw no hypocrisy in his actions, had no desire to become a martyr. Time, and God, would resolve the situation.

It actually turned out to be a politician named Mikhail Gorbachev who changed the climate, who made God officially acceptable, though not respectable, in the eyes of the Party.

Rostov was quick to embrace his childhood faith. He allowed his Party membership to lapse and attended prayer meetings as Moscow churches started cautiously to open their doors to their congregations. His superiors, both in the KGB and in Government, tolerated his actions. He was an exceptional officer and a loyal Russian. They needed him, both for his ability and as a symbol of their new policies. The result was that he was pushed even faster up the promotion ladder until he found himself, at the age of forty-six, the Deputy Director of the gigantic organization that was the KGB. Every day Rostov made a point of visiting at least one of the many churches that were opening up in Moscow. He would leave Dzerzhinsky Square at lunchtime and be driven in his official Zil car to his chosen place of worship.

Today, after a busy morning dealing with administrative problems that had arisen since they had decided to transfer decades of typed secret archives to a new computer, he had chosen to pray at the Church of the Resurrection in Kadashakh. One of the earliest and finest examples of Moscow Baroque, it is reached by way of Red Square, past the extraordinary domed St Basil Cathedral, across the Moskvoretskiy Bridge and into Bolshaya Ordynka Street. The district, Zamoskvorechie, literally means 'area beyond the Moscow River', and houses the four great churches that were built by the weavers who dominated the textile trade and made this the production centre for cloth over many centuries.

The Church of the Resurrection in Kadashakh, built by an unknown architect, is the most famous of the four. Unlike many of the Russian churches, this one had escaped the ravages

70

of Stalin's reconstruction, had not been vandalized and turned into a working man's club as had its sister down the road, the Church of Our Lady of Iberia.

Rostov sat on a bench at the back, his head bowed as he prayed. The church was half-full and the Russian Orthodox priest at the altar led the prayers. As he listened to the priest, he felt the peace that always came at such times envelop him. He took strength from such moments, found an inner calm that allowed him to deal expeditiously with the many unsavoury events that landed on his desk each day.

Out of the corner of his eye, where his KGB bodyguard stood, he was startled to see the black shiny shoes of his assistant. He turned his head sideways and saw the two men talking. He looked forward again, anger bringing a flush to his forehead. It was an easily recognizable trait, one that warned those who were confronted by him that they were in for a rough ride.

His rule was simple. He was always available, except when he was at prayer. That rule was sacrosanct and had never been broken.

He felt his assistant slide on to the bench next to him.

'Why are you here?' he asked icily without looking up.

'To fetch you, sir,' came the nervous reply.

'You know the rule, don't you?'

'Rule, sir?'

'That I'm not to be disturbed when I come to pray.'

'Yes, sir.'

'Then what's so important that it can't wait?'

'The Director would like to see you immediately.'

'You told him I was here?'

He heard the man gasp. 'Yes, sir,' he replied when he had caught his breath.

'That was a mistake.'

The assistant knew he was about to be transferred. 'It is the Director. His orders,' he went on, grabbing at straws.

'Nothing is that important that it couldn't have waited for another twenty minutes.'

'Sorry, sir.' The assistant gave in; Rostov was not known for changing his mind.

'Wait for me. Outside.'

'Sir.'

The assistant withdrew and Rostov went back to his prayer. But the moment was gone, he could only think of what was so important that he was being recalled to Dzerzhinsky Square immediately.

The Director was impatient. They should have found Rostov by now. He leant down and switched on the intercom, changed his mind and switched it off.

Outside, in her office, his secretary shook her head at his impatience. He had already called and asked where his Deputy Director was five times in as many minutes.

The Director turned to the window and looked down on Dzerzhinsky Square, at the people scurrying round, rushing to the shops in their short lunch breaks. Who'd be a member of the human race? Who'd be common man? Not Feliks Dzerzhinsky, the Polish revolutionary who had founded the KGB, or the Cheka, as it had been. His gloomy, unwashed statue had stood in the centre of the square, right there in the front of KGB Headquarters and had been pulled down unceremoniously by the citizens of Moscow in 1991. What would old Feliks have thought of it all now, or his discredited mentor, Stalin?

The Director remembered the report on his desk. It was a mess. The Americans, for all their fine words, were not to be trusted. He'd hated the new openness, the desperate urge to forget the Cold War and pretend it had never existed. While the Russians sued for peace and help out of the economic shambles they had got themselves into, the Americans had insisted on putting East Germany under NATO control, had tried to build bases all over the Middle East after the Gulf crisis. No, they were still the old enemy, still not to be trusted.

He saw the Zil pull up at the pavement and Rostov get out.

'Bloody Christian!' he thought. You never could completely trust a man with two masters. At least you could see proof of the State, however did these people see proof of their God?

His Deputy walked in two minutes later and the Director signalled him to take a seat.

'Sorry to drag you away from your prayers,' he lied.

Rostov shook his head, as if signifying it didn't matter. They both knew he also lied; Rostov's rule was well known in the building.

'I wouldn't have, had I not considered it to be of extreme importance.' The Director watched Rostov, who said nothing, knew it was best to remain silent when his superior was in one of his tetchy moods.

The Director pushed a copy of the report across the desk towards his Deputy. 'I only received this about an hour ago. It makes chilling reading. You can study the details later. I'll go through it with you first.' He reached over and took a cup, poured himself out some tea from the samovar that was on the trolley beside the desk. 'Want some?'

'No, thank you.'

'It's about our sleeper network in the West. Looking at the age of some of them, I wouldn't be surprised if they weren't planted before the Revolution.'

Rostov smiled at the weak attempt at a joke.

'One of them,' the Director went on, 'was in Canada, Goose Bay. The NATO airbase. Hans Putiloff. His record's in there.' He indicated the file. 'Like most of our people, as you know, we arrange for them to make contact with us once a year. Putiloff used to visit Niagara Falls for an annual holiday, always met one of our people. They never spoke, just verified that all was well. The meeting was scheduled for two weeks ago. Putiloff never appeared. Our agent, as was expected of him, went to Goose Bay to find out why Putiloff hadn't made it. He discovered that Putiloff had died, just outside an hotel where he'd finished a meal. There was no apparent reason for his death. No heart attack, no choking, no obvious cause. He just died.' The Director drank his tea, draining the cup totally. 'In Cannes, last week, a black man, a Senegalese pedlar, accidentally shot a German tourist. Killed him. The reason he shot him, according to the newspapers and the authorities, was that he was trying to rob him and was surprised by a passing gendarme. He panicked and, while trying to get away, opened fire and shot this Kraut in confusion.'

The Director poured himself some more tea, watched Rostov

over the tilted samovar. His Deputy revealed little, but the Director sensed his increased interest.

'Sure you won't have some?'

'I'm fine,' Rostov replied, reaching forward to pick up the file.

The Director turned sideways, opened a drawer and took out a steel tube, about nine inches long and as thick as an index finger. He laid it on the table. It was in three sections and he unscrewed them, separated them. The bottom section had a simple firing pin, like a pair of tweezers. From the drawer he took out a small powder charge and put it where the firing pin struck. When connected to the centre section, it caused a small metal lever to move. The Director took a small glass ampoule and slid it into the centre section. Then he screwed the three sections together, rose from his chair and went round the desk to where Rostov sat. He slowly brought the tube up, to no more than eighteen inches from his Deputy's face.

'Maybe you'd prefer this?' he stated, pulling the simple trigger. There was an inaudible pop as the powder charge exploded, kicked the middle lever which burst the glass ampoule and released its contents through the end of the tube.

Rostov never moved.

'Stashinsky,' he said.

'Very good. Top of the class,' the Director replied. He was impressed with Rostov's iron self-control. He couldn't have been completely sure that the ampoule contained air, instead of the customary and deadly prussic acid. He moved the tube away and returned to his desk.

'Is this what did in the sleeper?'

'Our man in Goose Bay searched the area where Putiloff was killed. He found such a tube. He's an old timer, knew all about Stashinsky. He took it back to Washington, to the embassy, and had it examined. There was no trace of cyanide, but there were marks where a trigger had been. We're convinced it was the method used.'

'Was the German one of our sleepers?'

'No. But this' – he held up the tube he had fired at Rostov – 'was found wrapped in a newspaper. Nobody linked it with the death. No, it was only afterwards, when our local operative asked some questions, that we found out about the weapon. To the police it was just some rubbish left on the beach. Our operative, fortunately, also remembered his early training and recalled Stashinsky.'

'KGB folklore. Sometimes I think it's all we have,' remarked Rostov.

Bogdan Stashinsky had been one of the KGB's most notorious assassins, had been nicknamed the 'Murder Machine'. A Ukrainian by birth, he was employed by Soviet Intelligence to spy on other Ukrainians. The main target of his observance was Lev Rebet, an exiled Ukrainian. In time he was told that Rebet was his target, that he was expected to assassinate him. The weapon to be used was simple and effective. Easily concealed, it also left no trace as to the cause of death. To avoid the prussic acid, a colourless liquid form of cyanide, from also killing the assassin, the KGB created an antidote. It was a tablet, sodium thiosulphate.

'From what I remember, Stashinsky was a lucky amateur,' added Rostov, ever the inquisitive historian.

The Director was of the old school, remembered Bogdan Stashinsky and the furore his defection to the West caused. It was as the Berlin Wall was going up in 1961 that Stashinsky caught the electric train in East Berlin at Schönhauser Allee Station and got off at Gesundbrunnen Station in West Berlin.

'I met him,' the Director recalled. 'In the OKR.' The *Otdely Kontrrazvedki* was the widely feared counter-espionage branch of the KGB that took over from SMERSH or Smyert Shpionam which translates into 'death to spies'. 'He was a frightened sort of fellow. A misfit. I don't know how he ever got his reputation. Of course, the Americans never found out whether he was a plant or a genuine defector.' The Director laughed as Rostov opened the report and flicked through it, stopping at the file photograph of Stashinsky, a dark-haired, attractive man.

'Is he dead?' Rostov asked.

'Probably. Changed his name so many times we lost track of him. Anyway, I can't see him doing all this. Bit old for that sort of fieldwork now, even if he is alive.'

'What about the German, Kushmann?'

'No link with us. Apart from the method used to kill him.'

'But he was shot.'

'Possibly. But I think he was already dead. The blackie panicked when the gendarme came after him. That's when he drew his gun. I think he'd already killed the German with the Stashinsky tube. It had already been fired when we found it.' The Director watched for Rostov's response and was quietly pleased when he saw his Deputy nod in agreement. 'There was also an American with the group. A top-level scientist. The Yanks rushed him straight back to America immediately after the shooting. I presume they think he was the target.'

'Have research come up with any ideas?'

'Nothing. No logic, you see. Even though I don't trust the Americans, I can't see what they'd get out of this.'

'And there're no links at all?'

'Nothing obvious. Apart from the fact that they're all Germans.'

'Putiloff had quite a record. Dachau. War crimes.' Rostov held up the file he had been skimming through. 'He could've been turned.'

'He wasn't a serious operative. If he'd lived here he'd have been on a pension. At least his death will save some of our foreign currency budget.'

Rostov smiled, stood up and placed the report under his arm. 'It's a starting-point.'

'Whatever. But this has to be resolved. After all, if they're destroying our sleeper network, that means they've got access to our most confidential information.'

'It'll take priority over everything.'

'Good. At least we've something on our hands that smells interesting. Different from guarding food supplies and helping the police marshal crowds. Our leaders sometimes forget why the Cheka was first formed.'

'We live in strange times.'

'We do. *Shpion*. They've all made it into a dirty word. Now they need us. Keep it on a need-to-know basis. And, I have been told from the Kremlin, don't rock the boat too much with the Americans. There are summit meetings planned, peace and goodwill are the passwords of the day. Remember Gary Powers and the U2 incident. We don't want that again, even if we did it deliberately last time.'

'I may decide to go through our diplomatic people in Washington.'

'Just don't upset the Yanks.'

'Even if it's them?'

'We'll worry about that when we get there.'

In the distance, muted and faint, a fire-warning bell started to wail.

'Bloody drills!' snapped the Director. 'Too many of them. If it is the real thing I think I'd rather sit here and fry.'

Rostov chuckled and turned to leave the office.

'Merry Christmas,' said the Director. Rostov was surprised as he turned back. 'Isn't that what you Christians say?'

'Yes. In two days' time.' He smiled, the Director was relaxing, becoming his old self. 'And Merry Christmas to you, too.'

The two men looked at each other, an understanding and warmth between them.

'I'm sorry I pulled you away from your prayers,' said the Director. 'But this is important. I don't like the feel of it. My instincts, as I said before, tell me that someone means us great harm.'

Rostov nodded and left the room. As he walked along the corridor, there was a stream of people rushing in all directions as the alarm clanged on from a lower floor. He decided to ignore it and went to his office. His secretary was out, probably checking to see if there was a real fire or this was simply another interminable safety drill.

He went into his inner office and sat down, started to read the report. It said little more than the Director had, gave detailed information on Stashinsky and the two dead operatives. The German, originally from Dresden but had ended up in Berlin, was an important corporate lawyer who was on vacation with his friends. There was little else, nothing that hung it all together.

He leant back, the fire bell still wailing in the distance, and considered the matter. After a while, when the bell finally stopped, he called his secretary on the intercom. She still hadn't returned. He then dialled the switchboard and asked to be put through to Dimitri Sorge of the Russian Embassy in Washington. He told the operator to ring Sorge's home and ensure it was a clean line, was not tapped by any outside agency. He waited for five minutes before he was connected.

'Dimitri. Sorry to ring you so early.' He knew it was only three in the morning, but this was something that couldn't wait.

When he had finished talking he hung up and went back to the report, rechecked to see if there was anything he had missed the first time.

'Didn't realize you were back,' said his secretary, surprised to find him there as she returned to the office.

'I had to see the Director.'

'Tea?'

'Good idea.'

'I was out because of the fire bell.'

'Another drill?'

'No. It was real this time. An electrical fire.'

'What do you expect in an old building like this? Where?'

'On the fourth floor.'

'Anyone hurt?'

'No. But the room was destroyed before the firemen put it out. A small room. In the filing section.'

'What filing section?' Rostov was alarmed suddenly.

'The old ones. Nothing important. I checked because I knew you'd want to know. Nobody's been in there for years. Trouble is, it's the next batch of information that was to be processed on to the computer.'

'What files were destroyed?'

'All the post-war ones. On agents and other Counter-Intelligence information from the end of the war up to 1956.'

San Diego

NOTHING. JUST BLANK after blank.

Billie stood at the window, her eyes smarting after hours of concentration in front of the computer screen. The bright sun, harsh in its winter clarity, added to her discomfiture and she turned back into the room.

She looked round the small office, the only workplace she had ever known. No high-tech, open-plan California space here. Just a darkened room, last on the right at the top of the stairs, on the first floor above the taxi company. She'd always hated this place, resented being pushed in here so as not to attract attention. And now she wanted to stay here more than anything else. She didn't want the faceless decision makers at Langley to take it all away in the name of economic necessity. This had been her sanity over the years, away from the cauldron of her personal life, away from Peter.

Forty-one and about to become unemployed.

What the hell would she do? What did she know about the outside world? Who'd want a forty-one-year-old collector and disseminator of Intelligence information who spent all her time in front of a computer? And then she wondered about all those files she'd collected over the years, information she'd pumped down the line to Langley. Had they used it, had they learnt anything from it? Had she been of use? Had Billie Wood been of any use? Had Billie Wood made a difference?

There was nothing new she could add to what Langley already knew. Which was nothing. An absolute zero.

She'd worked her way through the indexes, run all the relevant facts through her programme and still come up with nothing. No links, nothing between the few facts that tied Reindeer and a contaminated computer. Three days and nothing more than sore eyes.

She walked back to her desk and sat down again. The taste of a cigarette suddenly filled her throat and she wished she had one. After giving it up for all these years, she still yearned for that dry bitter taste when the pressure was on.

The phone rang and she reached over for it.

'Yes.'

'Billie?'

She recognized Tucker's voice. 'Hallo, Phil.' They were on first-name terms now.

'How are you doing?'

'Not good.' She sensed the disappointment in her own voice.

'Just give it your best. We're not doing much better here.' He'd picked up her disappointment. 'Anyway, there's new developments. Could be a breakthrough.'

'What's happened?' The excitement caught at her.

'Reindeer's not alone any more.' He was being careful, knew that however closed a phone circuit was, there was always the possibility of someone overhearing. 'West Wing's joined him.'

'Where?'

'Hannover. In Germany. He worked as a baggage handler. Had just loaded a small commuter plane when he walked into one of its propellers. The plane was starting to taxi, it was a late flight, so no-one found him, or what was left, till the next morning.'

'Anything unusual?'

'Only that he was sixty-five and about to retire.'

'Police say anything?'

'Our people are chasing that now. We've got to be careful. Can't use the usual channels. But, according to what we know, it's being treated as an accident. I think he had an alcohol problem. According to his wife.'

'You spoke to her?'

'She rang through. That's how we found out. She was also worried about her pension.'

Who isn't, thought Billie. 'Is that it?'

'For now. I'll get a full report, then modem it through to you.'

'Did the computer show anything?' she asked. She knew the answer before he replied.

'Didn't want to know. Just like before. Same pattern. Anyway, it just opens the door a little more. Gives you more to work with.'

'Was he German?' she asked, unsure about what had prompted the question.

'I don't know. Probably. Why?'

'Just looking for a connection. Not SS by any chance?' It was a joke and she said it lightly.

'Yeah, maybe we finally found Adolf Hitler. Hell, I don't know. And we'll never know now.'

'Thanks, Phil.' She knew he wouldn't miss the sarcasm in her voice.

Tucker laughed. 'Have a good day now.'

She sat still for a moment before replacing the receiver.

Two dead. While she sat here in front of this unblinking screen, people were dying out there. And they expected her to find the answer, just to snatch a solution out of thin air. So cold, so unemotional. Yet both those men had died, horribly and cruelly in countries she had only seen on maps.

She thought of West Wing, thought of him being sliced and splattered by the spinning propellor, just stamped out as if he'd never existed, not even a whole being to bury.

She shook her head, turned her mind away from the awfulness of it and started to enter what little information she had.

What she couldn't key in, because she didn't know the details, were those final moments of death. West Wing, turning away from the twin turbo-prop, nineteen-seater Swearingen Metroliner, saw two men approaching him. They both carried long poles and circled him. It was a quiet part of the airport, away from the main terminal and more busy areas. The plane had started to taxi, to swing round towards the runway, when the men had prodded him with their weapons, pushed him backwards towards the spinning blades. He'd cried out, but no-one had heard him above the roar of the turbo engines. Then, before he could duck away to escape the propellor, the first blade had sliced into his skull, sliced the back of his head off in a ball of matted bloody hair,

81

bone and brain. The second blade ripped his body in half, tore the torso from his arms and legs and left a fleshy mess on the tarmac for the undercarriage wheels to taxi over as the plane headed for the runway.

The two men who had caused his death returned to the distant terminal. They left the poles in an engineering shed where they had found them. Both men had short blond hair and walked in step, as soldiers would.

In California, Billie keyed West Wing into her computer.

It was only a small clue, but it gave her some glimmer of hope. Maybe, when they had modemed over more information on him, she would crack the problem. And then she'd be safe. Maybe then they'd keep her on.

She wondered what instinct had prompted her to ask if West Wing had a war record. She laughed at herself. Some instinct. It hadn't done her much good in her life.

She went back to her terminal.

Facts. That's where the answers lay.

Suck instinct. That was for the birds.

CIA HQ
Langley

PHIL TUCKER SAT on the edge of a table and watched the two computer programmers at work.

They were both young, in their early twenties, and more than capable of solving most problems. They had spent over a week trying to find the virus that had infected the Langley computer, but with no apparent success. The real problem was that every time they switched the system on, it simply continued to corrupt the information, continuing from where it left off when the computer was powered down.

All that the programmers had managed to identify was that the virus infected only part of the whole system. Most of the Langley data base was untouched, the CIA's day-to-day operations continuing unabated.

The sections corrupted by the virus were mainly of an archival type. Data on the activities of the Office of Strategic Services were the most affected, including the files on OSS Counter-Intelligence in Europe at the end of the war and up to 1947, when it ceased to exist and became the CIA. But the virus continued, still destroying those files which were a continuation of similar activity until 1958. It was these files which contained information on the early days of the Cold War, of the networks installed throughout Europe by the Americans as the tension between East and West grew, of the many military and scientific secrets that were seized by the OSS from Nazi Germany at the end of the war. Although most of the information was now defunct, there was still the occasional need for it, as in the case of Reindeer. The paper documents had long since been shredded as part of Langley's drive to a paperless situation. The back-up discs were also found to be corrupted with the virus.

He thought of the telephone call during the early hours of the morning. Only this time it wasn't 'Reindeer', but 'West Wing'. He'd known better than to dig into the computer, knew that the virus would eat away the information. So he'd kept the woman talking as he tried to find out who West Wing was. Karl Breitling, a sixty-year-old baggage handler with the airport authority. She knew little else and yes, he would make sure she received her pension. He had passed the information to the DDA's office, but knew they were as much in the dark as he was without the computer. They'd told him to pass the information on to California.

'OK, we're ready to give her another run,' said one of the programmers, breaking into his thoughts.

Tucker nodded his assent, then watched as they prepared to enter the corrupted files.

The first programmer loaded his floppy disc into the system, watched the icon come up on the screen to confirm it was loaded. Once satisfied, he switched to the Langley menu and punched up his authorization code. When the menu was opened, he typed in the code for the OSS files.

While he waited for the system to retrieve the information, he looked at his companion.

'If the antidote works, then it'll enter the system within ten seconds of the menu opening and stop the information from breaking up,' his companion said, speaking to Tucker, who had now swung himself off the table edge and stood behind them.

The three of them watched the screen.

'You know the difference between sex and computers?' the second programmer asked Tucker as they waited.

'No.'

'In computers, the software goes into the hardware,' the programmer paused and waited for Tucker's reaction.

'Go on. I'm slow today.'

'In sex, the hardware goes into the soft . . . ' the first programmer butted in.

'Why are you always spoiling my gags?' snapped his companion.

Tucker laughed as the screen came alive.

The file, an archive on Russian troop movements in Poland in 1951, spilled its information on to the screen, green type on a black background. When the screen was full, it started to break up, the letter As disappearing first, then the Bs and so on.

'One.' The programmer started his count.

The break-up of words continued.

'Two.'

No change.

'Three.'

The Cs started to disappear.

Tucker stood up and walked away. It was like waiting for a rocket launch. He looked out of the small, glass-walled room into the main area where the Communications section went about their normal business. It was a quiet day, but then things had died down a lot since the dawn of *perestroika*. Occasionally, when a crisis like the Gulf War exploded, things got busy again. But, all in all, life had quietened down. He turned back towards the programmers.

'Eight.'

The virus was busily destroying the Gs.

'Nine.'

The Hs started to fade.

'Ten.'

Nothing happened. The Hs turned to Is which turned to Js.

The programmer counted till twenty before they had reached the Rs.

'Crash the programme,' said his companion.

The counter reached forward and switched off the power; the screen went to black.

'Shit!' cursed Tucker.

'Exactly.'

'What next?'

'No idea. That's the sixtieth antidote we've introduced. I can't think of any more. From now on we'll have to design our own. Only trouble is, I don't know what the key is, what they've used for their code. The only way we'll get that is by letting the virus run. By the time we've tested it, got into the binaries, we could've lost most of the data.'

'We can't risk that. I've got to get to a meeting.' It was one that had been hurriedly called and he had received no papers on it. That meant it was an emergency, a crisis brewing. He hoped he could get home to Jean and the kids tonight. 'You're just going to have to go on, try and find another way into the system.'

'How important is this?'

'Top priority. You know that. Why?'

'Tomorrow's Christmas Day.'

'You're lucky. I hear the commissary serves a good turkey brunch.'

He grinned as he left the room, the howls of protest ringing in his ears. Welcome to Langley, boys.

The Office of Communication comes under the responsibility of the Deputy Director for Administration. He is also responsible for Medical Services, Internal Security, Finance, Education, Training, Information Technology, Logistics, Information Services and Personnel.

The virus had now, also, become his responsibility.

He and the Deputy Director for Intelligence had met with

the Executive Director to resolve the problem. The DDI's accountability was for European Analysis as well as his many other functions, which meant he was in charge of all Counter-Intelligence.

'It's not my fucking computer that's fucked up,' argued the DDI. He was a man known for his blunt manner, a brute who ruthlessly steam-rollered his way through any obstacle that stood in his path. Because of this single-minded purpose, and a natural cunning that came from his years in the field, he was one of the most successful DDIs the Agency had ever had. 'If you ran internal security as efficiently as you run the fucking kitchens, maybe we wouldn't be in this fuck-up.' The DDI was also well known for his hatred of all administrators, especially the Deputy Director for Administration.

'Personal attacks are not going to resolve this situation,' answered the DDA, irritated but not rising to his counter-part's usual boorish behaviour.

'Tell that to the poor shits out in the field. Tell them how you're going to resolve the fucking situation. That's if they're still alive to be told.'

'Let's not exaggerate. We've lost one, possibly two, assets. In Lapland and in Germany. That's not—'

'We also had an attempt on one of our top scientists.'

'We don't know that for sure.'

'Come on. Guy runs up, pulls a gun out and peppers away at one of our top people. Don't fucking tell me that's not for sure.'

'That point has yet to be proved,' interjected the Executive Director. He was the senior executive, below only the Director of Central Intelligence and his Deputy.

'Proved or not, we can't take any chances. This is a top-alert situation as far as my people are concerned.'

'Which is a wise precaution. But we need more information. Isn't there anything coming out of your contacts?'

'Nothing.'

'Is Trimmler home now?'

'Yeah. We flew him straight out once we'd heard what happened. He's in San Diego, safe at home.'

'And Reindeer?'

'Also nothing. He left no messages, nothing except a wife who's only worried about her pension.' He turned to the DDA. 'I hope you've resolved that issue.'

'Of course.'

'We haven't had time to get anything on West Wing. I've got people on it. But my gut tells me it'll be as fruitless as Reindeer. Damn it, these guys were sleepers. They were there only to be activated in the event of an emergency. They looked after themselves, were cut off from us. They just knew we'd look after them and their families if anything happened. Since the end of the Cold War, they've become an embarrassment. We don't know what to do with them. Can't pull them out because we might need them, can't leave them there because we could get found out and end up with egg on our face. We don't know who, or where, half of them are any more. Not without that fucking computer.'

'I can't see it being the Russians,' said the Executive Director.

'Why not?'

'Too much to lose.'

'Unless they're up to something.'

'Something so important that they're taking out everyone over sixty. I don't think so. Anyway, there's another point which we should resolve first. One much closer to home.'

His two Deputies looked at him, waited for him to continue.

'The only way that virus could be introduced into the system was by someone at Langley. I accept that we're having trouble finding out how to control it. But I also think it's time we concerned ourselves with who put it in there, and also how deep that person, or persons, went into the data base. It could just be that we don't have any secrets left. Could just be that they were milked out a long time ago.'

Carter, the DDA's assistant, was alone in the meeting room when Phil Tucker walked in.

The two men had met a week previously when Tucker had made the first report on Reindeer and the computer virus.

'Hi!' greeted Tucker. He didn't like Carter, found him too

87

aggressive in his manner, but appreciated they all had to live together and at least appear to be one big happy family at Langley. He pulled up a chair and sat down. 'Anybody else coming?'

'The DDA.'

'Big guns.' Tucker became alert, he hadn't expected the Deputy Director of Administration to attend.

'And the DDI.'

'Heavy stuff.' Tucker was impressed. He had never attended a meeting with two Deputy Directors before.

'Did you take the call about West Wing?'

'Yeah. I was on duty.'

'That's two now. Him and Reindeer.'

Tucker realized why he didn't like Carter. A stater of the obvious. Hard-headed, with not a lot between the ears. 'I heard there was an attempt to knock out one of our top scientists.' He decided to push for information.

'Jungle fucking drums. That's classified.'

'That he was on vacation in France.' Tucker pushed harder. 'Some guy just came along the beach and popped him.'

'Where'd you get this crap from?'

'Like you said. Jungle drums.'

'Who?'

'Someone. I overheard it when I was waiting in line at the commissary.'

'Don't bullshit me, Tucker.'

'Look, we're in this together. We're meant to be on the same side. I'm not going to tell you who said what. It's common knowledge anyway. I need to know. Especially if it's all related to Reindeer and West Wing.'

Carter thought for a moment and then sat down.

'What I tell you is for your ears only,' he said, keeping his voice low. 'I don't even want the DDA to know I said anything. If they want to tell you, that's up to them.'

'OK with me.' Tucker smiled. Gossip was one thing you could get out of people at Langley. It was part of the 'I'm-more-important-than-you' process. There were no secrets in the company.

'Heinrich Trimmler. One of our top rocket boys. At the

Mirimar Air Base, out at La Jolla. They have a research and development facility there. Don't ask me what they do, I really don't know. Except that it's top, top priority.'

'I presume he's American?'

'He is now. Came over after the war. Anyway, he was sitting on this beach in the South of France with some friends when this African, from Senegal, comes up and opens fire on the group. Missed Trimmler but killed a friend of his.'

'What did the African say afterwards?'

'Not a lot. A cop shot him dead.'

'What makes you so sure he was after Trimmler?'

'We ain't. Except that someone's after our assets and the African aimed his shooter at him and pulled the trigger. Only reason he's still around is because the gun jammed. Trimmler's pretty high-powered. Been on the Canaveral and Houston teams, was one of Von Braun's main people.'

'I guess he didn't stay on and improve his sun-tan.'

'Yeah.' Carter laughed. 'That was quite a moment.'

'Why?'

'We sent a G4 to pick him up at Nice Airport as soon as we heard what happened.' The Gulfstream G4 is probably the finest, long-range executive jet in the world and can fly at an altitude of forty-three thousand feet across the Atlantic. Faster than most commercial jets, it is commonly used by government agencies in America. 'When they got there, Trimmler and his wife were waiting at the airport, but there was no sign of their daughter. She's nineteen years old and, so they say, beautiful with it. So, one of our people went back to the hotel to find her. He did that all right. In bed with two guys, both old enough to be her grandfathers, in sex gear that you only see in the dirty movies. It was in her parents' bedroom, in the bed they'd just vacated. And the best of it was that she was being paid. Our guys got her dressed and dragged her out. And the clients were screaming after them that they wanted their money back.' Carter snorted as he laughed. 'I tell ya, that didn't go in any report. On the way back, she just sat there, demure as a kitten. And when she arrived in San Diego, she gave all the guys her business card, printed with her name and telephone number. Said to call any time they wanted.'

89

Tucker watched Carter chuckling to himself, could imagine him at a bar with a beer in his hand, a constant source of smutty jokes. He'd dine on that one for a long time. He wondered if Carter had a daughter, wondered how she'd turn out.

The door opened and the two Deputy Directors walked in.

Tucker and Carter stood up.

'It's OK. Sit down.'

The two men sat again as the newcomers joined them at the table.

'How big are these computer files we're talking about?' the DDI asked Tucker, getting straight to the point.

'Very. Just to give you an idea, in the late 1950s Russia's State Security Committee, which presided over the whole of their Secret Service, employed nearly a million people inside and outside the Soviet Union. Now, we didn't have every one of those people on our data base, but we were receiving information daily from all over the world on their personnel. That came under the Office of Soviet Analysis, one of your departments, sir. Then there was the rest of Europe, South America, Asia and Africa. On top of that, just dealing with the Russian personnel, we also had covert investigations running on students and other possible activists here in the United States. And let's not forget McCarthy and everything he drummed up. I've got one section which just deals with Hollywood and every actor, writer, director, producer and cameraman. Add to that the OSS records, the Nazi Spy rings, the Korean War . . . I could go on for ever. And all that information probably covers no more than 25 per cent of what we're talking about.'

'Always did have too much fucking paperwork in this organization,' said the DDI, looking accusingly at the DDA.

'And all this is at risk?' asked the DDA, ignoring his colleague's criticism.

'Could be, sir.'

'Explain.'

'We've identified that not all the files are contaminated. Asia seems untouched, as does Australia. Northern Africa too, but South Africa is almost wiped out.'

90

'South America?'

'Contaminated.'

The two DDs looked at each other, but Tucker went on, ending their sudden speculation.

'Funnily enough, the Cuban files are untouched.'

'Or changed,' said the DDI.

'No, sir. We would've identified that. Most of the South American cases are in the southern half of the continent, from Brazil down. But the heaviest contamination is in the European field. The whole of that data base, from 1943 onwards, anything to do with counter-intelligence or OSS activities, is under threat.'

'Are you any closer to tracing this virus?'

'No, sir.'

'Why not?'

'Because we don't know its code. It'll have its own logic, be designed to be activated at a certain time, or when certain information is called up. And it'll be trained to attack specific data, corrupt select fields. We don't even know what that logic is. And it's so advanced that it just reactivates every time we power up the computer to go into these files. It won't allow copies to be made, no data to be transferred. We've run over sixty tests, introduced as many antidotes and we're no nearer solving it than when we started.'

'The only way we can progress this thing is by trying to outguess whoever's put this game together. Do you have any idea why Reindeer and West Wing were taken out? Is there any link, however remote?'

'Not that I can find. We don't have much on West Wing, just what I learnt on the phone. Maybe there'll be more when our people go in.'

'From now on, you are to work directly to the two of us. I don't want it discussed with anyone, it's the only way we'll get to the bottom of this. Nobody is to be trusted. Understood?'

'Yes, sir.' Tucker decided to cover his back. 'We've already brought a dissemination expert in from California. She knows as much as I do.'

'She's cleared,' interrupted the DDA. 'Any progress there?'

'No, not yet.'

'OK. The following information is for your ears only.' The DDI then proceeded to tell Tucker about the attempt on Trimmler's life, about his importance and how he was to be protected. Tucker nodded, as if hearing it for the first time. Over his shoulder he could feel Carter's eyes piercing into the back of his head.

'You think this is all tied up?' asked Tucker when the DDI had eventually finished.

'We don't know. But we sure as hell aren't taking any fucking chances.'

'Our first task is to identify and wipe out the virus,' said the DDA.

'We're pushing ahead with that,' replied Tucker. 'But there's no guarantees.'

'Understood. We also need to consider three other factors. I would like your ideas, on paper, by tomorrow.'

Bang goes Christmas, thought Tucker.

'First, we need to protect Trimmler. Just in case he's a target. He's at Mirimar right now. Living in the officers' quarters. He's not too happy about that. We need someone to liaise with him. No high fliers, just someone who can respond quickly. Can California take it?'

'I'm sure she can,' responded Tucker.

'Any field experience?' interjected the DDI.

'No, sir.'

'We need someone with field experience. Gotta have that.'

'Everyone with field experience is on the computer.'

'Let's cross that bridge when we come to it,' returned the DDA. He brought them back to his own priorities. 'Second, we need to identify and then protect our asset base. Third, we need to come up with any ideas as to why this is going on. We don't have much to go on, but let's make a start on it.' He stood up, the DDI following. 'Tomorrow evening, seven o'clock sharp. At my house.' At least the DDA wasn't going to miss Christmas. The DDI looked disgruntled; the other two didn't know they had tossed for the choice of house. Like all fathers, they wanted to spend Christmas at home.

'If something comes up, who do I report to?' asked Tucker, hoping it wasn't Carter.

'To me,' snapped the DDA. 'Communications comes under my brief. If you can't contact me, then go directly to the DDI. Mr Carter is along to represent Internal Security.'

When they had left, Tucker spoke. 'You didn't have a lot to say.'

'Damn right,' replied Carter. 'This one's for the losers. It's your fucking computer. You sort it out.'

After he had gone, Tucker sat still, nervously working out what he was going to tell Jean and the children. Sorry kids, but it's only Santa and the CIA who work on Christmas Day. Even the President gets the day off.

Hyatt Regency Hotel
Washington DC

THE GIRL WITH the large black attaché case walked through the lobby, her striking dark looks attracting envious glances.

She was oblivious to the attention, it was something she was used to, as most really beautiful women are. In her mid-twenties, Mary Monicker wasn't just your everyday hooker. She worked for the most exclusive escort agency in Washington, her clientele carefully screened and consisting of the most powerful diplomats and government officials, elected or otherwise, in that capital city.

Dressed in a smart, dark grey business suit over a high-collared cream blouse, Mary looked like any other personal assistant or junior executive on her way to an important meeting. Her carriage, conservative and poised, was not one which encouraged men to approach her. Neither did the large, brutish gentleman in a black suit who walked beside her. It was her driver, her minder, the man who got the papers signed.

Upstairs, in a corner suite on the ninth floor, Philip Nowak, Special Assistant to the Secretary of State with responsibilities for European Security, poured himself a drink. Behind him, looking out of the window, already with a Scotch and soda in his hand, Dimitri Sorge, Deputy Military Attaché at the Russian Embassy, looked out on the street below.

'A lot of traffic for Christmas Eve, don't you think?'

'Busy time in Washington. All those bachelor boys and girls with no homes to go to. Party time for middle management.' Nowak joined Sorge at the window. 'What's so important, Dimi, that's got me away from my family on Christmas Eve?'

'I must apologize for my timing,' replied Sorge, turning away from the window and coming deeper into the room. 'But, as you know, when our masters call, we must react immediately.'

Nowak nodded and grinned. He knew Sorge's orders came directly from the top echelons of the KGB, just as Sorge knew that Nowak reported directly to the Executive Director of the CIA. Knowing where the other stood made life easier for both of them. They were the direct link between the two security agencies, the fail-safe contact which allowed the Directors of each Agency to communicate with one another when all else failed. Nowak and Sorge had known each other for over ten years, had seen the Cold War thaw, the Berlin Wall crumble and the rich promises of *perestroika* start to be fulfilled. Their loyalties lay with their individual agencies, but their friendship was as firm as could be expected under the circumstances.

'You've already told your superior that I wanted to meet?' asked Sorge.

'Of course.' Nowak had reported back to the CIA Executive Director and been surprised when he was summoned immediately to Langley for a meeting. After the briefing he was told to listen to what Sorge said and then only to engage in further discussion if the content of the Russian's interchange was similar to his own.

'You know why I want this meeting?'

Nowak chuckled to himself. It was typical of Dimi to call a meeting and then play dumb in an attempt to find out how much the American knew. No wonder the Russians made great chess players.

'No,' he replied.

'My people want to know if you are about to renew hostilities between our two countries.'

'What on earth for?' Nowak was genuinely surprised by the question.

'That is what we would like to know.'

'Come on, Dimi. Nobody wants to go back to how it was. You must have a reason for saying that.'

There was a knock on the door.

'Ah!' said Sorge. 'The evening's entertainment, I hope.'

He crossed the living area to the door and opened it. Mary Monicker stood there, her escort beside her. 'Good. You've arrived.' He stood back as they entered the room, closed the door behind them.

'Not on Christmas Eve?' exclaimed Nowak, a big grin spreading across his face.

'What better time? I thought it's when you Christians give presents.'

'Mister Sorge?' asked the escort.

'Yes.'

'I need your signature,' the escort continued, taking a carbonized sheet of printed paper out of his top pocket. 'Under the laws of this state, prostitution is illegal and carries heavy fines and a possible jail sentence. Our escorts are here simply to keep you company. No suggestion of sex, either for money or not, is to be made by you. The charge for this service is $150 an hour. There will be an additional charge of $150 per hour, or part of, for any extension of your companion's time. To make sure everything's to your satisfaction, and to ours, your escort will be required to ring in on the hour. As well as cash, payment can be made with American Express, Visa, Master Card or Diner's Club. If you agree to these terms, just sign this contract for an evening's companionship.'

'No sex?'

'No sex.' The escort ignored the grin on Sorge's face and took a pen from his top pocket. 'That's a fact.'

Sorge shrugged and reached over, signed the paper where indicated.

'Thank you,' said the escort, handing Sorge a copy of the agreement and pocketing the original. 'Have a nice day. Merry Christmas.' He turned and left the suite.

'Hallo, Mary,' said Sorge.

'Dimi,' she acknowledged, leaning forward and kissing him on the cheek.

'This is a friend of mine. Philip Nowak.'

'Hi, Phil.'

'Mary,' Nowak replied.

'The usual terms?' Mary turned her attention back to Sorge.

'Of course.'

'Well, you guys finish your little talk. I'll just go and freshen up.'

The two men watched her walk into the bedroom before Sorge went and poured himself another drink. Nowak sat in the armchair facing the bedroom and watched Mary put her attaché case on the bed before opening it. Sorge came and sat opposite him on the sofa.

'Is she safe?'

'These girls hear more classified information than the KGB and CIA together. They earn too much to risk talking about what they pick up. Their jobs depend on them being safe.'

'So, why the meeting?'

'As we both know, *perestroika* has left many loose ends as far as intelligence is concerned. Things started so long ago that it is sometimes impossible to stop them. It's no secret that we both have sleeper agents, all over the world. We have more than you, but that is only because you decided under President Carter to concentrate on satellite and aerial surveillance. Even if you've stopped spying on us, the satellites remain in position. It only takes a second to switch a camera back on. Our spies are on the ground. Europe, Africa, we have representation in most areas. Like you, we don't use them, but they're there . . . in case.'

'It's something we both accept. Even used it to our mutual advantage.' They both knew Nowak referred to the Iraq Gulf Crisis. He didn't allow his excitement to show. The conversation was going the way his Executive Director had hoped.

'One of our sleepers has been taken out. In the last few weeks.'

'What?' Nowak unwittingly showed his surprise. It was not what he had expected, not what Langley had briefed him on.

'That's right. I won't say where, but it was definitely assassination.'

'How do you know?'

'The methods used were KGB-style killing from the 1950s.'

'You're joking.'

'No.'

'What method is that?'

'It's not relevant.'

'And you want to know if we're involved.'

'Obviously.'

'If we were, we'd simply deny it.'

'Are you?'

'No.'

'Will you help us?'

'I would think so. But that isn't my decision. Are you asking for assistance?'

'Not my decision either. I was simply told to open a dialogue between us.'

'OK. I'll pass that on. Come on, Dimi. There's more, isn't there?'

'Of course. Your people rushed one of your scientists out of Cannes the other day. A black pedlar started shooting at a group he was with.'

'That's right. We thought he might be in danger.' Nowak leant back and looked into the bedroom. The main lights had gone out, but a light flickered on the bedroom wall. There was no sign of the girl, but he heard a tap running. She must be in the bathroom.

He decided to cross the line.

'I was called to a meeting at Langley before I came here,' he said. 'Just me and the Exec Director. We've also lost two of our operatives. Like you, in the last two weeks. One of them was only yesterday.'

Sorge looked disbelievingly at his old friend.

'It's true,' Nowak continued. 'There were no old-style methods used, but we believe the action was deliberate. Too much coincidence.'

'And you think it's us?'

'What do you expect, Dimi? After all these years. That's why we were concerned about our guy in Cannes. He deals with some pretty vital stuff.'

'We know the same method was used in Cannes as that which took out our sleeper,' Sorge stated flatly.

'No shit?' Nowak blurted out disbelievingly.

'Why should I lie?'

'Fuck it, Dimi. The guy used a shot-gun. Nothing strange about that. Even for your lot.' He regretted his own cheap distasteful joke immediately.

'He didn't. The Kraut was already dead. Before he was shot.'

'It doesn't make sense. Except that our people are convinced that they were after the scientist. You sure he was dead before he got hit?'

'As I said, it was a tried and tested KGB procedure.'

'So, why tell us?'

'Because our hands are clean. Because someone's taking us both on.'

'Hi, boys,' Mary appeared at the bedroom door. 'Look what Santa's brought you.'

They both looked in her direction, saw her standing there in a red, fur-lined top that barely covered her firm breasts, pushed out by the white lace bra that clasped together at the front. She wore no panties or G-string, only a Father Christmas false white beard that covered her most private part. Long suspender straps stretched down her thighs and fastened to sheer dark tan stockings.

It was definitely a conversation stopper.

'So. Do you boys want to fuck or do you want to make love?' she went on.

'What's the difference?' asked Nowak.

'Three hundred dollars or five hundred dollars.'

The two men laughed at her bawdiness and Sorge stood up.

'Let's talk in the bedroom,' he said.

The girl turned on her five-inch, red stiletto heels and went into the bedroom, the two men following her.

The lights were off and five slim candles in small, red-glass containers now flickered, lighting the room. The attaché case stood open on the floor, empty, its contents laid regimentally on the dressing table.

There were two whips, one with delicate leather thongs no more than ten inches long, the other much more brutal which Indiana Jones would have been proud to own. Next to these were a selection of dildos. The smallest was narrow, no more than three inches long, hard plastic and rough surfaced. The largest was what could only be described as an implement, smooth and pliable rubber, over fourteen inches long and with a large penis-shaped head at each end. The three that lay between them were of various shapes and sizes; it was a selection to satisfy all demands. There was also a variety of rubber underwear, men's leather briefs and a selection of pornographic photographs.

Mary swirled round, letting them enjoy her body, and envisage what was coming. She was in her element, a long way from the demure professional executive who had walked through the hotel lobby some fifteen minutes earlier.

Nowak walked over, picked up the smallest flesh-coloured dildo and held it up towards her. 'Bit out of its league, isn't it?'

Mary laughed and took it from him.

'Sit down, boys,' she purred. 'Show time.'

The two men sat, Sorge on the only chair in the room, Nowak on the edge of the dressing table. He picked up the photographs and started to leaf through them as she climbed on to the bed, rolling over on to her back so that she faced them, her legs splayed, visions of depravity opening before them. She slipped off the beard and started slowly to rub her opening, turning her warmth and dryness to wetness. They heard the sound of her fingers caressing her juices, saw her smiling face taunting them.

Once she had moistened herself, she slipped the little dildo into herself, probed her inner flesh with short, sharp jabs. Then, she pulled it out and licked it, rolling it with her lips. Finally she put it between her legs and slipped it into her other entrance, the hell to her frontal heaven.

Sorge unzipped his trousers and, pulling his hardness out of the shelter of his clothing, started to stroke himself. Nowak said nothing, just looked at her as he put the photos back on the table.

'Look at it, boys. Look at it,' she commanded, enjoying the power she knew she excited in them, urging them on as she rotated her hips invitingly.

'You ever do it for nothing, honey?' asked Nowak, his eyes transfixed by heaven and hell splayed before him.

She laughed, safe in the knowledge that these two tricks were good for the price. 'Once had a boy, no more than eighteen, who got me into his hotel room. Keep looking, you bastard,' she swore at Sorge, who had looked away from her openness to her face as she spoke. He went back to watch her seduce her own flesh. 'You just keep your eyes down there, baby, you keep your eyes on the action. That boy only had twenty dollars. Twenty fucking dollars, that's all. I told him I'd have the twenty, but only stroke him for it. But when he took his pants off, wow, when I saw what he had. He was big, something else. Well, I just had to have that thing in me, boys. Just had to. And did he go. Eighteen years old and the biggest cock I ever saw. After that, I just couldn't bring myself to . . . he saved himself twenty bucks. Boys, if you want my best, it's going to be worth every penny. Now, just keep looking, just keep your heads thinking.'

Nowak stood up suddenly and climbed on to the bed, lying flat, his head between her open legs, only inches from her.

'Keep looking, boy. Keep looking.'

Sorge leant forward in his chair, saw Nowak's head move sharply forward, saw it bob up and down as he manipulated his tongue into her; first by sliding it in long deep strokes up and down her valley, then rubbing his nose and full mouth into her wetness, washing his face with her juices, licking at her until she started to respond as he wanted, not as a $500-an-hour hooker, but as a woman. No eighteen-year-old boy was going to outdo Nowak. She moved sharply, bringing her legs upwards as she released the small dildo that she had inserted into her rear, grabbing the top of his head with her hands and pulling his face deeper into her. He stopped licking as he sensed her urgency, now jabbed at her small mound of heaven, probed that pointed peak that was hard and sharp under his tongue.

'Don't stop,' she ordered Nowak, her voice low and deep

in her hunger. 'For fuck's sake, don't stop. Don't stop.'

Sorge watched them, watched his friend's head bobbing up and down between Mary's wide-stretched legs, watched her arched body as this sudden unexpected passion absorbed her, saw the whore scream and release all over his friend's mouth and tongue. As her body suddenly went limp, as her legs straightened and collapsed back on the bed, Nowak looked up at her, then turned and grinned at Sorge.

'Yankee know-how,' he said, pushing himself up so he was now kneeling between her legs.

'The Nijinsky of cunnilingus,' Sorge joked back.

'Wow!' said Mary, turning her head to Sorge. 'What's he like when he takes his clothes off?'

'What evidence?' asked Nowak, taking his jacket off, followed by his tie and shirt. 'Your people in Cannes. What evidence did they find?'

'Something you wouldn't be looking for.' Sorge stood up and started to undress.

'The police, and our people, combed the whole beach. They found nothing. What sort of weapon is that good that . . . ' Nowak had kicked off his shoes and was now unzipping his trousers.

Mary watched him, her legs still open as he knelt between them.

'Trust me,' interrupted Sorge.

'Too much coincidence.'

'No. Not enough coincidence.'

'Langley is worried about our asset base. It's something neither side has turned their attention to.'

'So, who's going to be the first to call in their sleepers?'

Nowak shrugged as he slid his trousers off, his hardness not affected by the discussion with Sorge. The American kept his eyes on Mary's face, not wanting to lose the heat that drove him.

'Is it time to bring our people in from the cold?' asked Sorge, now almost completely undressed.

'That's not our decision.'

'But we need to know what your people want.'

'That's what I was asked to find out. What you want. It's

a fucking stalemate. I mean, who's going to be the first to make that decision. And how do we monitor it? Who's going to believe the other's pulled all his sleepers in?' Nowak stood up on the bed, straddling over the whore. 'You want to go first?' he asked.

'No, no. After you. This one's on me.'

'Ever the diplomat, Dimi. Ever the diplomat.' Nowak lowered himself over Mary's face, knelt over her and pushed his penis into her mouth. 'We need to know what's going on out there, Dimi. We need to know.' His voice was urgent and breathless, not because of the content of his words, but because the whore sucked him hard into her.

'It must be stopped. Before it gets out of hand,' muttered the Russian to a disinterested audience.

Sorge climbed on to the bed, behind Nowak and hoisted the whore's hips up with his arms, positioned her so he could enter her as she occupied herself elsewhere. He looked at the American's moving back, admired the firm muscles and wished the girl wasn't there. With Mary's legs now firmly wrapped round him, trapped by his bulk, he put his arms round Nowak, knew the American would think he was only holding him for support. Then he pushed with his hips and grinned as he heard her squeal as he claimed the hell hole for his own. She tried to yelp with the sharp pain, but there was little she could do, jammed to the bed by the weight of the two big men, both pumping at her as they worked towards their release.

Outside the candle-lit window, the first snow was starting to fall on the streets of Washington. People rushed by, cars were driven impatiently, the last few jets took off over the Potomac from Washington National Airport as travellers looked forward eagerly to the warmth and comfort of their suburban homes.

Hosanna. It was going to be a white Christmas.

San Diego

THERE WAS NO snow that Christmas in San Diego.

There never was, apart from what was sprinkled on the trees in the windows of the downtown department stores.

Billie Wood had never seen a white Christmas, except on television. She had once spent Christmas in Atlantic City. There had been no snow, only wind and rain and a bone-chilling cold that made her yearn for her native California. Her companion, an early lover after she had split with her husband, was as wet as the weather and spent most of his time at the dice table. She had left him there, spending the fortune he never had and was trying to win, and caught the only flight available back to San Diego, only to spend a lonely holiday by the TV set wondering where Peter was. And who he was with.

'You want some grapefruit juice for breakfast?' Billie called from the kitchen as she poured boiling water on the herbal tea in the pot.

'What d'ya say?' Gary shouted back at her from the exercise room.

'Do you want grapefruit juice?' she replied, louder so that he could hear.

'Yeah,' came the muffled reply.

She poured some grapefruit juice into two tumblers and put them on the large tray, next to the pot of tea, the two cups and the Swiss muesli that was all ready milked in the two bowls. She picked up the tray and left the kitchen, walked through the sitting area and bedroom and into the exercise area that opened on to the balcony.

'Hi, babe,' panted Gary, a gleaming muscle-machine, strapped to an exercise bench with weights above his shoulders as he pumped iron, the weights sliding up and down in the iron frame as he pushed himself beyond the limit.

She smiled warmly at him and put the tray on the table by the sliding doors. She turned to watch, admired his twenty-six-year-old body that was his pride and joy. His short jogging shorts were glued to his body by the perspiration he generated, his muscles straining as he lifted his inner self beyond pain and physical limits. She compared him to Peter, he of the burnt-out and wasted muscles, the bloated waistline and the thinning hair.

He'd be in his 'I-want-to-be-younger' designer clothes now. The girl on his arm his latest accessory. Designer woman to go with his designer clothes.

Go away, Peter. This day has nothing to do with you.

She walked over to Gary, letting her short housecoat fall open and reveal her nakedness, apart from a white G-string. She knelt by his head, pulled her stomach in and fondled his blond locks, ran her fingers through his hair. California blond. It's how she liked her men. Except for Peter, damn him.

'You OK, babe?' she whispered in his ear, gently blowing into it.

'Easy, baby. I gotta finish.' He was in his own world, trying to crash his own barriers, irritated by her interruption.

But she wasn't prepared to be dissuaded. It was Christmas. Even if there wasn't any snow.

She slipped off her housecoat and moved further down the bench, watched the sweat running off his chest and stomach muscles. She loved the smell of his body juices and she rubbed her face over his skin, tasted its salty wetness with her tongue. He ignored her, concentrated on his task. She moved lower, her tongue still probing as she neared the top band of his shorts.

'I gotta finish,' he gasped as he pushed the weight upward once again.

'Later, baby. Do it later.' She reached down and slid his shorts down to his ankles. It wasn't true what they said about body builders. They were as big, if not bigger, than most others. She reached towards it, tentatively and full of wonder. It always surprised her how this small tube of flesh grew and developed into the hard manhood that she craved for. It was a magic moment, that short instance between limp futility and hardened ecstasy. She leant forward, her mouth about to absorb his softness.

'For Chris'sake, Billie!' he shouted, the weight banging down on its stops as he let it go. He sat up suddenly, his anger obvious. 'I gotta finish my programme. You know I gotta do that every day.'

'You killed the passion!' she yelled back, picking up her robe as she stood up. 'It's Christmas, damn it. What's wrong with that? Fuck your programme. Just for one stinking day. Can't you do that for me?'

She wrapped her robe round herself and rushed to the door. She turned and looked at him, the hurt and humiliation wrenching at her.

'You look fucking ridiculous,' she derided him. 'Lying there, working out on your body, your pants round your fucking ankles.'

He swung his legs off the exercise bench and attempted to pull up his shorts, but they had twisted in their dampness and he struggled, tripping over them and crashing to the floor. He swore loudly as the pain stabbed at his knee and he gripped it tightly, the entangled shorts now forgotten.

She was suddenly concerned for him and she rushed forward to help, but he pushed her away.

'Fuck off!' he shouted. 'Don't treat me like shit. Just 'cos you pay all the bills. Don't . . . '

'I'm sorry, Gary baby.' She despised her own pleading, but couldn't stop herself. 'I didn't mean it. I just wanted you. I just . . . '

'I could've busted my knee. Damn it, I could've been hospitalized.'

'I'm sorry. I just wanted to share something with you. It's Christmas.'

'You should've waited.'

'I just wanted to be with you.'

'You just wanted to fuck. That's all you think I'm worth. Just someone to fuck.'

'No, that's not true. That's not—'

'That's it. That's all it ever was.'

He stood up and pushed her away, knocking her to the floor. He managed to pull his shorts up and left her in her misery. In time, when she had composed herself, she rose and went to the window and looked out on the Californian coast.

She hated her loneliness, knew he was right. But it wasn't

just the sex; like most women she could live without that. It was the loneliness. It was the emptiness that comes from going home and having no-one to share the day's gossip with.

She wished she could go to work. If only there was something worthwhile to go to work for. She'd got no further with the task Langley had set her, and now Tucker had called to say she was expected to nursemaid a scientist. She wondered if they knew what they were doing.

The dread of that awful memo on her desk, still not answered, sent her into a deeper depression. It wasn't right, taking away her job after all these years. Damn it.

It was a miserable Christmas.

In Washington the DDA put the phone down.

He was surprised the Exec Director had agreed so readily to his plan of action. He knew the DDI would be against it, which is why he'd gone straight to his superior.

The Exec Director had told him he would ring London direct.

The DDA hoped there'd be an answer by Christmas evening. He wanted to see the look on the DDI's face. He grinned as he imagined his colleague's discomfort and angry reaction.

He heard his wife calling. The first of their many guests were arriving.

Then he went through into the dining room to carve the Christmas turkey, to slice it as cleanly as he hoped his news would slice the DDI.

Dresden
Germany

THEY BURIED WILLI Kushmann in the city of his birth on the day after Christmas. It was a cold, bitter morning, still dark at 6 a.m., with storm clouds threatening a rain that never seemed to come.

The cemetery was on the southern outskirts of the old city, an overgrown place that had been little tended over the years. Many of the gravestones had been broken and lay littered over the three-acre site. Its appearance was of a disused and forgotten spot, not something amiss in an East Germany that was busily being reunified.

Dresden, like East Berlin and Leipzig and most of what had been East Germany, is a city where time has stood still. Its architecture, that which was left standing after one of the most devastating bombing raids of the last war, is a mixture of 1950s drab and fine German baroque. Its demeanour is pretty yet shabby, its people expectant but weary after nearly fifty years of Russian occupation and Communist rule.

The strength of the city and its people was their link with the past. Not so much in what Germany had once been, but what it could once again become. Their past was their hope. If they had achieved greatness before, then they could achieve it once again. The shining example of West Germany was their torch, the memory of pre-war days their ambition.

Unlike the West, without the freedom of a democratic society, many of them had secretly clung to their heritage. To them, the war had finally finished when the Wall came down and the Russian troops had evacuated their land. There was now an urgency to redress what was lost, a need to wear their nationalistic badge proudly once again.

Because of this stubborn conviction, there were now many separate nationalistic groups, embryo political parties who wanted a slice of power for themselves and felt they deserved a bigger say in a united Germany's future. Not all of them believed in the Western system of democracy. Some of these groups were secretive in their intent and their membership. Unlike their fellow countrymen in the West, whom they saw as softened by the extravagances of a modern society, the new freedom was the first step to their rightful place as the world's most powerful nation.

Old habits die hard. Especially when they've been suppressed for nearly fifty years.

Willi Kushmann had belonged to such a group and been one of its most influential members. A lawyer by profession, he had concentrated on corporate legislation as soon as he understood that the two Germanys were to be united. He realized, unlike his own experiences in the communist environment, that economic power was supreme. The leading corporations had a major say in, if not control of, the prosperity and destination of the more powerful states.

West Germany was one of those.

In his view, East Germany must join ranks with her sister country and together they would become the most powerful nation. His destiny lay in the West, so he concentrated all his efforts to that end. Within a surprisingly short time he had joined a competitive law firm in Frankfurt and was put in charge of a department that dealt solely with the legalities of Corporate Reunification. Mergers and take-overs became his speciality; he was the expert to whom everyone turned.

His list of contacts increased and he was seen at all the right functions, all the correct social gatherings. He became part of the establishment and no-one questioned why he had climbed the ladder to success so rapidly. But he knew, and more importantly understood, the significance of his link with the past. It was a chain that must never be broken.

Reunification wasn't just about the East Germans swopping their Trabants and Wartburgs for Mercedes and BMWs. It was about a dream that had been stifled fifty years previously. A dream that passed through the generations, lost for some but deeply yearned for by others. A secret shared over the years between many powerful people both in East and West Germany.

The dream had been kept alive by the older generation, kept alive through their shame and disgrace of the Russian jackboot. It had been handed down to those like Willi Kushmann, passed down, not as a memory or a footnote in history, but as a flame to be kept burning as strong as ever.

Willi Kushmann had been the bright hope who would turn that dream into reality.

Except that now he was being laid to rest in a neglected graveyard in the city of his birth and at a time in the morning when few people were about, when the funeral would pass relatively unnoticed. For such a seemingly unimportant funeral in such a forgotten place there were many more mourners than anticipated.

On the pot-holed road that skirted the mortuary, there was a line of cars, a confused mixture of black Mercedes, Trabants and Wartburgs.

At the entrance to the graveyard, where a large wooden gate had once stood between the stone wall, three men waited, one of them sitting on the wall, his legs idly swinging beneath him. The other two stood on the path that led to the graveyard and the mourners hidden by the trees that masked the scene. They were big men, short-cropped hair, skinheaded and brutish in appearance. They all wore dark overcoats, in order not to draw attention to themselves. Underneath the topcoats, they were dressed in identical mustard-brown shirts with a military insignia in the shape of a cross with the ends linked up and an eagle's head at its centre, stitched to an armband on their left sleeves. The breeches were of a darker brown shade, tucked into knee-length, black leather boots.

The graveyard was in the public domain, but no member of the public would be allowed to attend this funeral without the permission of those on the gate.

There were seven other guards scattered over the area, most of them hidden in the trees. Unlike those on the gate and in spite of the cold, they displayed their uniform proudly, their topcoats on the ground beside them. You could see they carried no weapons, apart from the short police batons that were strapped to the back of their belts. Each guard also had a scout's hunting knife tucked in to the top of his right boot with the same military insignia stamped in gold on its black handle.

The funeral was over and Kushmann's coffin had been lowered into the earth. The mourners, some forty of them, wandered around the graves in small groups, looking for forgotten names amongst the headstones. For many it had been the first time they had returned to the East, to this part of Germany that reminded them of their youth. Most of the mourners were in their sixties; some expensively dressed, the others in simple suits that had seen better days. Most surprising of all, there were no women present.

Grob Mitzer was amongst the mourners. The wealthy industrialist finished speaking to the priest before he moved away to a small group who had lingered by Kushmann's grave. This group, obviously the most senior members of those present, huddled together as they shared their secret discussion.

'A tragedy,' said one of the mourners, a bald-headed, stooped man in a threadbare suit.

'It's over now. We must move on,' replied Mitzer.

'Always it happens. Always so close and something happens.'

'Nothing comes easy. It only needs more effort, one more push,' urged the wire-haired man to Mitzer's left.

'He's right,' added Mitzer. 'Now is not the time to lose heart.'

'Who will replace Willi?' asked the bald-headed man.

'Whoever.'

'Frick is the only one.'

'That's up to the council.'

'It must be soon.'

'It will be.'

'We will have to have meetings. That'll draw attention to ourselves.'

'Not if we're careful.' Mitzer's anger suddenly flared and he turned his fury on the bald-headed man. 'Now is not the time to panic. We will replace Willi. We will succeed. Our enemies will not find out about us. Not if we keep our mouths shut. And stop being frightened. Understand?'

The others were silent, cowed by Mitzer's outburst. He suddenly took a deep breath, brought his temper under control.

'We are among old friends here,' he went on, calmer in his tone. 'Those who are alive and those who have died, many in our cause. Let us not be disrespectful to them. Come on, let's go and pay our respects.'

He turned to lead the group towards the headstones when the bald-headed man spoke.

'*Und die Lucie Geister?*'

Mitzer swung round sharply, his venom obvious but hushed so that no-one else near the group would hear him.

'*Die Lucie Geister.* I have told you. Never mention them in public. It is more than your life is worth.'

Georgetown
Washington, DC

TWELVE HOURS BEFORE they buried Willi Kushmann, the Deputy Director of Administration had sat down to his meeting with the DDI, Phil Tucker and Carter. It was still Christmas evening on the East Coast and the festivities were in full swing.

Unlike Dresden, Washington is the most modern of cities and Georgetown its cultural and residential jewel. Just north of Foggy Bottom is the oldest part of the city, having started its life as a tobacco port in 1751. Along its picturesque commercial centre there is a diverse and exciting selection of restaurants and shops designed to entice the many-cultured habitants of the area, mainly those who spend their working hours in the embassies and government agencies.

The DDA lived off Massachusetts Avenue, the thoroughfare that houses most of the embassies in Washington. Unlike most of his colleagues who lived outside the city, the DDA was never slow to flaunt his position and usually had a house full of guests, many of them diplomats from the foreign missions.

Christmas Day had been no different. Ostensibly a day for children, the DDA saw it as an opportunity to entertain and impress, an opportunity to pander to the whims of Washington society. Not much had been seen of his children all day. He didn't know they had gone to his wife's mother after lunch and wouldn't be returning until the following morning.

He had received Nowak's report at eight o'clock that morning. It had stunned him.

He opened the meeting with that information. Little was said. He knew they wanted time to absorb it before they responded. All except the DDI, who was furious that his colleague hadn't rung him earlier and passed the report on.

'Anything new on West Wing?' the DDA asked Tucker.

'Nothing concrete. He got married fifteen years ago, sort'a late in life. Had no kids. Liked his liquor and disappeared on the occasional bender. No idea where he came from, how we got him his identity. That's all locked up in the computer. We searched his home. Found nothing. Except he'd been a corporal in the Waffen SS during the war. Still had his identity papers. Stashed away in his bedside drawer. We checked back, but there was no war-crimes stuff.'

'Reindeer was in the SS, wasn't he?'

'Different outfit. We couldn't find any link between them.'

'That's all?'

'Yes, sir.'

'Anything on that virus?'

'No.'

'I think we should be addressing the point about why some-one's knocking out our asset base . . . as well as the Russians'?' interrupted the DDI, changing tack on the discussion.

'If you believe what they say,' answered the DDA.

'They always were tricky bastards.'

'Still can't see what they hope to achieve.'

'Unless they're after Trimmler.'

'What for?' asked the DDA sharply.

'Who knows? But they could've been after him. Christ, could he be a double?'

'He's a scientist, not a . . . I doubt that. Have we got anything on that Kraut who was shot, what's-his-name, uh, Kushmann?' The DDA swung round to Carter.

'Nothing,' answered the security man. 'Another East German lawyer who moved to Frankfurt. He was important, in a corporate way. But not that important, not enough to be taken out.'

'And the other guy?'

'Mitzer. Big industrialist. In defence. Aerospace. Big sup-porter of ours in Germany. He could've been a target for kidnapping by a terrorist faction. But they wouldn't have gone after him in a crowded restaurant in such a public place.'

Tucker suddenly understood that the security man had been given his own responsibilities, independent and classified from his own. He would have to be more careful in future as he realized all his thoughts and actions would be reported back to his superiors. He watched Carter lean back when he had finished and knew he was deliberately avoiding eye contact.

'Go back on it. Dig deeper into each one. Including the women. And Trimmler. There could be something there, something we've missed,' ordered the DDA.

'Can we get some help on it? I've only got two guys here in Langley. There's a lot of legwork that . . . '

'Shit, no,' interjected the DDI. 'Even the President doesn't know what's happening.' He realized he had gone further than he should have in front of the two subordinates. 'Look, you two better understand where we're coming from. This whole thing is just conjecture. It makes us look bad if we run to the White House with every rumour we come across. All we know for certain is that our computer's partly fucked, which is being dealt with; that we lost two agents, which is now under investigation; and that someone may have tried to take out one of our top scientists. Which is also being investigated. And while we're doing that we're also going to protect him. That's all there is to go on. We don't report this to anyone until we get some more facts. OK?'

'There is also one other slight problem,' added the DDA. 'We don't know who planted that virus. Which means we don't know how much they've infiltrated our intelligence system. If we start sharing this information with anyone else, including any special advisers to the President, can you guarantee it won't get out to those who mean to harm us?'

'Anyway, who can we go to? The Puzzle Palace is out.' The DDI referred to America's National Security Agency, the most secret agency within the US government. The NSA has a budget estimated to be far greater than the CIA and has a complex of electronic eavesdropping stations and satellites that cover both America and the globe. Its Director is probably the most powerful executive in the American Intelligence community.

'Why?'

'Because they could be involved up to their fucking necks and maybe just happened to forget to tell us.'

'Even they won't be knocking off our own people.'

'Oh yeah. They're as dangerous as the Russians. They play their own weird games. Yeah, and just think how easy it would be for them to get access to the computer.'

There was a silence round the room. At last the DDA spoke.

'We keep this thing in-house. Carter, you just keep digging as instructed. The DDI and I, we'll follow up on the Russians through our contacts. While that's going on we need to protect Trimmler. Just in case he is a target. As well as chasing this computer thing, I want you to look after that, Tucker.'

'I've never been in the field, sir.'

'Just do as we tell you,' countered the DDI. 'I'll bring some of my people across. All you have to do is—'

'No,' interrupted the DDA. 'Your people are out.'

'Who says?'

'The Exec Director.'

'We were going to keep this in-house.'

'Except for this.'

'Why? What's wrong with my people?'

'All their records are in the computer. Put them in the field and whoever's set this up will know we're protecting Trimmler. We want to use Trimmler as bait. We've already got a tap on his phone. If they're after him, let them think they've got a free run.'

'So, who do we use?'

'Someone outside the Intelligence community.'

'Cops? You gotta be joking. They've got the biggest mouths in town. They're not used to working alone. We need someone who is.'

'We appreciate that. And it's not the police.'

'Who then?'

'Two people. A professional field man and a partner who's used to sifting information, looking for something that everyone else's missed.'

'And they're in place?' The DDI's question was harsh, he knew he had been outmanoeuvred in front of the Executive Director by his counterpart. He cursed silently and regretted not moving with his own plan earlier.

'Not yet. I'd like to clear it with you first,' the DDA lied smoothly to the DDI.

'The Grombach Organization. These two part of them?'

'No.' In 1942 Colonel John V. Strombach had established an organization that was integrated into the CIA in the mid-fifties. It remained secret within the CIA, as it had originally been within the wartime OSS, and it concentrated on the collection and dissemination of Intelligence. Although it flirted with Counter-Intelligence, its main brief was information gathering. By 1960 it had been disbanded, but rumours persisted into the Eighties of a private firm that went under the name of The Grombach Organization which concentrated its information gathering in the private and industrial sectors. Certain sources believed the organization still existed and dealt directly with the Executive Director.

'So, who's being brought in?'

'Both these people are outside the mainstream of Intelligence. They're definitely out of the computer. The first is our woman in San Diego. You already know about her. Recruited by the Agency in the early Seventies, when we had regional centres. But things changed, we closed down the centres and most of the staff came to Washington. But, because of the nature of the Californian campuses, because of the drugs and protest movement, we kept a small unit going in San Diego.'

'She's a desk jockey.'

'Collection and disseminaton. She's been doing that ever since.'

'What's her cover?'

'She's a deputy in the Mayfair Cab and Taxi Company.'

'And not in the computer?'

'Only as a clerk.' The DDA didn't add that her section was to be closed down in the near future. 'She's experienced in the operation of computers and she's been looking at our problem with Tucker.'

'Who else?'

'Like I said, a professional in the field. Used to working alone and looking after himself. A soldier.'

'Special Forces?' The DDI referred to members of the Armed Forces who were trained for covert and dangerous missions.

'We wanted someone whom no-one could identify. We decided to go outside our normal sphere of operation. We decided' – the DDA knew his colleague was about to explode. Now was as good a time as ever – 'on someone who would be classed as a mercenary. A British soldier. A member of their SAS.'

'You're fucking joking?'

'One of their best. Used to working underground and part of their Intelligence arm. Just finished a tour of duty in Northern Ireland.'

'You're not fucking joking.'

'The Exec Director's already spoken to London. They're playing ball. He speaks German. Served some time out there. Could help with Trimmler.'

'I should've been brought in on this earlier.'

'Well, that's how it is.' The DDA turned to Phil Tucker. 'He'll be over in the next few days. Adam Nicholson. That's his name. I suggest he flies straight to San Diego, you'll need to be there to brief him. And the girl.'

'This computer's going to need a lot of my time.'

'Delegate someone. Everyone knows there's a virus. Just make sure they don't know how important it is.'

'I need to know my responsibilities. And how to progress the situation.' Tucker thought of Jean and the pressure he would be under at home. She had been married to an army officer before they met and hated the life, the constant separation. After nine years of marriage, he still hadn't spent a night away from home. It was something they both preferred, it suited their relationship. He suddenly dreaded going home, remembered the foul mood she had been in when he left to come to this meeting. To return and tell her he was going to San Diego and God knows where else for an undetermined period would cause havoc in the household. At least they had tomorrow, he would take them all out for the day.

'We'll meet in the morning and work out the logistics. 8 a.m. My office.' The DDA's words were like a death-sentence and Tucker groaned silently.

'How much information do we give this guy?' demanded the DDI, now aware that he had lost control of the situation. It wasn't his baby any longer. Fuck Administration! he thought.

'As little as we can get away with. Leave it till tomorrow.' The DDA slid his chair back and stood up. 'Well, thanks for coming. I suggest you all get back and enjoy what's left of Christmas. See you in the morning.'

Two minutes later they were out on the street, standing below the period lamp-stand that splayed its yellow light down on to the snow-covered sidewalk.

'Wanna lift?' the DDI asked Carter, signalling across to the chauffeur-driven government car that was parked across the road.

'Thank you, sir. I'd appreciate that,' answered Carter keeping his eyes away from Tucker.

'Good. See you tomorrow, Tucker. Sorry I can't give you a lift but we're going the other way.'

'No sweat. See you tomorrow.' Tucker stood back as the car pulled up at the kerb. Carter opened the door for the DDI, and after he had climbed in, followed him and shut the door.

Tucker watched the car drive off towards Massachusetts Avenue. The more he knew Carter, the more he disliked him. He was probably selling his soul to the DDI right now, in the back of the company car. He would always go to the highest bidder. A corporate whore.

He started to walk towards the main street, wished he had brought the car. Jean had kept the station wagon in case she took the kids out. He sure as hell wasn't going to find a cab easily at this time of night on Christmas Day. He couldn't even ring Jean, she'd have the kids in bed by now.

'Christ, I'm a fucking communications executive, not a fucking secret agent,' he shouted to the cold night.

Nobody heard. Nobody cared.

Botanicheskiy Sad
North of Moscow

'THANK YOU, DIMITRI Dimitrovitch. This has put a new slant on the situation. You must keep alert and concentrate your efforts on this matter. If there is any change, contact me immediately.'

Rostov put down the phone and looked out of the window. The snow was thick outside, the street blocked off with the latest heavy fall. The late afternoon sun shone brightly as he looked up, the glare from the window reflection making him squint. He tried to remember a document he had seen, a glimmer of everyday information that hadn't seemed important at the time but could tie in with what Dimitri Sorge had told him on the phone.

He heard one of the children, probably his youngest daughter, laugh from the living room. Then came the stronger tones of his wife admonishing her. Someone was being naughty. It warmed him, he loved the family, loved the days away from the office. He looked down at the phone. Not true, he was always at the office.

They may have driven the Jews out of Russia, but they and their religion had some good points. The Sabbath. They always switched off their phones on a Sabbath. It was a day of rest. He wished he could switch off the phone.

He picked up the receiver and dialled 2 Dzerzhinsky Square. When the operator answered he asked to be put through to the Director. He knew he'd be there.

He grinned as he waited.

He was certain the Director didn't believe in Santa Claus.

M1 Motorway
Luton

THE WHITE POLICE car, its red-and-blue lights busily flashing, spotted him in the heavy traffic and chased him for nearly two miles before pulling him into the hard shoulder.

'In a rush, are we?' was the sarcastic policeman's comment as Adam climbed out of the Ferrari F40. He added, 'Sir,' with the customary arrogance that is traditional in such situations.

'Not really,' smiled Adam.

'You were doing nearly a hundred.'

'Was I?' Adam knew that a hundred miles an hour normally meant a ban in most traffic courts. Which is why he'd held it at ninety miles an hour.

'The limit's seventy.'

'I know the highway code.'

'Then you should stick to it.' Once more the sneering, 'Sir. Would you follow me, please?'

Adam followed the officer to the patrol car where the second policeman was waiting.

'Mr Nicholson?' asked the second officer.

'Yes.'

'Would you get in the front, please.' He opened the door for Adam to slide into the passenger seat, then walked round and climbed into the driver's side. He leant over and picked up the radio telephone. 'I've got him here,' he said, then handed over the telephone to Adam.

'Nicholson,' said Adam.

'Where've you been this time in your little toy?' came the official voice that Adam recognized as his contact officer.

Adam put his hand over the receiver and turned to the policeman. 'Would you excuse me?' he asked politely. 'Official secrets and all that.' The policeman shrugged and climbed out,

119

annoyed at being asked to leave his own car. 'What do you want?' he asked into his receiver once the door had been closed.

'I wish you'd follow orders.'

Adam didn't reply. He'd spent the day at the Ferrari Owners' Association at Castle Donington Racetrack in Leicestershire. He'd come second in the unlimited class race and was still savouring the enjoyment of the speed and precision of the racing circuit.

'Anyway, we need you down here. Immediately,' went on the voice.

'Is this an operation?' Adam asked, suddenly excited with the possibility of action.

'So it would appear.'

'Where?'

'We'll tell you that when you get down here.'

'In my toy.'

The radio phone went dead. Adam put it down and stepped out of the police car. 'Thank you.' He walked towards the F40.

'Watch your speed, will you? Sir.'

Adam nodded and climbed into the Ferrari.

The police car followed him till the next turn-off and he cheekily kept the speed at eighty-five. He knew they wouldn't stop him, not when they knew he was important enough to be stopped on the motorway and given a message.

When they'd gone, he gunned Steed up to a hundred and twenty and drove his little red toy into London.

San Diego

THE BIG BRITISH Airways 747 is the only scheduled jumbo that lands at San Diego's Lindbergh Field.

Flight BA 285 flies direct from London Gatwick to Los Angeles, and then, once it has discharged the majority of its passengers and burnt up most of its fuel, carries on for the

120

short hop into San Diego. Lindbergh's 09 eastbound runway is only 9,400 feet long and the lightly loaded Boeing jumbo can be landed safely because of its lack of weight.

The approach to Runway 09 is over the mountains that leap up to the west of the city. It is an exacting approach for any pilot, leading down to the runway which is close to the downtown area. It juts out into the most spectacular bay and to watchers on the other side it appears that aircraft descend into the heart of the city, into the heart of the corporate skyscrapers that are clustered together as a beacon of a modern and prosperous San Diego.

Adam was one of fifteen passengers left on flight BA 285, and the only one still in First Class. He had fought the usual bureaucratic battle with the Admin boys who had insisted he use a travel warrant that only entitled him to an Economy-Class seat. In the end he had simply agreed because he realized he was wasting his time arguing with the form-fillers who were blindly carrying out their orders. As soon as he left them he called British Airways and bought a First-Class ticket on his American Express card. It was his usual way; he simply reported that he had lost his travel warrant and claimed the economy fare back from the form-fillers on his return. There would be the usual caustic remark about, 'Lose your head next time', or some similar comment that the form-fillers always seemed to dredge up from the safety of their filing cabinets and wooden government-issue desks.

The briefing in London had been short. He wondered how much his people really knew, or whether the Americans had simply passed on as little information as they needed to.

'The Yanks believe Mr Trimmler is in danger, that an attempt may be made on his life. They've asked for our help because they want to keep it out of their own sphere. Apparently there is some concern that security is not as tight as it should be' – the briefing officer, Captain Coy by name but not by nature, allowed himself the hint of a smirk – 'and that the danger to this scientist chap could come from inside their own organization. That's why we're involved.'

'So I'm the bodyguard.'

'I wouldn't class it as that. You're to protect where necessary, but your first responsibility will be to help discover if there is a plot against Trimmler.'

'Wouldn't a policeman be better for that?'

'They asked for someone with field experience. Someone who could look after himself if things took a nasty turn.'

'Will I be armed?'

'Yes. Nothing too extravagant, mind you. We don't want you getting off the plane with a sub-machine-gun and grenades strapped to you, do we? This isn't Ulster we're talking about.'

'Have you ever been to Ulster?'

'Hardly the point, is it?' answered Coy tetchily. Adam knew he'd scored a point, could tell the man had never visited the province. Bloody desk-soldiers. 'You can pick up a firearm in America. No need to get caught going through airport security and blowing the job before you've even arrived. You'll be dealing with two Americans. Both are, I believe, from the CIA. A Mr Phil Tucker and a Billie Wood. As this is an American operation, you will be directly responsible to them. Should something arise which causes you concern, then contact the British Embassy Military Attaché and ask him to contact us here.'

'That's it?'

'That's all I was told.' Coy pushed a small folder across the desk. 'There's a small bio of Mr Trimmler in here, including a picture, your voucher for a travel warrant to San Diego and another voucher for any petty cash you might need. The Americans have some credit cards in your name which you can pick up when you arrive. That'll be for additional and necessary' – he emphasized the word 'necessary' – 'expenditure. Hire cars, things like that if you need them. That's all.'

Adam took the folder and put it on his lap. He would check it later. 'Who chose me?' he asked.

'No idea. You were available and, as far as I can tell, still causing everyone here a headache.'

'So, cure the headache. Cut off the head.'

'You have rather an inflated view of yourself, don't you think?'

Adam laughed and stood up.

'Remember, even if this isn't under our direct control, that you are a member of the Armed Forces and still a representative of Her Majesty's Government,' warned the briefing officer. 'But you are on your own. Use your initiative as you see fit. That doesn't mean that we will support all your actions. Understand?'

Adam understood. He nodded his head, refused to salute the senior officer and left the office. He was looking forward to the exercise. He enjoyed America and sensed the whiff of oncoming danger. It was good to be back at work, even if he didn't know why he was going and what was expected of him.

The file on Trimmler wasn't very expansive. Heinrich Spiedal-Trimmler had been a brilliant young German scientist during the Second World War who got caught up in the swirl of things and became part of the famous rocket team that launched the V1 and V2 rockets. An expert in rocket guidance and gyroscope systems, he was given much of the credit for the unusual accuracy of the early rocketry as it blitzed London. When the war finished, he'd been part of the Peenemünde team who surrendered to the American Forces under Werner Von Braun and General Walter Dornberger in 1945. Like his colleagues, he settled into the American way of life easily and became a major part of the organization which started in the 1950s and had by the 1970s put a man on the moon. American money and resources were freely available to the scientists who, not long before, had been instrumental in directing their rockets at the Allies. Trimmler, now one of the more senior scientists in America, had become one of the world's greatest authorities on guidance systems and electronic navigational hardware. He was a valuable asset to the Americans, who had changed his records and shortened his name to give him a new identity, in an effort to wipe out his links with the Nazi Party.

There were also some notes on Trimmler's family which highlighted the fact that he was a wealthy man who lived in La Jolla, an exclusive and wealthy town on the outskirts of San Diego. Of his German past there was very little, except to say that he had not been a member of the Nazi Party and was born in Leipzig. He was first and foremost a scientist. Adam wondered why someone would want to kill him.

He had returned home to Lily's last meal before leaving for America. He rang her from the car phone in the Ferrari and the meal was ready for him by the time he let himself into the flat. It was steak and kidney pudding, cooked as only she knew how, and she fussed round him as he ate.

'I'm off to America tomorrow,' he said.

'Will you have time for breakfast?' she asked. He sensed the disappointment in her voice, recalled that she lived as lonely an existence as he did.

'No. I'll get it on the plane.'

'I'll get your pudding,' she said, scurrying off to the kitchen. Damn, he could have handled it differently. Then he remembered the Christmas present he had given her. A Sony CD Walkman with her favourite collection of Fifties songs. She'd had it strapped to her head ever since. It was an oddball sight, the old white-haired lady cleaning and cooking while she bopped her head to Max Bygraves and Bing Crosby. He smiled and knew she would be all right. He would be back soon.

He escorted her downstairs to wait for her taxi and kissed her on the cheek; she was obviously pleased. For all their closeness and dependability on each other there was little show of emotion between them.

Then he had driven to Woking, out into the Surrey country-side. He drove automatically, his mind locked into the past and the memories of where he was going. It took nearly an hour to reach the cemetery from the centre of London. The gates were locked, as he knew they would be, so he parked some distance away and walked back to the twisted and open railing he had discovered many years ago. He slipped through the opening and made his way towards the gravestones on the west hill.

He had sensed others around him, didn't need to see them to know they were there. Mostly kids, experimenting with drugs and sex, or tramps destroyed by their own experience with them. They were all harmless, but he hadn't thought so once, when he had first come here all those years ago. The hidden voices and movements had frightened him, filled the twelve-year-old boy with fear and visions of ghosts and ghouls and bodysnatchers. He laughed to himself as he remembered chasing through the undergrowth to find a naked boy running away, as frightened as he was. A girl was shrieking somewhere behind, interrupted in the act of losing her virginity.

The three graves, side by side in their loneliness, were well kept as usual. He had leant over his mother's and touched the flowers. They were fresh, as he had always insisted. He stood between the two headstones and touched them both, his two hands joining them again. It was a ritual he always attended to.

Then he had moved to the grave on the other side of his mother's.

MARCUS JAMES NICHOLSON. AGED NINE. BELOVED SON OF HENRY AND MARGARET AND BELOVED BROTHER OF ADAM. Underneath, much smaller in its print was the inscription, THE GODS LOVE THOSE WHO DIE YOUNG.

He had knelt beside the grave, reached forward and touched the earth.

'Hi. I'm going away again, Marcus. To America. California. You'd have liked California. Crazy people who've inherited the earth . . . I think I upset Lily earlier on. I was thoughtless. I forget she's old and she needs me around. When you're that age, moments count, time runs out, eh? I raced at Donington today. Had a great ride, the best time I ever recorded. That Enzo Ferrari, how marvellous to leave a legacy that people love and enjoy. To have a dream and make it real, to share it with millions . . . I don't know why they're sending me to America. The whole thing smells. I mean, I can understand Ireland and living rough, taking on an enemy you know is there. But this California thing, it's not something I'm trained to do. I still can't work out why they're sending me there. Still, it's action . . . Gives me something to do, eh? . . . I'm lonely, Marcus. Can't stop this feeling that I'm not all there, that so much is still with you, with Mum and Dad . . . I sometimes wonder if I get into danger just so someone'll put a gun to my head and take me out. I don't belong here, Marcus. I'm so fucking lonely. So fucking alone.'

Adam had left the cemetery five minutes later, driven the Gullwing back to London, gone to Tramps and picked up the first attractive girl he fancied. He had taken her back to the flat and fucked her in his loneliness until morning broke and it was time to leave for Gatwick and Southern California.

125

The flight had been uneventful, apart from the interlude of a young beautiful Englishwoman flying to meet her husband in Los Angeles. She had her two children with her, the youngest a toddler who was full of beans. A Californian yuppie had sat next to her and turned his bronzed charms on her. Adam heard the immortal line, 'I just love children', as he moved in on his prey. An hour into the flight he didn't love them quite as much. The toddler had crawled over him, first crumpling, then wetting, his new Italian suit. The second child, no more than four, had then knocked her mother's gin and tonic over the man, who frantically looked round for another seat. But all the First-Class berths were taken. He suffered silently until the children finally went to sleep. With twenty minutes to run into Los Angeles, he had shifted to go to the toilet. The toddler, now fast asleep against his arm, had been in the way and the mother reached over to move the child. 'No!' snapped the young man nervously. 'No. I'm all right. Don't wake him.' He finished the journey with his legs crossed. He was first off the plane, rudely pushing his way past the other passengers.

Adam helped the mother lift her hand luggage down from the overhead lockers.

'When I get married,' he remarked, 'I shall make sure my wife travels everywhere fully armed with at least two young children.'

'Works every time,' she said and they both laughed. Then she went off to meet her husband, out there waiting in the crowd. He envied them their marriage and their sharing. He settled back in his deep British Airways seat for the rest of the journey, only fifteen minutes down the coast.

The jumbo slurped its wheels on to the tarmac and rolled to a stop seven thousand feet down the runway, where it rumbled to the right and taxied to the terminal.

Billie hadn't expected him to be quite so short. She knew he was a field officer in the SAS and had expected the usual Californian tall, broad-shouldered illusion of a fighting man. His hair was too long at the back, too gelled and too crimped. Maybe she'd expected too much, after all these years waiting to become a real CIA operative.

'Hi,' she greeted him as he stood waiting for his contact in the small terminal arrival hall, a cigarette in his hand, the only passenger left. 'Are you Adam Nicholson?'

'Yes,' Adam answered cautiously.

'I'm Billie Wood. Welcome to San Diego. This is a No Smoking area.'

'I didn't expect a woman.'

His brusqueness shocked her.

'Well, that's what I am,' she replied defensively.

'Billie's a man's name.'

'Never heard of Billie Holiday?'

He shook his head. 'Only Billy Graham. But he was a fella. Nobody said I'd be working with a woman.'

'What's the difference?'

'There isn't one. As long as you're good at your job.'

'My car's outside,' she answered, furious with his whole macho approach. Bloody English. They thought they still owned the world. She turned and walked out into the car-park. He followed a short distance behind, the cigarette now dangling from his lips.

The car, Billie's brightly coloured Renegade, was parked by the pay booths.

'Could you . . . ?' she indicated the cigarette.

'Are we meant to be undercover on this thing?' Adam asked, tossing the cigarette on to the pavement and stepping on it.

'Yeah. Why?'

'I wouldn't exactly call this jam-jar low profile.'

'Jam-jar?'

'Car.'

'Then we'll change it. OK?' She turned and unlocked the car. He was getting worse, this was not at all what she had expected.

He walked round to the passenger side and put his Louis Vuitton suit carrier on the back seat. He climbed in the front and waited for her to start the engine.

'Where am I staying?' he asked.

'With me. It's OK. My fella thinks you're over here on a business visit from our British associate company. Anything else?'

'How old are you?'

The harsh directness of his question flummoxed her. The flush

127

grew deeper in colour, her discomfort obvious. She stared at him in defensive silence, said nothing. Then she turned and slipped the car into Drive. She kept her chin up, furious with him for his youthful, male arrogance, even more furious with herself for keeping her chin up so as to hide the age wrinkles that formed round her neck. She silently cursed her own vanity.

'Nothing personal,' he went on. 'I want to know if you can handle it.'

'I can handle it.'

'Look. I'm told this is a dangerous assignment. I don't know much more. I'm used to working on my own. If I'm part of a team, under someone else's orders, then I have to know my back's covered. So, how old are you?'

'Forty-one.' There was little point in her lying. She knew he would eventually look up a file on her.

'Have you ever been in the field before?'

'No.'

'Shit.'

'Can we go now?'

'Why not? It can't get any worse, can it?'

'What charm school did you go to?' she snapped, almost adding the expletive 'shithead' to the sentence. She released the brake and stamped on the accelerator. The Renegade squealed and jerked out of the parking slot.

They drove all the way to La Jolla, a forty-minute drive along Route 5, in absolute stony silence.

Welcome to sunny California.

KGB Headquarters
Dzerzhinsky Square
Moscow

'THE AMERICANS ARE either lying or telling the truth. The trick is to determine which,' said the Director as he poured himself another cup of tea from the samovar.

'We could always toss a coin,' suggested Rostov.

'I accept your religion, but I didn't appreciate how deep down the road to capitalism you had gone. Gambling? What next?'

The two men laughed, a joke shared at a time of crisis.

'There were two other, quite small things. Quite unimportant on their own, but possibly worthwhile, especially when you consider we have very little to go on,' went on Rostov.

'You're right. At this stage everything is important, however tenuous the link.'

'I was going through the travel lists a few weeks ago.' Rostov referred to the weekly reports that were screened through the KGB as to which people of note and special interest were requesting visas for foreign trips. It was a legacy from the old days, but one which still was useful to the spymasters. 'I recalled that there was a group of scientists due to visit America. For a space convention. One dealing specifically with rockets. A very high-powered convention. Our best people as well as theirs. It was the name Trimmler I remembered. He is leading the American delegation.'

'The same one?'

'The same.'

'Interesting.'

'That's all there was. Just a coincidence.'

'And the other?'

'Mitzer. The industrialist who was in Cannes. He's very

big in electronics. Built a vast empire in West Germany. He worked with the rocket scientists at Peenemünde during the war.'

'So, why didn't he come here, or to the Americans?'

'He was only an administrator. We only wanted scientists.'

'And he used his knowledge to build his business?'

'Yes.'

'He would've needed money. To become that big.'

'We think it was Lucy Ghosts' money.'

Then he posed the question, 'The Lucy Ghosts?'

Rostov shrugged. 'I don't know.'

The two men sat in silence for a long moment.

'We need the names of the other delegates,' said the Director.

'Being prepared.'

'Both sides.'

'That's what I've asked for.'

'Maybe we should tell the Americans. This is not a time to turn against each other.'

'I disagree. Not until we know they're not up to their old tricks.'

'The Kremlin wants us to open our files to the Yanks. To show them our list of sleepers in return for theirs.'

'That would be very foolish at this stage.'

'I agree. Let's keep this to ourselves for now.'

'I'll bring you the list as soon as I get it.'

'Keep in touch with Dimitri Sorge. He is our only contact out there. He might just stumble across something.'

'I'll follow that up.' Rostov had already done that, but it wasn't his intention to appear more enterprising than the Director.

The old man smiled. He knew Rostov had already contacted Sorge. He appreciated his tact and consideration. Russia needed people like him. He would get to the top, even if he was a Christian.

La Jolla

THE MUSCLE GRIPPED Adam's hand tightly and squeezed it in a show of strength.

Adam had known what was coming and winced accordingly; there was little to be gained by retaliating.

'This is Gary,' said Billie, her mood still black.

'Nice to meet you. I'm Adam,' he replied, the wince turning to a smile as the Muscle pumped his arm up and down.

'Nice to meetch'ya, too,' Gary replied, a satisfied grin across his face. He relaxed his grip and let go. This weak little wimp was no threat to him. He grabbed Billie and gave her a big kiss, held her pinned with his mouth. When he'd finished claiming his property for Adam's benefit, he said, 'Hi, babe. That guy Tucker's here.'

Adam saw that the girl was slightly embarrassed by this obvious show of emotion. 'I'd like to go to my room and freshen up, please?' he asked.

'This way.' She led him past the Muscle to a spare room. She opened the door and he slipped past her into the bedroom. 'I'd prefer it if you didn't smoke in the house.'

'Certainly,' he said, but the door was already closing behind him. He shrugged and threw his case on the bed. He zipped it open and took out a brown suit and some shirts.

It was a chintzy dressing room, very Californian chic and obviously designed for women friends. He decided to leave the rest of his unpacking till later and took out his matching Vuitton toilet bag. He walked into the *en suite* bathroom, once again very feminine in its fashion, and plugged in his Braun electric razor. He far preferred to shave with lather and brush, but the Braun was always on standby when he was in a rush.

Phil Tucker was on the balcony when Billie came through.

131

The Muscle, having maintained his position as pack leader, disappeared into his exercise area.

'Hi, Phil,' she welcomed him. They had already met the night before and had dinner at the Hard Rock Café in La Jolla Village. Tucker had taken her through the events that led up to their meeting, but had deliberately avoided any reference to the computer and its problems. They had agreed that the Englishman was there because of his field experience, and he would be useful if things turned violent. 'One of their heavies,' Tucker had remarked during the evening. 'To be used as required.'

'Hi. Our guest arrived OK?'

'Yes. Not at all what I expected.'

He looked quizzically at her, but decided not to push her as he sensed her antagonism. 'This sure is a nice place to live. Some views. Makes waking up that much easier, huh?'

'It does.' She looked out over the coastline, watched the surf breaking.

'It's snowing in Washington. We had three feet of it before I left.'

'Well, you certainly came prepared for California,' she joked, remembering how she had met him at the airport, he with an overcoat over his arm, a high-necked sweater under his suit and a scarf draped round his neck.

'I still don't believe it's seventy degrees. Seems wrong at Christmas time. Where's he gone?'

'Having a quick wash. He knows you're here.'

They stayed on the balcony until Adam joined them ten minutes later. He'd decided to change and the tailored jeans and blazer had been replaced by a monogrammed, button-down pink shirt, black tailored Bermuda shorts with turn ups and knife-edge creases, and tanned legs disappearing into black slip-on calf-leather shoes. His gold bracleted Ebel watch dangled on his right arm, below the cuffs which were rolled halfway up his elbow.

European beach chic was not what the Americans expected of the SAS, even in Southern California.

'You're Adam?' said a surprised Tucker, moving forward with his arm outstretched in welcome.

'Mr Tucker?'

'Call me Phil. Everyone else does.' They shook hands and Adam liked the American immediately, felt the confidence and warmth in the handshake. 'Flight OK?'

'No problems.'

'Good. Guess you're pretty tired.'

'Not really.' There was no need to add that he was used to living on four hours sleep a night, that he had often gone days without resting in the course of his duties.

'That's great. Means we can get straight down to business.' Tucker pulled up a chair at the table and sat down, the other two following him. 'So, what did they tell you about this little trip?'

Adam repeated what the briefing officer had told him in London and also about the contents of the folder he had read afterwards.

'That all?'

'That's all.'

Tucker thought for a moment; the Englishman knew less than he had expected. 'We think there's a leak inside the Agency. If someone's trying to get to Trimmler, we don't want to warn them about our plans.'

'Who do I see about weapons?'

'Weapons?'

'I was told I was to be armed.'

'What do you need?'

'A standard 9mm Browning High Power semi-automatic for starts.'

'OK. What else?'

'A Heckler and Koch MP5K sub-machine-gun.'

'That's powerful shit. Why?'

'I like to play safe. And because it's the shortest barrel available. In this case, we might just need something that's good at close quarters.'

'What unit were you with?'

'CRW.'

'CRW?'

'Counter Revolutionary Warfare Wing. Don't worry. I know how to handle the hardware.' Adam's answer mocked Tucker, but the American ignored it. 'What's next?'

'Nothing for now. Get some rest. Tomorrow we go to a wedding.'

'Wedding?'

'Trimmler's a guest. At the Torrey Pines Sheraton. Just down the road from here. It's the sort of public place they might decide to hit him. He's at the Mirimar Air Base at present. In officers' quarters. Desperate to get out and back home. At least we know he's safe there. But, after tomorrow, we might just arrange for him to go home. Maybe even get you to stay there. Well, that's it for tonight.'

'I suppose you'll both want something to eat?' said Billie, standing up.

'Hey, thanks. Sounds good.'

'Not for me, thank you.' The last thing Adam wanted was a pleasant evening at home with Muscle and his companions. 'I'll go into La Jolla. Have a look around. Seems a nice place.' He stood up from the table. 'Can I call a taxi or get a hire car somewhere?'

'Use mine,' snapped Billie.

'Thank you.'

'No sweat. I'm sure they'll all see you coming.' Her sarcasm was lost on Tucker, who didn't know of their earlier conversation. She stood up. 'I'll get the key. Are you going to be late?'

'I don't know. Probably not.'

'I'll give you a front-door key as well.'

She left them on the balcony.

'Something I missed?' asked Tucker.

'No.'

'You two seem pretty cool towards each other.'

'We get on just fine,' said Adam and left to follow the woman.

It was the last thing Tucker wanted. His first field assignment and two operatives who couldn't get on. Shit, life really was a bitch.

It was nearly four in the morning when Billie heard the key being twisted in the front-door lock, heard the door open and close quietly.

134

She lay next to Gary whose snoring was akin to a rumbling express train going through a long dark tunnel. It didn't normally keep her awake, she had got used to it over the months. But the Englishman had irritated her with his rudeness. She had prepared a meal for him and Tucker, but he had disappeared before she had had a chance to tell him.

But it wasn't that which got under her skin, after all he could be excused for not knowing about the meal. What really upset her was the way he was using her home as an hotel.

If this assignment hadn't been as important as it was, she would have had his bags packed and waiting by the front door.

She pushed Gary's arm away and slid out of the bed, picking up her robe from the end and wrapping it around herself.

Adam was about to enter his room when she came into the hallway.

'You're back,' she said softly, instantly feeling like an irate parent scolding a naughty child as she spoke.

'Yes,' he replied. 'Great place. Great action. Been to the Singing Canary.' It was a night-club on the outskirts of La Jolla.

He held his hand out and she saw he held a mixture of yellow and red roses.

'They're pretty,' she said, softening immediately as she imagined the offering was for her.

'Aren't they? I've never had a girl give me roses before. Very friendly people, you Californians. Very friendly. Good night.'

His door had closed on her before she could answer. She felt foolish. Why the hell did she think that rude bastard would bring her roses?

The Mirimar Road runs from the downtown area of La Jolla Town, not to be confused with La Jolla itself which is the beach-front village to the west, and runs through the commercial area and out past the Mirimar Air Base to the east. This stretch of office-blocks, billboards and single-storey shops, showrooms and eating houses is over four miles long. Like all American commercial centres, it is a mixture of urban sprawl, disorganized architecture, modern shopping malls and a thousand billboards and signs blasting their own visions of the American Dream.

They had gone to the Hertz Rent-a-Car outlet in the commercial area to hire a less conspicuous car than Billie's Renegade. Adam, knowing he had time to kill, had wandered past the Porsche and Jaguar dealerships to Cornes, the big Rolls-Royce and Ferrari dealership on the Mirimar Road. His passionate interest in cars led him to the Ferraris that filled the showroom window and he was soon in conversation with an attentive salesman.

The other two found him twenty minutes later at the wheel of the red Testarossa that was parked in the forecourt, the salesman next to him, as they enthusiastically discussed the merits and faults of various models, both old and new.

Tucker had hired a brown Granada and he pulled up next to the Testarossa and bipped the horn at Adam. Adam said his goodbyes to the salesman, put the holdall he was carrying in the boot, and slid into the back of the Granada.

'Where now?' he asked.

'To get Trimmler,' answered Tucker, 'and take him to the wedding.'

'Sounds good. Anything else happen?'

'No.' Tucker had already decided not to tell Adam too much. After all, he was here as muscle to protect Trimmler. Nothing else concerned him.

They drove to the Mirimar Air Base in silence, the journey taking little more than five minutes. Tucker swung the car into the Base entrance and presented his identity to the armed guard on duty. They were expecting him, and the guard waved Tucker through after lifting the steel barrier and giving him directions to the officers' quarters.

Adam reflected that this was the home of the best American jet fighter pilots in America, the home of the Top Guns. He ruefully wished he had joined the RAF instead of the Army. At least he wouldn't have been stuck here with these two amateurs.

Trimmler was waiting at the entrance to one of the largest houses on the base. He was dressed in a grey morning suit, a top hat in his left hand. They could tell from his demeanour that he was agitated. He bounded down the steps from the house and was pulling open Tucker's door before the car had come to a stop.

136

'You're late!' Trimmler snapped.

'Sorry, sir,' said Tucker, scrambling out of the car. 'We needed a new car. Is your wife coming?'

'Who are these people?' asked Trimmler, ignoring Tucker's question as he pointed at Billie and Adam.

'Your escorts.'

'All of you. This is stupid. Three people?'

'Those are my instructions.'

'And you expect me to get in with all of you, with these clothes on?'

'Yes, sir.'

'You want us to arrive looking like gangsters? You think I'm Al Capone, or something? No! I will not go with all of you.'

'My orders are—'

'I don't care about orders. Get me another car. If they want to come, they can follow.'

'That'll make us late for the wedding.'

'Stupid. This is stupid. We must leave them here.'

'I can't do that, sir.'

Trimmler slammed the door shut in frustration, nearly trapping Tucker's hands in the process. The two men stared at each other, a war of nerves and frustration.

'All right!' shouted Trimmler. 'But I sit in the front. The woman . . . in the back,' he ordered.

'Billie. Please?' said Tucker.

Billie climbed out of the passenger seat and slipped into the back as Trimmler stormed round and angrily sat in the front, slamming the door shut once he was in. Tucker climbed into the driving position and swung the car round and drove back to the entrance.

The trip took an uncomfortable and silent thirty minutes in the busy traffic. The only time anyone spoke was when Trimmler demanded that the air-conditioning be turned down. Tucker leant across and adjusted the dial accordingly.

'Is that better?' he asked after a few minutes.

Trimmler nodded, his top hat now balanced on his knee.

In the back, Adam and Billie studiously avoided each other, their gazes determined not to meet, their bodies apart and obvious in their language. Billie kept her chin up for the whole journey.

137

The Torrey Pines Sheraton is one of those low-level, sprawling hotels that Californians insist on building so as not to intrude on the environment. It overlooks the Torrey Pines Golf Course, a municipal track that is world class in design and has hosted many great golf classics. The hotel is shaped in a wide W, with the three wings reaching out towards the golf course. Between the outer wings and the centre index of the W there were two outdoor, terraced areas which were used for weddings and other similar functions. Although the hotel had only been completed in 1988, it was now seen as one of the fashionable venues for wedding services in the La Jolla area.

The wedding Trimmler was attending was one of his younger colleague's, a Jewish subordinate who worked on his team.

Tucker pulled the car up outside the canopied lobby entrance. Trimmler was out and on his way to the hotel before the parking attendant had reached them.

'How y'a doing?' He greeted Tucker through the open window. 'Want me to park it?'

'No, thanks,' said Tucker. 'I'll do it.'

He swung the car round the centre island and drove to one of the empty spots next to the hotel. When he had parked, the three of them climbed out of the car. They were surrounded by Bentleys, Rolls-Royces, Mercedes, BMWs and other expensive, mostly European, cars. Adam realized it was a top society wedding. It would be difficult to keep an eye on Trimmler with all those people milling about.

'Now what?' asked Adam.

'Just stay out of the way and keep an eye on him,' replied the CIA man.

'I need to get in the boot.'

'The what?'

'He means the trunk,' interrupted Billie.

'It's open.'

Adam went to the rear of the car and pushed the button that released the lock and allowed the boot lid to spring open. Tucker and Billie followed him round.

From his brown holdall he took out a Heckler and Koch

MP5K sub-machine-gun and a standard 9mm Browning High Power semi-automatic.

'Do we have to take those in?' asked a startled Tucker.

'If we're here to protect the guy, yes.'

'Come on . . . Not the machine-gun as well, are . . . ?'

'Don't be daft,' replied Adam curtly. He slipped off his jacket and looked round the car-park to make sure he wasn't being observed. Satisfied that all was well, he then reached down and lifted out a shoulder holster and strapped it on. Once he had checked that it fitted snugly, tight enough to stay firm under his left shoulder yet loose enough not to impair his breathing, he took the 9mm Browning and slipped it into the holster. Then he closed the boot lid and put his jacket back on.

'OK,' he said. 'You'd better make sure the alarm's on. We don't want that little number going walkabout, do we?' he went on, indicating the machine-gun.

As Tucker turned to switch on the alarm, Adam walked away from them and into the hotel. Billie and the CIA man followed at a distance.

LOPIAN-ROBBINS WEDDING ON THE GOLF VIEW TERRACE said the legend on the signboard in the entrance lobby. Underneath it, in bolder red print on a white background, shouted the words, THE TORREY PINES SHERATON WELCOMES ALL PHIL'S AND JANEY'S WEDDING GUESTS.

'Excuse me,' Adam asked one of the receptionists, a pretty redhead with DEBBIE HANNIFF – RECEPTIONIST printed on the badge perched above her left breast. 'Debbie?'

'How can I help you?' she smiled back.

'The Golf View Terrace, please?'

'Down there,' she pointed to the right corridor. 'Just keep following the hallway and you'll come to some big glass doors. Opens right up on to the terrace. You here for the Lopian-Robbins wedding?'

'Yes. Thank you, Debbie.'

'Have a good day, sir.'

Adam turned and walked down the marble-floored hallway with his two companions following. When he reached the big glass doors he found his way barred by an usher in a grey morning suit.

'Hi,' welcomed the usher.

'Hallo,' replied Adam, moving towards the open terrace.

'You got your invitation?' asked the usher, stepping forward and blocking Adam's way.

'Not on me.'

'Well, this is a private wedding. Invited guests only.'

'That's good. I just wanted to see how you do these things over here.'

'You from England?'

'Damn accent always gives me away,' Adam joked.

'I'm sorry, but it is a private wedding.'

'I appreciate that. But I really would love to watch the wedding. My friends here' – he indicated Billie and Tucker who were now standing behind him – 'they'll tell you I'm from *Tatler*. A big magazine at home. The biggest. We carry society weddings. Our readers love it. I just wanted to see what it's like over here. You never know, it might even make our pages.'

The usher looked over Adam's shoulder at Tucker, who nodded his agreement. 'OK. There's some spare seats at the back. And you'd better wear these.' He handed Adam and Tucker two skull caps, satin white *yarmulkes* with TORREY PINES SHERATON emblazoned across the back of them.

'That's fantastic!' exclaimed Adam. 'And maybe I could meet the lucky couple afterwards?'

'I'm sure they'll love to. I tell ya, this is one of La Jolla's biggest.'

Adam could see that most of the guests had arrived, some two hundred of them. The path from the glass doors led down to a large balconied terrace. Rows of white, slatted-wooden chairs spread out on each side of the path, most of them filled with immaculately suited men and expensively dressed, fashionable women. At the end of the path, a four-poster canopy, the *Chuppah*, had been erected, the Star of David proudly embroidered on the top. The rabbi and cantor stood next to the *Chuppah*, talking between themselves as Adam and the two American agents took their seats at the back. By the time Adam had sat down, he had identified where Trimmler sat, halfway down on the right-hand side of the path. He leant across the other two and told them where the scientist was.

'Wow! An accomplished liar as well,' said Billie sarcastically, referring to his exchange with the usher.

Adam grinned and said nothing, went back to surveying the area and its surrounds. If there was to be an attempt, then it would come from one of the many hotel-room balconies that ran the full length of the terrace. There were already many people on these balconies, no doubt hotel guests who had been drawn from their rooms to watch the ceremony below.

The music, piped, surged up as the first pair of ushers and bridesmaids walked down the terrace from the glass doors to the *Chuppah*. They came in single pairs, the usher on the left, the white, short-skirted bridesmaid on the right, carrying a posy of fresh cut flowers. When the first couple reached the canopy, they split, the usher to his left, the bridesmaid to her right. They waited there for the next couple to walk down the seventy-foot-long path.

There were ten pairs in all, ten couples dressed identically and separating as they reached the *Chuppah*. When they had finished, and formed themselves in a gently curved row facing the audience in the way of the Jewish faith where men and women are separated at their place of worship, the close relatives of both families walked down towards the canopy and took their places at the spare seats on the front row.

Then came the groom, escorted by two men, his father and his future father-in-law. They left him at the canopy, next to the rabbi. Everyone turned expectantly. The bride would soon be making her appearance. Adam watched Trimmler, then kept his vigil. If someone was to strike, it would be when everyone's attention was diverted elsewhere.

He saw nothing to alarm him.

The bride came through the glass doors, accompanied by her mother and future mother-in-law, all three of them carrying lighted candles. She was a plump girl, in her mid-thirties. Adam noted the small bump on her stomach, too big for the white wedding dress to hide. He watched them walk down to the groom and the waiting ceremony.

When they reached the canopy, the two elder women went

141

to their seats at the front whilst their respective spouses came forward to escort the bride on her last short journey. As the cantor started to sing 'Mi Adier', they led her round the groom and canopy seven times in the orthodox manner. They completed the last circle at the front of the *Chuppah*, where the bride joined her husband-to-be in front of the rabbi. The couple held hands as the rabbi recited his blessing over the cup of wine he held in his hand.

The movement was slight, but unusual enough to catch Adam's eye.

It was to his right, up on a third-floor balcony at the rear of the hotel.

The closed curtain had moved, not in the haphazard way that one would expect as a result of a sea breeze, but in a deliberate manner, as if someone was holding the curtain edge stiffly so they could see but not be seen.

It was then he saw the black shiny barrel slide out from the curtain. It was only out for a few seconds before being withdrawn.

By the time Adam had left his seat and was through the big glass doors he had worked out which room the sniper was in. Behind him, surprised by his sudden movement, Billie and Tucker decided to follow him.

The rabbi continued his blessing.

The guests and Heinrich Trimmler sat still and excitedly watched the ceremony unfold.

Adam didn't take the lift, but found the service stairs and climbed them, two at a time. When he had reached the third level he stopped at the steel door and waited. He heard the other two rushing up behind him.

'Quietly!' he shouted down the open stairwell. 'Quietly.'

He heard them slow down as he pulled the Browning 9mm from his shoulder holster. He didn't want their noise warning whoever might be on the other side of that door, any look-out who was in the hallway. When they had reached him, he motioned them to be quiet, then slowly turned the round knob and pushed against the door.

The hallway was empty.

He came along the hallway towards the room he believed the sniper to be in.

'What the hell's going on?' asked Tucker quietly as he followed Adam.

'I saw something. In one of these rooms.'

'What?'

'I don't know. Maybe a rifle barrel.'

'Shit. You sure?'

Adam had stopped outside the room door, his hand-gun ready for any quick response. He listened, and when he was satisfied that there was no movement from inside the room, he tried the handle. It was locked, as he had expected.

'Let me get a pass-key,' whispered Tucker behind him.

'No time,' answered Adam as he stepped back and fired the hand-gun at the lock, smashing it from the wood of the door and out of its latch. He lashed at the door with his foot and kicked it open, fell into the room rolling across the soft carpet with the Browning cocked and ready to fire. The room was empty but the balcony glass door was open, the curtain stretched across it and flapping outwards. As Adam came to his feet, a man stepped through the curtain, a long-nosed black cylinder in his hand. He was wearing a morning suit and Adam recognized him as the usher who had let them into the wedding.

'He's got a gun,' screamed Billie behind him.

The shriek startled the usher who stepped back out on to the balcony as Adam lunged across the room and dragged him down, ripping the tube from his hands and holding the Browning muzzle to his head.

The usher screamed and started to sob uncontrollably.

The wedding ceremony came to an abrupt end as the rabbi, the couple and all the guests looked up to where the scream had come from.

That was when Adam realized the usher had been holding a long-lensed camera, a Nikon F4 with a 300 mm lens, in his hand.

He'd been taking pictures for the family album from the vantage of the balcony.

Shit.

Adam put the gun into his holster and stepped away from the sobbing man.

'It's a fucking camera,' said Phil Tucker as he looked through the curtain.

Adam looked down on the assembled guests, saw them all looking up at him. He shook his head and turned away, stepped through the curtain and back into the darkness of the room.

'A camera. That's all it was.'

'Great trick, tough guy,' said Billie. 'What's next? Take out the groom?'

Behind him, from the other side of the curtain, he heard Tucker trying to calm the hysterical usher. He looked at Billie and grinned. She'd forgotten to keep her chin forward. Stupid girl, as if it mattered. She was attractive, anyway. Even when she stood sneering at him.

'Wimping bloody Californians,' muttered Adam as he walked past Billie and went down to wait for the others in the car-park.

This is it, Marcus. The home of the American Dream.

The ride back to the Mirimar Air Base was in equal silence to the one they had made to the wedding. This time Trimmler didn't ask Tucker to turn down the air-conditioning.

The police had arrived at the hotel, but Tucker had taken control of the situation and explained they were there on Agency business. The wedding had continued, albeit without the usher who had retired to his room in a state of shock, and Trimmler had demanded to leave immediately after the ceremony.

'I will contact your superiors,' Trimmler barked when he climbed out of the car at the Mirimar Air Base. 'I will not be put in such an embarrassing position again.'

The trio watched him storm off to his temporary quarters before returning to Billie's apartment.

'You'd better stay here,' said Tucker, 'until someone tells me what to do with you.'

'House arrest, eh?' said Adam.

'Look, just cut out the humour. OK. Damn it, you could've killed that guy.'

'But I didn't.'

'What's that mean?'

144

'Think about it,' answered Adam and he went to his bedroom.

'*But I didn't*,' Tucker mimicked Adam. 'The guy talks in riddles,' he slammed at Billie.

'He's just telling you he was always in control.'

'Some fucking control. Jeeze, what a mess. They'll love this at the Agency. Send Tucker out into the big wide world and he shoots up a wedding. That'll look great on my record sheet.'

'It could've been a rifle.'

'It wasn't.'

'But it could've been. And that's what you've got to tell Washington.'

Tucker thought about her advice, about her obvious logic. 'OK. So we support him. But if he blows again . . . Damn it, he's not stable.'

'He's another breed. Not like us. He's a professional. Just did as he was trained. We're in his office, in his space. We're the amateurs, Phil. And that's a fact.'

CIA Headquarters
Langley

THE DEPUTY DIRECTOR of Administration read the faxed report that Tucker had personally sent the next morning. Next to him, the DDI, not a man known for detailed study of written matter, sat back in his chair and waited for his colleague to finish. He had already skimmed the report and sensed events were turning to his advantage.

Phil Tucker was in on the meeting, linked on a conference call. They sensed his nervousness as he waited for the ordeal to begin. Tucker knew someone was going to nail him to the cross.

'Not good,' said the DDA, finally looking up from the typed sheets in front of him.

'Damn right it's not good,' came in the DDI, his patience snapping as he moved in for the kill. 'Who the hell OKed his hardware?'

'I did,' replied the DDA calmly.

'That wasn't very clever, was it?'

'The British wanted their man armed. We had to agree to that.'

'We?'

'The Exec Director and myself.'

'Hell, I should've been consulted.'

'Bring that up with the Exec Director.'

'Some professional. Shooting up a damn photographer.'

'Nobody fired a shot.'

'But everyone saw him. Jeeze, calling the damn British in.'

'Come on. We have to keep this thing under wraps. We still have a rogue computer out there.' The DDA turned to the intercom phone. 'Phil, have we got any further on that?'

'Not yet.' Tucker had already checked with the two programmers before calling. 'There's a consensus that we should put it out to some private specialists. In Silicon Valley.'

'That's great. Bring in the whole world,' snapped the DDI.

'Why?' the DDA asked Tucker.

'There're people out there we trust,' replied Tucker's metallic voice. 'Good programmers. Some of the best in the world. And they've done confidential work for us before. Government specialists. It won't get out.'

'OK. But make sure they understand the confidentiality of this one. Otherwise they lose all government contracts. Make sure they understand that.'

'Yes, sir.'

'Set that in motion now. I'll contact you if there's any change.'

'What about Trimmler?'

'Continue as before. Just . . . uh . . . tell the Brit to be more careful next time.'

'Yes, sir.' They heard Tucker click off the line.

'Clerks should be pushing pens. Not running field operations as important as this.' The DDI referred to Tucker.

'It's what we decided.'

'We?'

'The Exec Dir—'

146

'Why are you having these meetings without me?'

'Don't ask me, ask the Exec.' The DDA knew his colleague wouldn't dare, nor was he prepared to admit that he waited early each morning for the Exec Director to get in so that he could give him the daily reports personally and ingratiate himself with his superior. It was a simple tactic, but effective as it convinced the other heads of departments that he had a special relationship with the Exec. It was a relationship the Exec also fostered; he had always been a firm believer in maintaining tension between his subordinates. It helped keep them on their toes and protected his own position.

'Time to push the Brits out,' said the DDI, knowing he'd lost the advantage this time. 'And put our own people in.'

'Can't do that.'

'For Christ's sake, he pulled a gun in public.'

'We'd look stupid. You can't ask for help in the first place, then send him packing because he was trying to protect Trimmler.'

'What about New Orleans?'

'They'll have to go. Including the Brit. Maybe when that's over, maybe then we'll have a clearer idea of what's going on. Maybe then we can send him home.'

'Shit. Nothing's going for us. Nothing.'

The DDA felt a glow of satisfaction. His colleague was right. Nothing was going right for him. But, for the DDA, things were certainly looking rosier by the minute.

'Well,' he shrugged. 'We just need time. Then things'll come right. They always do in the end.'

La Jolla

ADAM WAS SITTING on the balcony minding his own business when he heard the doorbell ring.

'Billie, it's for you,' he heard Muscle call.

'Coming,' he heard her reply from the kitchen.

A minute later he heard her shouting, screaming obscenities, then slamming the front door.

'What the hell's going on?' he heard Muscle yell.

'That bastard!' she screamed. 'That bastard's served a writ on me. For a fucking divorce and no settlement.'

'What the hell else did you expect of the shit?'

She stormed out on to the balcony waving the legal sheaf in her hand and went to the balustrade, leant over to catch a view of the process-server. Muscle came out after her.

Then she saw him.

'You shit,' she screamed over the railings at the bright yellow Bentley Mulsanne parked there, the driver's face grinning up at her. 'Too yellow to do your own dirty work?'

It was Peter. Her husband.

'Get up here, just come up here,' Muscle joined in over her shoulder.

Peter waved, arrogant and mischievous, enjoying her discomfort.

'You said you'd wait,' she continued shrilly. 'That you wouldn't leave me high and dry. You lying shit.'

The process-server climbed into the passenger seat as Peter switched on the engine.

'I'll fight you for every cent. You promised me a fair share. Every fucking cent I can get.' Her words were lost as he waved a final indolent farewell and drove out of the car-park.

She swung round, wild fury still in her eyes. Then she saw

148

Adam, realized that he had seen her at her weakest moment.

'What're you staring at?' she hissed at him.

'Nothing,' he replied warily. Now was not the time to get involved in a domestic squabble. Over her shoulder, Muscle challenged him, dared him to respond. He saw a car pull into the front out of the corner of his eye. 'I think Tucker's back.'

She turned and saw the Granada pull into the lot. Tucker got out, waved at the group on the balcony, unaware of the drama that had just taken place, and entered the condominium.

'Let him in, Gary,' she told Muscle who left to open the front door. 'Don't laugh at me, mister,' she warned Adam.

'I'm not laughing,' he replied. 'We all have our problems.'

'And I don't need your bullshit.'

'You're not getting it,' he said as he got up from the chair. 'If Tucker wants me, I'll be in my room.'

'Hey.' Her tone suddenly changed. 'Don't go,' she appealed to him. 'I'm sorry. I just don't like . . . people seeing me with my guard down. Hell, I never expected that from him.'

'How about if I made you some coffee?'

She laughed. 'No. This is still my place. Why don't I make it?'

'Why don't we both make it?'

'Deal.'

He held out his hand and she took it, shaking it in mock welcome.

'Good to see you both on the same side for once,' said Tucker, walking on to the balcony.

'Where's Gary?' Billie said, pulling her hand away from Adam.

'Said he was going to the gym. I told him we had business to discuss.' Tucker pulled up a chair and sat down; Billie joined him at the table. 'Damned if I can get used to this heat at Christmas. Seems wrong somehow.' He took off his jacket and hung it over the back of his chair. Then he looked up at Adam, who now leant against the balustrade. 'You have caused big problems,' he stated flatly.

Adam said nothing, just waited for Tucker to continue.

'Even so, we have a task to finish,' Tucker went on. 'Important enough for us to stay together on this thing as a team. I

149

have to say this . . . because I've been told to . . . that you're to take it easy on the gun-play.'

'There wasn't any,' replied Adam.

'You know what I mean. Hell, I've done nothing but sort out police and Agency people since you pulled that little stunt. Not to mention calming down two hundred wedding guests, the bride and groom, and the whole damn Sheraton management. Shit, there's only the rabbi and the State of Israel left.' Tucker laughed at his own joke as he saw Adam smile. 'Look, you're on foreign territory, on official business. Just take it easy in future. OK?'

'The situation was always under control.'

'All right. It was under control. You can even have the last word. This time. But just take it easier next time.'

'I thought I was going to have the last word.'

'Touché,' said Billie.

'Hey. Don't gang up on me, you two,' Tucker continued in the new-found lighter vein. 'Anyway, we're still on the case, as they say.'

'What next?'

'New Orleans.'

'New Orleans?'

'Louisiana. That's where Trimmler's off to. Big convention with Russian Commonwealth scientists.'

'When?'

'Tomorrow.'

'I can't go.'

'Orders.'

'Something's come up. I've got to deal with it.' Billie looked at Adam as she spoke and he knew she referred to the divorce writ that had been served before Tucker arrived.

'It'll have to wait. Our duty is to protect Trimmler. Wherever he is.'

She stood up angrily. 'You'll have to carry on without me for now. I've got calls to make.' She stamped off the balcony, the papers in her hand.

'What was that all about?' asked Tucker.

'Divorce.'

'You're kidding?'

'No. I'd leave her alone for a while. You know what they say. Never come between man and wife.'

'This isn't what I expected. Field operations. Damn it. It's like amateur night out, kindergarten stuff. Some fucking operation. I need to use the phone when she's finished. Ring Jean and tell her what's happening.' Tucker dreaded the call, knew his wife was going to bitch about his trip to New Orleans and his extended stay away from home. Especially with the New Year holiday looming the next day.

From the sitting room they heard Billie switch off the television news programme and phone her lawyer. It wasn't a news item with which they were concerned. It was about Berlin: riots had erupted and were now tearing that city apart.

An unimportant matter in the great scheme of world events.

Bellevue Hotel
Dresden

GROB MITZER WASN'T used to being kept waiting, particularly on New Year's Day.

He was on the second floor of the Bellevue Hotel on the Köpckestrasse which runs along the banks of the River Elbe, pacing the sitting area of Suite 217.

Dresden. City of smashed dreams, the recipient of Churchill's last blow at Hitler's Third Reich in 1945 when British bombers virtually razed the city to the ground and wiped out thirty-five thousand civilians in one night. That terrible night became known as Churchill's Revenge.

Dresden. Since the end of the Second World War, the centre of National Socialist activity in the oppressive new world of Russian invasion. The movement built secretly and slowly, a covert political doctrine that was carried through the early days of defeat and occupation, through the new order of Communism and the GDR, and into the final freedom of a reunified Germany. It was a word-of-mouth movement, a secret dream between those who remembered what the Third Reich could have achieved and who now passed that dream down through the generations of occupied Germany. The dream had been easy to perpetuate and nurture under the Russians. Any existence was better than a nonexistent life under Communism. For many, the dream, as submerged as it was, was the gateway to the future.

And when Communism was defeated by the simple removal of a concrete wall, National Socialism remained a dirty word, a memory of baby killers and mass murderers. It may have evoked such memories for the rest of the world, but, to the dreamers, it was the path back to greatness, to what Germany should have become. So they kept their brutal secrets, but in their darkness they became organized. They turned on the Poles, Turks and other foreigners who worked in the East, smashed them with their lead pipes and baseball bats, sent them back to where they had come from. Germany, the Fatherland, for the Germans. It became a familiar and popular chant during this time of unemployment and listless wandering for an identity. Then the dreamers came together and word of mouth was supplanted by fax messages, meetings, big-business financial support and a realization of destiny. All they had to do now was wait for the chaos that would surely come, the very chaos out of which they would one day lead Germany. Just as Adolf Hitler had done in the 1930s.

Willi Kushmann had been the chosen architect and leader who would take them forward on the day that the National Socialists decided to show their hand. But Willi Kushmann was dead and the council of twelve, of which Mitzer was one, had chosen their new leader.

Peter Frick was, like the late Willi Kushmann, a laywer from Dresden. He had been, at thirty-six, Kushmann's organizer and private secretary, Iago to Kushmann's Othello, the man of steel behind the dreamer.

But Kushmann had been Mitzer's man. Frick wanted his own loyalties and his own programme for the future, was tired of the older men who only had dreams and talked of what had been. But he needed their money and their contacts. They were his credibility. He would play the game for as long as was necessary. He would keep Mitzer and the others on their toes, keep them edgy while he put his plans into place.

That was why he kept the great industrialist, Grob Mitzer, waiting in the ante-room while he carried on the pretence of having an important meeting which could not be disturbed.

Across the river, in the Theater Platz which was ringed by the Zwinger, the Hofkirche Cathedral and the Semper Opera, Mitzer could see the tourists milling around. It was a cold day, but clear and bathed in sunshine. A good day to see the sights, a good day to be alive.

'Sorry to keep you waiting, Grob,' said Frick from behind him, startling Mitzer. Frick came towards him, his arm half-outstretched in the familiar fashion, the palm of his hand turned upward.

'Peter,' Mitzer replied, holding his own arm up, but feeling strange with the unfamiliar gesture.

Frick, his welcoming smile topped with a wide blond moustache, walked up to Mitzer, adjusting his arm down to the more familiar handshake. Mitzer returned the greeting. Frick was, as usual, wearing a business suit, a grey woollen outfit that completed the image of the successful lawyer. Behind him, standing in the doorway, were the now-familiar skin-headed *Sturmabteilungen*, the brown shirts who would one day take their rightful place as the storm-troopers of the new movement.

'A Happy New Year to you. And, hopefully, this will be the start of a momentous year for our movement,' said Frick. Mitzer noticed he didn't apologize for calling a meeting on a public holiday, summoning the industrialist across Germany in his private jet. 'What were you looking at with so much interest out there?' asked Frick, walking to the window.

'At the Zwinger and the tourists there. It's good to see the crowds out again, after all these years.'

'It is. And that they should come to the Zwinger.' Frick looked across at one of Germany's finest baroque buildings, the seven connected pavilions that form Dresden's most famous landmark. 'It stood through all the bombs. It stood when all else had been burnt to the ground. Our past and our future. A great time, Grob. An historic time.' Frick turned back to his guest. 'Come through into the other room,' he said, taking Mitzer's arm.

The two *Sturmabteilungen* stayed guarding the door that Frick closed. The bedroom had been turned into a small office, a simple table and some armchairs the only furniture.

'You know Helmut,' said Frick. 'I have asked him to be present for this meeting. Just in case we need anything actioned.'

Mitzer nodded at Helmut Kragan, the bull-necked Rottweiler of a Prussian who was Frick's personal assistant. Kragan smiled back, the smile as warm as the embers of a fire that had long gone out. Mitzer sensed there was a difference about the assistant, but couldn't immediately place it.

'I thought it wiser we meet here,' Frick continued, his German more orthodox than Mitzer's as is the manner of the East Germans. 'Unfortunately, anonymity is necessary. But maybe not for long.' He signalled Mitzer to sit in one of the armchairs and lowered himself into the one next to his guest. 'I know you didn't vote for me during the leadership campaign. I understand your reason, the need for someone more' – he paused – 'mature. I hope my future actions will give you confidence in my ability.'

'That was yesterday. I pledge you my total support. I will be proud to serve your leadership.'

'Thank you. I shall not let you down. And I shall count on your support and advice when I need it.'

The two men sat in silence for a while, the formalities complete.

'Would you like a drink or anything?' asked Frick eventually. Mitzer shook his head.

'You saw the news from Berlin today?' Frick continued.

'Yes.'

'It's good for us. All these television pictures of riot police being attacked by thugs. Scares the hell out of the public, eh?'

'The New Forum people,' spat Kragan, standing beside his leader. Mitzer now realized what was different about Kragan. The man had treated his close-cropped, mousey hair with blond streaks. He remembered that was what Martin Bormann had once done to resemble a true blond-haired Aryan.

'The New nothing.' Frick's words cut across his thoughts. Mitzer realized he had turned to answer Kragan. 'Communists and Zionists. Anarchists. With their Mohican haircuts, their derelict dress. Leather jackets, jeans and, what do the British call it, bovver boots. The more they attack the police, the more the people will look for proper law and order.'

'Over three thousand police.'

'With bulldozers and armoured personnel carriers. Batons and tear-gas. Ninety police were injured, you know. And many of those arrested were militants from France, Italy and the Netherlands. They've crossed the old border, the old Wall to bring their radical political agenda into the rest of Germany. And the media' – he snorted in disgust – 'hiding the truth. But then it's easy to blame rising unemployment and a collapse of local and federal authority. Familiar stuff, eh?'

'Just like 1933.'

'Precisely. The chaos before the order. In 1933 it was the Führer. This time it will be us.' Frick laughed, a high-pitched gurgle, excited and girlish. 'You know the old joke. Give a German a rifle and he'll head for France.'

'I hope I can be of service to the Party at this time,' said Mitzer, bringing himself into the diatribe between the two men.

Frick swung back sharply to the industrialist. 'You are a corner-stone of that future. A leader of business. A veritable captain of industry.' He played to Mitzer's ego, saw his pampering was having the desired effect on the industrialist. Why, the bastard was positively preening himself. 'When the National Socialists came to power in 1933, it was with the support of big business. Successful industry needs an ordered society. That's why they supported us in 1933. And that's why they will support us now. That's where we need your help. To show the businessmen that we are their salvation, their bridge to success. And this time, we will not have to use military power to achieve our ends. With the single monetary policy of Europe, with the powers of the Bundesbank governing the financial policy of Europe, we can do it all without firing a shot. Even the bloody British will lose their sovereignty. But to do that we need to be in Government. For that we need chaos.'

'West German businessmen have been used by these groups

before. Baader-Meinhof, the Red Brigade. It has been a part of our life for thirty years now. It still continues with Rohwedder and the others.'

'You knew him?'

'He was a friend.' A good friend recollected Mitzer. He remembered the shock he had felt when Detlev Rohwedder, the politician responsible for much of the privatization of state industries in East Germany, had been shot dead at his home in Düsseldorf in 1991.

'Yes. The Reds.' Frick wasted no opportunity in reminding Mitzer that the Red Army Faction had claimed responsibility for the attack. 'Your colleagues must be shown that only we can lead them out of this mess. That we are the only alternative to anarchy and disorder. That is our joint destiny. And I count on you, my dear Grob, to show them the way to our door. To their salvation. To Germany's salvation.'

The force of the man engulfed Mitzer. In that brief moment he saw the power and charisma that Willi Kushmann never had. It was a time for radical action and Frick had the magnetism that such a leader would need.

'I . . . you have my loyalty . . . all my efforts,' Mitzer stated, not comfortable in calling Frick by his first name any longer. The leader of the party deserved more respect.

'No more than I expected, Grob. And I'll give you the means with which to achieve our aims. I won't concern you with those plans at this stage. But, when the time is right, they will give you all the ammunition you need to convince your colleagues. In the mean time, we must let the Communists and Zionists and the rest of the anarchists fight our cause for us.' The hatred built in his tone. 'Even the Jews are claiming their property back in what was East Germany. The shits. They bled us dry before 1930 and now they want to do it again. Our people will love that. Their homes, their land, were taken from them by the Communists, and now, when they have learnt to work their own property again, the Jews are using the courts, the German courts, to take back that property. Why? Because they say it was stolen from them before the war. Stolen from them? They are the thieves of history. How the fuck can you steal from a thief?'

Frick fell back in his chair, his anger suddenly released from his body. Mitzer watched him, saw his leader sit still while he gathered himself.

'We must never let them back,' said Frick quietly. 'Never.' He suddenly stood up. 'Time for you to go. We both have work to do.'

Mitzer levered himself out of the armchair and followed Frick to the door. Frick swung round and faced the industrialist.

'One more thing. The Lucy Ghosts.'

'That's going according to plan,' said Mitzer.

'Yes. But impractical. Wasted effort.'

'They're key people.'

'Past people.'

'With vital knowledge.'

'Twenty years ago. Not now.'

'We promised that—'

'We don't have the resources. Or the need. This Berlin thing, the way things are moving fast in our favour. We must concentrate our efforts here, in the Fatherland.'

'It'll be impossible to stop it. The whole thing's gathered a momentum—'

'I leave it in your hands. Deal with it in your way. But it has to stop.'

'It's their money that's made all this possible.' Mitzer regretted the words as he spoke them. He saw the fury in Frick's eyes. He changed tack quickly. 'There have been accidents.'

'Accidents?'

'Deaths.'

'What do you expect? They're old now.'

'Violent deaths. Murdered. Friends who wanted to come home.'

'Friends. No. People who were forcing us to bring them home before we were ready.'

The horror of Frick's words stunned Mitzer. His mouth fell open as Kragan realized what his leader had said.

'Not us, Grob. We were not responsible,' Kragan intervened.

'I'm sorry. It has been a great shock. Especially poor Willi's death.'

'What the Führer meant was that we have other priorities.

That we have enough on our plate now. We don't need people putting us under additional pressure.'

'How many have died?' asked Frick.

'Nearly twenty.'

'That many?'

Mitzer nodded. 'Unfortunately, three of them were agents. Two for the Americans and one for the KGB.'

'So?'

'It would be a tragedy if the truth were to get out.'

'Not with that lot,' interjected Kragan. 'They've got enough of their own problems to sort out. No, as the Führer says, we need to concentrate on more important matters. You must talk to them, tell them to be patient.'

Mitzer knew there was no redress. 'I'll arrange things.'

'I know you will,' said Frick. 'Remember, they died with Boorman. There're no ghosts, Grob. Only the memories of old men. I'm not interested in the past. Help me. To discover the future. Revolution requires a society of extremes. It's there now, as it was in 1933.'

Frick opened the door into the ante-room and signalled the *Sturmabteilungen* to escort Mitzer from the room.

'Thank you for your time. Remember, out of chaos comes order. But to achieve order, we must have chaos. Goodbye, my old friend.' Frick bade Mitzer farewell. He didn't shake his hand, simply gave him the Nazi salute.

Before Mitzer could return it, Frick had closed the door and left him with the two *Sturmabteilungen*, one of whom escorted him out of the room and into the corridor.

The interview was over.

Nobody said Happy New Year.

The promise was broken and Mitzer was the envoy who had to break it.

Inside the suite, Kragan watched Frick looking out of the window. He knew better than to interrupt. His leader's sudden change in mood was well known.

'He must never find out,' Frick said at last. 'He'd be a dangerous enemy.'

'Only a handful of our people know.'

'In Cannes. He wasn't one of ours.'

'We hired him. So nobody could trace it back to—'

'I know why. But I don't want any black bastards, or any foreigners, used again. From now on we only use our own *Sturmabteilungen*.'

'It could lay us open to risk.'

'Why? Our people are the best. They wouldn't have made a mistake. Not like the African.'

'He panicked.'

'Precisely. If he hadn't, if he'd carried out his orders, it wouldn't just be Willi we'd be mourning.'

'If the CIA and KGB are involved—'

'They won't find anything. Not until it's too late.'

'I suggest we should hold back on any more action on the Lucy Ghosts.'

'It's not my fault. Bastards shouldn't have been pushing to come back. The last thing we want . . . Shit to the Lucy Ghosts. I will not live in the past. They've served their purpose. Germany needs us to look to the future.'

KGB Headquarters
Dzerzhinsky Square
Moscow

'Is THIS ALL that was saved?' Alexei Rostov asked the Head of Archives as the two men entered the large room where the remains of the fire from the fourth floor had been moved.

'Yes, sir. But it's more than half the information we had stored.'

Rostov walked along the long line of charred and scorched filing cabinets, the bitter smell of burning lingering heavily in the room.

'Many of the filing cabinets were wooden,' continued the man from Archives. 'We lost all those. But the metal ones, like these, resisted the heat for much longer. We saved most.

Apart from those near the centre of the fire. The emergency fire crew arrived quickly. Thank God.' The man caught his breath. God was still a foreign agent as far as the KGB were concerned. He continued quickly. 'Without all these drills we've been having, we could've lost everything.'

'And the transfer on to the computer?' Rostov ignored the religious comment, but had chuckled inside.

'Back on schedule. I don't think we've lost anything of great importance.'

Rostov stopped along one of the rows and wiped the soot away from the front of a cabinet, revealing the insignia that was the symbol of the Nazi Party, the eagle straddled over the swastika.

'What's this?' asked Rostov.

'War booty. After the war, we *confiscated*' – Rostov grinned at the explanation for stealing – 'as many useful items as we could from the Germans. Filing cabinets, typewriters—'

'Tanks, V2 rockets. I know,' Rostov joked. 'I hope they never present us with an inventory of all that was taken and ask for them back. What caused the fire?'

'That's our problem, sir,' said the Head of Archives, suddenly lowering his voice. 'Which is why I asked to meet you outside your office.'

'Deliberate?'

'We think so.'

'We?'

'The Head of Administration and myself. And the Chief of Internal Security who came to us in the first place. Nobody else is involved yet.'

'Explain.'

'The room where the fire took place was rarely visited. But, due to the sensitive nature of some of the archives, those from the end of the war until 1956 dealing with Counter-Intelligence information, the area was sealed off with high-security locks and alarms. To gain entry, all the keys and alarm codes were kept in a safe in my office suite. There were also duplicate keys kept securely in the Administration Section. When the fire was discovered, fortunately by chance when a cypher clerk had to visit a nearby room for some information, our people reacted quickly in gaining access to the room and quelling the fire. Afterwards, when things returned to normal, they attempted to determine what the cause was. It was an electric heater, the open kind with filament bars running across it, which had shorted and caught fire.'

'Why is that suspicious?'

'Because it wasn't a room we normally heated, certainly not with a single electric fire.'

'Had someone been working there, wanted to keep warm?'

'Nobody has asked for a key to that room for over two months.'

Rostov said nothing as the real possibility of sabotage dawned on him.

'The consensus, amongst ourselves, is that someone left the fire on and draped a wet cloth over the fire. That would have given them time to relock the doors, set the alarms and leave the area before the indirect heat caused the cloth to catch fire. It was an old method we used to—'

'I know the methods we used to use,' interrupted Rostov. 'But even that would only have given whoever it was ten minutes at the most. Did the cypher clerk see or hear anything unusual?'

'No.'

'Is he above suspicion?'

'She, sir. We think so. She is an old lady, in her sixties. Due to retire soon. She was an Intelligence officer at the end of the war, a language expert who went with our troops into Germany. Was part of the Occupation army until 1975. Anyway, if she had started the fire, then she would have let it burn, not reported it before it got going.'

'Investigate her. You never know. The cabinets near the heater. I presume they were the ones which were destroyed. Do we know what was in them?'

'Some were totally destroyed. But others, of German manufacture, were designed to be fireproof. They were damaged quite badly, but we managed to salvage most of their contents. They're at the back, over here, sir.'

He led Rostov to the rear of the room, where some twenty scorched metal cabinets had been gathered.

'Much of the contents are singed, sir. The flames got through the metal joints and hinges. And, of course, the water and fire spray was everywhere. Ruined most of it.'

'I need a list of all those documents. And what they referred to.'

'It's being prepared now.'

'How long?'

'A week, sir.'

'Too long.'

'A lot of the paper is stuck together, because of the water that was used to put out the fire. We have to let them dry naturally, we can't force that process.'

'Then get me an index of what you have already identified. Within the hour.'

As Rostov returned to his office, an Aeroflot Ilyushin 62M with four Soloviev D 30KU jet engines strapped to the rear fuselage took off from Moscow's Sheremetyevo Airport.

On board were a group of Russian space scientists, some forty of them. They would change planes at Kennedy Airport to an American Airlines Boeing 757 which would transport them to the first joint-manned flight space conference between the USA and the USSR.

The final destination of the Boeing was New Orleans.

CIA Headquarters
Langley

THE DDA WENT through the list that had just been placed in front of him, an index of the files that had been contaminated by the computer virus.

The list, ninety-three pages in all, gave little away. It was no more than a list of single-line headings which related to events and personalities that the American Counter-Intelligence Agencies had been involved in in the European theatre from 1945 to 1958. There were one hundred and twenty lines to the page, over eleven thousand subjects to choose from. Each heading could have between one hundred and five thousand files dealing with that subject. That meant there were between thirty and forty million single items on that segment of the computer being systematically wiped out every time someone switched on the machine.

He put the list down. He was wasting his time. He'd been through it four times in the last few days with no idea of what he was looking for.

It was time to open up the game.

He decided not to tell the DDI. He'd object anyway.

He picked up the phone and asked his secretary to get Phil Nowak on the phone.

'I want to open up to the Russians,' he told Nowak. 'How far will they go?'

'I think they want this resolved as much as we do.'

'OK, I'm convinced that there is a direct link between the problem on the computers and this attack on our asset base. The fact that Russian agents are also getting hit means we're on the same side. Unless they're pulling a fast one on us.'

'I can't see what they'd gain.'

'Neither can I. I have a list here. Headings of the various files that have been contaminated on the computer. I think we should show them that list.' He heard Nowak draw his breath, they both realized the importance of what he was prepared to do. 'I know, but I don't think we've any alternative. I would like that list to go through you and your contact. There may just be something that is common to us both, something we can't see without the other half of the puzzle.'

'Is this cleared with the Agency?' Nowak meant the Executive Director.

'Yes.' The DDA didn't add that the Exec had told him he was on his own on this one. But then, if it produced the goods, the DDA was assured of his promotion.

'OK. I'll arrange that.'

'I'll get it sent over. But before you show your hand, tell them they've got to be as open as us. Tell your man Sorge what you're going to show him. Give him time to contact Moscow and see if they've got anything to share with us. I want to see how open they're being with us before we're committed.'

'I'll get on to it now.'

The phone went dead and the DDA put his own receiver down, gently placing it on the cradle. Before he had removed his hand it rang sharply. He picked it up once again.

'Yes,' he said.

'Any news?' asked the DDI.

'Nothing,' he lied.

'Where's Dirty Harry?' It was his nickname for the Englishman.

'About to leave for New Orleans.'

'Call me if anything breaks.'

'Of course.'

He put the phone down again. He picked up the list and flicked through the pages. The answer was in the computer. He suddenly regretted sending Tucker to look after Trimmler. Tucker was a computer man, would have the nose to dig into this thing and get an answer. But it was too late now. What they needed now was a sliver of luck.

Maybe the Russians would provide that. Or maybe they could just blow the whole thing up in his face.

The phone rang again. It was the Executive Director.

'You better come on up,' said his superior's voice. 'We've got to discuss the President's trip. The one to Berlin.'

BOOK THREE

Ghosts from the Past

American Airspace
Texas

THE DESERT LANDSCAPE had changed and Adam now saw rivers running like twisted ribbons through the green earth, the sand and water reflecting each other as the sun bounced upwards and glistened in blinding brilliance.

Very poetic, he thought as he looked down out of the aircraft window. Very bloody poetic.

Billie sat next to him, her head tilted down as she read the latest copy of *People* magazine. Across the aisle, Phil Tucker had fallen asleep, his head tilted sideways as his snores rumbled gently on.

They sat in Executive Class. Trimmler and his wife, Trudi, were up front in First. Adam had decided not to follow his usual habit and upgrade himself to First Class. It would have alienated him from Billie and Tucker and he felt no desire to do that, not at this stage anyway. He grinned as he thought of the effect it would have had on Trimmler. Maybe he should've upgraded, if only to annoy the touchy little scientist.

'Ever been to New Orleans before?' Billie asked, putting her magazine down. She was relieved the airline had a total restriction on smoking throughout their fleet, it was his one habit she couldn't tolerate.

'No. You?'

'Yes. For my honeymoon.'

'Good timing.'

'Isn't it?'

'Did you get hold of your lawyers?'

'Yes.'

'I thought in California the wife automatically got half her husband's money?'

'I signed a settlement waiver. When we got married.'

167

'Waiving everything?'

'Something like that. I was in love. You don't think about things like that when you're in love. And when I signed, he promised that he would always look after me if things went wrong. Some promise.'

'What do your lawyers say?'

'That I might have a case. They don't care, do they? They win either way.'

'That's the same all over the world. The worse the news, the richer they get.' He paused. 'How long were you married for?' he asked eventually.

'Twelve years. And separated for four. They were good and bad years. The highs were high and the lows were even worse. Shit. Some mess.'

'Miss him?'

'What are you? A detective?'

'Sorry. I just sensed it.'

'Well, you sensed wrong.'

They sat in silence for a while, still unsure of each other.

'There's nothing wrong with missing someone you lived with for twelve years.'

'I wasn't sitting in judgement.'

'Whatever. So, I miss him. So what?'

'No chance of getting back with . . . ?'

'If I want your advice, I'll ask for it.'

'OK.'

'There's no chance of getting back. I tried for long enough.'

'Why did you split up?'

'You really keep pushing, don't you? You can't let go.'

'It's terrible. The way I am. My mother always said . . . '

'Why don't you just leave me alone? We're here working, not on some agony-aunt tour.'

'I'll shut up.'

'Good. Anyway, what did your mother always say?'

'That my lips moved faster than my brain.'

'She was right.'

'So, why did you split up?'

'Because I grew too old for him. Just like you think, tough guy?'

168

'Who says?'

'You did. First time we met. Said I was too old for the job.'

'No. I wasn't talking about you as a person. I was talking about you as a field agent.'

'Old and inexperienced, huh?'

'Don't knock yourself. You don't need to.'

'You're right. I don't need to when you're doing it for me.'

'And stop feeling sorry for yourself.'

'Fuck off,' she hissed at him.

'Chance would be a fine thing.'

'What?'

'Chance would be a fine thing. It's an old English saying. You really want me to fuck off?'

'Course not.'

'So, why did you split up?'

She started to laugh, his cheek winning through her defences. 'I told you why. Because I grew too old. No, that's not true. He wanted to stay young. Suddenly developed an interest in teenage girls. The older he got, the younger they got. You know, I found him crying once. After we'd broken up and I called round to pick up some things. You know why he was crying. Because this girl of twenty, the one he was living with, didn't walk up to him and touch him. Said that made him feel old. Because, before he went out with her, he'd seen her with her boyfriend at a softball game in the park. She'd walked up to her boyfriend from behind and just put her arms round his shoulder. Hugged him, I guess. Peter said it was the most natural thing he'd ever seen. And he was fucking crying because in three months together she'd not done that to him. You know what I did? I walked up behind him and put my arms round him. I felt sorry for him. He deserved better.'

'What did he do?'

'Told me to fuck off. He didn't love them, you know. He was obsessed. By their fresh bodies, their soft pubic hair and their wide-eyed innocence.'

'Maybe you expected too much?'

'No. I knew what Peter was. I just didn't want to let go. I

never wanted anyone else. And here I am, sitting in this metal tube, going to New Orleans where I had my honeymoon, watching over some nothing scientist with a crazy gunman for my partner, and back home the lawyers are moving in to take away everything I've got. Not fair, is it?'

'Not fair. What about Gary?'

'What about him? Probably move out while we're in New Orleans. No, that's unfair. But he does his own thing. It's not . . . permanent. Not for Gary. Maybe Peter isn't the only one holding on.'

'To what?'

'To whatever it was we were. He's just frightened. Middle age is like sand. The tighter you hold it in your hand, the faster it runs through your fingers. You're a great person for asking questions. About other people. What about you?'

'What about me?'

'Don't answer a question with a question.'

'Why?'

'Because it's rude. I thought you English types were always polite.'

'Sometimes.'

'You married?'

'No.'

'Girlfriend?'

'No.'

'Divorced?'

'No.'

'Gay?'

'Only when I'm happy.'

'Meaning?'

'I prefer queer. When they adopted gay they took a great word out of the English language.'

'Macho-type, huh?'

'Just normal.'

'You rich?'

'A little.'

'And you like your job?'

'Yes.'

'You good at it?'

'Better than most.'

'Don't let much out, do you?' She ignored his arrogance, even if it rang true.

'No.'

'If we walk into trouble, and my back's against the wall, will you come and save me?'

'You'll have to wait and see.'

'Whatever happened to the age of chivalry?'

Adam laughed. 'I'll tell you that when your back's to the wall.'

KGB Headquarters
Dzerzhinsky Square
Moscow

'Dimitri tells me that the Americans have uncovered a problem with their records regarding all counter-espionage action from 1945 until 1958.'

'What problem?'

'There was nothing specific. But they believe it could be tied up with our common predicament,' said Rostov.

'And what do they want from us?' The Director knew everything had a price, that charity was not common currency in the espionage game, even in these enlightened days of *glasnost*.

'They have an index of all the subjects that their records deal with during that period. They would like to see if we would be willing to provide a similar list so that they could determine if there were any common factors which would help find the reason for these attacks on both our agents.'

'Our little fire in this building suddenly takes on a new complexion.'

'It'll be interesting to find out what problem the Americans have with their records.'

'There are things in those files, in those cabinets, that would

171

cause us great embarrassment if they were ever to get out,' stated the Director.

'We can't always be responsible for the past. It is a chance I feel we have to take.'

'And if the Americans are out to deceive us?'

'We have people on the ground over there.'

The Director raised his eyebrows. 'Nothing against the spirit of co-operation between our two great countries, I hope.'

'Of course not,' Rostov lied, as was expected of him. 'We'll follow their actions as closely as we can.' He wasn't prepared to say any more. They both understood that the Director was to be protected when faced with awkward questions from the Kremlin. 'We'll take it step by step. If they're prepared to show us the outline of their files, without giving away any specific details, then we can do the same. I already have an index prepared. It was for my benefit. Maybe there is some common ground.'

'We have little choice. Especially as the Americans are making such an obvious gesture. Be careful. Watch your back at all times.'

'Yes, sir,' replied Rostov.

'You know what the Americans call Counter-Intelligence?'

'Dante's Inferno. With ninety-nine circles.'

'Exactly. It'll be strange,' said the Director, 'working this close with them. Ten years ago we were at each other's throats. Now we're allies. But where, my dear Alexei, is the enemy?'

International Airport
New Orleans

THERE WAS NO delay and the twin-engined, wide-bodied Boeing screeched on to the runway exactly on schedule.

Tucker had slept for most of the flight and was now sleepily gazing out of the window, frantically trying to bring his senses into focus as the plane taxied in.

'Please stay seated until the seat-belt light goes out,' a stewardess shouted at Adam, who had stood up before the aircraft left the runway so that he could take his overcoat and Samsonite case from the upper lockers. His weapons were in the suitcase, cleared through security at San Diego by the local Agency operatives.

'OK,' said Adam as he continued dragging his belongings from the shelf.

'Please sit down, sir.'

'OK,' repeated Adam, finishing his task. He grinned cheekily at her and sat down, his coat and case draped across his lap. His duty was to protect Trimmler and he wanted to be ready in case the scientist was the first off the aircraft.

'Rebel without a cause,' quipped Billie.

'The lost generation. That's us,' he replied.

Adam's instincts were correct; and Trimmler had elbowed his way through the other passengers, dragging his wife by her arm, to become the first passenger off the plane once it had docked. The Englishman wasn't far behind, his passage far less strenuous and impolite.

The other two caught up with Adam at the baggage carousel, where he stood under the exit sign, watching Trimmler anxiously waiting to retrieve his suitcases.

'Why the rush?' said Tucker. 'He had to wait for his cases.'

'I hope he doesn't get his before yours arrives. Otherwise he's going to get away from here without you,' said Adam.

'Shit. I better go and tell him to wait for us.' Tucker turned to Billie. 'Transport ready?'

'Yes,' she answered. 'Two company cabs. They'll be outside.'

'OK. I'll go with Trimmler. You two follow. I'll leave you to organize the cabs.' Tucker left them and walked over to the Trimmlers.

'This yours?' Adam asked Billie, stepping back and revealing her ordinary leather case next to his Louis Vuitton suit carrier.

'Very impressive,' she said, trying not to show her surprise. She looked towards the carousel which remained still.

'Aren't you going to ask how I managed it?'

'No.'

'Then I won't tell you.' He grinned as he replied. Damn her

cool. She didn't know he hadn't loaded the bag at San Diego as he had offered, but simply bribed one of the stewards to put it on the plane as hand luggage. Amateurs never understood the need to be expeditiously mobile.

He picked up her case as well as his own, linking the two handles together in his hand so that he could carry them as one.

'OK?' he said.

'Thank you.' She turned and walked out of the baggage area, Adam following behind her.

There were two cabs parked side by side at the entrance. In the style of New Orleans they were large American cars, not the compact or special square-bodied ones that were used in most cities. Like most New Orleans cabs, and like the city itself, they were of a shabby appearance, old in design, a reflection of a greater age past. One was a blue 1988 Chevrolet Impala, the other a white 1976 Cadillac Fleetwood with a 1927 Chevrolet Qouta Trophy mascot on its bonnet, a cast zinc model of Lindbergh's Ryan monoplane supported by the Spirit of Victory.

They both bore the logo of the Mayfair Cab and Taxi Company.

Billie walked up to them as the driver from the blue car got out. He was black, in his early sixties, and his name, Marius Beiderbecque, was painted on the rear wing of the car in a classic Gothic style.

'Miss Billie,' he greeted warmly.

'Hallo, Marius,' she smiled back. 'This is Adam Nicholson. He's with us.'

'Mister Adam.'

'Hallo.' Adam nodded, his hands full of luggage which Marius came and relieved him of. Adam kept the Samsonite case to carry with him in the car.

'Put those in Frankie's cab, please,' stated Billie. 'We'll travel with him. We've got three more. They're getting their cases. You take them.'

'To the River Walk Hilton?' asked Marius as he opened the boot of the white Cadillac and put the cases in.

'That's the one.' Billie walked to the driver's door of the

Cadillac and spoke to the driver. His name, Frankie Mistletoe, was emblazoned on the side of his cab, in the same style as that on the blue Chevrolet. 'Any problems?' she asked Frankie.

'No. Apart from a ticket happy cop who tried to move us.'

'This is—'

'I heard. Hi, Adam. I'm Frankie.'

'Hallo, Frankie.' Adam came up to the car.

'You English?'

'I am.' As Adam leant forward he realized the driver was a cripple, his wheelchair folded and wedged in the passenger seat next to him, his hunched back pushing his head towards the windscreen. His hands were arthritic, his fingers arched stiffly. On the steering wheel there was a large plastic knob with which he steered the car. The column gearshift, an automatic box, had a long L-shaped extension which made gear-changing simple. He was no more than thirty years old.

'You never seen a cripple before?'

'Not one that drives cabs.' Adam tried to lighten the situation. He was annoyed with himself. The driver had surprised him and he had let it show.

Frankie laughed. 'Best driver in New Orleans,' he drawled.

'Bet you get the biggest tips.'

'Damn right. Works every time. Get in, limey.'

Adam climbed into the back of the car leaving Billie to wait for the other three.

'Now I don't want you worrying about me,' Frankie continued. 'My right foot's my good foot. Works the accelerator and the brake.'

'If you got here to pick us up, then I'm sure you'll get us to wherever we're going.'

'Well said. What you clutching there?' Frankie asked. 'Got to be important, the way you hanging on to it.'

'I've heard about the muggings in this town. I'm carrying twenty hand-grenades, a sawn-off shot-gun, three Kalishnikovs and a rocket launcher.'

'In this game nothing surprises me. Nothing.' The two men laughed, sharing their humour. 'I've been to England, you know. Oxford. You been to Oxford?'

'Yes.'

'Pretty place. I toured all round. About seven years ago. Spent two months there. Pretty country. But Oxford, that was the prettiest of all. What're you doing here, with our people?'

'Helping out.'

'That right? You must wonder what someone like me's doing here?'

'It crossed my mind.'

'Crossed your mind. More likely smacked you across your face. Ha! You heard of the Mayfair Cab and Taxi Company.'

'Billie told me. Big company. Across America, in most of the large cities. It's used by the Agency who put agents in as drivers.'

'Great network. Amazing what you pick up in a cab.'

They saw Tucker and the Trimmlers come out of the terminal entrance and Billie walk towards them.

'That them?' asked Frankie.

'Yes.'

'Good, we can get going. And don't let this body fool you, limey. It's supporting a brain up here' – he tapped his forehead as he spoke – 'that's smarter than you think. You just call when you're in the shit, and I'll be there.'

'You're on.'

The drive into New Orleans was slow, the traffic heavy.

New Orleans is a faded city, shabby in its disrepair and peeling past. Known as 'Big Easy' and sometimes 'Sin City', the city conjures up images of carnival, jazz, voodoo, sex and fun against a Caribbean-Gallic heritage in a predominantly Anglo-Saxon culture. This confusion of spirit was once described as a cross between Port-au-Prince, Haiti and Patterson, New Jersey with a culture not dissimilar to Genoa, Marseille, Beirut and Egyptian Alexandria. This is reflected in the names of the various city boroughs, Algiers, Arabi, Gretna, Westwego, Bridge City, Cajun County and the French Quarter.

Its aura of decadence is a true reflection of its poverty. And where there is poverty, there is invariably crime. Paid-for sex, paid-for drugs, paid-for violence and paid-for eroticism is the currency of the city, openly on display amongst the swirl of tourists on the look-out for that which is unattainable in the suburban homes, but openly on display where it can be watched from the safety of the crowd on the pavement.

The city's population is 60 per cent black, the highest ratio of any city in North America. With strong religious roots dating back to the discovery of Louisiana in 1699 on Mardi Gras Day by a group of French Canadians, this mixture of Roman Catholicism, Bible-Belt Protestantism and mass slavery resulted in a voodoo culture that still grips the dark side of the city.

New Orleans. Where everything is easy, where nothing is impossible. Home to one million people. Home to four hundred thousand tourists a year. And the largest convention centre in the United States.

Adam sat quietly in the back of the white Cadillac, looking out on the 'Big Easy'. In the front Billie listened to Frankie giving a guided tour of their route into the centre, his wheelchair now sharing the back seat with Adam.

'French Quarter's OK,' he heard Frankie expound, 'but you gotta remember it's for the tourists. Easy-money country. A jerk on every street corner, ready to be taken. If you get up there, just watch out for the hustlers. And don't go up Basin Street alone, not north of the Quarter. Even the twos of you. That's bad terrain. Bad people. Cut you for a dime. Hell, cut you for nothing, just for the fun of it.'

They came in on 61, the Airline Highway. It was a flat land, the city having been built on the wetlands and bayou next to the Mississippi River. They turned off the 61 at the Charity Hospital and continued down Common Street to the Trade Centre where the Hilton Hotel was located. To his right, Adam saw the huge, covered Superdrome, home of the New Orleans Saints. Ahead, as they drove down Common Street, he glimpsed the mighty Mississippi, Ole Man River, as it wended its way through the southern half of the city. He saw the busy river traffic, barges, tugs, steamers and pleasure craft, working the water as they had done since man first stumbled on the Mississippi; the main artery and heartbeat that was the south.

The Hilton, twenty-five storeys of twin towers, sits on River Walk, on the banks of the Mississippi.

The two cars pulled up at the entrance, Trimmler, in his

usual hurry, being the first to exit the lead cab, his wife scurrying behind him. By the time Adam had climbed out of the Cadillac, Tucker was organizing the bellboy to deal with the luggage. Adam followed Trimmler into the building still carrying his small case, and took the escalator to the third floor where reception was. He kept his distance as he took in the lobby and its occupants. There was nothing to alarm him, all things seemed fairly quiet at this time. He watched Trimmler book in, then turn and go to the lifts.

'I'll get your key,' said Tucker from behind him. 'We're all on the eighteenth floor. I'll meet you up there. You stay with Trimmler.'

Adam crossed the lobby area and joined the small group waiting to take the lifts. When the doors finally slid open, he followed the Trimmlers in. It was a viewing lift, glass-sided and fixed to the outside of the building so that hotel guests could look out on the city as the lift climbed up to the twenty-fifth floor.

Trudi smiled at Adam, but Trimmler ignored him. He had pointedly ignored the Englishman ever since the wedding incident. That didn't worry Adam; in fact it made life rather easier as he could concentrate on keeping a watchful eye on the situation rather than get involved in idle small talk.

He returned Trudi's smile, then turned and watched the city fall away below him as the lift shot up, stopping twice before it reached the eighteenth floor.

He waited for the Trimmlers to exit before he followed them, skipping through the lift doors as they started to close. Trimmler walked along the corridor to the left and Adam followed at a distance. When the couple reached Suite 1844, Trimmler inserted his pass key and entered the room with Trudi behind him.

The loud slam was for Adam's benefit.

He ambled back along the corridor and waited by the lift for the others.

'Everything OK?' asked Tucker when he emerged with Billie five minutes later, a bellboy with a loaded luggage trolley trailing them.

'Fine.'

'Good. You're in Suite 1842. Billie's in 1840 and I'm the other side of the Trimmlers. We'll work out a schedule when we're unpacked.' Tucker turned to the bellboy and pointed at the luggage. 'That's for Suite 1844, so's that. The blue valise . . . '

Adam took his and Billie's luggage from the trolley and turned back down the corridor. She followed him, leaving Tucker to sort out the remainder.

'Welcome to New Orleans,' she said.

'Is there something I don't know?' he asked suddenly.

'Like what?'

'Like why're we guarding someone who doesn't seem to be in any real danger?'

'We don't know that. Why?'

'Because if he's a prime target, then there'd be more security than this. Unless one of us is going to live in that room with him, we can't guarantee anything.'

'It's how they want it.'

'They?'

'Higher-ups.'

'I know I'm not being told everything, Billie. I just hope, if anything does happen, that I'm ready for the unexpected.'

The Lincoln Memorial
Washington, DC

A BLISTERY, COLD morning. The sort of morning when the air stays chilled in your lungs and your cheeks burn. But the sun was shining and the two diplomats had decided to meet in the open and enjoy the brief sunshine before the bad weather moved in again. Both men carried briefcases, two office workers on their way to a meeting.

A group of tourists stared up at the vast statue of a brooding Abraham Lincoln, so the two men decided to walk in order that they could hold their conversation in private.

'Moscow is worried that you might hold something back,' said Sorge, his feet crunching in the ice-hard snow.

'Just what my people said,' replied Nowak.

'Old habits die hard.'

'They said that, too.'

'How honest are your people with you?' asked Sorge, stopping sharply.

'Well, they haven't seen me eat pussy, like some have,' Nowak laughed. 'Sort of gives you a common bond. Hell, Dimi, I don't know. I mean, we all know that we get set up at times. By our own people. But they're nervous this time. They genuinely seem to want to know what's going on. I think they're being pretty straight.'

'I feel this also.'

'Have you been told everything by Moscow?'

'Yes. But they told me to let you speak first. To see how much you knew before I committed myself.'

'My lot read me the same scenario.'

'So, who starts?'

'OK. As long as I have your word . . . '

'I will tell you everything. At least we're honest between ourselves.'

Nowak walked over to a wooden park bench beside the path. He wrapped his coat round himself and sat down, Sorge joining him immediately.

'One thing I didn't tell you last time was that our agents, the ones who had been killed, were also in their sixties,' Nowak started off.

'So, you also employ pensioners.'

'*Touché*. In our case, they're all pretty ancient.'

'Why?'

'Because of President Carter. Once the National Security Agency went for satellite surveillance, the whole administration pulled back on agents in the field. But we kept a lot of the ones we had in place out there. Our secret army. Growing older by the day.'

'For both of us it is impossible to bring them back. How would we do it? Have an amnesty day. Hundreds of people all heading for borders. With wives, children, belongings. We don't even have borders to cross any longer. Not like the old days. No more Berlin Wall, no more Checkpoint Charlie. All we can do is leave them to fade away.'

'So, why's everyone going out with a bang instead of a whimper?'

'That, my literary friend, is what this is all about.'

'We lost another one. Just before Christmas. In Portugal.'

'Portugal? I thought they were on your side.'

'We had people everywhere. Allies have been known to change sides.'

'To our knowledge there have been no more deaths.'

'That you know of.'

'That we know of. What was the problem with your records that prompted you to suggest this meeting?'

Nowak told Sorge of the computer virus, of the electronic enemy within which was steadily wiping out the records. When he had finished, he leant back and watched the Russian who was playing noughts and crosses with his shoe toe in the snow. When he had beaten himself, and connected the line that joined the three crosses, he finally told Nowak of the fire in KGB Headquarters.

'Deeper and deeper,' commented Nowak when Sorge had finished.

'Someone has their tentacles in both our organizations.'

'Yeah. Who? Unless one of us is being set up. By our own people.'

'Or both of us.' Sorge shrugged, opened his briefcase and took out a sheaf of papers. He handed them to Nowak. The American took the bundle, opened his briefcase and repeated the exercise.

There was nothing else to say. They had known each other so long that both were aware when the other was telling the truth.

River Walk Hilton
New Orleans

JUST AFTER 9 A.M., Billie watched Adam through the glass entrance-doors of the hotel Fitness Centre. He was working out on the multi-gym, that modern torture chamber of pulleys, bars and stacked weights. He wore a pair of shorts and a sweatshirt, with a towel wrapped round his neck to keep the heat in. He was on his back, tilted head down, on a padded board with his feet tucked under a bar above him. His hands were clasped behind his head and he pulled himself upright into a sitting position before lowering himself down again. It was a painful exercise, one she did herself on her short morning sojourn in the gym at home. She usually managed twenty before her stomach muscles demanded that she rest before attempting any more. She knew Gary did one hundred every morning and another hundred at night. He had told her how difficult the last twenty were, how painful the exercise.

She watched Adam effortlessly on the board, counted him to a hundred and nine pull-ups before he swung his legs off and sat crosslegged on the floor. He saw her as he wiped his face with the towel, grinned and beckoned her in.

'Don't you ever sleep?' she asked, when she had let herself in.

'Not a lot. Waste of time.'

'Didn't know you were a fitness freak. Quite Californian.'

'Very funny,' he said, standing up. 'Goes with the job. Usually, when I'm in the field, it's easy to stay fit. But here, with all this soft living, this is the only way. You going to have a go?'

'No. I just wanted to check you knew what was happening.'

'The boat ride.'

'Yes. It leaves at twelve.'

There was to be a reception for the American and Russian

scientists later that afternoon, but Trimmler had insisted he wanted a trip on a Mississippi riverboat before that. The boat, the *Creole Queen*, left from the wharf next to the hotel and Tucker wanted Billie and Adam to accompany the Trimmlers. 'At a discreet distance,' he had instructed.

'I'll be in the lobby at eleven-thirty,' Adam said. 'Do we need tickets?'

'I'll get those.'

'Come on. Go and get changed and then jump on one of those machines. It'll do you good.'

'OK,' she replied. 'See you in ten minutes.'

She left the exercise room. It would be fun exercising with someone else, Gary always took it so seriously. She was beginning to enjoy the Englishman's company. Maybe he wasn't as hard-nosed and arrogant as he had first appeared. Then she remembered the bag by the side of the exercise room, remembered the weapons.

That was the difference between him and Gary. Gary worked at his exercises for self-achievement, for his own gratification. To Adam it was the difference between life and death.

And she, old collector and disseminator of information, was part of a real life-and-death struggle. The realization suddenly hit her, she felt the excitement rush through her.

She really was in the field.

And of all things, it had been the Fitness Centre that had brought about that realization. With Gary, exercise was something to do. With Adam it was for real.

She was a secret agent and she wanted to tell the world. It was her secret and she regretted not being able to shout it out as she walked back through the lobby.

Twenty minutes later, as Adam watched her on the jogging machine, with her full breasts bouncing up and down under her tight T-shirt, he hoped she wouldn't be faced with what he knew could well happen. Violence was his estate. If it came, sudden and harsh as is its nature, he knew she couldn't cope.

What he didn't say, his real reason for coming down to the exercise room, was that he sensed that instinct, that flash of the unexplainable, that warned him of danger. He needed his fitness, his agility, his strength.

He knew things were suddenly going to change.

He didn't try and define his feelings.

His instinct had held good in the past.

The road was about to become rocky.

The *Creole Queen* is a paddle-bashing, white-painted, single-smoke-stacked river boat.

It recalls days of Rhett Butler gamblers strolling the decks with a thin cigar clamped between their teeth; of smart-suited men and elegantly frocked women on their way to the American dream; of little boys fishing on the banks of the Mississippi hearing the toot-toot of the river boat as it rounded the bend; of cotton and steam; of the old captain up on his bridge sailing into the wilderness; of the Deep South, of Mark Twain, of all that made America great.

That's as it was. Today, the *Creole Queen* and its sister ships that ply on the reminiscence trail are a sham. Only half the size of the original river queens, they are designed purely for the tourist market.

Adam watched the Trimmlers walk down River Walk and up the gangplank on to the boat. He and Billie kept their distance.

Trimmler seemed nervous, anxiously looking round for something, yet not wanting to appear to be doing so. At one stage, as they were climbing the steps down to the restaurant gallery, he whispered conspiratorially into Trudi's ear, then seemed to point across the boat to the other passengers. Trudi glanced in their direction.

Adam looked over to where he had indicated. A group of people stood there, a mixture of ages and sexes. There was nothing extraordinary about them, they were simply tourists like the others on the boat.

Across the river, a tug, pushing a line of five heavily laden barges, blew its horn, warning a small, motorized pleasure craft going in the opposite direction to keep clear. The sound, loud and nearby, attracted the attention of the tourists on the *Creole Queen* and they turned as one to look at the tug-train bearing down on the smaller boat. The pleasure craft, with six revellers on board, swung hard left and skirted the barges on their port side.

'Did you see that? That was close,' said Billie.

'Wasn't it?' he replied. But he had ignored the incident, kept his attention on Trimmler. The scientist had also chosen to disregard the near-accident and had signalled, with a small wave of his hand, to one of the group on the opposite side of the deck. A distinguished, older man with a heavily lined face framed in a grey shock of wavy hair with his back to the railings, had acknowledged Trimmler. The two men had held their gaze and Adam immediately sensed their closeness. Then the grey-haired man smiled gently and turned away to watch the scene on the river. Trimmler, obviously excited by the encounter, took Trudi's arm and led her down the stairs to the restaurant. The man who had been the object of his attention stayed with the group, but moved along the railings to get a better view of the pleasure craft as it passed the tug-train. He walked with a limp and Adam realized he held a walking-stick which he had not seen because the man had hung it on the top railing of the balustrade.

That was when Billie spoke to him about the incident on the river. When he had answered he crossed the deck towards the tourists on the other side, first ensuring that Trimmler hadn't left the boat before they pulled the gangplank up.

'Trimmler's gone,' nudged Billie, rushing after him.

'It's OK,' he replied. 'He's all right.'

They reached the opposite side and Adam leant against the railing, looking out at the accident that never happened.

'What's going on?' asked Billie, leaning next to him.

Adam put his finger up to his lip, signifying her to keep quiet. She shut up, her curiosity blunted, her frustration sharpened.

Behind them, the group of tourists chatted amongst themselves, obviously excited to be there. They were foreign, their language was Russian.

After a minute, Adam led Billie away towards the stairs down which Trimmler had disappeared. To his left, away from the group, the grey-haired man stared out at the Mississippi.

'Are you going to tell me what's going on?' Billie asked again.

'When I know, I'll tell you.'

'They're Russians.'

'So are the scientists at this space convention. The one Trimmler's here for.'

'Damn. Are you saying . . . ?' She stopped suddenly.

'What?' He never stopped, kept going and started to descend the steps.

'I don't know. If they're Russians, and' – she rushed after him – 'what if they are Russians and scientists?'

'I don't know. Just interesting. Don't you think?'

'So, it's a coincidence.'

'So it is. Just like Trimmler, not exactly your every-day tourist, is also a scientist and comes out on to this boat for a joy-ride. Just coincidence.'

She caught him up at the bottom of the stairs and was about to answer when another group of laughing tourists made their way towards them, Americans this time from Tennessee.

'You'all having a good time?' shouted one of them at the couple.

'Great,' replied Adam. 'Real fun place.'

'Sure is. Sure is,' replied the Tennessean. Above them the whistle blew and the *Creole Queen* slipped its mooring for its daily run down the Mississippi.

The loudspeaker voice blared out, 'Brunch is now being served on the lower deck. Creole brunch and original cajun cooking. Right now on the lower deck.'

'Where's Trimmler?' Billie asked.

'He came down here.'

They found the Trimmlers in the restaurant at the front of the queue, their bowls already full of seafood gumbo. A small jazz band played in the corner, the sound an explosion in the confined and crowded restaurant. Conversation was only possible by shouting above the din.

They joined the queue, watched the Trimmlers sit at a window table and settled themselves on the opposite side of the restaurant. The Russian party came in five minutes later, without the grey-haired man, and the Trimmlers rejoined the queue for their jambalaya and red beans.

'I can do without all those red beans and sausages,' said Billie, the gumbo already taking its toll on her Californian stomach. Adam nodded agreement and lit up a cigarette. She shook her head, her views on his nasty habit were already known. 'That's a disgusting habit. Smoking's for jerks.'

'Let's not get into that. Politics, smoking and religion. I don't discuss those with anyone.'

She shrugged and turned away to watch Trimmler.

'If they split, I want you to stay with her.'

'What makes you think they'll split?'

'He's restless. She's eating, he's playing with his food.'

She watched Trimmler. 'Maybe he doesn't like jambalaya.'

'We'll see.' As he spoke, Trimmler spoke suddenly to Trudi, then rose from the table. He checked out Adam and Billie, but didn't acknowledge them.

'Here we go,' said Adam, pretending to eat his gumbo. When the scientist had left the room, Adam got up from the table and went to join the food queue. 'Stay there,' he said to Billie. 'Stay with her.'

Trudi looked towards them and then went back to her meal. Adam got lost in the queue and then, when he was shielded from Trudi, broke across the room and went out through the kitchen area.

'Hey, what're you doing here?' shouted one of the chefs.

'Sick,' returned Adam, holding his throat in a mock grip as if he was about to throw up. 'I need fresh air. I need . . . quick, I'm gonna . . . '

'Out'a that door,' yelled the chef, not at all bothered about his professional ability being under question. 'Get out'a here quick. Up the fucking stairs.'

Adam rushed out of the kitchen, stifling his grin as he went, and up the stairs on to the middle deck. It was empty. He moved up to the next level, the top deck, and looked round. There were a few people still looking over at the Mississippi, but no sign of Trimmler or the grey-haired man. He descended to the middle deck and crossed slowly to the rear of the boat.

He saw the grey-haired man cautiously limping his way towards the conference rooms. Adam slipped under the stairs and watched the Russian enter one of the rooms, waited until he heard the door close. Then he moved forward and looked in through the porthole.

The two men, Trimmler and the grey-haired man gazed at each other, examining each other as friends would who had not seen each other for a long time.

'Heinrich,' he heard the grey-haired man say.

'Albert. Albert. After all these . . . ' Trimmler was overcome, tears filled his eyes.

Adam realized Trimmler had instinctively spoken in German.

He saw the two men step forward and embrace. They held each other, thumped each other on the back, both started to laugh and enjoy this most personal and joyous moment. After a while they stepped back and looked at each other again.

'I could say you haven't changed,' said Trimmler. 'But I would be lying.'

'At least success hasn't gone to my stomach,' replied the other, prodding Trimmler's pot-belly, making him squirm. 'Apart from that, you look well. Western living, eh?'

'I can't believe . . . after all these years . . . Oh, Albert. After all these years.'

'Who would have thought it? All that time ago . . . that we would meet here, on a boat in America. Now I know the war is really over.'

'Just as Grob Mitzer said it would be. Just as he said.'

Adam rejoined Billie at the table.

'Well?' she asked.

'He met an old friend.'

'Who?'

'One of the Russians.'

'Really?'

'Really.'

'Why would he do that?'

Adam shrugged. 'That's up to Tucker to find out. We're here to guard and report back.'

'And you just do your job?'

'That's me.' Adam took out another cigarette and lit it. She shook her head in disgust. 'By the way, they spoke in German.'

'A Russian-speaking German?'

'A German-speaking German. Name's Albert. That's all I picked up.'

'Are you sure he's with the Russians?'

'He sure as hell isn't from Tennessee.'

One hour later, when the boat docked, Albert was the first off. He never looked back.

The Trimmlers followed not far behind.

There was no indication that the two had ever met.

Hamburg
Germany

IT WAS TO be an historic day.

The first new synagogue built in modern times in the city of Hamburg was due to be opened at noon that day.

Rabbi Levi Shamiev and his wife, Juliet, went into the synagogue before dawn to continue their preparations and ensure that all would be ready for the opening ceremony.

Rabbi Shamiev, British by birth, of German origin, was in his early thirties and had been rabbi in a Birmingham community when he was asked to head up the new Hamburg synagogue. There had been many synagogues in pre-war Germany, the largest in Berlin, the massive city synagogue on the Oranienburger Strasse, which was in the process of being restored. There had been some trouble during the restoration work, the usual daubing of swastikas and Communist emblems. But the work had gone well and the Berlin synagogue was now a faithful reconstruction of what had been.

The first thing Shamiev found was that there are few Jews in Germany; not many had returned to the country of their origin after the war. But, with the coming of a single Europe, some of the younger Jewish community had decided to try their fortunes in Germany, despite the natural fear that a reunified nation would release all the prejudices brought about by the Holocaust. Maybe it would be all right this time.

With that as a background, fund-raising for the Hamburg synagogue had been relatively easy and the square, bricked building was completed within a year. Now, twenty months after the project had first been mooted, Rabbi Shamiev was about to open the doors to the outside world. There were to be honoured guests that day: politicians, religious leaders, captains of industry, social officers of the highest office.

It was to be a truly historic day.

Juliet Shamiev had left the two young children with their grandmother. The family lived in a small house lent to them by the city on the southern outskirts of Hamburg. The children would be brought along later to see the ceremony. As she checked the seating arrangements and made sure the dignitaries' name-cards were in the correct places, she turned and watched her husband.

He stood at the arc in his black canonical robes. The arc is the cupboard at the front of the synagogue, where in a Christian Church one would find the altar. It represents the Holy Arc in the temple where the tablets of stone that Moses received were stored. The arc is the home for each synagogue's *Sefer Torah*, that most holy of Jewish books, their bible. Each year the five books of Moses are read aloud; it is divided into sections, one of which is recited each week from the *Bimah*. The *Bimah* is the central podium of the synagogue, surrounded by a low railing; it has two sets of steps, one used to enter the *Bimah* and the other to exit it. Juliet watched him prepare the scrolls of the *Torah* ready for that first historic reading that would take place later in the day, the same *Sefer Torah* that had only arrived two days earlier from Jerusalem and had been specifically prepared and blessed by the Chief Rabbi of Israel.

As he went diligently about his work, she smiled, proud of what he had achieved and was about to achieve.

It was when she turned back to the seats, her list in her hand, that she saw the first intruder. He wore a black sweater and black trousers with a red sash around his waist. Over his head there was a balaclava. In his hand he held a wooden baseball bat which he swung threateningly against his thigh.

'Levi!' she heard herself call, the sudden fear nearly choking the words. 'Levi!' she shouted louder.

The rabbi swung round as more intruders burst in. Some carried baseball bats, others spray cans of paint. One man, out of sight of the Shamievs, hauled a large can of paraffin into the entrance.

'What do you want?' asked the rabbi, running forward to protect his wife. She moved backwards until he was beside her and had put his arm round her shoulder. 'What is it?'

The leader of the group rushed forward menacingly to confront the Shamievs.

'This is a House of God,' continued the rabbi. 'A House of God and . . . '

'A House of Jews. A House of Filth,' said the first man who had entered the building. Then he swung his baseball bat and smashed Levi Shamiev across the skull, smashed him before he had a chance to defend himself, smashed him repeatedly until he was dead.

As the others watched this deadly débâcle, one of them laughed. 'Fucking Oven Dodgers,' he crowed as the deadly act continued in front of him. 'Jews in a House of Filth.'

Juliet Shamiev tried to scream, but a second intruder battered her and destroyed her young life just as ruthlessly.

Then the invaders painted red hammer and sickles across the walls, destroyed the arc and the *Sefer Torah*, and set fire to the synagogue.

The whole incident took no longer than seven minutes.

When he was satisfied, the leader of the terrorists took off his balaclava. He was a young man of medium height, blond-haired with curls that ran down to his shoulder-blades. He was thin-faced and thin-lipped, not a man given to emotion. Across his left cheek there was a raw-looking scar. It was a knife wound he had received ten years earlier when, as a policeman, he had stumbled on four thugs robbing a store in East Berlin.

He signalled the others to remove their masks. When they had done so, he calmly led them out of the building to which they had just set fire and disappeared before morning broke above the commuters flooding into Hamburg.

When the fire brigade arrived fifteen minutes later, the

synagogue was a burning inferno. But the firemen could still recognize the red hammer and sickles daubed on the walls.

'Poor bastards,' said the fireman who found the charred bodies of the Shamievs inside the remains of the building. He didn't know his father had once been a member of the Hitler Youth movement at the end of the war.

'Fucking Reds,' he said, turning to his compatriots. 'Why the fuck can't they let the Jews live in peace? Fucking bastard Communists.'

His colleague said little. He was from Leipzig and had moved to work in the West immediately after the Wall came down. He had nothing against the Jews, but remembered his father's words. They were the cancer that had caused Germany to fall, the cause of the pain endured by all Germans since 1945. He kept his silence. To him, the Jews had only got what they deserved.

They've got Israel, he remembered his father saying. We don't need them back in Germany.

River Walk Hilton
New Orleans

THERE WERE NINETY American delegates to the Russian Commonwealth's sixty. Gone were the days when the Russians always sent along an equal number so that they could save face and be on a par with the West. Economics and a new order dictated otherwise.

The scientists covered all aspects of space, ranging from metallurgy and fuel experts to dietary and public relations advisers. They were the world's best, there for a common purpose, to divert the developments of war to the fruits of peace.

They were attending a champagne reception, a social coming together before the hard work started. Many of the Russians were excited to meet Von Braun, eager to touch the legend.

192

Adam noticed the grey-haired man wasn't present. He had checked the lists and discovered his name was Albert Goodenache and he was the Russian expert on solid fuels. Trimmler was present, as ever with Trudi, and he stayed near Von Braun for most of the reception.

'Ladies and Gentlemen,' said the smart silver-haired American administrator who had already made a play for Billie when she came into the room. Adam had taken an instant dislike to this smoothie, saw him as one of the army of useless men who administered the experts and often claimed the glory for themselves. 'Ladies and Gentlemen. Please,' he said into a microphone at the top end of the hall. He smiled, the winner's smile, and held his hands up for silence. Slowly, the sound in the room quietened as the scientists and their guests turned towards the smoothie.

'I am honoured to be here,' he said, then paused. Behind, the interpreter repeated his words in Russian into another microphone, the two of them carrying on like two dancers always out of step. 'Honoured and privileged . . . to be here, among some of the greatest scientists in the world . . . and I mean that, to be here at such an historic time, at the threshold of what will, one day, be seen as the greatest of man's scientific achievements . . . From now, we can work together on other things, on medicine . . . on the environment . . . on the opportunity to let science give all people, from the poorest to the most fortunate, the opportunity of a better life . . . So welcome, my friends and colleagues, to this, the first joint space venture between our two great countries . . . and what a great ambition. To put man farther into space, to find out about the universe, and to do that together by pooling all our resources, all our talents, all our future . . . as one great scientific movement . . . We start work tomorrow, today is so that we can get to know each other. I won't say any more, except please raise your glasses and join me in toasting the joint space venture, our great opportunity and our hopeful future. To you all . . . '

'How's your bullshit?' whispered Billie, as the crowd applauded the speaker as he left the microphone.

'From the way he came on, I thought he was your type,' said Adam.

'Yuch. I hate them when they come on that strong.'

'Where's Tucker?'

'Reporting back to Washington. I can't see Trimmler's German friend.'

'Probably ducked out on the reception.'

'Wouldn't it be something if Trimmler turned out to be on their side?'

'Don't wet your knickers. That's . . . '

'That's the most sexist thing I've ever heard.'

'Why?'

'It just is. Demeaning.'

Adam shook his head. 'You people take things too seriously.'

'Forget it. It's not important.' She was annoyed with herself, angry at the way she was so quickly irritated by the young Englishman.

Tucker was making his way through the guests and Billie waved in his direction to catch his attention.

'Happy party,' he said when he reached them. 'Where's our boy?'

'Over there,' indicated Billie, pointing to the other side of the room where Trimmler was deep in conversation with a group of American and Russian scientists. 'Did you speak to Washington?'

'I did. They want us to increase our awareness.'

'What does that mean?' asked Adam.

'What it says.'

'Increase our awareness? Do we move in to his hotel suite? Go to the loo with him?'

'The loo?'

'The men's room,' interpreted Billie.

'Look,' snapped Adam, irritated by the interruption. 'I just want to know what they mean. How far are we allowed to go?' Adam was a soldier by instinct, orders were his staple, even if they were to be broken.

'OK, OK,' replied Tucker, taken aback by Adam's sudden intensity. 'I guess we've got to make sure we're covering everything.'

'The only way we can do that is by gluing ourselves to him.'

194

'They also said we weren't to make it too obvious.'

'That's ludicrous.'

'I'm just telling you what they said.' Tucker was exasperated with the Englishman. 'Let's just be more watchful, OK?'

Adam shook his head. If someone was after the scientist, they could hit him at their leisure. The whole thing needed more resources. 'Can we get some more support?' he asked.

'People?'

'Yes.'

'I'll put it to them. When I ring later. In the mean time, we just continue as we are. Take turns and keep close to him. I'll stay with him till he goes to bed. There's an official dinner later, here in the hotel. I'll attend that.'

'What if he leaves again?'

'Washington have asked him not to go out alone, unless it's an official trip. You two take the afternoon off. I'll see you back here at about ten-thirty, eleven.'

Tucker left them to join Trimmler.

'Wow, a free evening,' said Billie.

'Yes. Very secret service.'

'What's that mean?'

'It's like a bloody holiday outing. With time off for good behaviour. I'm sorry. When you've been in some of the places I have . . . We're either guarding this chap's life, or we're not. There's no in between.'

'So, do you want to see New Orleans or not?'

'Hell, why not?' Adam laughed. 'I'm not paying for this jaunt, am I? Where do you suggest?'

'Let's become tourists. Let's go to the French Quarter and see the sights.'

'Zis eez good,' he mimicked in Franglais. 'Zis is vot ve vill do. To ze French Quartair. To ze naughty place, eh?'

He made her laugh. Then she remembered why they were here. It was a shit life. Some way to earn a pension.

CIA Headquarters
Langley

'WHO THE HELL'S Albert?' asked the DDI.

'One of their scientists,' replied the DDA.

'Did Tucker say anything else?'

'No. Apart from their operational report. They're running shifts on Trimmler.'

The Exec Director watched the two of them across his desk. Each one of them was on their best behaviour so as to impress him. In truth, neither was a natural successor. The DDA was an exceptional administrator, the DDI an aggressive field leader. But both had their limitations, neither had that extra dimension that you needed to fill the top slot. What was it Confucius had said? *The Master must teach the pupil everything, except how to be the Master.* An apt saying, an exact hypothesis, thought the Exec Director.

'And Grob Mitzer? I'd never heard of him. Not until he popped up in Cannes,' continued the DDI.

'Big German industrialist.' The DDA scored a quick point. 'Big in electronics. Heavily involved in the European space programme. And in ours.'

'Is that right?' stalled the DDI, not wanting to lay bare his ignorance of Herr Mitzer. 'God-damn funny. Him sitting next to Trimmler when that black boy took a shot at them. There were three possible targets. Trimmler, Kushmann, and Mitzer.'

'New doors opening all the time,' commented the Exec Director. He turned to the DDA. 'I think we should also explain your ideas on the work we're doing with the Russians.' He watched the DDI's face, there was no flicker of surprise. That came from years out at the sharp end of Intelligence. At least by highlighting the DDA as the prime mover in contacting the KGB, the Exec Director had shifted the onus of responsibility away from himself. 'There have been some interesting developments on both sides. Intriguing and similar.'

He sat back and watched the DDA explain the recent events that had taken place between the CIA and the KGB. The DDI gave nothing away as he listened, apart from a reaction from the left eyebrow when he was told that the two sides had exchanged information regarding their most secret files.

'Well?' asked the Exec Director when the DDA had finished.

'We should protect my people in the field,' came the reply, the DDI's drawl more pronounced and deliberate than before. 'We could be putting their lives in danger.'

'No individuals' names were given out. We only showed them an index of what was in the computer,' snapped the DDA. 'The secrecy of the asset base, and its protection, is still a major priority.'

'Can we trust them?' The DDI's instincts were to trust no-one, especially those who had been his direct enemies as long as he'd been in the Agency. 'It all sounds a bit too slick. We lose an agent, so do they. We have a computer glitch, they get a fire in their filing room. We both lose the same data, dealing with the same period in time. It smells. Too damn neat.'

'We can't ignore it,' said the Exec Director, turning to the DDA. 'Have we come up with anything since we got their list?'

'Yes, sir. We listed their headings and ours on to a data base, then ran the whole thing through to find any common denominators.'

'What sort of stuff did you feed in?' asked the DDI.

'The locations of the killings, ours and the Russians'. The dates and times they happened. The methods used to see if they cross-linked in any way. Any outside organizations which could have tied up with our agents as double agents. Foreign Secret Services, both friendly and otherwise, that could have run doubles. Any war-time operations that were trying to hide their past records. Computer companies that had links into our computer, assassinations from the past that had a similar *modus operandi*. Hell, we fed in over four thousand

197

different clues. My people are still coming up with ideas where there might be some connection.'

'And you've still drawn a blank?'

'We've still got a long way to go. I've got thirty programmers working on this, all under the strictest security, and over fifty operatives coming up with ideas. The only connection we've got, and this doesn't involve the asset base, is the one between Trimmler, the computer and the period of 1945 to 1958 which has been affected by the virus, Grob Mitzer and the Paperclip Conspiracy. In addition to that, the Russians have determined that Albert is one Albert Goodenache, a German scientist they captured at the end of the war. He's been heavily involved in their rocket and space programme.'

'And Mitzer?'

'He was picked up by our troops at the end of the war. With another scientist, Heinrich Spiedal. Mitzer was heavily involved with the administration at both Nordhausen and Peenemünde. Our people didn't feel we had a need for Mitzer and he stayed on in Germany. With his knowledge, it doesn't take much to see why he became such a high flyer in West Germany.'

'And this Heinrich . . . Spiedal-Trimmler, was it?'

'That's Trimmler.'

'An ex-Nazi?'

'Name change because of past connections. You know what happened with the Paperclip Conspiracies. We just hijacked them over here, changed some of their names, and conveniently forgot about their war records. When the Press got their hands on it, it created one helluva stink.'

'At least it got us going in the space race.'

'And the computer?' asked the Exec Director.

'Most of those scientists had links with our computers. Hell, they were in on the ground floor. In the early days, every government department was helping each other. They could've planted a virus.'

'Sounds unlikely.'

'We also deal with a company in Germany called Mitzer Metelwerk GmbH. They supply various hardware parts for us. Their people come over here and install and service some of our machines. Usually in non-secure areas, but still linked to the main frame.'

'Mitzer Metelwerk. I don't have to ask who owns that?'

'Grob Mitzer.'

There was silence for a while as all three absorbed this latest information.

'Industrial espionage?' asked the DDI eventually. 'Maybe Trimmler's been helping Mitzer gain access to our space technology and now he's running scared.'

'No,' replied the Exec Director. 'They wouldn't knock off our asset base for that. And the Russians?'

'They could've stumbled on to something.'

'That don't stack up. Nobody's going to take on the CIA and the KGB. What've we got on Trimmler's past?'

'Not a lot,' said the DDA. 'When we accessed his file, the virus went to work. Operation Paperclip, in its early days, was handled by the OSS and then the other secret services. All that information is under the 1945 to 1958 file. We can't get to it without corrupting the system.'

'Then how did we find out about Mitzer?'

'He's only come to prominence in the last twenty years. We picked him up through the German station—'

'You contacted my people?' barked the DDI.

'Yes.'

'You should've gone through me. Fuck it, it makes me look like I don't know what's happening. Even in my own department.'

'I said you were aware of the situation.' He lied in front of the Exec Director.

'You should've still cleared it with me.' The DDI sat back huffily, irritated with himself for letting his cool exterior slip.

'We needed the information fast,' the DDA purred on, pleased that he had needled his counterpart. 'The information on Goodenache and Spied . . . Trimmler was on their file. We also dug up that Mitzer gave a magazine interview where he talked about how he had been at Peenemünde and how he escaped with two scientists.'

'And he named those scientists?' asked the Exec Director.

'Yes, sir.'

'Has he any links with the Russians?'

'None. He kept his head down and built up his business. No known involvement with any political organizations whatsoever.'

'Any other way of finding out about Trimmler?'

'Now we're looking harder something could break. Most of those old scientists are dead. So are the soldiers and people involved with Operation Paperclip. Hell, it was nearly fifty years ago.'

'Let's not discount the Israelis,' said the DDI.

'Why?'

'They could've stumbled on to something about Trimmler's past, or even Mitzer's. Hell, they'd love another Eichmann Trial.'

'I don't see it. And what are the Russians up to?'

'They could be sandbagging us. We don't even know if they've really lost people. We know we've lost ours. They gotta be front runners.'

'No harm in being cautious,' interrupted the Exec Director.

'What about this latest information?' the DDA asked him.

'Give it to them. There's nothing in there to cause us any embarrassment. In the mean time, see what you can dig up on Trimmler. About his present activities, his connections and his war record. Hustle it. Those older colleagues, those who're still alive, they need to be seen and interviewed.'

'I'll deal with that,' the DDI reacted quickly, determined to regain the lost ground.

'All right. But keep us informed at all times. I also want information on Mitzer. Get that from the German station,' the Exec Director swung back to the DDA. 'See what the Russians have got on Mitzer and on Goodenache. I'll give you fifty-to-one his files were in that fire. That's if we believe Moscow.'

'They'd say that even if they weren't,' interjected the DDI.

'And keep a close watch on Trimmler. He could still be a target.'

'Can I put a team in?'

'Not yet. Until the computer snag's resolved we keep everything under wraps. Get Tucker to report his movements back to you.'

'He might need some help,' said the DDA.

'OK, but low profile.'

The DDA nodded. He would send Carter down to New Orleans in the morning.

'Can we pull out the Brit?' asked the DDI.

'No. We don't upset London. If things go wrong, we can always pass the buck there. Keep him in the dark. Just tell him he's there to protect Trimmler, as he always was. Limeys! Too bloody polite. They were always the easiest to fuck. And thanked you for the privilege afterwards.'

New Orleans

BRIGHT WINTER SUNSHINE, 70°F and a swirl of colour, sound and people on the streets as the clock clanged 6 p.m. in Jackson Square where they once hung thieves, beheaded murderers, burnt witches and broke rapists on the wheel.

New Orleans. The French Quarter. Watch your fantasies be born, flourish and die in the time it takes you to walk from one end of Royal Street to the other. A place where anyone can make a dream come true, as long as they've got the endurance and the dollars in their pocket. How the American Dream was before popcorn, Coca-Cola and Tyrone Power.

Adam and Billie, having agreed to meet Frankie in his cab at seven-thirty, had walked up Canal Street from the Hilton, past the new department stores and turned down Royal Street into the area known as the French Quarter.

Lined with elegant, Spanish colonial-buildings, their upper balconies jutting out over the sidewalk with their slim, cast-iron balustrades, Royal Street stretched from Canal to Esplanade, parallel to Bourbon Street. Sealed off to traffic, with the exception of black-helmeted policemen who rode the streets on their futuristic-shaped scooters, the street was crowded with the swell of tourists.

A fat boy, all three hundred quivering pounds encased in a tight white T-shirt and black elastic shorts with a zip up the back, was the first musician they saw. He walked along, twelve-string guitar strapped over his shoulder and cardboard box in hand, looking for a place to park and troubadour the crowd. They followed him, but never heard the curly-haired fat boy sing.

'Maybe he just doesn't,' said Billie. 'Maybe he just likes everyone to think he can sing.'

Adam was surprised by the lack of jazz players; he had expected to see them on every street corner. She told him they worked in the clubs and only came out at night when the quarter livened up.

'This is just for the gawkers,' she said. 'No-one makes money out of gawking.'

He was happy to listen, to take it all in. Dressed in a pink cotton shirt and pleated, charcoal-grey trousers he had bought in a local shop, Adam was the cultured European out on the town. Over his arm he draped his black blazer, elegant in style, heavy enough to carry the Browning 9mm in the pocket.

She liked walking with him. Short as he was, he attracted the attention of others. He was a man women liked to admire. She was pleased to be next to him, even if her clothes were California casual and not European chic.

Further down the road, a clown, white-faced and red-nosed in a multi-coloured jump suit, handed out balloons to passing children. A folk singer, singing Kristofferson songs in a Dylan voice, leant against the wall behind him, his efforts unrewarded by the lack of pennies in his upturned Lennon hat. The fat boy avoided the singer and crossed the road, his guitar wobbling along with him. The singer grinned as he saw the fat boy, *'wearing yesterday's misfortunes like a smile,'* he sang.

They stopped for a Häagen-Dazs ice cream at the next corner, Billie savouring a chocolate-chip special while Adam licked his way through a blueberry cone. The shop signs fascinated him, the impact of tourism shabby on this beautiful street.

ORGY FRENCH STYLE. GIRLS, GIRLS, GIRLS.

FEMALE AMATEUR WRESTLING. AUDIENCE PARTICIPATION.
WE COME TO THE STREET TO FIND A CHALLENGER.
MASK FACTORY.
GURU T-SHIRTS.
DEE-SIRE IS YOURS – THRU THESE DOORS.
LESBIAN ORGIES – WOMEN ONLY.

And those were just the ones he could see from where he stood.

'What're you thinking?' she asked him through a mouthful of chocolate chip.

'How about something to eat?' he lied back.

The Court of Two Sisters is housed in a building that dates back to 1832 and has one of the most beautiful courtyards in the quarter. It is called after two sisters who ran a dry-goods shop there at the turn of the century and is now one of the finest outdoor eating places in the street.

Adam led Billie through the darkened archway to the courtyard and they were shown to a table. Within minutes a black waiter, MATEUS according to the badge on his lapel, had poured them iced water and taken their order.

'What do you think of it?' she asked him.

'Interesting. And different.'

'What do you want to do tonight?'

'Not bothered. What about you?'

'I'd like some excitement.'

'Any ideas?'

'Yes. I've never been to one of those sex shows.'

'The lesbian ones?'

'Yup.'

He grinned. 'Women only.'

'Damn.'

'Shame.'

'Liar.'

He laughed. 'So, where were we? I know, we were talking about your marriage. You said you honeymooned here.'

'That was yesterday. On the plane. And I'm not talking about myself any more.' He saw the hurt in her eyes and regretted mentioning the honeymoon. But she pushed it aside and went on, 'Let's change the subject. Let's talk about you.'

203

'Nothing to say.'

'Like hell.'

'Wouldn't know where to start.'

'At the beginning. What were you like at school?'

'Terrible.'

'Why?'

'A right little tearaway.'

'I don't believe it,' she mocked him.

'I was. You really want to know?'

'Yes.'

'OK. I went to about six different schools in the same time that most kids go to one.'

'Why?'

'Because I was kicked out of every one. Expelled.'

'I don't believe that.'

'Listen, if you're not going to believe me, then I won't tell you.'

'Oops. Sorry.'

'Didn't see the point of school. Waste of time. So I played truant. Hookey to you. I got in with an older crowd, we all had a bit of money, you see. So I used to disappear each day and play cards with these guys. Poker. *Chemin de fer*. It was great. I won a car in one game. An old Mini. You remember them?'

'The little cars.'

'Yes. Except my Mini was big to me. It had no heater.' He laughed. 'I went to a garage to get one fitted. But they wanted too much. The mechanic told me that every time I'd pull up at some lights or come to a stop, then I'd have to wiggle the long gear lever up and down and stamp my feet on the accelerator and clutch pedals. Gets the circulation going, he said. Best way of keeping warm.'

'And you did that?'

'All the time. Stamped and shook my way all round London. I ran the car for three months before I lost it in another game. I used to arrive at the gates after school and pick up all my chums. Then we'd all go off and blow my winnings. Best time I ever had.'

'How old were you?'

'Fourteen.'

'You're kidding?'

'I told you. You have to believe me.'

'I'm sorry, I'm sorry,' she said, holding her hands up in mock apology.

Mateus brought them their wine and they waited until he had uncorked and poured it.

'I was broken up when I lost that car,' Adam continued when Mateus had gone. 'So I stole one of my guardian's Bentleys.'

'Stole it?'

'Borrowed. Except he didn't know. He had this old Bentley. Kept it in a lock-up garage round the corner from his flat. Only ever used the car at weekends. So I got a spare garage key cut and used to take the car from Monday to Friday.'

'What happened?'

'I took this girl out. You can imagine how popular I was with the birds. Not everyone at fourteen, going on fifteen, runs round in a Bentley. Anyway, I dropped her home, somewhere in the country, then got caught in the snow coming back. Bloody thing just buried itself up to the axle. Wouldn't have been so bad if it hadn't been Thursday night. When he went to the garage Friday lunchtime, of course, it wasn't there. I owned up. No point calling the police in. They'd have traced it anyway.'

'I bet he was pleased.'

'Just a little. Refused to speak to me for a week. Then I bought him a bottle of Scotch and he forgave me. He wasn't a bad chap. For one of the guardians.'

'Where were your parents?'

'Away,' he lied. 'Out of the country most of the time.'

She sensed his reluctance to speak about them, felt him tighten up. He picked up his glass and drank from it. It would be the only glass he would drink all evening. She changed the subject. 'So how many exams did you pass?'

'Hell, you can't pass them if you don't take them.'

'None?'

'Never sat one. Now that's what I call an achievement.' He grinned. 'Not true, of course.'

'What is?'

'That I passed none. I got my one-length swimming certificate.'

'Your what?'

'One-length swimming certificate. But even then I cheated. My legs were walking the last bit in the shallow end.'

They both laughed as the waiter arrived with the first course.

'So that was your secret life. Then. What about now?'

'Ah! There are things we all feel are better hidden.'

'Why? What makes people so . . . insular . . . that they can't share with others.' She was thinking of Peter and how he could never admit his infidelities, even when she had found him out.

'Don't ask me. Maybe, we just need our own space. Somewhere that no-one else can get to.'

Behind them a jazz band began to play. It was as life should be, sitting there in that sunlit courtyard before night fell, cast its shadow and opened the lid on Sin City.

They were ten minutes late for Frankie, but he'd waited for them.

'Any messages?' asked Billie, sliding into the back followed by Adam.

'No. Tucker said to make sure you're back by eleven.'

'Three hours to purgatory,' said Adam. 'What do you want to do?'

'I told you. Excitement,' she replied.

'Any ideas?' Adam turned to Frankie.

'In this town? Huh! I don't know if you guys could take it. We got jazz clubs, naked wrestling, men and women. Sex shows, even ones you can take part in. You wanna be a star? Hey?'

'No, thanks,' said Billie.

'How about cards? All the games you want. And whatever the stakes. Not just money. You can even roll dice for a woman, or a man. Anything you want. Wanna gamble, limey?'

'Not tonight. What else?'

'You're choosey, aren't you?'

'In a town like this, there's got to be something different. I mean, really different.'

'It's too early for what I think you'd like.'

'What's that?'

'A ceremony.'

'Tell me.'

'Voodoo.'

Adam grinned. 'Now that would be different.'

'Most of these ceremonies don't happen till late at night. I mean the real stuff, not this tourist shit.'

'Fancy it?' Adam asked Billie.

'Why not? Long as we're back by eleven.'

'OK, Frankie. Let's see how good you really are.'

The white Cadillac pulled away from the kerb and headed north, up Canal Street before turning east on to Burgundy Street.

Adam watched the crowds as they cruised past. The gawkers had been replaced by a new class of gawker. This time there were no children, only their parents out to explore the fleshy side of life.

The clown with the balloons was now handing out leaflets inviting passers-by to Chris Owen's Club on 500 Bourbon Street, the last of a tradition of one-woman shows in the quarter. The fat boy and Kristofferson weren't to be seen and had been replaced by a young boy, no more than sixteen and five feet nothing tall, painted white from head to toe, wearing a white traditional angel's dress, who now propositioned lonely middle-aged men walking the strip. He was just one of the many whores and pimps who worked the strip.

The erotic sex shops were doing a brisk trade. Billie pointed out a dildo, bright gold, twelve inches long and six inches in diameter. It was under a handwritten sign which proclaimed THE GOLDEN HORN – ONLY $25 – ONLY SIX LEFT IN STOCK. From the way the sign curled at the edges, the six in stock had been there a long time.

Music blared from the clubs, the crowds shouted above the cacophony. Sin City was waking up.

Frankie turned down Dumaine Street and pulled up to the kerb.

'Heya, Julie,' he shouted to a plump girl in a short working skirt that made her appear even plumper.

'Heya, Frankie baby,' she called back as she strolled towards the car. 'You got me some customers.'

'Maybe later. I'll see what I got. You seen the Fruit Juice Kid?'

'Nah.' She turned and looked down the street, across Bourbon which was sealed off to traffic, towards the New Orleans Voodoo Museum. When she had scoured the area, she turned back to him. 'Nah. Can't see him outside the museum.' She leant into the car, past Frankie and smiled at Adam. 'Heya, you're nice. Whadd'ya want mess round with that magic shit for? I got better things to keep you two occupied.'

'Not tonight, honey,' replied Billie tartly, irritated at being ignored by the girl. Adam grinned back and shrugged.

The girl stood up again. 'You want me to tell him you're looking for him if I catch him?' she asked Frankie.

'Yeah. I'll be around. If you see him, tell him I'm up at the Congo.'

'See ya, Frankie baby.'

'Take care,' he said, putting the car into reverse and backing up the street to Burgundy.

'And don't forget the customers,' Julie shouted after him.

'Sure thing. Later,' he yelled back. He spoke to the others as he reversed the car, his eyes fixed on the rear mirror because he couldn't swivel round with his disability. 'The other side of the CIA. Pimping on Bourbon Street. How do you put that down in a report?'

'Do you get a cut?' asked Billie.

'Damn right. You don't think I can live on that pissy salary the Agency pays, do you? Not here in New Orleans.'

He turned the car into Burgundy and took the next left up St Philippe Street, northbound and away from the tourist centre.

'Who's the Fruit Juice Kid?' asked Adam.

'The man,' replied Frankie. 'The drinker of blood.' He laughed and said nothing more. 'If anything's going on, he'll know where,' he added.

The Cadillac crossed over North Rampart towards Louis Armstrong Park, the large park named after the city's most famous native son. His statue stands proudly at the brightly lit entrance, looking out on the area where he was never welcomed to the better clubs during his acclaimed career.

'This used to be Congo Park,' said Frankie as he dragged himself from the parked Cadillac and into his wheelchair. Like many disabled people, he was proud of his independence and didn't readily ask for assistance. Adam, mindful of this, had simply pulled the wheelchair out and opened it up for Frankie, handling it as if he was simply helping someone with their luggage. That was when he noticed the satin-finished 9mm Heckler and Koch P7 strapped to Frankie's chest.

'Didn't know you guys carried,' he said.

'This isn't for the Agency,' Frankie replied, tapping the weapon. 'This is for New Orleans.'

They followed Frankie into the park, now mostly in darkness, the meandering paths illuminated by overhead lights.

'Slaves used to come here,' recalled Frankie. 'Used to dance and fuck all over the place. Big religious meetings, too, with drums and fired-up voodoo preachers. All that black magic started here, where the whites used to come and gawk at the antics that went on every Sunday. That's why they call it Black Sabbath. Used to slit the chickens' throats over there, by that little fountain. Sacrifice anything to their heathen gods. Now that fountain, that was the centre of Congo Park. And that's sometimes where these guys hang around.'

There was no-one there, no Fruit Juice Kid, only the occasional swish in the trees as unseen people watched them.

'Don't worry,' said Frankie. 'They're just drugheads out to see who they can rob. As long as you walk on the path, they don't come at you. Not unless you really looked helpless. Anyway, they know me. They know I'm armed.'

A tall black man in a white suit was waiting by the Cadillac when they returned. He had white curled hair, knitted tightly to his scalp, but the face was young, no more than twenty. The eyes were slit, Chinese-style, but the nose was flattened, his nostrils flared, in the Negro manner. His lips were thin and mean-looking.

'Heya, Frankie,' he called. 'I hear you been looking for me.'

'Heya, Fruit Juice. How'ya doing?' replied Frankie as he pulled up alongside the car. He held his hand out and the tall man slapped it in welcome. 'Meet my friends. They looking for some action.'

'Action? What kinda action?'

'A ceremony.'

'Ceremony? Hell, you know those ain't legal, Frankie.'

'Come on. These ain't tourists. These're friends. That's Billie, from California. Known her for years. And Adam. He's from England.'

'England? Shit, what's a nice boy like you doin' over in this neck of the woods?'

'Seeing the world,' replied Adam.

'New Orleans is the world, boy. There ain't nowhere else.' He reached in his pocket and took out a slim tall bottle filled with a red liquid, the dark red of blood. He twisted the top off and offered the drink to Adam. The hands holding the bottle were old and gnarled, in complete contrast to the youthful face. Adam realized his age was impossible to determine. 'Share a drink, boy?'

'What is it?'

'Blood and piss. Of a baby girl child.' He grinned at Adam. 'Keeps you young for ever.'

Adam shook his head. 'I'll pass this time. If you don't mind?'

'Don't mind at all.' He laughed and swigged from the bottle, took a deep mouthful and relished the taste. Then he screwed the top back on and slipped the bottle into his pocket. He turned to Frankie. 'You sure got polite friends, Frankie.'

'That I have. You gonna help us?'

'Too early for that sorta action.'

'Dark enough.'

'Mebbe.'

'And no tourist shit.'

'Would I do that to you, Frankie?' Fruit Juice laughed, a singular high-pitched shriek.

'So, whadd'ya say?'

'Depends.'

210

'How much?'

'You tell me.'

'A thousand dollars,' interjected Adam.

'Two thousand.'

'A thousand.'

'No American Express,' Fruit Juice joked. 'Even if it's platinum.' He leant forward and peered closely into the Englishman's face, stared at him for a full minute in silence. Then he stepped back.

'You troubled, boy. Your eyes, they got the death-wish.' Fruit Juice turned and started to walk away.

'We got it on, or not?' shouted Frankie after him.

'Mebbe. If so, see you at Old Number One. In one hour. If not, ya'll have a good day now.'

Fruit Juice disappeared into the darkness, beyond the lights that filled the street.

'Well?' said Adam, turning to Frankie.

'Just sit and wait.'

'What's the Old Number One?' asked a nervous Billie.

'Old cemetery. St Louis Number One. Big place on Basin Street, at the end of the park. Takes up most of the block. You see the movie *Easy Rider*? Well, Old Number One was in that. Big fancy mausoleums, white marble and all that. Full of tombs and vaults.'

'Gruesome,' commented Billie.

'Well, you ain't gonna find voodoo in a shopping mall, that's for certain,' Frankie grinned. 'You coming tonight?' he asked Billie.

'I'm not going to miss this for anything.'

'Why call him the—?' asked Adam.

'—the Fruit Juice Kid?' interrupted Frankie. 'Cos nobody knows what's in that bottle. Ain't nobody ever drunk from it. Most people think it's tomato juice with lemon juice swirling around inside. But it's easy to think. No sucker's taken the risk yet.'

'How old is he?'

'You tell me. He's been around ever since I can remember. And I been cabbying here for ten years. Don't look no older than the first day I saw him.'

KGB Headquarters
Dzerzhinsky Square
Moscow

ROSTOV WATCHED THE old lady across his desk.

She was nervous, it wasn't every day cypher clerks were called up to be interviewed by the Deputy Director of the KGB.

'This fire' – he said – 'has caused us some considerable concern. You understand why?'

'Yes, Comrade Deputy Director,' she answered softly, her head slightly bowed in acquiescence.

'Not comrade any more,' he replied, equally softly to try and win her trust. 'Deputy Director, or sir, in the Western manner, is adequate. May I call you Ivana?'

'Certainly, comr . . . sir.' She was taken aback with his informality. The young bastard downstairs who ran her department could do with a lesson in manners from this man.

'Good. Would you like my secretary to get you some tea?'

'No, thank you.' She suddenly hoped he wouldn't be insulted. 'I have already had some before I came up. My tea-break,' she explained.

'Good. So, tell me how you discovered the fire.'

'I had to get some files for the office. When I went down there I could smell something odd. After a while I realized it was something burning. I tried to see if I could find where it was coming from. There are, as you know, many, many rooms there. And corridors. When I found it, I saw there was smoke coming from under the door. I rushed back and reported it.'

'You saw nothing unusual there?'

'No, sir.'

'Think back. After all, the fire had only just been started. No sounds, no-one running.'

'No, sir. Nothing at all.'

He nodded, then picked up one of the sheets of paper in front of him. 'You have a good record. You have served the KGB well.'

'Thank you, sir.'

'It is us who should thank you. After such a lifetime of service. Not only here, in Moscow, but also during the last war. You were a heroine of the intelligence service.'

If only the bastard downstairs could hear this now. 'I was only a interpreter, sir.'

'In Berlin.'

'Yes.'

'Marvellous. I was hardly born then. It says here that you saw the bunker.'

'Where Hitler died. Yes.'

'History. And to have been such a part of it. I envy you. But why did you not come home when it was over?'

'It was because of my language ability, sir. Our troops needed someone who could talk to the Germans.'

'You stayed until 1975. Which part of Germany?'

'Dresden.'

'A beautiful city.'

'It was. Before it was destroyed by the British.'

'Ah! Sad, but war makes some things necessary.'

'Not to kill when there is no need. They bombed and killed many thousands. All civilians. There was no need.'

'You grew to like the Germans?'

'Some of them.'

'You lived there for thirty years.'

'Yes.'

'In the barracks.'

He sensed her caution before she spoke. 'No, sir. Not all the time.'

'In the town?'

'I had a small apartment.'

'You enjoyed your freedom away from your daily duties. I can understand that. It is always good to have your own private place, somewhere of your own.'

'It was only a small apartment,' she emphasized.

'You lived there alone?'

'Yes, sir.'

He knew she'd lied. He'd sat through too many interrogations to know that. He decided to change tack.

'Why did you go down to the records area?'

She sensed his sudden change, the sharpness in his voice. 'I had things to find.'

'What?'

'Information. On what I was researching.'

'According to your superior you asked to go down and find a file for a colleague.'

Superior. That little trumped-up turd who spent all his time pinching the office girls' bums. He couldn't run a party in a vodka brewery. 'I might have done,' she replied.

'He says you did.'

'I remember now. I wasn't feeling well. Too much smoking in the office and all the windows were shut. I wanted some fresh air.'

'Do you frequently have headaches?'

'No.'

'Your superior also says you rarely go down to the records area.'

'Does he?'

'He says he never asks you because of your age.'

'Then he's lying. The only reason he doesn't want me there is because I'm not young like the rest of them. You should see what he gets up to with them. Thinks nobody's watching. He's down in the records area all the time, with one of his little tarts.'

'But he wasn't down there when the fire started.'

'No.'

'We've checked every department in this building. Nearly everyone is accountable for their movements at the time of the fire.'

She suddenly realized the seriousness of her situation, how her hatred of her superior had allowed her defences to slip. She thought she'd been summoned because he was trying to get rid of her, not because she was the prime suspect.

'Which leaves us with you,' said Rostov, now menacing in his tone.

'Why should I . . . ?' she stopped as she desperately tried to clamber out of this awful predicament.

'I will use every means at my disposal to learn the truth. I don't need to tell you of our ways. You, you have lived through the war with the Nazis and through the Stalin purges. Do I have to show you what this organization is capable of?'

Rostov saw the spirit start to ebb out of her body. Now was the time to push on, he had her. Her age wasn't important, only what she had done.

'You have been a heroine of the state,' he said coldly. 'And now you are caught with your hands in the till. You will be disgraced. Your past deeds, your medals, your honours, even your pension, will be stripped away as though they never happened.' He saw her start to sob as she put her hands up to cover her face.

'Don't,' he snapped. She looked up sharply. 'To me, you are a traitor. I will break you if I have to. You're an old woman who can be broken easily. Tell me why you started the fire. Tell me everything. And then, maybe, I will allow you to leave this place with your dignity intact. Even your pension.'

When she had finished, when her tale was complete, he flicked the switch on the intercom and called his secretary through.

This time he wanted a record of what was said. Any future action he initiated had to have good reason.

It was time he started to protect his own back.

New Orleans

'SO MUCH FOR an evening of excitement,' said Billie, leaning against the Cadillac. They had been waiting for an hour outside Old Number One.

The high white wall of the St Louis cemetery stretched the length of the block. Over the top of it, in the harsh winter moonlight, they could see the shaped domes and pitched roofs of the ornate vaults and burial chambers.

'Used to be that the coffins floated to the surface when the rains came,' Frankie had explained. 'Water level's too damn high round here. That's why everyone ended up getting buried on top, in these vaults.'

They were parked by the Basin Street entrance, the high metalled gates closed for the night.

'Come on,' Billie continued. 'Let's get back to the hotel.'

'Give it time,' said Frankie. 'New Orleans folk never do nothing till they're ready.'

Ten minutes later, just as Adam had lit another cigarette, they saw the fat boy walking towards them, his guitar still strapped over his shoulder and the cardboard box in his hand. When he reached them he stopped and held it out to Adam. It was empty.

'You've got to sing before I give you anything,' said the Englishman.

'What you wanna hear?' asked Fat Boy, his voice high-screeched and irritating.

'What've you got?'

'Not a lot.' He put the box down on the sidewalk and swung the guitar over his ample belly. He strummed it twice, hit an A chord and an E, then swung the instrument back over his shoulder. He picked up the box and held it out to Adam. 'How's that?'

Adam reached into his pocket and took out a dollar bill. He dropped it in the box.

'Ain't much,' said Fat Boy.

'It's enough.'

'Hell, you want more than that for heaven. Or you planning on going to hell.' Fat Boy tilted his head back and let out the most piercing long scream that brought Billie to her feet and Frankie leaning out of the cab window.

'You promised. You promised,' ranted Fat Boy excitedly at Adam. 'You did. You did.'

'What did I promise?' asked Adam warily.

'A thousand bucks. A thousand bucks.'

Adam started to laugh as Fat Boy danced around him, still shrieking, 'A thousand bucks, a thousand bucks.'

The metalled gates of the St Louis Old Number One swung open and Fruit Juice came out to them.

'Cut it out, Arbi,' he shouted at Fat Boy. 'Cut it out.'

'But he promised. He promised.'

'And he's as good as his word. Ain't ya?'

Adam grinned and took out some banknotes from his jacket pocket. 'Five hundred now. And five hundred after.'

'He broke his promise. He broke his prom—' shrieked Fat Boy.

'I said cut it out,' Fruit Juice snapped at him. He turned to Adam. 'But he's got a point.'

'I just want to make sure.'

'Money. Hell, it's a terrible thing between friends. OK, boy. We do it your way. But don't change your mind. I have friends . . . in low places.' He turned and led the way back into the cemetery. 'Come on. Voodoo time.'

Adam walked over to Billie and took her by the elbow.

'OK?' he asked.

She nodded and he sensed her nervousness. He squeezed her gently to reassure her.

'Frankie?' Adam turned to the cabbie.

'No. You guys enjoy yourselves. I'll wait for you. Remember, we need you back at the hotel by eleven. And take it easy. You're off your turf now.'

Frankie watched them pass through the doors, Fat Boy behind them. The metalled doors closed and the stillness of the night returned. Frankie closed the door, wound the window up and locked the doors. This wasn't a place to be on your own at this time of the night. He settled down to wait, his hand-gun resting next to him on the seat.

There were only six others, standing by the tomb with freshly chalked Xs marked on it.

Adam had expected more people but his recollection of voodoo ceremonies was confined to what he had read in papers and seen at the movies.

Set back from the main paths that ran through Old Number One, the group was clustered together, chattering amongst themselves as they waited. The small clearing was lit by a

217

number of flaming torches, unnecessary in the bright moon-light, but as Adam realized, necessary for the right effect.

As they approached, the group fanned out in a welcoming V. Beside them, near the base of the tomb, were three large boxes, their lids sealed on.

'Where are the dancing girls?' asked Adam.

'I thought you wanted to see a *real* ceremony?' drawled Fruit Juice, stretching out the word 'real'. 'All them dancing girls and jazz bands, that's for the jerks. There's no Baron Samedi here.'

They stopped by the group and Adam saw it consisted of four men and two women. The men were dressed in long black coats and top hats, their faces covered with animal masks, each one different and powerful in its design. They represented a monkey, a goat, a chicken and a pig. Each mask was painted white.

The two women, both short, wore long satin dresses in a style reminiscent of the 1820s. One of them wore a monkey's mask, the other showed her face. It was a striking face, her Creole mixture of African and Spanish heritage producing a hypnotic beauty that was stunning.

She moved towards Adam and Billie and took their hands. She drew them towards the tombstone and beckoned them to sit at its base. One of the men, the goat, picked up a drum and began to play softly on it. It was a steady rhythm, a simple beat, little louder than the ticking of a grandfather clock.

'Voodoo, the real voodoo,' said Fruit Juice, 'ain't like what you see in the movies. The Yoruba, that's where it came from, say that there's a life-force that joins the living, the dead and the unborn together. That's why we wear the masks. 'Cos all life is one, all things are spirit. When we sacrifice, it ain't a chicken or goat or snake we killing, it's a life. Like our own.'

The drumbeat was joined by a second, this time the man in the monkey mask. The rhythm was intense, the first drum echoing the second, but the softness of the sound continued.

'The mask and the drum are one,' Fruit Juice went on. 'They are the language and the image of the spirit. When our forefathers were forced into the Catholic religion, all those years ago in Haiti, they mixed the best of the two religions.

218

They took the High Mass and they turned it to our ends. The blood the Catholic priest drank became the blood of a sacrifice. In that way, we finally linked the dead, the living and the unborn. The spirits were one.

'The tomb you sitting on is Marie Laveau's. She was black, Indian and white blood. She was the Voodoo Queen of New Orleans. Was the first one to stick a pin in a doll and hurt the spirit of a person through pain and even death. To her, sex was the union, the passing of a spirit through the fluids of the body. When she died, it was her daughter, also Marie, who went on and started the exotic dances and sex orgies that people call voodoo. Hell, you want sex, then go down Bourbon Street. Suit everyone's taste. But, if you want the spirit, then this is where you find it. This is where the voodoo lives.'

'At a thousand dollars a throw,' Adam whispered to Billie.

'No, brother,' screamed Fat Boy from behind the tomb. 'You wanted to pay for it. It was what you wanted.'

Adam was startled, not aware that he had been overheard.

'That's enough,' ordered Fruit Juice. 'Remember, you privileged to be here,' he yelled at Adam. 'Your money just buy you time. You here to see a ceremony. No point in a ceremony if you ain't involved. We going to find your spirit, boy.'

He came towards them, the Creole beauty next to him, and they took one hand each and pulled him to his feet. Billie moved back nervously, suddenly frightened without Adam in front of her.

In the background the drumbeat increased, all four drummers now in a simple harmony.

Adam was led to the front of the tomb and turned round, facing the headstone. The three of them stood still, the Creole girl, Fruit Juice and Adam.

'What you carrying armour for, boy?' Fruit Juice asked Adam as he pushed up against his side and felt the gun in his pocket.

'Same reason you have. For my health.'

Fruit Juice laughed, partly surprised that the Englishman had noticed the gun he was carrying. Then he held out his hand to Adam. 'Lemme hold it for you.'

'No.'

219

'Come on.'

'Why?'

'Just in case. Some people get carried away, don't always know how to handle it. Don't like seeing inside themselves.'

'No. I never let it go.'

'And if you—'

'I never lose control.'

'OK. But if things go wrong'– Fruit Juice looked round at the others –'we're all carrying.'

'I hear you.'

Fruit Juice stepped away and signalled the Creole girl to do the same. Then he looked up to the moon, bright and high over the city. In the distance you could hear the occasional police siren of a marked car that raced through the streets, but little more.

'Let it begin!' he cried, his arms held out to the moon. 'Let the man meet his spirit. Oh Vadun, let thy summon the loa. Let thy blood of the past mingle with what is yet to come and what is as it is.'

As he chanted upwards to the spirit of the Vadun, the Voodoo God to summon the loa that is the spirit of life, the Creole girl danced in front of Adam, a sensual slow dance. Then she sprinkled the white spell-casting powder known as gris-gris dust over Adam as a symbol of protection.

The woman in the monkey mask joined the Creole girl, but she danced and slid along the ground as a monkey would, kicking her heels upwards, moving her posterior towards the four drummers. As she moved, trying to excite the drummers, pulling her satin-hooped skirt up so that she bared her behind and they could see her nakedness, the monkey-faced drummer started to moan, moved his body as though possessed.

'Vadun, bring down thy godliness to us here on earth. Vadun. Vadun. Let us hear your word. Let us see your juice. See how we prepare ourselves for your coming. Vadun. Deliver to us thy loa. Give us the juice.'

The others joined the chant. 'The juice. The juice. Vadun, Oh great Lord, release thy juice.'

The monkey man, now wildly gyrating his body, moved away from the other drummers and approached the girl with the bared behind. He knelt down behind her and unzipped his trousers. Then he lifted her upwards, from the rear and stroked his manhood against her. It grew, long and hard, bigger than anything Adam had ever imagined. Then he pushed it into her and the monkey woman screamed.

'God,' Adam heard Billie gasp, but he ignored her, could not bring himself to believe what he saw in front of him.

The monkey woman had stopped screaming, had her knees braced in the ground to take her assailant, but didn't move. The monkey man had also stopped moving, knelt there, his pelvis nearly twelve inches away from the woman's rear. They were joined by his black penis, rock-hard and gross in its texture. Whereas they were now still, the penis moved of its own accord, backward and forward in its own frenzied sex act, driving into her softness in its animal fierceness.

That's when Billie clutched at Adam.

He later swore he saw the penis turn into a snake, twist and bend, and disappear into the monkey woman.

Her partner, with nothing left to protrude from his unzipped trouser opening, groaned and fell to the ground, unconscious.

Vadun had released his juices. The chanting stopped.

Adam knew it was a trick. Damn it, how the hell had they pulled that off? But there was nothing to see, only the kneeling girl, her naked behind still held high and open, and her now-unconscious mating partner.

The drums started again, louder this time.

The Creole girl moved closer to Adam and started to chant, indecipherable to him, but African in its rhythm.

Fruit Juice opened one of the three boxes and took out a large machete, its sharpness highlighted by the way it glinted in the moonlight. He held it up to the night and chanted, 'Vadun, Vadun', repeatedly. The goat-faced drummer left his instrument and opened the second box and dragged out a white chicken by its feet. He held it up high, the bird frantically clucking and flapping its wings, and came towards the Creole girl who had swung round to face him.

The goat man held the bird high over the girl, directly over her face and breasts. Then Fruit Juice slashed at the chicken, the sharp machete slicing through its neck, severing off its head.

The headless bird, now in its death dance, gushed blood over the girl, over her face and breasts. Adam saw the blood stain into the satin dress, saw the girl's eyes roll upwards in an emotional trance. She continued to chant, her body moving with the lilting music of her own words as the drums beat behind her.

Then she reached up with both hands, took the chicken and buried her face in its bleeding throat.

Adam saw her gorge herself on the still thrashing bird. Billie, still clutching him, had her head bowed. The whole thing had become too unbearable. As he comforted her, Fat Boy stepped out from behind the tomb.

There was no guitar this time, no cardboard box. Fat Boy, in his obesity and rolls of hanging flesh, was disgustingly naked.

He moved past where Billie sat and came to the kneeling monkey girl. He put his arm round her and swung her up, right there in front of Adam, and then, with his two arms round her as he gripped her naked buttocks, forced his mouth on to hers through the monkey mask and kissed her long and deep.

'Vadun. Let us see thy juice,' screamed Fruit Juice. 'Vadun, show us thy spirit. Be thee the Lord that we might see ourselves as thee see us.'

As he chanted, and as the couple kissed in their obscene manner, the Creole girl threw away the chicken and came close to Adam, grabbed a handful of gris-gris from her pouch and rubbed it over his cheeks and nose, rubbed it deep into him.

She stepped back and Fruit Juice turned to him.

'See thyself as the Lord Vadun would see you,' he cried.

Fat Boy pulled away from the monkey girl and turned to Adam as Fruit Juice stepped back.

Fat Boy opened his mouth and put his hand into it.

Adam watched in fascination as Fat Boy pulled the head of a snake out of his mouth, then the rest of it, dragging it out from inside him.

Fruit Juice moved alongside Adam and grabbed his arms, held them tightly.

Adam never flinched, never tried to pull away.

The drumming stopped. Billie started to sob quietly but he never turned towards her.

'See thyself as the Lord Vadun would see you,' Fruit Juice repeated as Fat Boy held the snake's head up towards Adam's face, held it tight so it wouldn't strike. The snake was nearly four feet long and at least six inches in diameter round its body.

'The water moccasin,' Fruit Juice went on. 'Vadun visits us in the form of the deadliest of the spirits.'

The snake's head, now no more than three inches from Adam's face, flicked its forked tongue at the Englishman.

'Very good. What's it do next?' Adam asked calmly. He hated snakes, but there was no way he would show them his feelings.

Fat Boy moved his own face menacingly beside that of the snake and stared closely at Adam.

'There are two,' Fat Boy said, his voice now deeper and threatening.

'Two?' asked Fruit Juice from behind.

'Two souls in one pair of eyes. Two spirits. One body.'

'Piss off,' said Adam, suddenly visibly upset.

'Two souls. Of what is and what was. Of what can never be. Two troubled souls. Two. Two. Two faces making one. Two of you.'

Adam tried to turn away, the memory of Marcus and his lonely grave burning through his emotions, bringing tears to his eyes. But Fruit Juice's grip was vice-like.

'Two. I see two. Good and bad. Bad and good. Which is which? Is good bad and bad . . . ?'

The snake flicked its tongue again as Adam shouted back, 'Fucking tricksters. Go on, you bastard, let's see how real that thing is. Go on, you bastard. Bite. Bite me.'

Adam broke free and went to grab the snake, but Fat Boy pulled back and, in his surprise, released its head. It lunged for Adam, its fangs drawn. But Adam had it by the throat, its head firmly trapped in his hand. The others fell back and watched him with the reptile, watched the battle at a safe distance.

The snake, its head now in strange hands, the smell not one it was used to, knew it was in danger and quickly wrapped itself round Adam's forearm.

Adam held it tight by the neck, yet felt the reptile squeezing

223

hard, starting to cut off his blood supply. He squeezed back, but it had little effect. He wished he had its head in his hand where he could have crushed it with his fingers. He tried to claw its head down into his palm, but the skin, dry under his touch, presented nothing he could grip on. He brought his left hand over and tried to catch the snake's head, but it was too fast for him, he knew it would sink its fangs into him before he could trap the head in his free hand. After a few moments he felt his grip begin to weaken, the tourniquet pressure of the entangled snake taking effect. He knew he couldn't let go of its head, knew that it would strike at him immediately. He tried to reach into his inside top coat pocket for his gun, but it was impossible, his left hand couldn't get into the pocket as the jacket flapped uselessly.

He heard Fruit Juice laughing, then Fat Boy and the others joined in the merriment. He dropped to his knees and tried to smash the snake's head against the base of the tomb, but it had no effect.

'Heya, what you doing?' he heard Fruit Juice shout.

He turned sharply and saw the machete glint, saw it come down towards his hand, then veer off and slice into the snake's head.

He looked up at Billie, the machete in her hand, pushing down with all her strength and pinning the snake's head to the stone.

The grip round his arm began to weaken as he heard Fruit Juice shouting. He saw Fruit Juice try to wrench the machete from Billie. Adam managed to shake the snake free and finally let go of its head as he stepped back.

By the time Fruit Juice had snatched the machete from Billie, the near-dead snake had wriggled off the stone and into the undergrowth.

'What the fuck you do that for?' yelled Fruit Juice, his young face suddenly looking very old and tired. 'That fucker cost me a hundred dollars. You owe me a hundred.'

Behind him the others were still laughing.

'It was going to kill . . . ' said a startled Billie.

'Gonna kill nobody. Shit, we already drained its poison. Capped its fucking fangs also. Couldn't kill a butterfly.'

'That's not . . . ' She was beside herself with fury.

'Mebbe woulda scratched him. Mebbe just tore a little skin. Shit. That was a good snake.'

Adam put his arm round Billie. 'Relax,' he said. 'And thank you.' He turned to Fruit Juice. 'Any more? Or is that it?'

'You owe me five hundred bucks.'

Adam reached in his pocket and took out the notes. He added another note to the pile and handed them to Fruit Juice.

'A hundred more for the snake.'

Fruit Juice didn't bother counting the notes, simply put them in his coat pocket.

'Trust me?' asked Adam.

'You ain't a shyster. But you sure gotta death-wish, boy.'

'He got that,' said wobbling Fat Boy. 'He sure got that.'

'I ain't seen no-one like that before. You woulda let that snake bite you. Fuck me, you woulda done that.'

'I never seen that either. A real fucking death-wish.'

'Why you wanna die, boy?'

'Nobody wants to die,' replied Adam quietly.

'Mebbe you don't wanna die, but you sure don't care if you live.'

'Interesting show,' said Adam, changing the subject. He took Billie's arm. 'It was quite an experience.'

'You OK?' he asked her as they walked towards the entrance.

'I am now. God, what were we doing there?'

'Thanks for helping out.'

'I couldn't believe it. That snake . . . yech . . . I thought you'd had it.'

'I wondered why they were all laughing. The bastards had drained its poison sac.'

'Some performance.'

'Wasn't it? Showtime in New Orleans.'

'Was it all just a show?'

'Who knows?'

'What did he mean? Two of you? Two spirits in one body?'

'I don't know.' Adam decided not to tell her about Marcus. But it was the one part of the ceremony that had shaken him. How the hell did they know?

'It shook you up. You went crazy.'

'Of course. I had a snake staring straight at me. About to have its dinner,' he joked.

'You holding something back?'

'No. You see that sex thing between them?'

'I couldn't believe it.'

'Clever. Clever. I wonder how they pulled that trick. Just like getting that snake out of his mouth.'

'Wasn't up his sleeve. He was bare naked.'

'In his fat. In the rolls of fat round his belly.' He relaxed as he joked, pleased that he had got her off the subject of Marcus.

Marcus, Marcus. So, someone else had finally seen you. And who was good and who was bad? Am I bad, Marcus? Me? The one with blood on my hands. That fat bastard saw me for what I am. Bad. At least you're there. At least you're the one who keeps me straight.

Sverdlova Prospekt
Moscow

THE BIG ZIL limousine was stuck in a traffic jam, not uncommon in these days of cheap imported cars and unrestricted travel across Russia.

'It gets more like the West every day. The people are starving, but they'll give up everything to be seen in a new car,' remarked Rostov to his Deputy as he looked out on the motionless traffic.

'Keeping up with Boris is how *Time* magazine reported it. The new snobbery,' replied the Number Two, a younger man in his early thirties destined for greater things. Like Rostov, he was a practising Christian and both men felt comfortable in each other's company. It was a trust they had shared since the early days when their practice of religion had been a secret thing. 'Those journalists are quick to criticize. They should try and live in a revolutionary society that is changing day by day. I'd like to see how well they would cope if their beloved capitalism had been taken over by our system.'

'It never happened. Which is why we're stuck in this jam. We should never have closed the central lanes. It's not dignified to be sitting here in this big car with nowhere to go.' Rostov referred to the central lane on the major routes into the city which had once been reserved for party officials and official motorcades, now a casualty of the new regime. 'Is New Orleans in place?' he asked, his voice suddenly lowered.

'It is. Nobody expected us to move so fast.'

'An opportunity not to be missed.'

'One problem has arisen.'

'Only one?' came the laconic reply.

'I'm sure there will be more. The person we are dealing with is a double.'

'Damn. I don't want the Americans to know.'

'It's our only contact in the city. If we had to move someone else in it would take time. Possibly days.'

'Then we must proceed and take a chance.'

'I've already actioned it.' The Deputy noticed Rostov's quizzical look. 'I took your order of immediate response to mean just that.'

'And the rest?'

'Being prepared. We shall play it by ear.'

'And the old woman?'

'Pensioned off and sent to a state home in Perm.'

'Under surveillance?'

'Like a hawk. Including the phone she has access to.'

'Good. If you use the German station, be careful. Trust no-one. Especially the Germans. They're either at your throat or up your arse.'

Rostov settled back. Actions had been put into motion. Hopefully they would force a reaction that would open up the way to a satisfactory conclusion. A little bit of pressure here, a little there. Push down in one place and it pops up somewhere else. That was the only way.

River Walk Hilton
New Orleans

'THEY WENT TO their room early,' said Tucker. 'As soon as the speeches finished.'

Adam and Billie had met him in the corridor outside Trimmler's suite. He had pulled a chair from his room and sat near the scientist's door.

'Bit obvious, isn't it?' commented Adam.

'Listen, wise guy, I was told to watch them. And that's what I'm doing.'

'And what if someone had come down here with a gun?' Adam held up his hand, his forefinger pointed at Tucker's head as one would a gun, and clicked his thumb. 'Bang. You should know better.'

'Why? I'm just a fucking clerk.' The other two joined in the laughter with Tucker. 'So, what should I do?'

'Keep out of sight. If they don't think you're there, then they won't expect you.'

Tucker stood up. 'Well, it's your watch now.'

Adam turned to Billie. 'I'll take it.' He could see she was tired, that the evening's events had exhausted her.

'You were on watch all last night,' she replied.

'I can handle it. Bed.'

'Thanks. Good night, tough guy.'

'Good night. And thanks for the help.'

'What help?'

'With the snake. I owe you.'

Tucker picked up his chair as Billie went to her room. 'What snake?'

'Nothing. Just a joke.'

'You two obviously enjoyed yourselves.'

'New Orleans. What a town!'

'Some chance I got of seeing New Orleans. Good night, Adam.'

'Good night, Phil.'

Adam watched Tucker let himself into his room, dragging his chair behind him. He decided on the same watching place he had used the night before.

Trimmler came out an hour later, first opening his suite door carefully and checking there was no-one outside. Satisfied he was on his own, he set off for the fire stairs.

Adam slipped out of the closet and followed at a distance and saw him go through the fire-escape doors. Adam listened until he heard a door close below him. He descended the stairs quickly and came out three floors lower, just in time to see Trimmler disappear down the corridor.

He already knew where he was going. Room 1589. Adam had checked that was where the grey-haired man was registered.

Inside, the two men embraced once again.

'My dearest Albert.'

'My dearest Heinrich.'

'Schnapps,' said Goodenache, holding out two glasses.

The two men drank together.

'A day I sometimes thought would never come,' said Trimmler.

'I never doubted,' replied Goodenache.

They talked for a while of their families, of old friends. Goodenache had never married, his work and the dream of a return to Germany had been his only preoccupation. He explained how he had been found by a Russian platoon who had an English-speaking political commissar with them. He had told them he was a rocket scientist, just as Mitzer had instructed. Realizing the importance of his discovery, the commissar commandeered a doctor from another unit to fix Goodenache's smashed knee. It had been a field medical unit and they had operated with the most rudimentary instruments. After that he had been taken back to Moscow and ridden on trains where he shared his compartment with wounded soldiers, German prisoners and even a sheep. Once in Moscow, with the war finally won, he had joined other captured German scientists and worked with them on rebuilding V2 rockets.

229

It was an ironic situation, but one in which they had little choice. Their living quarters were sparse, their food simple, but they had the best Russia could offer. Not much by Western standards, but enough for scientists who were hiding the shame of the war in the efforts of their work.

'How did you get up there before us?' asked Trimmler.

'Surprising, wasn't it?' Albert laughed. 'There was Werner telling the world the Americans would be the first into space, you know, with that smug little smile he has, and we decided we would beat him. While he talked, we worked. And we had nothing to work with. Only our hands and our "ingenuity".' He tapped his forehead as he spoke. 'It was just like the end of the war, when Berlin gave us nothing.'

'Berlin had nothing left to give.'

'Neither did the Soviets. But when we heard about Project Vanguard we thought you would beat us. What with your WAC Corporal and Viking rockets, you had such an advantage.'

'Damn thing. We used a Redstone rocket, an advanced V2. Werner jumped the gun when he announced we were ready for space. Just like when everybody promised Hitler we'd be ready. The Press, the television, film cameras, all the world is on our doorstep waiting for it to happen, and you go and put Sputnik into space.'

Goodenache laughed mischievously. 'We knew you weren't ready. Your rockets weren't up to seven miles per second. They weren't reliable enough. Ours were. Only if the satellite weighed under one hundred kilos. But it was a Russian who led the project. A quiet man. Not like Werner and his publicity machine. Sergei Korolev. He fought for us, for every little thing that we needed. We got into space in spite of the Kremlin and all those *apparatchiks* who thought we were wasting our time. And their money.'

'I cursed you when they told me of Sputnik. Then you put that little dog . . . ' Trimmler paused, trying to recollect.

'Laika. Sweet little animal.'

'Barbarians. That's what the Western media called you. To stick a little dog like that into space and then leave it to die.'

'Ahh! Your people would have put up a pedigree dog and spent millions to bring it home again. So different to the war, eh? We didn't need to mess around with animals, not when we had people.'

'I swore even more in '61, when Gagarin went up in your Vostock spacecraft.'

Goodenache continued to chuckle.

'But we passed you when we got to the moon.' Trimmler finally scored a point.

'We had to let you win something,' Goodenache shrugged it off. He reached over for the bottle and offered it to his friend who held out his glass.

'It should have been for the Fatherland,' Goodenache said.

'It was for the Fatherland. And they never knew. They never understood why one side never went too far ahead of the other. But now it can be for Germany.'

'It's too late. We're old. Yesterday's men.'

'We have knowledge.'

'All kids these days have that. Our knowledge is what they learn in their elementary school books. The young ones, like we once were, they're the ones who will break new horizons. They don't realize most of us were only twenty when we were at Peenemünde.'

'Germany will need us. That's why it is being cleared for us to go home.'

'No more.'

'Then why have we waited all these years? To get those bloody records off our files so that we could go home without the shame of being called Nazis. Damn it. Once we were proud of being called Nazis. A Master Race. And now, because they've rewritten history, we're ashamed of what it was that made us great.'

'You were wrong to go to Cannes,' admonished Goodenache.

'We always go. Every year. Kushmann and Grob were also there.'

'But it made the Americans watch you.'

'Damn it, the assassin aimed his gun at me. Pulled the trigger. It was me he was after,' said Trimmler defensively.

'Are you sure?'

'Of course. If it hadn't jammed, I wouldn't be here now.'

231

'Why should someone want to kill you?'

'I don't know. Ach! Maybe, it is just my imagination. Maybe he just wanted to rob us. And then it all went wrong.'

'It doesn't matter now. With Willi gone, they don't want us any more.'

'Who says?' Trimmler was suddenly alarmed.

'Frick.'

'What about Grob?'

'He was the one who told me.'

'But he's one of us.'

'He's frightened. For himself.'

'The Lucy Ghosts. That was the dream. The way back.'

'Frick isn't interested. If we come back, we do it on our own.'

'Bastards.'

'It's a new order, Heinrich. Maybe we've waited too long and now we're paying the price. We should've gone home before, in the early days when Germany was recovering from the war.'

'They wouldn't have let us.'

'Whatever. But we should have tried.'

'I don't care. I still want to go home.'

'So do I, Heinrich. So do I.'

'Then let's do it.'

'If they use our past against us, which they well might, then the Israelis and others could come and hunt us down. Do you want to stand in a glass box like Eichmann?'

'He was a murderer. We're scientists,' dismissed Trimmler.

'To them, there's no difference.'

Trimmler thought for a while before answering. 'If we're on our own, then we need to go home and see for ourselves. Talk to Grob, talk to Frick. Face to face. Damn it, Albert, I want to be home. Did you ever go back to Peenemünde, or to Nordhausen?'

'Once. To Peenemünde. It's all still there. The buildings, even the rocket ramps. Rotten and rusty but still there.'

'I would love to see it. Look, when this conference is over, let's meet there. I have some time off. I will go to Germany. To Nordhausen first.'

'I don't have your Western freedom yet.'

'Don't tell me you can't go back to Russia through Germany. In these days?'

'And if I could?' asked an interested Goodenache.

'Meet me there. In Nordhausen. Near the Metelwerk. At the Kurhotel.'

'It's not that easy.'

'In'– Trimmler thought for a while –'seven days' time. The conference is over in three days, then we'll have enough time to settle our affairs and meet there.'

'I don't know. What about Grob?'

'What about him? We'll ring and tell him to meet us there. If he wants to. Damn it, he's already in Germany. We're the ones who are on the outside. Albert! Let's stop talking and wishing about what we're going to do. Let's do it. Damn it, if we don't do it now . . .'

'All right. Let's see. We'll decide tomorrow.'

'In seven days. That's where I'll wait for you.'

'We'll see.'

The two men drowned their sorrows together, the schnapps bottle rapidly emptying.

'Frick and the others,' said Trimmler. 'We made it possible and he wants to discard us.'

'That's the way of the world, my friend.'

'No. It's wrong. It was never planned this way. It was for our return. The money, everything. It's wrong and it must be righted.'

Trimmler left Room 1589 half an hour later. He was unsteady on his feet and this time he took the lift to the eighteenth floor.

He never saw Adam come out of Room 1591, slip silently from the empty bedroom which he had broken into so that he could overhear the conversation between the two men.

Fifteen minutes later Tucker had contacted the DDA at his Georgetown home and relayed a full report to his superior.

Twenty minutes after that, Nowak's bleeper went off with a message to ring the DDA.

'Where the hell are you at this time of the morning?' asked the DDA. 'I tried your house and the office.'

'In a poker game. With some friends. I was just about to leave,' replied Nowak.

'OK. Don't respond. But I want you to get out of there when I've finished and pass this on to our friends. Understood?'

'Understood.' Nowak knew he meant the Russians. He listened attentively while the DDA went through Tucker's report of the two scientists' conversation. When he had finished, Nowak said, 'I'll pass that on right away.'

After he hung up, he leant back on the hotel sofa and ran his hand over his penis, stretching it as he did so. He was almost naked, apart from his socks, one shoe and his shirt.

'Two jacks,' said Sorge, holding up his cards. He, too, was in a state of undress.

Mary Monicker giggled and threw her cards on the table. 'A pair of deuces,' she said as she stood up and started to take her bra off.

'Hey, you ain't see my hand,' yelled Nowak.

'The only place I want to see your hand is up my fanny.'

The men laughed.

'That was the company. They want me to contact you,' Nowak told Sorge. 'Things have moved on.'

'Can't it wait?' asked Sorge.

'Of course. Until this game's over.'

'Good. What was your hand, anyway?'

Nowak stopped stroking himself and picked up the cards beside him. He turned them over and threw them, face up, on the table.

'Three kings. You win,' said Sorge.

'No. In this game, everyone wins.'

Frankfurt *Daily News* offices
Frankfurt

THE NEWS EDITOR was winding up his morning conference when the call came in.

'Mickler's on the line,' said his secretary, buzzing through on the intercom. 'Another terrorist attack. Bomb's gone off at the Gravenbruch Kempinski in Neu-Isenburg.'

'Shit!' swore the news editor, picking up the receiver. 'Put him through.' He cupped the phone in his hand and spoke to the others in the room. 'Put everything on hold. And be ready to change all the pages.' He uncupped the receiver and barked into it, 'What's going on there?'

'There's been a big explosion in Neu-Isenburg. Fire engines are being called out from the city centre, so it must be big. My contact there rang me and told me that he believed it was a bomb. Also something about Stars of David and other slogans being painted on the walls.'

'Where are you now?'

'In the car. On my way.'

'Photographer?'

'With me.'

'How long before you get there?'

'Twenty minutes. I was lucky. We were on our way to a police briefing when I got—'

'Call back as soon as you're there. And keep me updated as you go along.'

'OK.'

But the news editor had already slammed the phone down and was on his way out of the office to see the editor.

'Could be a bomb,' he said to his subordinates as he left the room. 'Put a back-up team on with Mickler. And leave one communications line open exclusively for him. Otherwise just chase everything else as we discussed this morning.'

The editor was in a meeting with a local politician when his secretary rang through and said the news editor needed to see him urgently. He put down the phone, excused himself and came into the ante-room. He was a big man, more fat than muscle, a roly-poly shaped man with large waddling hips on short legs. He hadn't been a great journalist, was an even worse editor, but he did as his proprietor told him. He was, in truth, a tenacious arse-crawler who used his editorship shamelessly to his own ends.

'Sorry to pull you out,' said the news editor.

'I'm glad you did. He's driving me crazy. Politicians, all they ever do is moan.' He enjoyed that, flexing his power in front of his subordinates.

'We think a bomb's gone off in Neu-Isenburg.'

'Hamburg all over again.'

'Possibly. We're getting feedback on some East Germans who want to see a Communist State again. Apparently they've picked up a lot of support from others, including the Red Brigade.'

'Any neo-Nazi activity?'

'No. Apart from the usual nuts.'

'So, it's the Communists?'

'Looks like it.'

'OK. Then we attack the New Forum and the other radical groups. Trying to divide a unified Germany. That's what the leader will say. I'll do it myself.' The editor paused. 'Damn. I've got this politician here.'

'I'll arrange it, sir.' The news editor was used to the buck being passed. 'I'll get Korda on to it.' He mentioned the senior leader-writer. Korda was a safe bet; he always followed the proprietor's line. 'We've plenty on these terrorist groups. What about the Nazi factions?'

'No. Let's not drag up the past. This isn't a right-wing effort and they're a harmless bunch.'

'I'll report back as soon as I've something more concrete.'

An hour later the worst was known.

Seven people had died in the explosion. The bomb had

236

ripped the conference room of the hotel to shreds. The Gravenbruch Kempinski, an exclusive residence in its own private thirty-seven-acre park on the outskirts of Frankfurt, is a favourite venue for conventions and other large meetings. The Euro-Israeli Trade Conference was such a group, where the delegates could stay in the hotel and attend the conference without leaving the premises. Normally ideal for security.

It was later found the bomb had been planted in the air-conditioning system some time earlier.

When the firemen had brought the blaze under control they found the Star of David painted on the outside walls in white paint with a red hammer and sickle daubed over it. DEATH TO JEWS AND ISRAEL was another slogan painted on the garage wall at the rear of the building.

Nobody had noticed the slim man with the raw scar on his left cheek. He had left the scene of devastation two hours before the explosion.

It was considered fortunate that only seven had died. Of the other forty-two delegates, three were still critically ill in hospital while the rest had minor injuries.

Of the seven dead, three were Israeli, one was an Irish Jew, one Italian and the other two were German.

One of the Germans was recognized as Grob Mitzer, a leading industrialist. He was the last to be identified.

Washington DC

'THINGS'RE MOVING TOO fast.'

Traffic jams are the same the world over. Moscow and Washington, for all their difference in styles and distance, suffered from the same traffic congestion. The whole thing was made worse by the thawing snow, the dirt-grey slush and the drip-drip of the water that fell everywhere. It was winter at its most boring.

The black government limousine, a Lincoln Town Car, was beached between a 1964 Toyota Corolla and a 1990 Ford Turbo Mustang. The drivers of both cars, one a seedy long-haired college student in a torn T-shirt and leather jacket, the other a dark-suited woman business executive, stared into the limousine, trying to make out who was inside.

The DDA, on his way to brief the Executive Director on the latest developments, ignored them. He was a tidy man with a liking for tidy things. The Trimmler affair wasn't only untidy, it was rapidly spiralling out of control. That is, if it ever had been in control.

'Just too damn fast,' he repeated.

The student, the driver of the Mustang, leant towards the Town Car and tapped on the window. The DDA ignored him. If this had been Russia, he would probably have had him lined up against the nearest wall and shot. He supposed there were some advantages his counterparts in the KGB enjoyed. Not a lot, but some.

The student knocked again, then turned and shouted something obscene to the woman in the Toyota. She shrugged and turned away. In frustration she banged her horn and added to the general cacophony of the stilled traffic; tempers were rising as rapidly as the heat in the automobile engines.

The DDA, through his darkened glass, saw the student turn away and go back to picking his nose, obviously something he enjoyed from the enthusiastic and aggressive way he went about his task.

'Little shit,' said the DDI, sitting next to him. 'You notice how everyone in parked cars always ends up picking their noses. Shitty habit, that.'

'And who the hell are the Lucy Ghosts?' snapped the DDA, wanting to change the subject.

'Code name, I guess. That is if the English guy heard right.'

'His report to Tucker was pretty thorough. He definitely heard the words, Lucy Ghosts.'

'And Frick?'

'Haven't traced that one yet.'

The traffic edged forward and stopped again.

238

'Have we passed it on to the Russians?'

'Yes. But nothing's come back yet,' the DDA responded. 'They drew a blank on Mitzer. And Goodenache was one of their top people on their space programme. Was being the operative word. He's seen more as a figure-head now. They couldn't find any link between him and Mitzer, or with Trimmler. All I know is that Goodenache's file was in the room that caught fire.'

'Was it destroyed?'

'Didn't say.'

'We getting anywhere with this virus thing?'

'No. But it all points to Mitzer's organization. Hell, it was easy for them to introduce a bug into the system. They've been working with us for over twenty years. It could've been triggered off at any time.'

'So, why go at our asset base?'

'That's what doesn't fit in. But it's all pointing to Trimmler and Mitzer. Maybe there just was a big network there, something beyond Fuchs and the Atom Ring. Just like the Brits had people left behind when Philby escaped to Moscow. Shit, we could be sitting on the biggest spy ring in history, right to the top, and it's taken us working with the Russians to dig it out.'

'So, whose spy ring is it, if it isn't theirs?'

'I think it's to do with these damn scientists. We're getting a breakdown of Goodenache's career. Maybe we'll find a link there.'

The DDI shook his head. 'It's crazy. Us having to protect war criminals as if they're heroes. Stupid. We shoulda got everything we wanted out of Trimmler and his cronies after the war, then turned them in.'

'Well, we didn't. They're our responsibility now. Hell, can you imagine what would happen if all this got out? The political fall-out on the White House would be catastrophic.'

'That reminds me. I gotta stay with the Exec after this meeting. My car's picking me up, so no need to wait.'

'What are you seeing him about?' The DDA was intrigued by the sudden change of direction.

'Oh, nothing. The President's trip to Berlin. Just briefing

them on the situation over there. With all this trouble on the streets we need to make sure there's no problems.'

'You seeing the President?' It was something the DDA rarely did. He hoped the DDI didn't sense the envy in his question.

'Yeah. I think so.' The DDI didn't know whether or not he would be seeing the President, but it didn't do any harm for the others to think he was.

The car-phone warbled and the driver picked it up.

'It's your office, sir,' he said to the DDA.

The DDA took the phone. 'Yes,' he said, then listened. When his secretary had finished he spoke again, 'OK. If anything else comes through get me straight away.'

He put the phone down and slowly blew the air out of his lungs as he gathered himself. 'Fucking traffic!' he said.

'What's wrong?' asked the DDI, sensing that the news affected them both.

The DDA paused before replying. He would have preferred to wait until he got to the Exec Director's office.

'There's been an explosion in Germany. A bomb. According to Associated Press, one of those killed was Grob Mitzer.'

'Shit!' swore the DDI. 'Fucking traffic!' he added.

The student in the Turbo Mustang, bored with excavating his nose with his index finger, turned back and once again stared into the limousine.

'Shit to them all,' said the DDA.

River Walk Hilton
New Orleans

THE CONFERENCE HAD started well.

Billie was on the morning shift. She sat at the back of the conference room where she could keep an eye on both Trimmler and Goodenache. She tried to follow the gist of the conference, but soon lost interest. She realized that these meetings were for the media and that the serious work would begin when they were away from the public eye.

Goodenache enthusiastically applauded each speaker when he had finished. Trimmler seemed strangely quiet and had positioned himself in a dark corner away from the rest.

Adam slipped into the empty chair next to her just before lunch.

'You really can do without sleep, can't you?' she remarked.

He grinned. 'A trick of the trade. How's it going?'

She told him about Trimmler's lack-lustre interest. 'Probably tired after his late night.'

'I'll take over. You grab some lunch. Give yourself a couple of hours.'

'All right. I'll be back before then.'

The conference broke for lunch twenty minutes later and Adam followed Trimmler into the lobby where he was joined by Goodenache. They huddled together, away from the main group, and Trimmler excitedly jabbed his finger at his companion as he made his point. Goodenache tried to answer, but Trimmler wouldn't be interrupted. It soon took on the look of a heated argument and suddenly Trimmler walked away. Adam followed him into the lift. Trimmler stared angrily at the Englishman, but Adam ignored him as they rushed up to the eighteenth floor. The scientist stormed down the hallway to his suite. When he'd slammed the door, Adam went into his own room, left the door ajar and waited for the scientist.

An hour later he emerged and went back to the conference hall, Adam once more in attendance.

The afternoon watch was taken over by Tucker who had a full report on Trimmler's odd behaviour. While Tucker stayed in the conference hall, Billie and Adam went up to the gym where Adam once again set about his rigorous exercises. She thought of Gary and excused herself while she went up to her room to call him.

Still no answer. She ignored the panic in her stomach. Then she rang her lawyers. There had been no further response from Peter with regard to the divorce and they advised her to sit and wait it out. She slammed the phone down, her emotions now at a raw edge, and immediately dialled Peter to shout at him. No answer . . . Damn it. She decided to stop thinking at that stage, showered and went down to wait for Adam in the lobby.

Things broke after the conference had ended for the day.

'You call this a serious occupation?' growled Trimmler as Adam took over from Tucker. The scientist had turned to confront his watcher. 'This is not a job,' he went on, 'this is baby-sitting. You should have grown out of this a long time ago.'

Adam said nothing, he realized that the pressure was getting to Trimmler. Over the scientist's shoulder he saw Tucker disappear down the escalator to the lobby, on his way to buy presents for Jean and the kids.

Trimmler spun away and walked rapidly towards the lifts. Adam followed at a safe distance, not wanting to inflame the situation. They both climbed into the lift together; there were no other passengers.

'You're my baby-sitter,' Trimmler was sulking. 'You know where we're going. Press the button.'

Adam pushed the button for the eighteenth floor. The lift started its upward journey.

'You're not American. Why are you here?' questioned Trimmler.

'To protect you.'

'Rubbish. I'm in no danger.'

'People think otherwise.'

'People. What people? *Schmucks*. Secret agents. They're not people. They belong in the comics.'

'Shouting at me isn't going to get me off your tail. I'll go when I'm ordered to.'

'Baby-sitter. A joke.'

Billie stepped out of her room as Trimmler slammed his door.

'Problem?' she asked Adam.

'No. Just a tantrum.'

'Are you on all night again?'

'Of course.'

'Then let me watch him now.'

'No.' It was an instinctive answer, and as he said it he knew

242

that he needed to be on his own. Danger, its bitter taste, was ever present and he needed his own space. He didn't need Billie, or Tucker, cramping his judgement. 'No. I'll be fine. You take it easy and I'll catch up with you later.'

He took her arm and propelled her gently back into her room, pulling the door shut behind her.

Almost immediately Trimmler came out into the hallway, his topcoat over his arm and his hat rammed on to his head.

'My wife' – he declared loudly – 'has gone shopping. I am going into the French Quarter. Instead of following like a dog behind, I will let you walk next to me.'

They rode down to street level in silence and then walked out on to Canal Street. Adam saw Frankie parked and waved him over. The white Cadillac lurched forward and slid in front of another cab that had pulled up for them.

'Heya. What you doing?' yelled the cab driver at Frankie.

Adam opened the back door for Trimmler and slid in after him.

'French Quarter,' he instructed Frankie. 'Anywhere special?' he asked Trimmler.

'I want something to eat. And somewhere quiet.'

'OK?' Adam asked Frankie.

'I know a place,' said Frankie as he swung the car up Canal Street followed by a torrent of abuse from the other cab driver.

They drove to Chartres Street where Frankie pulled up outside K-Paul's Louisiana Kitchen. 'Best Cajun meals in the city,' he said, but Trimmler was already out of the car and on his way into the restaurant. 'Maybe I shoulda said an ice-cream parlour. Cool him down a little, eh?'

'Don't go too far,' instructed Adam as he followed Trimmler.

'Do I ever? Hell, do I ever?'

Trimmler had found a corner table. Trimmler signalled Adam to sit down as the waiter approached.

'Heya all. Welcome to K-Paul's Louisiana Kitchen,' he chirruped as he put two glasses of iced water on the table. 'This establishment is named after the greatest Cajun chef, Paul Prudhomme, and his wife, Kay. And we got the best cajun cooking any side of Louisiana.' He put the menus on

243

the table. 'Now you just cast your eyes over them and I'll be back soon as I can to get your orders.'

'I would like a drink now,' said Trimmler.

'OK. We got cocktails starting with—'

'A Scotch. Just a Scotch. On the rocks.'

'OK. You want anything?' he asked Adam.

'Orange juice.'

'That all?'

'That's all.'

'I would like my Scotch quickly.'

The waiter pranced off and the two men sat in silence until he returned.

'Another one,' ordered Trimmler as he took his and started to drink.

'You the customer,' smiled the waiter and disappeared to the bar to get a second Scotch.

Adam slowly sipped his orange juice and said nothing.

'What's the matter, baby-sitter? You don't like alcohol?'

'Sometimes.'

'Ah! You are on duty. Is that it?'

'Yes.'

Trimmler laughed. 'On duty. To change my diapers. Is that what you're paid for? To be a baby-sitter would drive anybody to drink.'

'Mr Trimmler, insulting me isn't getting you anywhere. It has no effect. But, if it makes you feel better, then you just go ahead. But I'd rather go and sit at another table so that I can enjoy my meal in peace.'

Trimmler rocked back in his chair and studied Adam before he spoke. 'Life is easy for you. You know that. You just do as you're ordered. No thinking, just do it. I have spent my whole life thinking. Then the day comes when you think – what am I thinking for? Just to benefit science. Just to put another man in space. To make it all possible and never feel what it is like, to never really understand what it is to be weightless as you hang over this small planet, floating in space. All the science in the world, all the thinking, it can never be like being there, like actually doing it.' He deep-gulped his drink, drained the glass as the waiter arrived with his refill.

'You ready to order?' asked the waiter.

Trimmler shook his head and waved him away.

'OK. I'll be back.'

'Another one of these,' demanded Trimmler, raising his now-full glass. Adam realized he was not a man who could hold his drink. The glaze in his eyes confirmed that.

Trimmler leant across the table conspiratorially as the waiter went back to the bar.

'Dreams,' he continued, 'are not just the preserve of the young. And it is arrogant of you, of all young people, to think so. As you always do. Too many people confuse success with dreams. I have success. The sort other people dream about. I am rich. I am famous, not like a pop star, but in my own world. I have been involved in, and touched, history since I was seventeen years old. But I have never been part of it. I have never ridden in one of my space ships, never . . . the dream I had as a young man was someone else's achievement, in someone else's country. And dreams are more important when you get old. You know why? Because there is so little time left to achieve it. And then the young come along, and they crush your dream, as if it never existed.' He drank deeply again. 'You have no idea what I'm talking about, do you?'

'I understand what you're saying.'

'Hmm,' Trimmler snorted disbelievingly. 'You're English, yes?'

Adam nodded.

'European. Like me. Closer to me than these Americans with their barbaric ways. This country, it's a cultural wasteland. The dollar. That's all they care about. Their dollar and what it buys for them. When I was thirteen, my father used to take me to concerts. I heard some of the greatest musicians in the world before the war. I have waited here for nearly fifty years. For what?'

Adam saw the waiter approaching again. 'I think we should order. Otherwise they're going to throw us out.'

'You order for me. Anything. Chicken if they have it.'

The waiter put a fresh Scotch on the rocks down and took Adam's order. He asked for Chicken Cajun for Trimmler and blackened redfish for himself. The redfish platter was once so

245

popular that a commercial fishing ban was levied on the fish in the late 1980s. To fit in with Adam's style, it was also the most expensive dish on the menu.

Frankie wheeled himself in at that stage, caught Adam's eye and signalled him over. Adam excused himself and crossed the restaurant to the cabbie.

'Gotta message for you. From Tucker,' said Frankie. 'He said you should know that someone called Mitzer, Grob Mitzer, just died. He was in a building that got blown up. In Germany. Says not to say anything to your friend over there, unless he already knows. Just wanted to make you aware of it.'

'OK. See you later.'

Mitzer, Adam thought as he walked back to the table, was the name mentioned during Trimmler's meeting with Goodenache. Trimmler had said they should meet him in Nordhausen. And now he was dead. The danger signals were growing by the minute.

'What was it?' asked Trimmler as Adam sat down.

'Tucker. He wanted to know what time we were coming back.'

'That driver. He was at the airport to meet us.'

'He's part of Tucker's team.'

'They like playing games, these Americans.'

'If you miss Europe so much, why not go back?' There you go, he thought. In for a penny, in for a pound. 'If Germany is still your home, why stay here?'

Trimmler looked up sharply, then smiled and shook his head. 'If only life was that easy.'

'It's not the money that keeps you here. You've made yours. What is it?'

'Everything. Forty-five years. That's how long I have lived here. What are you? A detective as well as a baby-sitter?'

'No, sir.' Adam could butter up with the best of them. It was like pulling a bird. No different than clinching a business deal. 'I just feel that you've achieved so much, unimaginable to the rest of us. But you did that here, in this country. And Germany has changed since you left. I can tell you that because I live in modern Europe. Nobody gets taken to concerts at thirteen any more. Hell, the parents spend all their time trying to stop their children going to pop concerts. We also have drugs, high crime, AIDS and every other problem that America's got. It's the same wherever you are in the world now.'

'Maybe in the West. Not in some other places.'

'Like where?'

'In Eastern Europe, even after the Russian invasion, there are still old values.'

'And poverty. And starvation. In the West we have progress.'

'Economic problems. They can be resolved. But you can never bring back the moral loss, the drop in human standards. You talk about progress. Do you know what that is to a scientist? Progress portion?' Trimmler downed his drink and signalled the waiter to bring another one. The drink was opening the man up. 'Let me tell you about progress. When I first left university, hardly more than a schoolboy because of the war, I was sent to the air research unit in Bremen. In 1939. We were testing for aircraft pressurization. We wanted to see the effect high-altitude flying had on people. We couldn't put rats or mice into those decompression chambers. We couldn't see what was going to happen to them, couldn't hear how they reacted. We had to use humans. First we had volunteers, from the *Luftwaffe*. After we'd blown a few ear-drums and sent some people imbecilic after oxygen starvation, we realized we wouldn't have an Air Force left by the time we'd found a solution. So we used other volunteers. Criminals, people like that. No good people. And because of those tests, because of the risks we took, passengers now fly across the world in perfect safety, at whatever height they go to. It was our experiments that made it possible. That, my friend, is where progress comes from. From the risks of others.'

Yes, reflected Adam, and the pain of the Jews, Poles and other Eastern Europeans that Trimmler and his friends had experimented on. He fought his revulsion, controlled it before continuing.

'I didn't appreciate that,' he heard himself lying.

'No-one ever does. They forget the hard battles you fight to win an easy life.' Trimmler reached across the table and held up one of the small plastic butter cartons. 'This is margarine, you know. In the war, that's all we could get. Not butter. But this, because it was easier to produce. We used to call it Hitler butter. You see, even this legacy lives on.'

'Why is Eastern Europe different now?'

'Because they still have the old values. Because for forty-five years they have been subjugated. Because they still remember how it was. And that's where the new Germany will come from. And the new Europe. From the old values. From the way it was.'

'And that's why you want to go back?'

'So I believed. Until I was told I was too old. I have waited all these years. For what?'

'Who told you?'

Trimmler shook his head, his face twisted in bitterness and anger. Then he suddenly stood up. 'I can't wait for this food. It's too long. I'm going.'

He stormed out of the restaurant, unsteady on his feet as Adam handed the surprised waiter a hundred-dollar note and followed him.

Trimmler turned into Toulouse Street, crossed Royal and stopped on the corner of Bourbon. Adam had followed at a short distance, not wanting to further upset the scientist. Frankie, blocked off by the increasing crowds and pedestrian areas, had stayed where he was. If they wanted him they'd find him. The crowds, the night-time activists, were once again on the move, mixing with the hookers and other pleasure dealers who were out earning their daily crust.

One of the hookers, a buxom-blond girl in pink-satin hot pants and a tight-ribbed sweater, came alongside Trimmler and smiled brazenly at him; that thousand-year-old smile full of meaning and erotic promise. Trimmler shook his head and crossed the road, then turned and watched her from a safe distance. He saw her proposition another man, then take his arm and lead him away.

Trimmler waved Adam towards him.

'I don't want you to follow me any more,' he ordered.

'I can't do that.'

'I'm telling you to stop following me.'

'And I'm saying I can't.'

'I am entitled to my privacy.'

'Get my orders changed and I'll be happy to leave you alone.'

'Then keep out of my sight, you bloody baby-sitter.'

Adam realized Trimmler had lost control. Whatever it was that had aggrieved him was now secondary to the hate he directed towards his watcher. Adam shrugged and moved away, melting into the crowd that had started to form as Trimmler's outburst poured forth.

At a safe distance he spent the next ninety minutes watching Trimmler visit a series of bars along the strip. The scientist stuck to his staple Scotch on the rocks, grew more morose as he sat in dark corners and disappeared into his own thoughts. The only times he looked up was when single, unattached women, nearly always hookers, appeared near him. But he never took the initiative, always returned to the comfort of the glass in front of him.

On his sojourn between the various watering-holes, he occasionally looked back to see if he could spot Adam, but the Englishman used all his experience to stay well out of sight.

The Afro-hair-styled man in the jeans and '49'ers letterman jacket appeared for the third time outside the latest bar Trimmler was visiting when Adam decided he was following the scientist. He'd already recognized the man, his tall and slim stature easily recognizable as the goat-masked drummer from the night before.

Adam checked the road behind and saw no-one he recognized. But he kept his distance. It didn't mean there wasn't someone out there he hadn't come across yet. His shortness was his advantage, he could easily just become another gawker in the crowd.

Trimmler's next port of call was to a strip-and-sex club, SEX LIKE YOU'VE NEVER SEEN proclaimed the sign outside. AUDIENCE PARTICIPATION FOR ONLY $20 blared the legend under the sign.

Goat Face followed him in.

Adam knew that the alcohol had boosted Trimmler's bravery, he was ready for action. It was the last thing he wanted, a randy scientist hell-bent on dipping his wick before Adam could take him back to the hotel and tuck him up for the night.

'Hi,' he said to a girl who didn't look like a hooker, but was plying her trade like the rest of them.

'Hi,' she replied, the smile and the eyes giving away her intentions.

'I need some company.'

'Who doesn't? You English?'

'I am. Let's get a drink.' He took her arm and led her towards the strip club.

'Come on,' she said, holding back at the entrance. 'We don't need all that. Or maybe you do.'

He grinned. 'I said I wanted company. And I want to see one of these places. Never been in one before.'

'OK. But my meter's running. One hundred fifty an hour.'

He pulled two hundred-dollar bills from his pocket and slipped them into her hand. She smiled and linked her arm through his. He led her into the club.

Adam found a table at the side away from the stage.

'You like dark corners,' she said, sitting down in the chair he pulled out for her. 'What're we going to do here?'

'Watch the floor show. I hear it's the best in town.'

A waiter crossed over and they ordered their drinks. Adam surveyed the room and saw that Trimmler was near the stage, seated alone with a drink already in front of him, watching the simulated sex show taking place a few feet from his table. He stared with open lust at the naked threesome who rolled collectively on the mattress spread out on the wooden stage, two well-endowed women with slim bodies and a blond, twenty-year-old who was probably earning his way through college and whose parents would be horrified if they knew about their son's holiday job.

Goat Face sat with a tourist couple at another table on the opposite side of the room. The way they sat told Adam that Goat Face had simply joined them and that they were not known to each other.

'I can give you more excitement than you're getting here back at my place,' the girl broke into his deliberations.

'I like it here. You don't get this in the pubs in London.'

On the stage, with Nancy Sinatra belting out *These boots were made for walking*, one of the girls left Blondie and her companion and slipped on to the floor. She snaked her way over the tables around the stage and draped her naked body over a paunchy man next to Trimmler. As she sat on his lap, rubbing herself over him, she whispered dirty intentioned words in his ear. He shook his head, embarrassed at this public display, whilst the rest of the audience whooped and shrieked their support. The girl, feigning disappointment moved on towards Trimmler, but on seeing the drunken glaze in his eyes, jumped to the next table where she went to work on a younger man. This time, the recipient of her attentions was much more forthcoming and, to rapturous applause, she soon had him stripped and being led on to the stage.

The action reached new heightss as the four of them writhed with each other, the three professionals simulating sex whilst still ensuring the newcomer didn't get too carried away.

'You really like this stuff, huh?' said the girl as she watched Adam inspecting the room.

'As I said, it's different.'

'You could've come alone. If eyeballing's all you wanted.' She slipped her hand slowly up his thigh, towards his crotch. 'Or maybe this is what you want? Huh? Taking part without anyone seeing. You like that. Is this what turns you on?'

He put his hand under the table and took hers, held it firmly and placed it back on her lap. She mocked him with her smile. He sure was a strange one.

The blond hooker who had first accosted Trimmler on the corner of Toulouse and Bourbon came into the club as the foursome on stage became so entwined that it was difficult to tell which limb and which private part belonged to which participant. Trimmler's eyes had popped out on stalks, the thrashing flesh within touching distance now turning his brain into a muddled vision of eroticism and sexual need. She recognized Trimmler and crossed the room to him, slid her satin-covered bottom on to the empty chair next to him. She leant towards him, her heavy breasts resting on his arm and she whispered in his ear. He nodded, eager to be with her, and she stood up, took his arm to support him and led him through the crowded club out on to Bourbon Street.

Adam didn't move until he saw Goat Face follow the couple out.

'Thanks,' he said to the girl. 'Time to say goodbye.'

'Hey. You still got forty minutes left on the meter.'

'Listen. I wish I could. It would've been fun.'

'Yeah. Well, no sweat. Just don't like leaving you boys short-changed,' she acknowledged good-humouredly.

He left her there and went out on to Bourbon. Trimmler was northbound on Toulouse, the girl hanging on his arm and leading him towards the Spanish-fronted houses that opened on to courtyards and apartments from where most of the girls worked.

Adam followed at a safe distance, not seeing Goat Face, but intent on keeping Trimmler in sight.

He saw the apartment she took Trimmler into, on the first floor behind the iron balustrade that curved up the line of the stair. When the door had shut, Adam surveyed the area. He knew there'd be a window at the rear, but he couldn't watch both sides at the same time. He took up a safe and hidden position across the street and waited. Of Goat Face there was no sign, but Adam knew he was around. He hoped he hadn't been discovered.

Trimmler came out twenty minutes later. It had obviously been a quick transaction.

Adam waited for him in the street before he crossed over to him.

'I think we should go back to the hotel now, Mr Trimmler,' he said quietly.

The scientist said nothing. Adam could smell the vomit on his breath. He doubted Trimmler had managed anything with the little blonde, probably spent most of his time knelt over the toilet bowl.

Frankie was where they had left him, deep in conversation with two locals.

'I kept checking with Tucker and he said to wait here,' said the cab driver as he watched Adam help Trimmler into the back of the Cadillac.

They drove the short distance back to the Hilton and Adam helped Trimmler out of the cab and into the lobby. Goodenache was there, anxious and desperate to see Trimmler. He took his arm and led him away to a secluded corner.

Adam stayed close enough to pick up the odd word but not appear obtrusive.

He heard Goodenache mention Mitzer.

Trimmler, even in his inebriated state, reacted with horror. He seemed to fall forward, but Goodenache held him up by his shoulders.

It didn't take the tears in Trimmler's eyes for Adam to realize he had just been told of Mitzer's death. Trimmler shook his head repeatedly, then slumped into one of the leather couches that were spaced intermittently along the wall. Goodenache sat down next to him and put his arm round his shoulder.

At that moment, Goat Face came up the escalator, accompanied by a man. His hair was short-cropped, but not curly, nor white. He limped alongside Goat Face like an old man, but the face was the clear face of a twenty year old while the gnarled hands that held the walking-stick confirmed the old man's age. It was Fruit Juice.

They didn't see Adam as he slipped behind one of the vast square pillars. Goat Face, as soon as he saw Trimmler, took Fruit Juice's arm and led him, as a son would an elderly father, towards the coffee shop. They sat at a table from where they could watch the lobby.

Goodenache helped Trimmler to his feet and the two men walked slowly towards the lifts. Adam couldn't follow without being recognized by the two voodoo men, so he ducked across to the emergency stairs and climbed to the fifteenth floor, taking two to three steps at a time. He checked that level, and when satisfied that the two men weren't there, took the emergency stairs to the eighteenth floor.

'Where the hell have you been?' said Tucker.

253

'Have you seen . . . ?'

'Yeah. They're both in Trimmler's room. His wife's in there, too. You look like you've been in a marathon.'

Adam grinned, his breath short and the sweat running down his face. 'I got left behind.'

'So, where've you been?'

'You know damn well where I've been. Watching Trimmler drowning his sorrows. Our friend Goodenache just told him about Mitzer.'

'Well, that, and the booze, should keep him in his room. I'll take over now. You rest up.'

'OK.'

'Did nothing else happen out there?'

'No.' Adam decided not to mention the watchers downstairs. It would only alarm Tucker. And there was another way of dealing with the problem.

Adam caught the lift down to the lobby.

'Hello, chaps.' He greeted the watchers in his best laid-back English as he entered the coffee shop. He pulled up a chair and joined them. He was the last person they had expected and he relished their discomfort.

'Well, what you doing here, boy?' said Fruit Juice.

'I stay here. What about you? This is a bit out of your province, isn't it?'

'Everybody needs new space. Even them in their graves, boy. Even those who ain't got no use for this earth.'

'I see you've got a new hair-style.'

'Street cut. The other's for the tourists.'

Adam signalled the waiter over and ordered a coffee.

'I don't wanna appear pushy,' said Fruit Juice, 'but this was a private meeting.'

'But I paid a thousand dollars.'

'That was yesterday, boy. You gotta start again.'

'Another dollar, another day?'

'Something like that.'

'Heya, you could be the snake this time,' interjected a leering Goat Face. 'Just slide into that nice warm pussy. Hot and steamy. That what you looking for?'

'I tried that. I was watching the same sex show you were.

Saw four people performing on a stage on Bourbon Street. Naked. About an hour ago.'

'Weren't me,' Goat Face replied as a quick look of concern passed between the two black men.

'Don't be embarrassed about it. We all do these things, have a need for the seamy side of life.'

'I said it weren't me.'

'I know what I saw. There were two of us there. Me and an older chap. You may have seen him. He was sitting near the stage. Grey-haired, German. Left with a blonde in pink-satin hot pants. Remember him?'

'You got the wrong man,' shrugged Goat Face. 'But then, we all look the same to you, don't we?'

'Time to go,' said Fruit Juice, standing up. 'You sure got bad manners, boy. Private means private.'

'Sorry, chaps. My misunderstanding. Why don't you stay and have another coffee? On me.' Adam knew they wouldn't stay. Whatever mischief they had planned, probably to rob Trimmler, was blown now.

'Keep away from what don't concern you, boy. This ain't a town you wanna get into trouble in.'

He turned and started to walk away with Goat Face a few steps behind.

'Keep away from the dirty shows,' Adam said to their disappearing backs. Goat Face stopped sharply, then when he had decided to ignore Adam's comment, followed Fruit Juice down the escalator and on to the street. The big clock overhead the lobby clicked past nine-forty-five.

Tucker was positioned back in the hallway outside Trimmler's suite. Adam decided not to warn him again about being an obvious target. You could give them a handkerchief, but you couldn't blow their noses for them.

'I'm going to have a workout, then something to eat,' he said. 'I'll take over about twelve.'

'Billie was looking for you.'

'I'll be down there if she wants me.'

He went to his room, changed and took the lift down to the Fitness Centre. It was empty and he settled down to his series of exercises, warming his muscles first with gentle movements before entering his strenuous and punishing schedule.

When pain came, that point when muscles cramp in torture and refuse to be driven any further, Adam, as always, turned to Marcus. He drew from his strength, knew it was Marcus who drove him on to cross the barrier. He could feel him, somewhere deep inside, giving him that extra power that lifted his mental and physical being above most others.

The pain eased, his strength grew, and Marcus filled his vision, his senses, his whole being. The two became one, fused in their life-and-death partnership.

Dresdener *Heide*
Dresden

THE BLACK MERCEDES 300 SL, chauffeur-driven by a *Sturmabteilung* in a dark grey suit, bounced up the Strasse Otto Buckwitz. One of the main roads leading northwards towards the airport, the Strasse Otto Buckwitz was like many of the thoroughfares in what was once East Germany. Occasionally pot-holed, heavily cambered and uneven in construction, it was, in essence, a bone-shaker.

In the back, like any two ordinary business men on their way to a meeting, sat Peter Frick and Helmut Kragan. They were on their way to a meeting, but their business was anything but ordinary.

'Did you contact all the members of the council?' asked Frick.

'Except Lieder. He's on a skiing holiday in Val d'Isere. But I've made arrangements for him to be reached and flown back for the meeting.'

'Good. Have we had any comments from them?'

Kragan knew he referred to Mitzer's unexpected death. 'No. Not on the phone. I expect they will comment at the meeting.'

'We must keep them under control. Especially the older ones. Now is not the time for panic.'

'They're the ones least likely to panic. They've waited a long time for this.'

'I meant that my position must be protected. Mitzer was a romantic, a dreamer of the past. But he had influence. His contacts in the business community were second to none. He will be difficult to replace. The others know that. Somehow, I must reassure them that we can still proceed.'

'There are other industrialists sympathetic to our cause.'

'Not as powerful as Mitzer.'

'I can prepare a list of those who have shown an interest in joining us.'

'Do that. But first we must clear it with the council. Make them feel that they are actively chasing Mitzer's replacement. The involvement will make them think of the future, not of the past.'

'I'll have the list ready for the meeting.'

The Mercedes had followed the line of blue prefabricated concrete slabs, the long four-kilometre wall that separated the Dresdener *Heide* from the Strasse Otto Buckwitz. The car pulled off the road and stopped at a gatehouse with double steel doors that blocked any unwarranted entry into the *Heide*.

A *Sturmabteilung* in a grey suit, like that of the driver, saluted the car and signalled his colleague to swing the gate open. The Mercedes moved through the gate and into the *Heide*.

The Dresdener *Heide* was the city's greatest park until the Russian tanks rolled in in 1945. Within weeks they had ringed it off and turned it into their barracks. Over the years, until their withdrawal in the 1990s, they had built a vast tank training ground through the woods and parkland, thrown up a series of yellow-and-black painted apartment blocks, and built a four-thousand-foot runway from which they flew small transport aircraft and helicopter gunships. Apart from the Army, it had also housed the KGB and other Military Intelligence. It had become a war zone, a centre of death in a conquered city.

Large tracts of the Dresdener *Heide* had been snapped up

by developers when Germany was reunified. One of those developers had been Ritz Frankfurte GmbH, a subsidiary property company privately owned by Grob Mitzer. It had taken the largest part of *Heide*, had sealed it off and kept it very much as it was under the Russians.

The official story was that it was an investment for the future and would be developed as the need required. Part of it was leased to a company that ran action and survival courses for executives and others who felt they would benefit from the service.

The truth was that it became the training ground for the *Sturmabteilungen* and other groups involved in the growth of the National Socialists. It was their base, the headquarters from where the party would move to head the political agenda of a new Germany.

The car swung up the cobbled road towards the big old house that stood deep in the trees, a baroque four-storied building that was home to Frick and his staff. Outside the small wooded area, it was surrounded by the old Russian barracks, now home to nearly a thousand *Sturmabteilungen*, the storm-troopers of the future.

As the Mercedes drove towards the house, small groups of them snapped to attention and gave the traditional Nazi salute as their leader passed.

'The newspapers are reacting as we expected,' said Kragan as he watched Frick return the salute in that same arrogant way that he had seen Hitler react in the old film footage. The man was already picking up his hero's mannerisms, thought Kragan.

'They follow the herd. That's all they're good for,' replied Frick. 'Feed them gossip and they call it news because it sells papers and makes them feel important. What the hell was Mitzer doing there?'

'It was a last-minute decision. According to his secretary the invitation had been declined, but a friend called him and said they should go together and then on to a business lunch.'

'Couldn't we have stopped him?'

'We would have done if we'd known. He always kept us informed of what he was doing. This was totally unexpected.'

'We needed him. Mitzer opened doors that others couldn't.'

'Then find new ways.'

'Take too long. No. Let's give those people a reason for opening the doors to us. We must speed up our programme.'

'The faster we go, the more chance there is of us making mistakes.'

But Frick was beyond caution. 'No!' he ranted. 'Now we go faster. Now we cause chaos. Then Germany will beg us to bring about order. Just like it did with Hitler.'

The car pulled up outside the building and a guard came down the steps and opened the car door for Frick, once again giving the customary salute.

'We will not waste unification,' continued Frick as he climbed the stairs, Kragan following just behind. He stopped at the top and faced his assistant. 'If Mitzer is gone, then there are others of the old ones who can help us. Trimmler and Goodenache. And the rest who are waiting to come back. Mitzer wasn't the only one who knew how to access the funds. But that doesn't mean we want the rest of them back. Not yet. Not until we have what we want.'

River Walk Hilton
New Orleans

HE WAS FAST asleep under the two-sided sun-lamp when they came for him.

Adam had finished his training session uninterrupted, apart from a short visit from Billie who had dropped in to see how he was. Having seen the sun-room next to the Fitness Centre, he decided to tone up his appearance in line with his physique. A naturally dark person, he always built up a tan once he was clear of his normal covert duties.

The sun-room was locked for the night, but he slipped his Visa credit card from his wallet and slid it into the crack between the door and the jamb, then clicked the Yale lock open and let himself into the room. There were three sun-beds, laid out side by side like mortuary tables. He closed the door and checked the controls on the middle machine.

It was a double-sided contraption, one where you lay on a bank of tanning tubes and lowered the canopy electrically, which also housed a series of tubes. A sort of fluorescent sandwich with a human filling, it was effective and toned up a tan within thirty minutes.

He undressed, picked up the small green goggles that he needed for his eye protection and slid between the two sections. Once he had lowered the canopy, he switched on the timer and had dozed off within five minutes.

Adam lived in that world of half-sleep, always enough to catch up with his rest, but never enough to be surprised by those out to harm him. In his mind he believed it was Marcus who watched over him, who warned him of any approaching danger.

They were good. They had to be not to wake him.

The first warning he had was when someone gripped his arms, which were crossed behind his head as a pillow, and pulled them outward and straight.

At the same instant, another intruder had grabbed his legs and held them rigid.

'Don't move, or I cut your throat,' said a third man to his right. 'You better believe it, boy.'

Adam felt the sharpness of a knife prick his neck. He decided to lie still. The men who held him down were strong; he couldn't see them as he was blinded by the brightly lit tubes. The rest of the room still remained in darkness.

'What do you want?' he asked. There was no emotion in his voice.

'Just wanna talk,' said the Knife. It wasn't a voice Adam recognized.

'I'm a captive audience.'

'Don't get fresh, jerk.' The Knife pricked him harder. Adam felt his skin break.

'You bleed nicely, jerk. Any more funnies?'

Adam shook his head.

260

'Good. Now tell me what you doing here?'

'Sun-tann . . . ' Adam stopped. His cheek was going to shorten his life if he wasn't careful. 'You mean in New Orleans?'

'You learning.'

'I'm here covering the space conference.'

'That all?'

'Yes.'

'Reporter?'

'No. I'm a special delegate. I've got to make a report for the British government.'

'Why?'

'We have a European Space Agency. We're not in your league, but we need to know what's going on.'

'You lying to me?'

'Why should I?'

'You tell me.' The Knife pushed the implement sharper into Adam's neck, the cut got deeper.

'I told you the truth.'

'We going to teach you a lesson, jerk. Don't mess with what don't concern you.'

'I'm happy to mind my own business.'

'Still going to teach you a lesson. I'm going to cut your toe off, boy. If you resist, I'll slit your throat. If you got any sense in that bone-head of yours, you'll just lie still.'

Adam knew he would do that, so he lay still. *Come on, Marcus, let me take this. Damn it, help me keep still.*

'Do it,' the Knife ordered the man who gripped Adam's legs.

The grip tightened round his ankles. He felt the Knife move away, down to his feet.

Then he felt the pain, sharp at first, then burning as it entwined the base of his toe. The pressure tightened, twisted into his flesh and to the bone; he and Marcus fought it and took the hurt and withstood the pain as his toe was cut from his foot.

'Tough bastard,' he heard the man who held his arms say.

Then it was over.

One of the men, he took it to be the Knife, punched him sharply in the side, forcing him upwards so he slammed his head into the canopy and broke one of the tubes.

261

They left him as quickly as they had come.

He lay still, collecting himself before he slid sideways out of the sun-machine and on to the floor.

He sat up and reached for his toe. They hadn't cut it off, just tightened a strand of barbed wire round it, twisted it so it cut right into the skin and some of its barbs had sliced through to the bone. Slowly he loosened the wire. They had taken away his dignity and fucking played with him. He felt the anger build within him and tried to control it, bring it down. Anger wasn't one of the weapons in his arsenal.

The bottle mocked him from across the floor, sitting in the corner. A simple bottle with red fluid inside.

A baby virgin's blood and piss.

He remembered they had been watching Trimmler.

He got dressed as quickly as he could. The gun was still in his brown bag and he slipped it into his belt.

He caught the lift to the eighteenth floor.

Neither Billie nor Tucker was there.

A baby virgin's blood and piss. They had to be after Trimmler.

A door opened across the hall and he had the Browning aimed straight at the person who came out.

'For Christ's sake!' said Billie, suddenly scared by his manner.

'Sshh!' he warned her. 'Where's Tucker?'

'I don't know. He was watching . . .'

Adam cut her off by turning away to Trimmler's door, the gun poised in his hand. He turned the handle; the door opened easily, it wasn't locked.

He quietly let himself into the room. Billie stayed where she was at first, not knowing what to do. Then she followed him.

The lights were on. There was no-one in the sitting area.

He saw Trudi first, on the floor, by the dressing table in the bedroom. There was no blood. Her neck had simply been broken, wrung like a chicken and twisted almost at right angles to her naked body.

Trimmler was on the bed. There was a lot of blood there, soaked into the sheets; the blankets had been peeled back and lay across the floor.

262

Adam checked the rest of the room before he approached the bed. Whoever had carried out the deed had long since left.

He'd seen death in many forms, in many different places, but he wasn't prepared for what they had done to Trimmler.

The scientist was naked, his body appeared whiter than it was against the redness of the blood that framed it on both sides. It wasn't an attractive body in the best of circumstances, but in death the fatness had spread, even his large paunch had slipped to his hips; his stomach was almost flat.

It was a grotesque sight, made more gruesome by the fact that both his arms had been sliced off just above the elbow. They had been placed over each other, the limbs forced and bent in such a manner that they formed a fleshy swastika.

Adam stayed in his room for nearly an hour before the Chief of Detectives knocked on his door. During that time he saw Tucker twice: 'Why the hell did you call the cops?' and 'The Agency's going bananas'; Billie once when she came and spent ten minutes with him and said little; and the house doctor who bandaged up his toe and told him to rest it up for a few days and take some time off work.

There was little he was prepared to tell the policeman, apart from what he had already gathered.

'You didn't see anybody? Nothing suspicious, anywhere in the hotel?'

'Nothing,' he replied.

The policeman shook his head. He was in a quandary, he knew there was more to this whole affair, but the CIA had banged heads somewhere above him in the department and he had to limit himself to simple questions. If he'd had his own way he'd rush them all back to headquarters and make sure he got answers to all his questionss.

When the policeman left, Adam lay down on the bed. He knew what was happening inside his head, that the forces of good and evil were at war.

Walk away from it. It's over. Go home to Emma, Steed and Lily's home cooking.

You know who the bastards are. Get them. You've never walked away from a job before, never left it unfinished. And they tied a bloody piece of barbed wire round your big toe and laughed their silly little heads off at you.

Go home, Adam. This is not your place. Mind your own business and go home.

I can't, Marcus. They ran rings round me and I can't let go.

Leave it.

How? It's not my way.

The dark side, as always, won.

He put his coat on, the Browning safely tucked away in the shoulder harness, grabbed some extra ammunition clips which he slipped into his pocket and went out into the hallway.

The area had been cordoned off and there were police at both ends of the corridor. He looked into Trimmler's suite and saw the hive of activity that was taking place. Doctors, police photographers, every Tom, Dick and Hank from the police department. It must have been a quiet time in the old town tonight.

'Where're you going?' asked Tucker as he saw him.

'To get some fresh air.'

'You shouldn't leave the building.'

'Why not? No-one to protect any more.'

'You should stay in.'

'I don't work for your people any more.'

'I still don't think . . . '

'So, have me arrested.'

'You fucking smart-arse.' Tucker knew he'd lost control. 'They'll want to see you.' He desperately tried one last time. 'Come on, they'll want to know what happened.'

'Ask Billie. She walked in there with me.'

'She says you already had a gun in your hand when she saw you. That you expected something to be wrong. Did you?'

'Don't be stupid. Do you think I sliced his arms off with my gun?'

'Why the gun?'

'What did you expect me to do? Get a hot-water bottle and tuck myself up in bed. You weren't here, Tucker. I was on my own.'

His attack on Tucker worked; the CIA man visibly paled

as he recalled his blunder. 'I told you. They said you wanted to . . . shit.'

'Your people. Your problem.'

Billie caught him up as he waited for Frankie to draw up in the street outside. The brown bag was slung over his shoulder.

'Tucker said you were going out. Why?' she asked.

'No point hanging round here. It's over now.'

'Can I come with you?'

'No. You're CIA. They'll expect a report from you.'

'I'm getting to know you, tough guy. You've got that look in your eye.'

'Don't look for what isn't there.'

'They said you had a death-wish.'

'Wrong. I don't like being set up.'

'Who?'

'I just need to get away. You feeling better now?'

She ignored his concern. Her sickness had been unnecessary. As he reminded her again, she felt the bile rise in her throat, fought to keep the retching back. 'Can I come with you? I don't want to stay here alone.'

Adam slipped his arm round her shoulder. 'You have to. Don't ask me why. Just . . . stay here until I get back.'

He climbed into the cab and shut the door. Billie stood at the pavement and watched him; he waved at her, tried to reassure her. When she could hold the retching no longer, she spun and rushed back into the hotel.

'Where to?' asked Frankie.

'Drive slowly up towards the quarter. Come on, let's go.'

The Cadillac pulled out from the kerb and turned up Canal Street. Behind him, through the rear window, Adam saw Billie turn and run into the hotel. He regretted leaving her at such a time, but he needed to be on his own.

'You heard what happened back there?' he asked Frankie.

'Couldn't miss it. Marked cars, sirens flashing, half the New Orleans police force falling over themselves to get into the hotel. Where we going?'

'I want to see some more voodoo.'

'You gotta be joking.' Frankie looked at Adam's face in the

rear-view mirror and answered his own question. 'No. You ain't joking.'

'I need to find Fruit Juice.' Adam pulled the bottle he had found in the sun-room from his pocket and held it over the seat so that Frankie could see it clearly. 'I think this is his.'

'Looks familiar. Where'd you get it?'

'Doesn't matter. But I need to see the man.'

'We can try. Don't you think you should tell the Agency?'

'It's personal. To me.'

Frankie shrugged and drove up Canal Street and turned on to Basin Street. Life in the quarter continued at its full frenetic pace, but here, northside, the streets were deserted, the overhead lighting poor and the ambience menacing. Frankie pulled up at the kerb.

'Why here?' asked Adam.

'He's going to be round here someplace. At this time of night this is his territory. It's a bad place. Not somewhere you wanna be on your own.'

'How do I find him?'

'He'll find you. If he wants to.'

Adam opened the door and got out.

'You're crazy,' said Frankie. 'They already know you here. Soon as they saw this car.'

'They?'

'The voodoo men. Why the hell do you want to see Fruit Juice?'

'Because he killed Trimmler. And he left his calling-card to tell me he did it.'

'You gotta tell Tucker.'

'He wouldn't know where to start. Even if he brought in the whole fucking CIA, they couldn't do a thing.'

'Then leave it. Don't go where you got no chance.'

'Not my nature, Frankie. It's how I am.'

'OK, but you can't just walk the streets. Not these streets.'

'So, where do I start?'

'Old Number One.' As Frankie spoke, Adam remembered the St Louis cemetery where the voodoo ceremony had taken place. 'But you gotta walk in the dark, be as black as the night and as empty as a shadow. I mean it when I say they watching you.'

266

'I'll start there.'

'Why? They'll be waiting for you.'

'First rule of combat. Fight on territory you know. Second rule. Take the bastards by surprise. It's the only fucking place I know round here, Frankie. See you back at the hotel.'

'Hold it. You better take some help.' Frankie reached over to his glove compartment and pulled out two hand-grenades.

'You carry these in the car?' asked an amazed Adam.

'You don't know what else I got on board this Caddie. It's more a tank than a car. I like being a secret agent. Beats working in a cripple factory. There's no Christmas decorations got my name on it.'

'Thanks,' said Adam, taking the two grenades and putting them in his bag.

'You OK for everything else?'

'I've got all I need now.'

The brown bag still slung over his shoulder, Adam disappeared into the shadows, out of the cab driver's view as he moved stealthily along the decayed walls of the old buildings that had long since been in need of a face-lift. Frankie suddenly understood why Adam was dressed in black. Maybe he stood a chance, not much, but just a hint.

Adam's toe throbbed as he moved along, hugging the walls that were his cover. But he didn't let the pain touch him. As he moved, he called to Marcus, called to the other dark half that would watch through this night with him while he set about exacting his revenge.

The voodoo men had seen his death-wish; they understood what drove him on. It was his natural advantage, the ability to face death and not fear it. And they would be frightened of it. Because they feared death. He would use that against them.

There was little point in hiding his presence. He knew they were watching him, that he couldn't hide. He also knew that he couldn't see them and that made a surprise move almost impossible.

They made a fool of me, Marcus. They bloody stuffed me and then took Trimmler's life.

Don't let it get to you. Stay cool. Sense the danger. Ride it. Make it work for you.

267

*Made a fucking fool of me. I'm going to ram his bloody blood
and piss down his fucking throat.*

Think.

I can't. Everything's red.

Think. Why did they kill Trimmler?

God knows. I just . . .

Why? Why did they kill Trimmler?

I don't know.

Why them?

Because they're part of something bigger.

They could be agents.

Whose?

Anybody's. Russian. Even American.

Someone's setting you up.

Why?

Don't know. Do you really want to get Fruit Juice?

Yes.

Why?

Because he knows the answers.

Now you're thinking. Let's go.

Adam knew he must create his own surprise. He could only
do that by doing the unexpected. He smiled to himself. That was
easy. And it put him on terrain he knew something about.

Straight into the lion's den, Marcus. That's the only way.

The stillness of Old Number One was as it had been the
night before, but it was darker. Thick clouds covered the
sky; there was a dampness that signalled rain. Adam hoped
it would come soon, the noise and wind that accompanies
rain would be to his advantage.

He followed the main footpath round the cemetery, at first
keeping clear of the tomb where the ceremony had taken
place the night before. It didn't take long before he heard
the first rustle in the bushes behind him. They were coming
in, the enemy was on the move. He kept walking, studying
the terrain as he did. He was certain they wouldn't shoot him.
Fruit Juice would be intrigued by his visit to Old Number
One, and if he were to die, then their instinct would be to
couple it with their sense of theatre.

When he had completed a circuit of the cemetery, passed the grand tombs and vaults, he followed the smaller routes that led to the poor graves as well as the middle-class tombs.

Twenty minutes later he was making his way to Marie Laveau's tomb. If Fruit Juice was as smart as he believed, he would be waiting for him there.

'What you got in that bag you carrying?'

Fruit Juice was standing in front of the tomb, dressed as he had been the night before, his hair now reverted to white and short-curled. As he spoke it started to rain.

'The rain-maker. Down to you, is it?'

'Everything come from voodoo magic, boy.'

'Where're your friends?'

'They here. I only got to call. What you got in that bag?'

'Magic tricks. My sort.'

Fruit Juice laughed. 'Guns. They no good. Not here. Not in the Magic Kingdom.'

'Don't tell me. You're Walt Disney reincarnated.' He heard the movement in the bushes. The troops were getting into place. He would have to move soon. He was glad the rain was getting heavy, didn't realize that's how it came in Louisiana, fast and furious and in short bursts.

'Different kinda magic, boy. This is for real.' He moved towards Adam. 'How's the toe?'

Adam's instinct told him that they were closing in, that Fruit Juice was spinning it out while they positioned round him.

'Why Trimmler?' he asked.

'Orders.'

'Whose?'

'From those who have the money.'

'Russians?'

'That ain't for us to discusss.'

'Why? You going to let me out of here alive.'

'No chance.'

'Then tell me who gave the orders.'

'Fuck you, boy.'

Adam swung the bag off his shoulder, startling Fruit Juice who stepped back sharply. He took out one of the hand-grenades and popped the safety-pin. He crossed over to Fruit

269

Juice, pulled his trouser waistband open with his left hand and slipped his other hand with the grenade down into Fruit Juice's crotch, into the softness of his balls.

'If someone shoots me, then this thing's going to go off. Before you can unzip your flies. Make one hell of a mess.'

'Stay clear!' screamed Fruit Juice. 'Don't nobody do nothing.'

'That's good. So, tell me. Who gave the orders?'

'Fuck you, boy.'

'You go on like that and you won't be fucking anyone.' He pushed the grenade harder into Fruit Juice's scrotum.

'You let that thing go and you're a dead man. You know that. Hell, I don't know who gave the orders. We was just paid. Just told to knock out the guy in 1844. After you gave us a hard time in the lobby, shit, I just decided to have us some fun. That was personal.'

'So, why cut off his arms? Or was that orders, too?'

'Look, I did like I was told. Just make a mess, they said. It's crazy, but I did it just like they paid for.'

'Who paid?'

'Usual channels. Could be anybody, even the Mob. You can't trace these things.'

Adam believed him, he could read it in his eyes.

'Just cool it, huh?' continued Fruit Juice. 'Come on, this thing's outta hand.'

'He was my responsibility. You made me look bad.'

'Weren't deliberate.'

'Neither's this.' Adam moved behind Fruit Juice and, with his arm now wrapped round the voodoo man and using him as a shield, dragged him backwards towards the bushes. Fruit Juice yelped and others started to shout from their hidden vantage-points.

But it all happened too fast. Before anyone could react positively, Adam was in the protection of the bushes.

'Was it blood or was it tomato juice?' he asked Fruit Juice.

'You shit crazy, man,' screamed Fruit Juice.

A gunshot exploded from near by.

Adam would never know. He closed his eyes to accustom himself to the darkness and then pushed Fruit Juice back towards Marie Laveau's tomb. He turned and ran, low to the ground, through the undergrowth.

He never saw Fruit Juice fall to the earth, never saw him writhe and twist on the ground as he frantically tried to pull out the grenade that was trapped in the tightly tailored cloth of his trousers. The more frantic his actions, the more difficult it was to dislodge the bomb. And then time ran out.

Adam only heard the explosion. Didn't know whether Fruit Juice had avoided death or not. It wasn't his problem. The others would be after him and he needed to prepare his ground.

The earth was soft under him, the rain now beginning to take its toll as it fell. His senses were fully alert and he heard shouting from behind, then a few gunshots followed by people crashing through the bushes. Someone yelled for quiet, but it had little effect and he heard the order being repeated.

He spun round, pulled the Browning from his waistband and fired three rounds towards whoever was giving the orders. He heard someone yelp in pain and yell he'd been hit. But he knew it wasn't serious, otherwise he wouldn't be complaining so vigorously.

Another voice now pleaded for calm. 'Shut yo' fucking mouth fo' I fucking do it fo' ya!' it screamed. This time the others listened and the shouting faded to nothing. From the noise Adam knew there were no more than seven or eight people, not a number that couldn't be dealt with.

Adam could still hear the recipient of his bullet moaning some forty yards away. As he moved towards another part of Old Number One, Adam knew he had to confuse them, scramble their knowledge of the cemetery until they didn't know where the next area of conflict was coming from. He knew he didn't have long. The grenade, as muffled as it was by Fruit Juice's body, would have been heard and someone would probably have told the police. Even in Sin City, grenades were not the norm.

He worked his way round to the west side of the cemetery and entered an old vault he had chosen when he had first circuited the cemetery. The door, steel, had been slightly open and he slipped in through the narrow gap.

It was cold, a dry chill that hung still. His eyes made out large stone shelves, four deep, that ran round three sides of the vault. There were coffins on each shelf, some resting directly on top of others, more than thirty, ornate wooden boxes in the mausoleum.

Glad of the respite from the rain, he wiped the water from his hair where it had run into his long waves. Then he opened the brown bag and took out the Heckler and Koch MP5K sub-machine-gun. He rammed a clip in, swung it over his shoulder, rammed two more clips and the remaining hand-grenade in his pockets, then waited by the door for whatever came next.

It didn't take long.

Two of them came into his line of vision, moving in the bushes on the opposite side of the park, both with hand-guns ready. They moved like amateurs, street bullies used to having their own way. They were sitting targets, too easy for Adam.

Killing was a way of life to Adam, something he did without considering the consequences. But that was when the odds excited him, when he felt there was real danger. It was his buzz, his church. These were fun-fair targets, something to hit and take home a prize Teddy Bear for. He let them pass, heard their whispers as loudly as if they were in conversation with him, and waited to see who followed.

No-one.

His pursuers had obviously spread out over the cemetery.

He came out of the vault and followed the two Teddy Bears. He caught them up quickly and stayed close behind. The heavy rain and its resultant sound on the bushes made his task easy. They split up to go around a large tree whose trunk was surrounded by big bushes. Adam decided to go after the man on the left.

As soon as he was out of sight of his companion, Adam was on him, the knife he always carried slashing down and across his throat.

By the time his partner had stumbled on the fallen corpse, Adam was nearly fifty yards away in the safety of the old vault. He heard the man scream, then stifle his fear. There were shots, four of them, as he either blasted at thin air in panic or signalled his cronies to him. Adam heard them collect where he had felled the man, saw the torchlights shining in the dark.

'He fucking killed him. He fucking cut his throat.'

'Take it easy, for—'

'Sliced him right next to me. He was only next to me.'

'Lay off. We got—'

'Fuck you. They said he got the death-wish. He a fucking spook, man.'

'Don't talk shit.' It was Goat Face.

'He fucking invisible. Right under my fucking nose.'

Adam grinned as he stepped out from the vault entrance and sprayed the Heckler and Koch in their direction. It was a short burst, enough to send them diving for cover into the undergrowth. When he had finished there was an absolute quiet. Nobody was saying anything now.

As he turned to retrace his track, he heard the police sirens in the distance, growing closer as they approached. He headed for the entrance to Old Number One, heard the shouting start up again behind him as his pursuers hastily prepared their exit, walked through the gates and out on to Basin Street.

'You causing trouble again?' was Frankie's caustic greeting.

He was in his wheelchair on the pavement, an old 1950s Reising M50 sub-machine-gun across his legs. Adam walked past him, packed his weaponry back into the brown bag and tossed it into the boot.

'Let's go,' he said.

The first police car, an unmarked Ford with a red flashing light stuck to its roof, was at the scene two minutes later.

By then, Frankie, having slid himself and his wheelchair back into the car with surprising ease, was turning towards Canal Street and back to the safety of the hotel.

Georgetown
Washington DC

'This had better be good at this time of the morning.'

'The Russians know who the Lucy Ghosts are,' said the DDA into the phone receiver. He'd just received that message at home from Nowak. He'd stayed there, trying to co-ordinate the problem in New Orleans while his assistant, Carter, had been sent on ahead in a private Agency jet to take over from Tucker.

'Who are they?' asked the Exec Director as he struggled out of bed.

'They're not prepared to give that information over the telephone. But they say it needs executive approval.'

The Exec Director knew that meant the President. Damn it. The last thing he wanted was this blowing up in the White House and on Capitol Hill. One always followed the other. 'Why?'

'Because their own executive has been informed. It's sensational, according to Nowak.'

'Does he know?'

'He says not. Just what his contact tells him.'

'OK. I'll take it from here.'

'They want urgent action.'

'I'm not waking the Pres . . . anybody . . . at this time of the morning. I'll put a call through at seven.'

'That's four in the afternoon over there.'

'I told you. First thing.'

'I've also had a call from Tucker . . .' The DDA'd saved the best for last.

'Tucker?'

'Our man in charge in New Orleans.'

'And?'

'Trimmler's been assassinated.'

'Shit. You're . . . I don't believe . . . When?'

'About two hours ago.'

'Why wasn't I called immediately?'

'I rang, sir. There was no answer.'

The Exec Director, recently married to a twenty-six-year-old daughter of one of the leading society hostesses in Washington, remembered that he had switched his phone off when he set about proving his youth in one of their nightly bedtime romps. He'd forgotten to switch it back on and only remembered when he went to relieve himself in the bathroom fifteen minutes earlier.

'Something wrong with the phone, I guess. What happened?'

'Killed him and his wife. With a knife. Then hacked off Trimmler's arms.'

'What?'

'That's right. Left them shaped in the form of a swastika.'

'Jesus!' came the unbelieving answer.

'Maybe you should take executive advice, sir.'

'OK. You at home?'

'Yes, sir. I'm running it from here.'

'You told the DDI?'

'No. I wanted to talk to you first.'

'OK. You tell him. Call him over to your place. And don't use the phone too long. I'll have to get back to you. We need a stenographer. I want a full report faxed here straight away.' The Exec Director was about to call the Head of the CIA, the Director himself. If anyone was going to ring the President of the United States of America at 3 a.m., it sure as hell wasn't going to be his arse that was going out on a sling.

The phone went dead in the DDA's hand. He put down the receiver. He'd already called in a stenog. She was next door, in his living room. Before he could get up from his desk the phone rang. He picked it up.

'Yes,' he barked.

'Tucker, sir.'

'What is it, Tucker?'

'More trouble.'

'It can't get any worse.'

'The Englishman went out after he discovered Trimmler. Our driver took him up into the French Quarter. They just got back. I've had the Chief of Detectives call me. Says there was a shoot-out in the quarter. Machine-guns and grenades. Says one of our people was involved. I'd like to remind you that we authorized the Englishman to carry arms. He had a machine-gun.'

'What makes you think it was him?'

'Because that's what our driver just told me. Seems he went after the guy who killed Trimmler.'

'How do you know that?'

'Driver told me. Something to do with a baby virgin's blood and piss. Sir.'

River Walk Hilton
New Orleans

ADAM WAS STILL asleep when the DDA's trouble-shooter, Carter, hit New Orleans at five-thirty in the morning. He'd brought two assistants with him, Windrush and Favor. They were runners, like Carter, but they were assistants to the assistant runner.

Marius, the other CIA driver, had met them off the private jet from Washington and driven them in his cab to the Hilton.

Their first meeting had been with Tucker, sleepy-eyed and relieved to hand over responsibility to Carter. He had given them a full report on the activities, including his conversation with the DDA, as he saw them right up to Adam going to bed.

'Snotty bastard,' remarked Carter. His two colleagues nodded. 'But he's right. We can't let the cops take him downtown. Any idea why he should go on the rampage?'

'No. I think you need to speak to Frankie Mistletoe.'

'What sort of name's that?' sneered Favor to no-one in

general. Windrush nodded agreement as a matter of course.

'What about the girl?' went on Carter.

'She's been fine. Just kept a watch on Trimmler like the rest of us,' replied Tucker.

It took nearly an hour for Tucker to complete his de-brief and Carter took him over the events of the last few days twice, just as the book said he should. The report included Frankie's trip to the cemetery with Adam and the ensuing squabble with the Chief of Detectives.

'Does Nicholson know that the cab driver's told us of his trip up there?' asked Carter.

'No. I got that out of Frankie after Nicholson went to bed.'

'Do the police know?'

'No. Only those of us in this room.'

'OK. Leave it like that for now.' Then he sent Tucker down to get Frankie.

While he waited he rang the Chief of Detectives at the New Orleans Police Headquarters. Their conversation was brief; Carter knew Washington had already contacted them and warned them off. The biggest battle had been with the FBI who wanted to stick their noses in. But that had now been cleared and the field was left to the Agency. But they had to move fast. The New Orleans PD would only sit still for so long before they'd want to resolve their own murders.

The Chief of Detectives, having been told to hand over responsibility to Carter, was understandably edgy, and Carter appeased him by telling him he needed all his assistance and would like them to work together on this one.

By the time Frankie wheeled himself in, Carter had pacified the policeman and agreed to meet him at 9 a.m.

Nobody had told Carter that Frankie was disabled and his surprise showed.

'We got equal opportunities in everything,' quipped Frankie. 'You're looking at your token cripple.'

Carter was embarrassed and angry at not being told. 'So, you took Nicholson up to the French Quarter?' he started, after giving Tucker a reproachful glare. 'Take me through it, would you?'

There was a long silence when Frankie had finished. 'And he took his arms with him when he went into the cemetery?' Carter finally broke the quiet.

'Yes.'

'Where did he get the grenade from? We didn't authorize that.'

'From me.'

'What the hell you doing with grenades?'

'This is a rough city. When you're committed to a wheel-chair, you prepare yourself for all eventualities.'

'You didn't have to give him a fucking hand-grenade.'

'He saw it and he wanted it,' Frankie lied. 'Hell, we're meant to be on the same side.'

'Did the girl know what was going on?'

'No. Not to my knowledge.'

'But she went to the voodoo ceremony.'

'I think that was more a night out.'

'So, why did he think it was this guy Fruit Juice?'

'I already said. I don't know. He just got in the car, showed me this bottle and said it was Fruit Juice's calling-card. Had to be Trimmler he was talking about. Nothing else was going to get him that mad. I mean, he's a pro. Trimmler's death makes him look bad.'

'Bad. And crazy,' chirped in Carter's assistant, Favor.

'He don't come over as crazy to me. He's bad, but he went in there after Trimmler's killer. Got him, too.'

'We don't know that for sure,' cut in Carter. 'And, even if he was right, he should've waited for orders. Damn it, he was under our command, not a fucking freelance.' This whole thing was already getting bigger than Carter. Nobody'd told him about the Englishman's action, but then nobody'd known at that stage. It was taking on diplomatic proportions that were above his realm of responsibility. But it was also an opportunity to be taken. He had to rock the boat without sinking the bitch. 'Unless he had another motive.'

'Sir?' asked Tucker, not comprehending Carter's gist.

'We're assuming that Nicholson was acting in our interests. It's time to consider if he had a different motive.'

'Why should he . . . '

'You tell me. You've been with him.'

278

'I can't think of anything . . . not one thing that would make me be suspicious. He . . . he took his duties seriously. Never allowed a situation where Trimmler was in danger. Hell, he even took him off for the evening. If he was after him, then he'd have done something then.'

'Not everything is as obvious as it seems. That's the first law of investigation. Is he still in his room?'

'As far as . . . Yes, sir.'

'Windrush. I want you up there. He doesn't go anywhere until I say so.' Carter turned to Tucker as Windrush left the room. 'I want to see him later and I don't want him to know about our conversation.'

They didn't see Adam because events changed everyone's plans.

Marius, Frankie's colleague, heard that another cab driver had taken a fare to the airport. The passenger had been a Russian or German and he wanted to catch the first plane direct to Germany or to New York where he would make a connecting flight. The cabbie had discussed it with his co-drivers as they waited for the morning rush to begin.

'Shit scared,' said the cabbie. 'Just wanted to get outta New Orleans. Hell, he musta had a bad night.'

The other men, including Marius, laughed and reminded each other of the wild nights and frightened tourists who went away and never forgot New Orleans.

Fifteen minutes later Marius had reported the conversation to Tucker who went to find Carter at the breakfast bar. When they checked with reception they found that Albert Goodenache had checked out over two hours earlier. By the time they contacted the airport and pulled strings to find out what Goodenache's destination was, the scientist was on his way to New York where he was to switch to a jumbo direct to Frankfurt.

Adam had shaved, showered, put on a fresh shirt and was heading for the breakfast bar at nine-thirty before Carter caught up with him.

'I want to see you,' he snapped at Adam, recent events now shortening his temper.

279

'Fine. Over breakfast,' Adam replied, coolly.

'No, damn it. We can't discuss these matters in a public place.'

'Well, I'm starving. So, either join me or arrange to see me later.'

'I think we should talk now.'

'Suits me,' said Adam with a smile, as he walked towards the breakfast bar.

'Hey, I meant before . . .' yelled Carter, but it was too late and he had little choice but to follow Adam into the open-plan restaurant where they were seated at a corner table. Carter nodded when Adam asked if he wanted a coffee, then sat back and waited while Adam painstakingly worked his way through the menu before ordering two fried eggs, double bacon, three sausages, grits, blueberry muffins and Darjeeling tea with milk.

'You like your food,' commented Carter, his irritation coming through.

Adam ignored him. When he was ready he said, 'Well, Mr Carter. What can I do for you?'

'You're heading for trouble. Did you know that?'

'My cholesterol level's fine. I've always liked greasy fo—'

'Don't get smart with me.'

'Would I?' Adam grinned. The CIA man was easy to needle.

'Why didn't you tell us that you'd been out shooting up half of New Orleans?' Carter watched Adam closely, but was disappointed that he drew no reaction from the Englishman. 'We know what went on up there.'

'Where?'

'At the fucking cemetery. We know what happened.'

'Then tell me.' Adam decided to play ignorant. He didn't believe that Billie had said anything. It had to come from outside, possibly from the police. Or Frankie.

'You're meant to be working for us.'

'No. I'm working for my own Government. On loan to you. I was sent here to help protect Trimmler.'

'Not exactly a success, was it?' Carter smirked.

'Your man, your Agency, were on duty when they killed Trimmler. You shouldn't forget that.'

'Fuck you.'

'Chance would be a fine thing.'

'What?'

'Nothing. I did what I was asked to do. Your people slipped up.'

Carter changed tack. He smiled magnanimously and held up his arms, palms forward, in a symbol of truce. 'We know you were involved in the shootings. Shit, I'd be happy to let the cops run you in. Except for one thing. You believe those guys up in the cemetery were involved in Trimmler's death. That means they could be under the control of a foreign agency. We've got to follow that through.'

'What makes you think they were involved with Trimmler?'

'We don't. You do. That's what we want to find out.'

'Then I'll make a full report when I get back to London.'

'I'd like to move a little faster than that.' He leant across the table. 'I know about the bottle.'

'Bottle?' Adam guessed it was Frankie who had told the CIA.

'Yes. Bottle. With blood and piss in it.'

'A baby *virgin's* blood and piss.'

'A baby virgin's blood and piss.' Carter was pleased he had got him to open up.

'Don't know what you're talking about.' He grinned as he watched the anger in Carter's face. 'Hey, take it easy. Bad for the blood pressure, you know.'

Before Carter could reply the waiter returned and laid out Adam's breakfast on the table. The two men sat in uncomfortable silence until they were on their own again.

'Looks good,' said Adam, tucking into his meal.

'You're asking for trouble. I should just hand you over to the cops. Let them do it their way.'

'You can't do that. You wouldn't be allowed to.'

'Then tell me what happened. What the hell made you go up there? What do you know that we don't?'

'It'll be in my report. Soon as I get back.'

'We'll talk to London.'

'Fine. If they clear me, then I'll give you a full report.'

Carter stood up abruptly, the chair nearly falling over as he pushed it back. He grabbed it and rammed it under the table. 'Don't leave until I come back to you.'

'Do you know what I don't understand?' said Adam.

'What?'

'Why, with all your technology and expertise, you Americans can't cook bacon like it's meant to be.' He held up a rasher on the end of the fork. 'Too crisp. Too damn crisp.' Carter stomped off, unable any longer to control his emotions. Adam grinned. 'Don't get the hump just because I don't like your bacon.'

The Oval Room
The White House
Washington DC

THE DDA KEPT quiet on this one.

He was sitting with the Director and Exec Director of the CIA as they made their report to the President. He knew he was only there for background information. He was the flunkey, the nowhere man, in this room of history and decision.

When the Exec Director had finished his report, the President leant back in the big leather executive chair and swivelled round to look out of the window.

'Thing's moving at one helluva pace,' said the President's Chief of Staff, Charles Magey. 'You sure nothing's happened since we started this meeting.'

'My office was told to inform me immediately of any significant developments,' replied the Director.

'This thing could run a million different ways. It could be anybody out there trying to damage us. Even the Russians.'

'We appreciate that.'

'And you're still getting nowhere with the computer?'

'No. But we're narrowing things down.'

Magey flared up. 'Hell, you won't have anything left on those data bases to narrow down.'

'Getting heated . . . is not going to solve this problem,' said the President as he swung the chair round so that he could face them. 'Could it be the Russians?' he asked the Director.

'I don't think so, Mr President.'

'Why not?'

'Because I can't see what they'd gain from it. They've got too many problems to get up to their old tricks. And if they wanted to, why bother knocking off agents who're too old to really threaten them.'

'The Chinese?' asked Magey.

'Once again, nothing to gain,' replied the Director.

'When do we find out about the Lucy Ghosts?' said the President.

'There's a meeting this afternoon. In my office. Our Russian contact is going to brief me on what they know.'

'OK. Keep me informed. Trimmler. Did I ever meet him?' the President asked Magey.

'Yes, Mr President. I think he was introduced to you. He attended some of our functions. Three in all. Scientific exchanges.' Magey always did his homework and the President depended on him.

'And is he an ex-Nazi?'

'Yes, sir. We don't know all the details. They're on the computer and it's difficult getting eye-witness information on something that long ago. We hid a lot. The then Secretary of State for War, Robert Patterson and General John Hildring just wanted to hide the true identities of the Nazis. Hildring said it was time to bury the dead Nazi horse.'

'Didn't bury it deep enough, did they?' commented the President drily. He addressed himself to the Director. 'That computer's important. It could give us the answers we need.'

'We're doing our best, Mr President,' the Director replied.

'I appreciate that. But we need some positive movement on this. Let's not forget the British are also involved. We don't want to look bad against the Russians. There's still plenty of tension there. We've seen the failure of some of their policies, and of their political change of direction. More than once. If

283

we mess up on this, the British, and the rest of the Europeans, will know. We can do without that. Don't forget, my trip to Europe is imminent. I have no intention of arriving with an empty suitcase in my hand.'

'Talking of the British, how much does their guy know?' asked Magey.

'Not too much. He knows he was here to protect Trimmler. I think he just wants to go home now,' said the Exec Director.

'After shooting up half of New Orleans. They've got to be crazy to send over someone like him.'

'As I said before, he believed it was Trimmler's killer he was after,' cut in the Director.

'You mean, *we* believe. From your report, he didn't say anything.'

'Not yet. We've contacted London. They'll be giving him orders to report directly to us. Even so, with all that evidence, we think—'

'Circumstantial evidence. Hell, your agent didn't see anything. He could just've been having a good night out. Drugs, anything. He's got to be weird to attend a voodoo ceremony. Maybe things got out of hand. And he's making no report because he doesn't want to be caught. This whole thing about the ceremony could just be a wild-goose chase.'

'Is that possible?' asked the President.

'Yes, sir. Anything's possible,' replied the Director.

'This whole thing's so damn mixed up, he could even be part of the conspiracy. How do we know he didn't take out Trimmler? After all, he was the first one to find the body.' Magey pushed harder.

'Unlikely.' The Director was sweating.

'Tucker says he was called away. When he left Trimmler.'

'Yes, by Nicholson. But it's unlikely he used his own name to get Tucker down there.'

'Why? Using his name was one way of guaranteeing Tucker went down to the lobby. Did your people check if anyone was recognized by the hotel staff for calling Tucker down?'

'They used a house phone to get the message to reception.'

'OK. But don't discount anything. This thing's so mixed up that anyone could be in play. That much is obvious. There's holes so damn big, Saddam Hussein could have driven his whole tank division through it. You have absolutely no idea what's behind it? That's how we started in Kuwait when the Iraqis went in. Because you guys had no idea that trouble was about to blow.'

'That's crap.' The Director defended himself. They always went after the failures, never the successes. Then he regretted his outburst in front of the President.

'That's what happened, isn't it?' Magey pushed again.

'Everyone was caught short on that. What do you expect with the cutbacks we had to take?'

'There's always the Israelis. Maybe they found out about Trimmler's past. It could be simple revenge. Or even a spy ring like the Fuchs episode. That would look great for us. Don't you people realize how bad any of this would make us look?'

'All right,' refereed the President. 'I don't think there's any need to turn on each other. But Charley's right. We could be following too narrow a band. Open it up. Look for things that aren't there. Put more resources on it. Find out what's happening. I do not want a political bomb exploding in my trousers.'

The CIA men were ushered out into the corridor.

'Get it done,' said the Director to his Exec. 'Find out what's going on or your backside's on the line.'

'You heard him,' the Exec Director told the DDA when they were on their own in the Exec's car. 'If I go, so do you. Find out why the Englishman went berserk in that cemetery. I don't care how, just find out.'

'What about diplomatic fall-out.'

'What about it? Kill the bastard for all I care, but find out.'

285

Frankfurt *Daily News* offices
Frankfurt

'THAT'S ONE HELLUVA war record.' The editor threw the notes he had been given to read on to his desk. His vast bulk spread as he leant back in his swivel chair and he fastened his most penetrating look on the news editor. 'That is, if it's true. We've been set up before.'

'That's never stopped us following something through,' replied his news editor, quite unabashed by his chief's attention.

'I knew Grob Mitzer well. I was a guest at his home here and also at his country estate.' The editor didn't mention that Mitzer had also been a great friend of the proprietor's, that they often spent weekends in the mountains on boar shoots or skiing. 'This was a great German. This filth'– he indicated the sheaf of papers in front of him – 'isn't true.'

'Then we prove his innocence.'

'It doesn't need proving. Not to those who knew him.'

'If we don't take it, then some other paper will. We can't tell them not to print.'

'Nobody's trying to stifle anything,' barked the editor, realizing he was stepping beyond the bounds of impartiality. 'Shit, I just want to save the reputation of one of the great men of modern Germany.'

The news editor picked up the notes. 'These need to be answered. Even if they're lies, they need to be answered.'

'All right. All right. Look, I don't expect us to hide the truth. I could never condone that. But, take it easy. I believe . . . these are lies. I don't want the usual newspaper trick about threats and innuendos producing the truth. This time let's presume the accused to be innocent, and let's make damn sure he's guilty before we print anything.'

'OK. But there is a lot of information here. True or not.

286

A Nazi membership card . . . the mass murder of imported workers at Nordhausen and Peenemünde . . . personally responsible for the transport which carried the workers to these rocket plants, transport so basic that hundreds died before they even got there. A specific accusation that he shot workers, too feeble to be of any further use, to save food rations for others. And that he used the knowledge of the Nazi rocket effort to build and further his own interests at the end of the war, information that should have been shared with other people, both in Government and in Industry. This is the sort of stuff the Israelis go after. If any of this is true, we're talking major war crimes.'

'They can't prosecute a dead man. But they could destroy his reputation. I mean, why didn't it come out when he was alive? Who would want to send us this information?'

'God knows. To hang on to this stuff for all these years. It's unreal.'

'If it's true. If it's true . . .' The editor shook his head. 'Do you remember that British paper, *The Sunday Times*, when they published the Hitler Diaries? Shit, that was the biggest con of all.'

'We're also getting feedback on a National Socialist group.'

'Nazis?'

'Nothing as bad as that. Just National Socialists.'

'Fringe politicians.'

'This could be something bigger. It's just a guess, but it could have something to do with the synagogue murders – and the Neu-Isenburg hotel bombing.'

'The National Socialists are more involved in trying to build a credible party, rather than blowing people up. I can't see it.'

'It could happen,' the news editor persisted. 'The time could be right for new attitudes, new political parties. Subjugate a people for over forty years and you've got a ready springboard for Fascism.'

'Possible, but unlikely. I agree we're in a mess and that's how Hitler came to power. By putting the economy right and uniting the country. And whatever people say, a party that could do that for East and West, with the right leader, has

287

got to be taken seriously. Hitler's downfall was his paranoia about the Jews and his greed for new territories. A new leader wouldn't concern himself with that. The Jews are no problem; I mean, we don't have any in Germany any more. And, as for invading other countries, no, not these days. For some war-mongering Arab, maybe. But not for us. The Russians and Americans wouldn't allow it to happen. If there is such a movement, then let's find out about it. But let's not condemn it out of hand, it could be what the country wants.' The editor was beginning to sound like his proprietor. 'Right now I want to find out who sent us these files on Grob Mitzer.'

'And if they're true?'

The editor sighed, then nodded, his triple chin bouncing down his neck. 'Go ahead. *If* they're true . . . '

River Walk Hilton
New Orleans

ADAM STAYED IN the hotel because he'd nowhere else to go.

There was no point in booking an air ticket home. He'd already spoken by phone to Captain Coy in London, and received little joy from him. 'Stay put until I come back to you,' was all Coy had said after listening to Adam's lengthy story and growing more appalled by the minute. Adam had expected little else. After all, Coy was just a briefing officer.

Billie had rung through on the house phone and asked him if he wanted to have lunch. They met downstairs in the lobby restaurant.

'I hear you had a run-in with Carter,' she said, when the waiter had taken their order.

'News travels fast in New Orleans.'

'Tucker told me. He's concerned.'

'Not about me?'

'No. His own position.'

'Ever the desk clerk . . . '

'Don't be too harsh,' she admonished him. 'It's all he's been trained for.'

'What else did he tell you?'

'That they don't trust you. That you're hiding something.'

'Sharp, aren't they?'

'Why not tell them what you told me?'

Adam shrugged and drank from the glass of iced water on the table.

'Why not?' she asked again.

'Not my nature.'

'What's that mean?'

'That I never disclose anything until I have to. I want to know why you didn't report back to them what I told you.'

'You trusted me enough to tell me. Why break it?'

'Thanks. What about you? Did you get in touch with home?'

'You bet I did!' Billie recounted how she had rung home to find a message on the answerphone informing her that Gary had left her to move in with a new girlfriend whom she knew was fifteen years younger than her.

'Didn't even have the guts to tell me to my face. Had to do it by tape.'

She suddenly hoped Peter hadn't rung; she would hate him to know that she could not hold on to her men.

'Sorry I asked,' he commented, when she had finished.

'Don't be. I envy you.'

'Can't see why.'

'Because you just do your own thing. For your own reasons. I always try and keep everyone happy. And in the end, it's always Billie who gets kicked in the teeth.'

'Stop feeling sorry for yourself.'

'I'm not.'

'Yes, you are.'

'Maybe just a little. Anyway, that's a woman's prerogative. I don't want to talk about it any more. They're all shits, every man I've ever known. Says something about me, doesn't it?'

'Unlucky. It happens.'

'You ever been in love, Adam?'

'No. Never had the inclination. Too mixed up with myself, I suppose.'

Billie gazed at him. 'They won't let you go back to England yet.'

'I know.'

'Who else was involved?'

'No idea. I don't even know why they killed him. I know who did it, but not why.'

'Are you sure it was Fruit Juice?'

'Oh, yes. And I believe he had no other motive apart from killing for money and fulfilling his contract. It's easy, that. Getting someone killed for a price. Especially in a city like this. I really believe there are no answers here. Apart from one.'

'Which is?'

'Goodenache. I think he knows . . . '

'But he's gone.'

'What do you mean?'

'This morning. Caught a plane out of here.'

'Who told you?'

'Tucker.'

'Damn.' Adam slapped his fist on the table. 'Where's he gone?'

'Germany. According to Tucker.'

'That fits. Damn and blast.'

'Why, Adam?'

'Because he's the key, he's got the answers. Not Fruit Juice, nor any of that lot.'

'How do you know?'

'I just do. Instinct, whatever. Look, I need to know what's going on. I was only sent here to protect Trimmler. And going after Fruit Juice, well, that was just anger at being made to look bad. I didn't go out to kill him, but to find out what happened. His death just happened. His life or mine. It could've gone either way. But now I'm getting sucked in to something I know nothing about. Except that it's dangerous and I'm in the middle. I haven't asked before, because I didn't want to compromise you. But now I need to know

290

why Trimmler was important and what's really behind all this.'

The waiter arrived with their brunch and they waited while he served them.

'So. What's going on?' he asked, when the waiter had gone.

'It mustn't get back. I mean—'

'Come on, Billie. These things don't have to be said. Not between friends.'

She sighed, then picked up a french fry with her fingers, blew on it to cool it and chewed it slowly. Then she told him everything. Told him about the computer and its virus, about the death of the agents and the attempt on Trimmler's life in Cannes, about there being some contact with the Russians, although she had no idea why.

'You'd better eat up,' he said when she had finished. 'Your food'll be cold.'

He said nothing until she pushed the plate away.

'Confused?' she asked.

'Totally.'

'Where now?'

'We'll see.'

'I'd rather you didn't tell your people.'

'Nothing to do with them. I was just told to stay here and protect Trimmler. That's all I report on.'

Coy's call that afternoon ordered Adam to prepare a full report for the Americans. 'And stay there until they tell you to come home,' Coy added. 'By the way, our side is disappointed with the course of action you took. You were there to support, not to instigate. We'll find it difficult to endorse such action. Unless, that is, there were exceptional circumstances which led you either to determine the truth, or defend yourself.'

Adam knew he was on his own; as usual, the faceless desk people were leaving him to sort out his own mess and absolving themselves of any responsibility.

In his typically mischievous mood, he decided to let Carter come looking for him and he headed up to the clothes shops on Canal Street. He left a message for Billie at reception telling her where he had gone.

The shops were not as impressive as he had hoped. Most major American cities have stores which carry a range of merchandise far in excess of their European counterparts, which are always cheaper. Unfortunately, New Orleans didn't meet that standard.

Frankie and Billie, cruising Canal Street for Adam, saw him come out of QuarterMan, one of the many boutiques near the strip.

'They want you back,' said Billie, shouting out of the Cadillac.

'Who's they?'

'Carter. He's pretty mad. Says London told you to report to him. He's really blown a fuse.'

'Never, not Carter. You know, this is a terrible place to shop. No choice. I expected better.'

'Doesn't anything get to you?'

'Not if it doesn't matter.'

Adam slid in beside her.

'I didn't get a chance to tell ya,' said Frankie, pulling away from the kerb, 'but they buttonholed me about Fruit Juice and Old Number One.'

'So I found out.'

'I just said you went in there . . . '

'Fully armed.'

'I didn't say I saw you do anything.'

'You didn't, anyway.'

'They'da found out soon enough. Even in them circles, the police've got their informers.'

'Wasn't he at the voodoo ceremony?' interrupted Billie, leaning forward and pointing at three men who were walking northwards up Canal Street.

In the middle of the three, laughing as he led the conversation, was Goat Face.

'Stop. Pull in!' shouted Adam, his sense of immediacy superseding his caution.

Frankie pulled the Cadillac over to the kerb, cutting across the inner line of traffic and causing a vociferous outburst of indignation from the other vehicles. Adam was out of his door, on the street side of the car, before it had stopped. As she saw the Browning in his hand, Billie knew he was heading into trouble again.

'Shit!' She heard Frankie curse, then saw him swing the driver's door open and clamber, with his crutch, to get out of the Cadillac. Out of the back window she watched Adam cross the pavement, gliding more than running, and catch up with the three men. Frantically, she opened her own door, her heart pounding. She could hardly breathe as she pulled herself on to the pavement and heard Frankie straighten up behind her, the crutch now supporting him under his left shoulder. She caught a glimpse of the Reising M50 in his right hand.

'Hey, Goat Face!' Adam called from behind the three of them.

Billie saw them spin round in surprise. The outer two stepped back in alarm, but Goat Face stayed his ground. He threw his head back and laughed.

'Fuck you, jerk,' he shouted.

She felt Frankie brush past her as he manoeuvred to support Adam, not wanting to be blocked off from the three men.

'You've certainly got a way with words,' said Adam. 'So much so that I'd like you to come and meet some people with me. Some people who'd like to hear what you've got to say.'

'I ain't going anywhere. You hear me, jerk?'

Billie saw Goat Face laugh again, then signal the other two to move away, to spread outwards and split the space that Adam had to contend with. Around them, passers-by had seen what was taking place and were now scattering along the pavement, clearing out of the way as they saw the guns being brandished.

'You gonna have to take us all out,' Goat Face spat at Adam. 'Otherwise one of us gonna take you, shitface.'

Adam moved sideways, the gun aimed at Goat Face as he did, cutting off the angle as the outer two separated.

'Keep back,' Frankie said to Billie, his sub-machine-gun now pointed at Goat Face.

'This what you call support?' Goat Face laughed. 'Fucking cripples?' He reached into his side pocket and pulled out a hand-gun, a .45 'Sin City' Saturday Night Special.

'You're going to be a dead man,' stated Adam.

As he spoke, he heard the shout from up the hill and turned to see a policeman running towards them, fumbling with his holster gun, trying to draw. The man farthest from him turned and plunged through the doorway of a shop, hell bent on escaping out of the back.

Momentarily distracted by the sudden movement, Frankie swung his gun off Goat Face, and it was at that instant that Goat Face brought his gun up and shot Frankie in the leg.

Adam pushed aside the man nearest him and crossed to Goat Face, swinging his Browning down across his head. 'Don't shoot!' he screamed. 'I've got him.' Before Goat Face, now confused by being attacked on both sides, could fire at Adam, the Englishman had smacked him across the forehead with his gun barrel and dropped him to the pavement.

As he lay there, his gun sent sprawling by the force of the impact, as Adam turned to stop the other man escaping, as the policeman ran on down Canal Street waving his gun, as the shoppers screamed and took cover, Billie saw Frankie, still standing there as though nothing had happened. Then he calmly raised his gun and she heard the rat-a-tat tat as he shot Goat Face in the head. The blood and bone spattered the pavement and she turned away in horror.

The policeman started shooting at them, panicking as he ran. Adam turned and pushed her down.

Frankie stood there, still on his crutch, then threw down the gun as the policeman approached.

'Hold it!' shouted Frankie, waving his arm at the policeman. 'We're government men. Hold your fire.'

The policeman stopped firing and approached cautiously.

'CIA,' re-affirmed Frankie as he got closer. 'Get some help. For fuck's sake, get some help.'

The policeman, his gun still held in front of him, used his other hand to summon help on his radio.

Adam helped Billie to her feet, his gun still in his hand.

'Fucking shit shot me in my bad leg,' she heard Frankie say, heard his unbelieving laughter as he stood there on his crutch. 'He shot me in my dud leg. How about that? Can't feel a fucking thing. In my bad fucking leg. No respect for a cripple.'

Adam let go of her arm and turned on Frankie. 'I told you not to shoot,' he said. 'We wanted him alive.'

'Didn't hear you. Thought the bastard was going to—'

'Half the street heard me.'

'Put that gun down. Now!' the policeman ordered Adam, pointing the barrel straight at him. Adam nodded, and lowered the Browning to the pavement. 'Now stand back and clasp your hands round the back of your neck.'

As Adam complied he heard the sirens approaching.

Things had got out of hand. He sighed.

Shit, Marcus. It's getting tougher by the minute.

Carter had ordered Adam straight to his room as soon as he returned from Canal Street. 'I'll talk to you when I've got this fucking mess sorted out!' he snapped, red-faced and furious. 'You must've been crazy, getting out of that car in broad daylight and starting a shoot-up. A fucking meathead.'

Adam didn't react. He wasn't going to get into a shouting match with junior management and explain that he hadn't started anything, had only meant to bring in Goat Face for questioning.

As soon as Adam was on his own he started to pack. He'd already decided on his plan of action. Trouble was brewing and he needed to distance himself from this place. He remembered Coy's words in London. *You're on your own*, he had said.

'Where're you going?' asked Billie, when he let her in.

'Not for you to know.'

'Why?'

'What you don't know, you can't tell.'

'I'm not a kid.'

'No.'

'I know what Carter's got planned for you.'

'That's blackmail.'

'That's trust.'

'So, tell me.'

'And what if you don't keep your end of the bargain?'

'That's trust.'

'Funny. He thinks you're more involved than you say you are. Even said the British government could be in on this.'

'That's daft.'

'It's as good as any other scenario in this crazy mess. I mean, they could blame the Pope and someone'd believe it. Anyway, he wants you packed off to Washington for interrogation.'

'Which is why I'm leaving. I want to resolve this thing, Billie. I won't do it stuck in Washington. And all the leads here are cold.' He smiled at his own unwitting joke. 'Cold and buried.'

'So, where're you going?'

'After Herr Goodenache. To a place called Nordhausen. Could be a dead end, but it's all there is. And no-one else realizes it.'

'Let me come with you?' She was surprised by her own question. It wasn't what she had opened her mouth to say.

He looked up, startled, from his packing.

'I mean it,' she continued. 'I've nothing here.'

'You're a CIA operative.'

'I'm a clerk. A disseminator of information. Yes, and I'm over forty years old, pal. You don't have to remind me. I'm also about to lose my job.'

'Since when?'

'Since I get back. That's when. Come on, I've got nothing to lose. Maybe it's just my new-found sense of adventure. Always talked about it, never did much. Hell, I've got nothing here, no-one to go home to, except a battery of lawyers and bad memories.'

'You're risking everything. For nothing.'

'It's as good a reason as yours. And don't give me that loyalty shit next. Unless you're a spy. Which I doubt.'

'You'll lose your pension.'

'Very funny. I think we should go now.'

'And if I say no?'

'I'll just make sure you don't get out of here.'

'I'd have to shoot you.'

'Too noisy.'

'Then I'd cut your throat. And put my hand down and pull out your vocal chords and . . . ' Adam paused.

'And what?'

'If you come, you do exactly as I tell you.' The wisecracking had stopped. 'Your life could depend on it.'

'OK.'

'I mean it. I don't want to be worried about you when somebody's having a go at me.'

'I understand that.'

'I hope so. Now go and pack. Just your necessaries. We can buy stuff on the way. Be ready in five minutes.'

'How're we going to get to Germany?'

'We'll worry about that when we get out of the hotel.' He suddenly saw a way out. 'Have you got your passport?'

'Yes. Agency regulations. Always be prepared. Hey, tough guy,' she said softly. He looked up at her quizzically. 'What if I was with you just to keep an eye on you? For the Agency.'

He grinned. 'It'd be interesting, wouldn't it?'

'What I said to you, about my reason for coming. Do you understand that?'

'Some people, when they approach the amber light, they put their foot on the brake. Others take a chance and slam down on the accelerator. Which are you, Billie? Are you ready to jump the lights?'

Getting out of the hotel unheeded presented no real problem. The CIA men, unused to having their orders ignored in their world of grey suits and corporate ladder-climbing, weren't expecting Adam to leave the building, let alone New Orleans.

He knew that was how they would react. They were Head Office men, not honed by the death-force of the field. They were out-of-touch men fighting for the glory of the top-floor, wash-room key.

He still took precautions. By descending the eighteen floors down the emergency escape stairs, he led Billie down to the rear exit, out on to River Walk and the Mississippi. She kept up with him and he remembered she was an exercise freak.

They walked along the north bank, the river barges towing their long cargo busily along the Mississippi, blaring their warnings as they passed each other, their horns the will of prehistoric monsters. There were no pedestrians and they turned north past the Riverfront Aquarium and up Spanish Place towards Tchoupitoulas Street.

297

'Heya. Where you going?' asked Frankie as he pulled up at the kerb, having spotted them as he returned to the hotel after dropping a fare on St Charles Street. 'Looks like you guys need a cab.'

Showing no surprise whatsoever, Adam opened the back door for Billie and ushered her in. He took her case from her, walked round to the boot and opened it, dropping their bags in the back. Then he joined her in the rear, his brown bag on his lap.

'Where to?' asked Frankie.

'The airport,' said Adam.

'Anybody know you're going?'

'Who's going to tell them?'

Frankie looked in the rear-view mirror and saw the Browning in Adam's hand and the lop-sided grin on his face. He was some crazy son of a . . . 'Not me,' he replied emphatically, putting the car into gear and joining the traffic flow. 'I owe you, anyway. I mean, they made me tell them about Fruit Juice. Didn't want to, but I had to.'

'Just get to the airport.'

'No sweat. Where's she going?'

'With me.'

'They gonna ask why.'

'Because she's my security.'

'Is that right?' Frankie asked Billie.

'Yes,' she replied, joining in the charade. 'Bastard forced me. With his fucking gun.'

'You getting into deeper shit. Back off now before this thing really gets ugly.'

'Don't make me repeat myself. Drive to the airport,' snapped Adam.

'Who the hell are you? You more than you seem.'

'So are you, Frankie. Just shut up and drive.'

The rest of the trip was made in silence, though Billie did ask Frankie how his leg was.

'No problem. Just dug the bullet out and bandaged me up. Wanted to give me a fucking anaesthetic. When I said no, they insisted on giving me a local one. In my damn leg. Shit, I've had no feeling in that leg for ten years. And they gave me a fucking anaesthetic.'

Adam directed Frankie to park in the C long-term park area, at the farthest corner under the flyover. He took the key out of the ignition, disarmed the cab driver and took his other weaponry from the glove compartment. Then he opened the bonnet and ripped out the carburettor head. As he pulled out Frankie's wheelchair and crutch he told Billie to get the bags out. He tied Frankie's hands behind him with his necktie. Frankie didn't say a lot, didn't shout in protest. The handkerchief stuffed in his mouth ensured that. It would be a long time before anyone found Frankie.

Using the wheelchair as a trolley, they took their luggage to the main terminal where they hailed another cab.

The cab dropped them at the entrance to New Orleans Station in front of the big AmTrak sign, and Adam led Billie to the booking office. Two queues had formed, one for all the local commuting traffic and the other for the Eastern Regional Pass, the routes that covered the East and Central areas from Grand Rapids to New York, from New Orleans to Miami. The long-distance queue comprised four people and Adam and Billie joined it.

'New York. Two, please,' said Adam to the booking clerk five minutes later.

'You got reservations?'

'No. We only just decided to go by train.' As Adam replied, Billie smiled, impressed with his Deep South accent.

'You need a reservation.'

'Don't you have any cancellations?'

'You gotta wait. Train for New York don't leave till seven in the morning. Won't know till then.'

'That's ten hours away. We can't just hang around till then.'

'Train's only just got in from New York. It's gotta be cleaned for the return trip.'

'Are you sure it's fully booked?'

'Won't know till everyone turns up. People could be booking outta town now. We have no way of knowing, not at this time of night.'

'Can I reserve two? In case someone doesn't turn up.'

'Yeah. We can do that. But you can't board till 5 a.m.'

'OK.'

'Good hotels round about. Should find a bed. You want bedrooms?'

'Yes.'

The clerk reeled off the various coaches and Adam standby-booked a deluxe double Superliner bedroom. The clerk wrote out a Pass and handed it over. 'Pay here at five. If there's any cancellations.'

They found a small hotel, Beiderbeck's, in the next street and booked in as Mr and Mrs Archer from Des Moines, Iowa. Billie giggled as Adam signed the register for the receptionist behind his steel-meshed counter. This was a working hotel for working girls. The clerk insisted they pay twenty dollars in advance. It wasn't the type of establishment where guests spent a whole night.

'What's so funny?' he asked as they climbed the stairs to the first floor.

'I've never booked in to a whorehouse before,' she said.

'Don't worry. I won't ask you to earn the fare to New York.'

The room was small, the walls dark. The bed was a cot and the mattress had long since given up its firmness. There was one wooden-backed chair and a cheap dressing table with a small cracked mirror standing on it. It was the pits, but it was safe.

'Why we going to New York?' she asked, settling on to the end of the bed. He took a cigarette out, but she stopped him. 'Can you *not* do that? In a room, this small . . . '

He shrugged and put the cigarette away. 'Because we can't just catch a plane to Germany. They'll be watching for us.'

'So why New York?'

'To get north. We won't be stopping there.'

'Are you going to tell me how you plan to cross the borders and get over to Europe?'

'Trust me.'

'It could all go wrong.'

'That's what makes it so exciting.'

Billie curled up on top of the bed and eventually snoozed, uneasy in their unfortunate resting place. Adam settled into the chair to pass the night away.

At four-thirty he woke her and, after the most rudimentary of toilet preparations, they left for the station. They were lucky. There had been cancellations and they found themselves climbing on the Crescent train just after five-thirty. Their bedroom far exceeded the hotel room they had just left and Billie settled down gleefully on the single swivel window seat. Adam leant over and drew the curtains shut. He didn't want to be discovered by Carter and his people when they had finally found a way out of New Orleans. She grumbled, but knew he was right. Their escape would've been discovered by now. They were fugitives and Billie enjoyed the sense of adventure that tingled her.

The room, as it was called, was designed for two adults, with a large sofa and a swivel chair. It converted to a bedroom with two fold-down berths, one of which was the sofa, the other folded into the wall. There was also a shower, toilet, sink and cupboard area. It would be a fun way to spend the thirty hours it took to travel to New York. Billie wondered how they would be travelling after that.

'All aboard,' she heard the conductor shout as he walked along the platform, hurrying his charges along. This was his fiefdom, his area of total authority. 'All aboard for Birmingham, Atlanta, Charlotte, Washington, Baltimore, Philadelphia, Newark and Penn Station, New York. All aboard.'

The Crescent pulled out of the station on time at 7 a.m.

Billie finally opened the curtains and settled back to enjoy the view. She had never travelled on a train before.

Frankie, now released from his uncomfortable entrapment, watched the Crescent rattle out of New Orleans. It hadn't taken him long to trace them; he knew his way round the Big Easy better than most. The cab driver who'd taken them to the station had been traced by a radio call and the rest had been simple.

So long sucker. You wuz easier than I thought.

BOOK FOUR

The Long Road Home

CIA HQ
Langley

SORGE HAD NEVER been to Langley before. It was not something a Russian expected to do.

It was after 9 a.m. when Nowak drove him through the gates, past the guards, and into the vast underground car-park.

'Why Langley?' Sorge had asked him on the way out of Washington.

'They want to show you that they trust you.'

'I don't expect I'll see much.'

Nowak laughed. 'Damn right. We park in the underground car-park, catch a special lift to the fifth floor and walk across the corridor into a special conference room.'

'That's trust?'

'That's trust.'

The Executive Director was already in the meeting room. 'Welcome to Langley.' He held his hand out in welcome.

When the introductions were complete, the Exec Director, the DDA, the DDI, Sorge and Nowak settled themselves round the small conference table.

'We have a new problem,' kicked off the Exec Director. 'The English operative who was guarding Trimmler has taken off. He's also taken an agent of ours with him. As hostage. A woman. We believe they're still in New Orleans.'

'Why?' asked Sorge, concerned.

'I don't know yet. What about Goodenache?' He decided to turn the pressure on the Russian.

'He caught a flight to Frankfurt. The he hired a car, but the car was found abandoned on the outskirts of Frankfurt. We are trying to find our missing scientist now.'

'Are the German authorities involved?'

'No. We have our own means.' Sorge saw the Exec Director look up, his eyebrows raised suddenly. 'We both have our methods. Even in an independent Germany. After all, it was the death of our people in these situations that has brought us together.'

The Exec Director shrugged. Bastard Russians were still up to their old tricks. He ignored the pointed look the DDI was giving him. 'I thought it best if the Director of our operations in New Orleans gave you a run down of what has taken place up to now.'

He sat back and let the DDA give a full report, including the trip to the voodoo ceremony and all that followed. Sorge didn't stir, even when they mentioned the gruesome spectacle of Trimmler's arms folded in the sign of a swastika. 'We still aren't convinced that Trimmler's death has anything to do with the death of our agents. There's no definite link.'

'The situation might be clearer when I've finished.' Sorge looked round the table, saw their undisguised curiosity. 'In 1942, in Germany, we had a GRU network named the *Rote Kapelle* . . .'

'What's that?' asked the Exec Director.

'Red Orchestra. The Nazis called it that because we had radio operators we code-named musicians. Their leader, the Chef, we called him, was Leopold Trepper. It was this group that radioed the warning of Operation Blue, the attack on Stalingrad that led to Hitler's biggest wartime disaster on the Russian Front.'

'Who was feeding you all this information in Germany?' asked the Exec Director.

'High-ranking officials. Both in the military and in the Government. They saw the damage Hitler was doing. They didn't disagree with his aims, only his methods. When they saw that the war could not be won, even as early as 1941, some of them opened up lines of communication with us and the British.'

'We didn't get that sort of stuff till late into 1944,' said the DDA.

'You weren't Europeans. We had centuries of contacts to fall back on. For all their bravery and resourcefulness, their

306

information was often wasted, because Stalin didn't believe them. But then, he found it difficult to believe anyone. The Germans, with more sophisticated radio-tracking equipment, started to track down the musicians. Even Trepper was captured and the *Rote Kapelle* was wound up at the end of 1942. Our information continued for a while, but it was of doubtful origin. Trepper was interrogated by the Gestapo and we believed he became a double agent, a lot of misinformation was received in Moscow.' Sorge leant across and finished his coffee before continuing. 'But we still needed information. The overall network with sources inside Germany was the *Rote Drei*.'

'The Red what?' said the Exec Director, pleased that he had deciphered the first word of the new code-name.

'Three. The Red Three. Based in Switzerland and named after the three transmitters that they used. The most important source of information, from agents inside Germany, was from a group under Rudolf Roessler. His code-name was Lucy and his network, the Lucy Ring. Roessler, or Lucy, was a Swiss Intelligence Officer of German extraction. He had many contacts in Germany. Lucy's four main contacts were Major General Oster who was the head of the Abwehr; Admiral Canaris who was later hanged for his part in the 1944 bomb plot; Carl Goehdeler who was leader of the official opposition to Hitler; and Colonel Boetzel, the commanding officer of Intelligence Evaluation. There were others, but Lucy never disclosed any of them to us.'

'Even after the war?' asked the DDI.

'The Lucy Ring was disbanded in 1943, after being responsible for some invaluable work. I won't go through all their successes, but it was substantial. The British were involved with them through us and it was their advanced work on breaking cyphers that enabled the ring to establish such a great record. But the ring disbanded, once more because of Stalin's penchant for secrecy, after Moscow tried to bypass Roessler and go direct to his Number Two.'

'So, where's the link?' interrupted the DDA, impatient as ever.

'It's important you understand the background,' said Sorge, not allowing the American to get under his skin. 'Nothing further came from the ring until the last few weeks of the war. With the Allies advancing on the Eastern and Western fronts, many high-ranking Germans were out to save their own necks. The Lucy Ring was reactivated, this time without the knowledge of the British.'

'Or the Americans,' commented the Exec Director.

'I suggest you take that up with Comrade Stalin,' replied Sorge drily. 'It was an impressive list. They didn't just have knowledge. They also had wealth. In all forms. Art, cash, in every form possible. They used the ring because of their line into Switzerland. They wanted the security of the Swiss banks and the Russian Bear. One was dependent on the other.'

'So they bought immunity. While our boys were still getting killed,' snapped the DDI.

'As were ours,' snapped back Sorge. 'But your hands weren't that clean. You were bringing scientists and others into America just as we were. Scientists with Nazi records, scientists with a history of brutality, war criminals.'

'Gentlemen, please,' said Nowak, ever the diplomat. 'Can we just stick to what we're here to discuss? Go on, Dimitri.'

Sorge was annoyed with himself, irritated that he had allowed the Intelligence man to get under his skin. 'Of course,' he smiled back. 'Now . . . ah, yes . . . we used the Lucy Ring. Many Germans, with their prizes, crossed safely into Switzerland. They came in cars, army lorries, even an aeroplane. Their riches were stored in the banks under private accounts and then they were brought through Czechoslovakia and East Germany into the Soviet Union.'

'All of them?' asked the DDA.

'Those who broke their word were hunted down.'

'And disposed of?'

'Some needed reminding that we expected them to honour their word.' It was a cold reminder of their world, of the business they traded in daily. 'We had a large colony of Nazis living in the Soviet Union. They weren't all scientists, in fact we had little use for most of them. They had their own estates and farms to the west of Moscow. They kept their secret identities and paid for it through their Swiss bank accounts. But they remained Germans, always dreaming of going back to the Fatherland one day.'

'How many Nazis did you take to Russia after the war?'

'The Narodnyi Kommissariat Vnutrennikh Del, our People's Commissariat for Internal Affairs, was responsible for —'

'I never heard of them,' the DDA stopped him.

'NKVD,' explained the DDI patronizingly. 'Wiped out twenty million Russians for Stalin. That right?' he challenged Sorge.

'More. Thirty million. According to official sources,' Sorge riposted. 'A most useful organization.' That should shut them up. He felt the look of disbelief pass between the Exec Director and the DDA. The other just watched him, the mocking smile still on his lips. He would be the one Rostov had warned him to be wary of. He decided to wipe the smile off his face. 'Thirty thousand. That's how many East Germans we deported into the Soviet Union after the war.'

The DDI's smile disappeared. 'Thirty thousand Nazis? Jesus.'

'Yes. And we kept another hundred and twenty thousand between 1945 and 1954 in Hitler's old concentration camps. Many were Nazis, but businessmen and professionals were also our targets. A third of those died. The others were eventually released and absorbed into the Democratic Republic.'

'Including Nazi sympathizers?'

'Probably.'

'Doesn't that concern you?'

Sorge shrugged. 'Not really. I was eight years old at the time.' It wasn't the answer that the DDI expected and Sorge regretted his words. He wasn't here to make jokes. 'The thirty thousand in the Soviet Union, as I said, became a community in their own right. Without our knowledge, over the years, with the use of their money and supportive people in the Swiss banks, they forged contacts with those left behind in East Germany. They all had one dream. To see a unified Germany. To regain what they had lost. They had a code-name amongst themselves. Something that linked them, was a reminder of how they had got there. It had to be a safe name, innocuous, nothing that would draw attention to the past. They remembered the Lucy network, their gateway out of Germany. They called themselves *Die Lucie Geister*.'

'The Lucy Ghosts.'

'Yes.'

'Did the organization extend to America?' The Exec Director was alarmed. How the hell did they . . .

'Goodenache. I guess he was one of them?' asked the DDI.

'We weren't sure, but in view of his sudden departure, I would say yes.'

'Which ties Trimmler in. And God knows who else. The name Grob Mitzer mean anything?'

'He was one of their leaders. It was the Lucy Ghosts who supplied him with the cash that helped him build his empire.'

'Why didn't you stop it? Damn it, you knew about it for long enough,' snapped the Exec Director.

'We didn't realize how important it was. We thought they were like any other wartime group, nothing more than reminiscences and marching songs. Old men remembering their youth. The importance of it didn't surface until Germany was reunified. And it was only the Englishman overhearing the conversation between Goodenache and Trimmler that finally bridged the gap.'

'So why should the English guy take off with the girl?' The DDI changed the subject.

'He's not one of us. I suggest you ask your Allies about that. Maybe he's just an adventurer. No more. You must have cleared him.'

'Of course.' The Exec Director didn't want his dirty washing wrung out in front of this Russian. 'Was there anything else?'

'Only that the GDR, East Germany, as it was, is different to the West. There are still many there who haven't forgotten the war. Their attitude is different to us. Some are still waiting for the war to end. They're a traditional people. Many ex-Nazis, even Gestapo, working and living normal everyday lives.'

'Working for the Stasi.' The DDI reminded them all of the secret police who had run East Germany with an iron fist.

'Some, yes. Others returned to the jobs they had before the

war. Within the new Germany, many of them have become frightened. Their secrets are no longer safe. Most of all, they fear the Israelis.'

'Is Frick one of these guys?' asked the DDA, remembering the name picked up by Adam in New Orleans.

'No,' lied Sorge. His orders were quite specific. Don't ratify any names. They didn't want the Yanks stumbling in and screwing up in an attempt to force the issue.

'So what's all this got to do with the deaths of our agents?' continued the DDA.

'We're not sure. Except that a lot of the information we have both lost was about the Lucy Ghosts. Link that with Trimmler's death, Goodenache's sudden departure for Germany and the mention of the Lucy Ghosts during their conversation, and I think you will agree that is the strongest lead we have to follow.'

Nobody spoke for a while, then the Exec Director re-opened the discussion. 'Has Moscow any suggestions as to how we should proceed?'

'No,' replied Sorge, which was what he'd been told to say. 'We hoped you would come up with something.'

'I'm sure we will.'

'Can you tell us the names of some of these Lucy Ghosts?' cut in the DDI. 'The ones in Russia. How high up the ladder did they go?'

Sorge enjoyed his reply. 'In time, yes. But I can tell you you're wasting your efforts looking for Martin Boorman in South America. He died twenty years ago.'

He watched their stunned faces across the room. Well and truly shafted.

They said little after that and Sorge was soon being escorted, with Nowak, down to the underground garage. Five minutes later they were on their way back to Washington.

'Boorman. Fucking Boorman. They had him all the time,' said an astonished DDI. 'Would'ya believe it? They probably got Hitler stashed away too.'

'Well, it's been a real eye-opener,' said the Exec Director. 'But let's not forget we've still got a crisis on. Find the Englishman. That's our first priority. Find him and see what the son of a bitch is up to.'

The AmTrak Crescent
Atlanta
Georgia

THE TRAIN PULLED out of Atlanta Station at 7.39 p.m., four minutes behind schedule.

They had slept well, eaten well, slept again and eventually got bored with the passing countryside. Adam had insisted they stay in the room and she hadn't found a good enough reason to change his mind.

He was thumbing through *USA Today* for the umpteenth time, looking for something he might have missed, when he heard her giggling. She was in the swivel chair, reflected in the window with the dark night as a backdrop, her head angled towards him.

'What's so funny?' he asked pleasantly, putting the paper down.

'You sure know how to give a girl a good time.'

'Don't I?' he grinned back.

'According to all the books, a secret agent's life's meant to be glamorous. We've spent twenty-four hours together and in that time I've been bitten by bugs in a hooker's bed, tied up a guy with no legs and stolen his wheelchair, stayed cooped up in a train for twelve hours with an attractive man and behaved like a virgin. Don't take that the wrong way. But James Bond would've handled it differently.'

'He was Scottish. I'm English. They prefer the ram 'em and bang 'em method. We're more sophisticated in our approach.'

'What happens next?'

'In which department?'

'In the where're-we-going department.'

'To Nordhausen. That's where Trimmler said he would meet Goodenache.'

'Trimmler's dead.'

'And Goodenache's running from the Russians. He can't go back there. From what I heard, Germany was still their home. And Nordhausen was where they shared something special. They wanted to go there. If Goodenache's frightened, and he wants to hide, that's as good a place as any.'

'Nordhausen. Where is that?'

'Central Germany. South of Berlin, near what was the old East-West border. An industrial town. It was also where the Nazis built most of their rockets, the V1s and V2s, during the Second World War. From what I remember, they moved most of the rocket manufacture down there so that our bombers couldn't get to them. Built the factory right in the heart of the mountains. Used slave labour. I think a lot of people died in the making of those weapons, before they ever got launched and blew up half of London.'

'Why would they want to go back there?'

'Who knows. Maybe it was a job they never finished.'

'But they did. Those guys put people into space, put our people on the moon. That's enough for most people.'

'That was just their work. And they didn't do it for Germany. They did it for their conquerors.'

'You telling me that all those scientists spent their time in America and couldn't wait to get home?'

'Not all of them. Most of them became good Americans. And good Russians, I suppose. But these two wanted to go home. They never stopped being Germans. Maybe it's the only thing they ever dreamt about.'

'Weird.'

'Is it? To want to go home?'

'All they're after is their youth. Catching up with what they thought they'd lost.'

'Aren't we all?'

She shrugged and looked thoughtful.

'Penny for them,' he said.

'I was . . . uh . . . just being a woman.'

'Tell me.'

'Thinking of Peter.'

'Ah! The venerable ex.'

'I know. Here's us, heading for trouble and God knows what else, and in the middle of you talking about Nordhausen, I start thinking of Peter. Wondering what the hell he's up to. The emotional mind of a woman.'

'Stop knocking yourself.'

'Makes a change. I usually leave that to you.'

He burst out laughing.

'OK, tough guy. What's got you so tickled?'

'Here we are, crammed in a small compartment in a train, hurtling across America being chased by the CIA, the FBI and god knows who else, and you're worried about your ex-husband's sex life. Christ, he must've been good.'

'He was a shit.'

'So, why . . .?' Adam stopped and shook his head.

'Because some of us like shits. Don't ask me why.' She laughed with him. 'He's cheap, too. He once bought me a Louis Vuitton handbag. Your travel case reminded me of it when we left the hotel. It was for our second anniversary. I broke the lock and took it back to the shop in La Jolla. They told me it was a fake. A fucking Hong Kong fake. Can you believe that?'

'What did he say?'

'That he'd bought it in New York when he was there on a visit. And if he could remember where the shop was, he'd go back and sue the bastards. That's Peter for you. A cheapskate liar and womanizer. And I can't let him go. That's really pathetic news. Isn't it?'

'No. Just human.'

'Very understanding. What would you know?'

'Maybe not women, but . . . my parents. And my twin brother.'

'You're a twin?'

'Was. They all died when I was nine.'

'You said they were out of the country. That you had guardians.'

'We all have things to hide.'

'Was he an identical twin?'

'Yes.'

'That means you came from the same egg. That right?'

'Something like that.' He, in his usual stoical manner, didn't

314

tell her that he had studiously learnt everything about twins and their relationships.

'I had a boyfriend in High School. He was a twin and his brother played on the football team. If he got hurt, my guy used to suffer, too. We used to watch the game together and I'd suddenly see him wince in pain. Just like that. And I'd look on the field and it was his brother who'd been tackled.'

'Yes. Something like that.' He laughed. 'I remember once getting a tap round the head from my dad. I'd done something wrong. I remember him saying it was a shame that he had to punish us both when only one of us was being naughty. That tap sorted us both out.'

'Do you still feel he's with you?'

'He is.'

'Then you're lucky. You're not alone. Is that so bad?'

'I don't know why I'm alive and he's dead.'

'What's his name?'

'Marcus.'

'Nice name. I'm glad you've got someone to love. It's important.'

The Kremlin
Moscow

THEY CAME OUT into the corridor together, Rostov holding back as he allowed the older and more senior man to go before him.

'Your head's on the block,' said the Director as Rostov caught him up. 'You know that, don't you?'

The younger man shrugged. It came with the stripes he wore on his shoulder.

They walked along, slowly, at the old man's pace. This was

not the place to talk, here in the corridors of power where every wall had ears.

'Not a job I would want,' said the Director, 'being President at this time. With all the problems we have between the republics. But then, there are always problems. It is not a job I would *ever* want.'

They had spent half an hour with the President, the Director sitting back and letting Rostov take him through all the details of the last few weeks.

'A confused sequence of events,' the President had said when Rostov finished. 'No doubt there is a logic to it. There always is. My main concern, after the safety of our people, is to ensure that the Americans and ourselves don't turn on one other. It's always difficult to trust old enemies. When I meet with the American President in Berlin, I want him to believe he can trust me.'

He said little more, only asked to be kept informed. He respected the American President. He didn't want this to come between them.

'He doesn't totally trust them either,' the Director said to Rostov as they came out into the open. It was a bright day and the official Zil lurched towards them. The Director waved the driver to stop where he was. There were still things to be said out of earshot. 'But he has to try. Just like we do. And, I suppose, the Americans. It was easier in the old days. We knew where we were. Now, in this time of peace, it's a fragile trust. So easy to be tested and broken. I hope it went well for Dimitri Dimitrovitch.'

'His report should be ready when I get back.'

'Was it wise to tell them about Boorman?'

'It was only a titbit. To excite them.'

'I suppose they'll think we have Hitler as well.'

'Our sources always reported that they believed Boorman had come here. He was seen by that general's daughter.'

'He was seen everywhere. Excellent misinformation. Now that they know about the money, there is always a possibility that they'll tell the Germans. They could ask for its return.'

'That's between them and the Swiss Banks. What's left of it.'

The Director laughed. 'Not much. It all helped fund Stalin's five-year plan.' He paused, then turned to the younger man. 'The Lucy Ghosts. It's important they don't leave Russia. Not until this matter is settled.'

'We deported over thirty thousand Germans after the war. It's not going to be easy. Not in this time of *perestroika*.'

'I know. I know. But Germany has been peaceful because the East Prussians were under our control. You know ... as I do ... that the Prussians have always been the war-mongers. We cannot allow them ... the neo-Nazis ... to stir up trouble. Not at a time when the rest of Germany is in turmoil, when the economy is struggling.'

'Neo-Nazis ... it's in the Prussian's nature. That won't change, however rich they become.'

'Are you sure you are taking the right course of action?' The Director couldn't ask what it was, not without implicating himself if it went wrong.

'Yes.'

'And if it fails?'

'That will be my mistake.'

'It's a sad moment when a man realizes he is expendable.'

'I won't be the first.'

'No. We've all been through it. When you have to stand by your own actions. You appreciate why, don't you?'

'Yes. Nothing must damage the relationship between us and the West.'

'If it works, nothing will ever be known. If it doesn't, then ...' he shrugged. They both knew that was the end for Rostov. The Director signalled his car over. 'Are you coming back with me?'

'No, sir. I want to walk. It's a nice day.'

'To church?'

'To church.'

'Well, I hope He can help where the rest of the KGB can't.' The old man instantly regretted his mocking answer. 'Take care. Come and see me when you're back. With Dimitri Dimitrovitch's report.'

Rostov walked out of the Kremlin, past the KGB guards with their blue-ribboned caps, and along the river. He mixed with the tourists and other passers-by, enjoyed being nobody in a bustling city.

He thought of the action he had instigated. He knew it was dangerous, knew that his only hope was to flush them out.

All they could do was watch and wait, trigger off several fuses and watch them burn until one of them, hopefully, ran its full course. His instinct told him the Englishman's disappearance was the best chance. He wasn't in hiding. He wasn't the type. He was after something. He could be their salvation.

He would pray for the Englishman's safety.

He needed all the help he could get.

Dresdener *Heide*
Dresden

THE AMTRAK CRESCENT was stopping at Culpeper, Virginia, when Peter Frick called the council meeting to order.

The twelve were there, in the big room that had once served as a dining room in this grand old house. Frick sat at the head of the long table, in his rightful place as their leader. Helmut Kragan sat on his right, his seat away from the table, as befitted the recorder of minutes who wasn't a council member.

'We are' – Frick said, after a long pause, well over half a minute, until he was certain he had everyone's fullest attention – 'at the beginning of history. All we have waited for is now possible. Germany is divided. Reunification has resurrected the class structure, not based on background, but on wealth. The haves and have nots. That is the clay we work with. It is our duty, as National Socialists, to unite Germany. To give those who have, the security to keep what they have earned. And to give those less fortunate, the ability to lift themselves into the prosperity that is the right of all Germans.'

He looked round the room slowly at the other eleven council members. Karl Schiller sat on his immediate left. He was the newest member of the council, hurriedly elected to replace Mitzer in a series of anxious and hushed telephone calls. He

318

was an investment banker and financier, in his early fifties, with contacts and influence into all reaches of Industry and Government. A new German, with a formidable international reputation in the United States and Japan, having developed, through his investments, a wide array of associates in the upper echelons of those countries.

Frick knew that Schiller was also greedy. His family had owned considerable estates in the East, lost after the First World War when raging inflation destroyed his grandfather's estate. Lost to a rich Jewish family who were eventually to die in the concentration camps after Hitler had promised to return the estate to his father for duties performed. But the end of the Second World War and the separation of East Germany under Russian control brought that agreement to an abrupt conclusion. As soon as Reunification came about, Schiller applied for the return of his family's estates. He was horrified to find that a British grocery family, close relatives of the Jews who had taken over his lands, had title to the property. The will that gave them title had been written on a torn-out page of a 1938 diary, the only paper available when the family learnt of their imminent fate in the gas chamber. The estate had been willed to another prisoner, a distant cousin, on the clear understanding that should it ever be returned to Jewish hands, the monies and profits taken from it would be devoted to the creation of a Zionist state. The estate itself was to be used for the well-being of those Jews who had also suffered at the hands of the Nazis and other oppressors of the faith.

Schiller now found himself fighting those whom his father had always taught him were responsible for the break-up of Germany and all she had stood for. They were thieves, and once again they would be stealing the land that was not theirs, the land and estates that were Karl Schiller's by right of inheritance.

He had been a keen and willing convert to the cause, his hatred fuelled by Grob Mitzer whom he knew and trusted as a friend and corporate colleague. Over the past few years, he had helped fund the Party, had worked closely with Mitzer in building a financial base from which their dreams of a new Germany could be launched. Mitzer's death had stunned him, but not for too long. Within half an hour he had contacted those he trusted on the council and given a good account as to why he should fill the vacant seat. His last call had been to Frick, the man he knew that he must convince.

'I hadn't considered you ready for the council yet,' said Frick, when Schiller had finished. He lied, for the financier was the obvious choice. He knew Schiller's history, knew his greed for what he felt was rightfully his, knew of his birthright hatred of the Jews. They had known each other for some considerable time and Frick trusted Schiller as much as he could trust any man.

Schiller had pleaded, once again going through the many reasons why it was right for him to gain a seat on the council. Then he pledged loyalty to Frick and to his leadership. When he had begged enough, when there was nothing else to repeat, Frick had appeared to surrender to Schiller's request. That would guarantee the financier's loyalty.

'When we come to power, my dear Schiller,' Frick had concluded, 'we shall return what is rightfully theirs to those who have supported us. That is the least we can do.' Over the phone he sensed Schiller's shiver of anticipation.

Now Frick continued his scrutiny of the room. He paused at Klaus Buhle, the Frankfurt *Daily News* proprietor and television-station owner. More pressure would have to be applied in that area, before the newspapers started to look in the direction of the National Socialists. Buhle must point the finger at the other radical groups. Other newspapers would follow his example, the media was well known for its sheep-like character.

'But,' Frick went on, 'if we are to take our rightful place in history, then it's time we came out of the woodwork.' He paused, sensed their uneasiness. They were used to working in the dark; they had become a secret society. They had sat with their friends and heard the vilification of Hitler and the Third Reich at dinner parties, in the cinemas, on television and in books and newspapers. Nazi-hating had become big business. And they had kept their counsel, never spoken out about their own beliefs.

And now they were being asked to come out in the open.

He felt them shudder; they were in the tunnel and the thunder of the oncoming express train was rattling the rails.

'We have nothing to be ashamed of,' he stated, clinical in his delivery. Now was not the time for emotion, but for logic. 'We can't always apologize for the past. Germany has moved forward. If we're not careful, we will always be looked on as yesterday's men.'

He stood up, aware of them all watching him. They were scared men, even Schiller was ramrod straight in his seat. What the hell had they expected, after all these years?

'It's easy to be frightened,' Frick said as he walked round the table, behind them, their eyes following him. 'I, also, am frightened. But we mustn't let our fear overcome our purpose, our duty. There have been far greater forces of darkness in our land than the Third Reich. The Americans, the British, the French. Even the poodle French. They told us how to live our lives, occupied us until we lived our life their way. Whatever nice things they said to our face, they always had their troops in the background, on our soil, waiting to beat us if we suddenly changed our minds. And we had the Russians. They hid their dark deeds behind the Wall. But they still raped our country, disgraced us, pissed all over us for the crimes of fifty years ago. And, however bad their crimes against us were, they always justified them by saying ours were worse. We became two countries. Two countries, until the will of the people decided we'd had enough and they went out in their hundreds of thousands and pulled the Wall down. With their hands. Like I did. On that great night, I stood with them and chipped away with my bare hands, until my fingers were bleeding, to bring down that iniquitous wall. But, like Nietzsche said, no herdsman and one herd. They have earned their freedom and don't know how to spend it. Our people need direction. And while they're looking for that direction, they are vulnerable. Vulnerable to the rabble rousers, to the Communists, to the Fascists, even to the hated Zionists. You've seen the riots in Berlin, the destruction of the synagogues, even the bomb that killed Grob Mitzer. Surely his death must show you that we can't stay hidden any longer. That it is time for us to take our rightful place. Time for us to be the herdsmen. We have the means. We even have our own secret police. The Stasi, Hoenicker's secret police, have been good *Sturmabteilungen* for us. An army of men with nowhere to go.'

As he looked round, he saw that his words were starting to have some effect. One or two of the older members were nodding in agreement. They had waited for so long that some of them had forgotten what they were waiting for.

'Do you know how many Stasi members there were?' he asked suddenly. 'Do you?'

'More than twenty thousand, mein Führer,' said Buhle, putting himself at the top of the class.

'More than that, my dear Klaus. That's how many full-time staff there were. There were another ninety thousand part-timers. Members of the reserves, the Army, informers and part-time officials. Imagine. We have an army of more than one hundred thousand trained soldiers to choose from. That is bigger than the whole British army. Not all will come with us. But even if only one in four follows us, we will have nearly thirty thousand people under our command.'

'A unique position,' commented Buhle.

'Unique indeed. To have that and also face a Germany which is being torn apart. It must have been the same in the early days of the Reich.' He appealed to their greed for power. 'Imagine. The day he came to power.' They all knew who 'he' was. 'Imagine. After all the turmoil, after the years of shame, to be in a position where power is absolute, where the future of Germany is in your hands. Can't you see him? Standing there, in Berlin, being sworn in as Chancellor in 1933. What a momentous time, what a magnificent occasion. Surrounded by his lieutenants, his architects of government. Believe, and it can happen again.' He urged them into his vision. 'Believe. Believe. All this can be ours. But it won't jump into our laps. It's a prize we have to take. And to take it, we have to show ourselves. Otherwise, all we've believed in, all that we and those before us have suffered for, will be wasted. Our time will not come again.'

He went back to his seat at the head of the table.

'Reunification . . . cannot be wasted.' It was the newest member of the council, Schiller, who spoke. The others looked up in surprise. They had not expected the newcomer to speak so soon. 'Grob Mitzer, our friend, my closest friend, gave his life for this chance. So have countless others, thousands upon thousands who have waited, and many have died, in South America and Africa and other hideous, secret parts of the world. They have, throughout their exiles, sent us money and resources to help us fuel our movement. Our Führer is right. Delay means termination. I, like many of you, have so much to lose if this goes wrong. I don't want them to brand me a bully-boy because I'm a National Socialist, to discredit me through their media. But the prize is worth the risk.'

'Well spoken,' applauded Frick. 'Bravo. Well spoken. We are all respected men. We all have positions of influence. But as anarchy increases, so we will be expected to use that influence. Klaus Buhle, through his papers and television interests, can sow the seed for us. He can defend us, can separate us from the past, from the concentration camps and lost wars. He can compare Germany with what it was in the Thirties. The National Socialists led us out of depression then, and the National Socialists can do it again. We're not warmongers, but liberationists. Fighting for the values of our heritage. The media will make us respectable.' He already knew that Mitzer's record was under scrutiny, but that could wait. Buhle was bringing that situation under control. 'Against the anarchists, and the Communists, that is the only way they can portray us. And with your names leading the Party, how can we be taken as warmongers and murderers?'

'That's if the riots and bombings continue,' said Swingler, one of the old crowd. 'The police say they have everything under control.'

'They always say that,' replied Frick. 'They have no idea what's going on.' He didn't add that he was responsible for much of the terrorist acts, and that he would ensure they continued. 'These things always run on longer than people imagine.'

'Even so,' Swingler persisted, 'it's the Lucy Ghosts who'll haunt us. It's their money that made this possible. When they return, their records will brand them as war criminals. Associate with them and we'll be attacked as Nazis.'

'We leave them where they are. Until we're in power.'

'But they want to come back now.'

'They must wait their turn.'

'They've waited a long time. In their swamps and forests, hidden from the world.'

'Then they'll have to wait longer. There's nothing I can do about that.'

'But we spent millions on destroying their records. We—'

'*Willi Kushmann* spent millions. Wasted money. I had the highest regard for him, but he was a dreamer. Now's the time to be practical Realists. The only way to bring back the Lucy Ghosts is to prepare a Germany that wants them back. Help win this fight and we'll have them back sooner than you expect.'

Newark Station
New Jersey

THEY NEVER COMPLETED the train journey to Penn Station.

Adam insisted that they left the AmTrak Crescent at its penultimate stop in New Jersey. They ate an early lunch, packed their bags and stepped off the train at 1.19 p.m. Adam was impressed; the train, after nearly thirty hours and one thousand miles, was only two minutes late.

They heard the final 'All aboard' as they left the station and took a cab to Teterborough Airport. It was some distance and they refrained from talking throughout the hour-long trip.

Teterborough serves private aircraft with the same intensity that Le Guardia and Kennedy serve the commercial routes in and out of New York. As executive jets and smaller piston-engined aircraft fly the final approach to Teterborough's runways, the twin towers of the World Trade Center in Manhattan are only five miles away.

Almost touch them with my hand, thought Jenny Dale as she looked out on the skyscrapers, then turned her attention to flying the small, six-seater, twin-engined Piper Seneca on to the final approach. She had maintained two thousand feet for the last five miles.

'Cleared to land,' crackled the tower operator over her headset.

'Roger.' She eased back on the twin-power throttles and pushed the mixture and prop levers fully forward.

She looked to her right once again, savoured Manhattan outlined against the afternoon sky. She smiled, it was a good feeling to be in charge of your own destiny. She thought of all the rats scurrying through the streets, hustling for a crust. It was good to be a flyer, up above it all, godlike in your vision. She pushed the yoke forward and the plane's nose dipped as it started descending towards the runway.

Jenny Dale, dark-haired, tall with a buxom figure, and twenty-nine years old, was a ferry pilot from Dagenham in Essex. She had been flying for twelve years, had studied with her father who flew Concorde as a senior British Airways captain, and had soloed on her seventeenth birthday. Flying was in her blood; she was the son her parents had never had. After she gained her private pilot's licence, she was an instructor at a flying school at Biggin Hill before sitting for her commercial ticket at the age of twenty-one. By then she had accumulated over two thousand hours.

But commercial flying in bloody great buses in the sky never appealed to her. She was an adventuress and she soon turned to ferrying. The easiest way to deliver a plane that someone has purchased is to fly it to them. As most light aircraft are either made in the United States, or sold on the second-hand market there, she learnt to fly the Atlantic in small planes. The northern route from Canada to Europe often included landing in Greenland and Iceland. It was a difficult journey, especially in the winter months when the vagaries of intemperate and often violent weather meant that remote airports could be closed down within minutes.

It was an exciting, yet dangerous, life, but one that suited her nature.

She greased the Seneca on to the runway and cleared left, towards the small, but busy, terminal and the parking ramps in front of it.

'To the top,' she told the refueller, 'and that includes the ferry tanks inside.' She opened the double rear doors and pointed out the two forty-five-gallon tanks which were her emergency supply if an airport closed down on her. They were lashed together, upright and side by side, between the rear four seats. A series of switches and fuel locks allowed the pilot to change tanks in mid-flight.

She left the refueller and walked into the terminal.

'Hallo,' said the Englishman as she helped herself to a mug of courtesy coffee at the desk.

'Hi,' she smiled back.

'You going across the pond?' he asked.

'Yes.'

'Where?'

'Manchester.'

'Could do with a lift.'

'Not insured for it.'

'Worth a thousand pounds to you.'

'Why?'

'Just fancy it. Never done it before and we fancy the trip.'

'We?'

'My friend,' he pointed to where the woman sat, 'and me.'

'People try and get drugs through this way. We're told not to do it.'

'I'm a soldier.' He showed her his passport and warrant card. 'Not a drug dealer.'

'Can't you manage more than a grand? I'm just a simple working girl, you know.'

'Fifteen hundred?'

She nodded. 'OK. Be ready to go in half an hour. She'll have to sit in the back. Bit cramped, but I need the heavier weight up front. Weight and balance of the plane.'

Adam knew she was lying. She just wanted male company to talk to.

'No problem,' he said and went back to Billie. 'We've got a lift.'

'Why this way?' she asked.

'Because your Customs and Immigration never check on people leaving the country. Only on those coming in. This

326

way we won't be on any ticket manifesto, not until we get across to Europe.'

'Smart.'

He introduced Billie to Jenny and saw her disappointment when the pilot explained she'd have to sit in the back with the ferry tanks. She would be even more disillusioned when she saw how limited the space actually was.

Forty minutes later the small plane, now over its weight limit, due to the extra passengers, clawed its way into the sky, its two, turbo-charged, 220 horsepower engines screaming at full power, and headed northwards at eleven thousand feet towards Canada and its overnight destination of Goose Bay, Labrador.

It was an eight-hundred-mile trip, flown in murky conditions with moderate turbulence. They rarely saw the ground, only snatches of lakes or wooded countryside appearing through the rare break in the stratus cloud.

The twenty-knot tailwind helped, and their airspeed of two hundred knots reduced the journey to just over four hours.

That was four hours too long for Billie wedged in behind the ferry tanks. The bumpiness had churned her stomach and given her a headache, but she kept her complaints to herself. She started to regret her impulsiveness in joining a wild-goose obstacle chase.

Up front, Adam watched the girl handle the plane with an ease that comes only with experience. She had left the plane on autopilot as they flew north over Massachusetts, Maine and crossed the border into Canada at Presque Isle. As she flew, Jenny explained to Adam how the controls worked, let him manoeuvre the plane on the co-pilot's yoke. His handling was light on feel and positive in action.

'You sure you've not flown before?' Jenny asked him, obviously impressed with his instinctive handling skills.

'No.' He didn't add that controlling the Seneca was child's play compared to the brute force of the Ferrari F40. Wow! It was good to be in control of a powerful machine again.

They came in to land in a snowscape, the lights along the thin ribbon of recently cleared runway coming into view and stretching out in front of them as the Seneca descended on its final approach. She had already explained the full landing procedures, the control of the plane by power and rudder, the way the ailerons were only used to hold the plane level. She kept her hand on the pilot's yoke and followed through on his movements in case of trouble, but without any qualms he greased the Seneca on to the eleven-thousand-foot Runway 27 at Goose Bay.

She then took control and taxied off the runway as three Canadian Air Force F11s blasted into the sky on a training mission farther to the north. As she taxied in to the small civilian terminal, Adam watched the three fighter planes ease their pointed noses skyward and climb at over thirty thousand feet a minute. Now that was power. His F40 was a Dinky toy compared to them.

Billie couldn't believe the cold and she rushed towards the warmth of the terminal. Adam and Jenny followed her, carrying the bags.

'Are you crew?' asked the Customs man.

'Yes.' Adam indicated Billie who was now stretching her legs in the terminal. 'She's my girl. She's along for the ride.'

'We're off at the crack of dawn,' added Jenny.

Customs nodded. He was doubling for Immigration who had gone home to babysit while his wife went to the movies with her sister. He signalled the three of them through. No record was made of their arrival. But then ferry flights were the order of the day at Goose.

Both the Aurora Hotel and Labrador Inn were fully booked and the cab driver finally deposited them at the Royal Inn. They were lucky; there were two rooms and the women decided to share.

Adam was in Room 17, little knowing that this was where the Russian agent Hans Putiloff had been killed in the early days of this affair. He locked the door, showered and freshened up for supper. When he left his room, he knocked on the women's door; he would wait for them in the small restaurant at the front of the hotel.

They joined him ten minutes later. He was at the bar, audaciously flirting with the shapeless young waitress in the even more shapeless sweater. She was enjoying every minute of it; men of this calibre were not something you came across every day, especially in Happy Valley, Goose Bay.

'I'm having mooseburger,' he said, directing them to the table by the window. 'Mooseburger! What about that?'

The waitress took their orders. Her dream of an exciting evening had abruptly disappeared.

The discussion was general; Jenny talked about her flying experiences whilst Billie reminisced about the warmth of her native Southern California. It was easy to do, as she shivered and looked out of the window at the thick snow that reflected the street lights upwards. She had come totally unprepared for the northern climes and, at Adam's insistence, had bought some clothes near to Newark on their way to Teterborough Airport. Her new coat was now firmly wrapped round her as she waited for her meal.

'You two spend time together?' she heard Jenny say as they sipped their coffees.

'No. We're good friends,' replied Adam, knowing what she meant.

'That's wrong,' interjected Billie. 'It's, we're *just* good friends.'

'What are you doing travelling together?' Jenny pressed them.

'Seeing the world.'

'There's got to be easier ways than this.'

'A sense of adventure!' exclaimed Adam.

'Rubbish.' Jenny turned to Billie. 'This is the last place you want to be. You don't like the cold. You hate it. All you have to do is hire a plane out of here and go back south. You could have both gone direct to England from New York. But you wanted to come up this way. If you think this is cold, you wait till we hit Greenland. With the chill factor it's nearly minus forty. It's only minus ten here. Are you two on the run or something?'

Later, when the women let themselves into their own room, Billie sensed she was being watched.

'Something the matter?' she asked Jenny.

'You sure there's nothing between the two of you?'

'I'm sure.'

'Then why're you along with him? He's the sort who travels alone.'

'How do you know?'

'You recognize your own.'

'I just wanted to. It seemed a good idea at the time.'

'Doesn't seem enough reason. Why don't you go next door?'

Billie was taken aback by the girl's directness. 'I'm not here for that.' She hated her own prim words. Shit, she was too old for this. With a fucking twenty-nine year old.

'You sure?'

'Of course I'm sure.'

'Then do you mind if I go?'

The directness shocked her. The girl was doing what she wanted to do. If it hadn't been so fucking cold. 'No,' she heard herself reply. *Yes. Yes. I do mind.*

'OK. I'll see you later,' said Jenny. 'Mind you, he could toss me out. You never know with some people.'

Billie heard Jenny knock on Adam's door, heard it open and close again. She waited for a while, then she undressed and climbed into bed, the coat thrown over the top to add extra warmth. Her head lay next to the thin wall that separated her from the two of them.

She didn't want to hear, but she held her breath and listened for any sound.

The bed creaked, and she lay even stiller, listening intently, conjuring up the pictures the sounds made in her own mind.

'Don't do anything. I'm in charge,' she heard Jenny say. It was all so terribly clear. She hated it and listened harder.

He laughed. The bastard laughed. He was enjoying it. You stupid dame, Billie told herself, what did you expect?

'You always like being in charge?' she heard him ask.

'Always. You sods don't have the automatic right to do it your way. Keep still,' warned Jenny. 'Don't fucking move.'

Billie lay there, imagining Adam with that smart-arse grin across his face, as he watched the girl abuse his body, lick it from toe to top. 'Keep still, you bastard, I told you.' She would be playing with his genitals with her tongue and then her fingers, building his erection. Was he fucking circumcised? They were prettier that way. Work him up and down while she licked the rest of his body, work her way up, lift herself over him, her fingers now slipping inside herself.

'Lick, now lick me and what I am ...' Ready and wet for him. Slide on top of him and slip him into her, gasp with the pleasure and the size of him, warn him to keep still as she reached her first wet climax on top of him, side to side, circular motion, up and down ... 'Keep still, you bastard, keep fucking still.'

The sounds built, the creaks got louder, her mind was absorbed with the two of them together. She turned on her back and slipped her fingers between her legs. She felt the wetness spread, down over her fingers and her thighs. She was drowning in her own juices as they soaked the sheet. The sound from next door had risen to a mechanical drumbeat, like a pneumatic drill hammering away, it was him, banging and banging away at Jenny, she could almost hear the girl's screams. Shit, shit, shit. Why did she always have to fuck herself ... Why?

'You all right?' said Jenny, shaking her.

'What?' Billie came awake, wondered where she was, saw the girl looking at her with concern. She quickly sat up in the bed, the blanket wrapped round her.

'Are you all right?' repeated Jenny.

Billie nodded. She'd been dreaming. But the wetness was still there, all over her.

'You're too hot,' continued Jenny, lifting the coat Billie had placed for extra warmth on her bed. 'You don't need this. It may be cold outside, but these people know how to keep warm inside.'

'What's the time?' Billie was fanning herself with the blanket to cool the sweat that was running down her body. She'd damn well been dreaming.

'Just gone eleven.'

'You're back soon.'

Jenny laughed. 'He wanted to talk about flying. I offered him my body and he just wanted to talk about flying. Funny bloke. Nice, but weird. You all right now?'

Billie smiled. 'I'm fine. Come on, you'd better get to bed if you're going to take us to England tomorrow. You need your beauty sleep.'

'What for? It's bloody wasted here, isn't it?'

Olympia-Stadion
Charlottenburg
Berlin

THE RIOT HAD started from nothing; nobody had expected any trouble.

It had been a march for the jobless, organized by the socialist opposition parties. The police, notified about the demonstration, sent fifteen uniformed men and two vans to marshal the crowd. It was to be a small rally, starting at the Olympic Stadium and ending outside the rebuilt Reichstag building at the Platz der Republik in the Tiergarten. There was to be an estimated crowd of one thousand people.

The organizers, loudhailers in hand, were corralling the crowd into marching formation when the first group of skinheads appeared. There were some forty of them, moving in from all directions, in gangs of no more than three or four.

The police, still clustered by their vans, were not watching out for trouble. They were relaxed, joking amongst themselves; it was a relief to be on a march where they didn't expect trouble after the last few weeks of demonstrations and violence. Some of them sat on the grass, smoked cigarettes and watched the organizers' bumbling attempts to set the rally in progress. The buses and coaches which had brought the marchers into town were parked opposite the entrance in a long line down the road. Behind the police stood the vast, ninety-thousand-seater Olympic Stadium. Built in 1934 for the infamous 1936 Hitler Olympics, when the black hero of America, Jesse Owens, smashed the formidable sprint opposition of Germany, the stadium had withstood the Allied bombings during the war and became a symbol of a new Germany when Berlin was split in half by the Wall.

It was a good starting place, this symbol of a united past,

for the march of hope that was about to begin. But it was about to become a symbol of all that was going wrong in Germany, a symbol of the divided factions that were driving a wedge into the heart of the nation.

The skinheads and punk rockers, sensing easy meat, mixed with the crowd, their red Communist-starred sweatshirts hidden under their coats. There were five pack leaders, whose responsibility was to incite violence from those who were always prepared to join in. The others, the storm-troopers or *Sturmabteilungen*, would spread through the crowds, wielding clubs, baseball bats and sometimes knives. It was to be an ugly demonstration; damage limitation was not on the agenda. Do what you want, boys, but make sure the television cameras get great pictures.

When the leader, a young man in his early twenties, saw that his *Sturmabteilungen* were in place, he walked towards the steps that lead up to the grand entrance. He stood there, red-shirted, on the steps, his coat wrapped around his waist. He would need it when he made his escape.

'Workers unite,' he shouted through the loudhailer. 'Communists, friends of the people, unite with us to drive out those who are profiting from your hard toil, those who steal the food from your tables and live off the sweat of ordinary people. Workers unite. Don't let these people, these pawns of the capitalists . . .'

As he shrieked through his loudspeaker, the *Sturmabteilungen* started to stream through the crowd, their red shirts now on full display, hitting out at all who stood before them.

The police were slow to realize that there was trouble, but now they moved into the crowd, attempting to find the troublemakers. But the crush of those fleeing was too much and the officers were swamped.

On the steps of the stadium someone had erected a red hammer-and-sickle flag and was waving it towards the crowd and the few media people present.

A woman with a child fell and the child was trampled in the rush and killed. A few feet away, a baseball bat crushed a schoolteacher's head, smashed his skull into a pulpy mess. It was carnage.

Two policemen, near the coach line, saw the waving flag and decided to try to arrest the two men on the steps. But, as they approached, the men broke up and ran into the stadium, vaulting the entrance turnstiles as they went.

A pack leader saw the police in hot pursuit, called six *Sturmabteilungen* to him and led them into the stadium. The two policemen hadn't expected to be followed; they were concentrating on their efforts to find the men who were now hiding in the covered area amongst the seats that were tilted upright in their stored position.

The pack leader grabbed the first policeman from behind and wrestled him to the ground, knocking his revolver from his grip.

The second policeman managed to get a shot off in panic, but before he could take aim properly, one of the skinheads smashed his shoulder with a baseball bat and knocked him down the aisle steps. Before he could rise to defend himself, four of them were on him with their clubs, battering the life from his body. He was dead within ten seconds. A coroner would later record that his body was hit over sixty times. Only his card allowed him to be identified.

The other policeman struggled uselessly, deeply stunned by the death of his colleague. Then he saw one of the men pull out a machete from his deep-lined overcoat pocket. He was grabbed by the shoulders and forced to his knees. He screamed, fought back, but it was futile. His attacker's grip was too strong.

The *Sturmabteilung* with the machete sliced off the top of his skull. The blood gushed out and he was thrown to the ground. The man continued to hack at the body, right down to the bone and intestines.

They threw the red Communist flag over the policeman, draped it over his cut and bleeding body, then they left the stadium by a side entrance.

The riot had now spread. More police were called, and the troublemakers of Berlin, always looking for new violence, joined in the fray. It was to last for nine hours, spreading from the Olympic Stadium into the streets, houses and offices of Charlottenburg, before the riot police, with their armoured vehicles and water canons, brought the whole thing under control.

Fourteen people were killed in the demonstration for the unemployed.

Three of them were policemen.

There were over six hundred arrests.

The white Mercedes bus that had waited at the end of the line for the red-shirted storm-troopers left twenty minutes after the attack started. The young man with the curly hair and the scar on his left cheek was nowhere to be seen. It had not been necessary for him to be there.

By the time the riot was brought under control, the white bus was already back in Dresden.

North Atlantic Airspace

SHE LET HIM fly.

Adam's natural ability impressed Jenny. He instinctively held the aircraft on course without being intimidated by its power or his lack of experience. He was a natural in a world where most pilots are made, not born.

After Goose Bay, where she had controlled the plane as it climbed through thick ice-laden cloud to eleven thousand feet, they had flown direct to Narssarssuaq on the southern tip of Greenland. Once clear of the cloud, she had handed over the controls to him and taught him how to use the power and propeller pitch levers, how to bank the plane sharply, how to descend and climb with power and nose attitude. She enjoyed it. It took away the normal drudgery of long flights with little radio contact and constant headings.

Billie, now having accepted Jenny as someone who could be trusted, settled herself down in the rear, albeit cramped, and spent most of the flight asleep. The dream about Adam had distressed her, and she had spent most of the previous night awake thinking about him, about her own life and where she was going. Wherever she turned, there were few answers to her frustration. Her life had simply come to a full stop.

Narssarssuaq, a small settlement of Danish scientists and westernized Eskimos, is a seven-thousand-foot runway cut out of a glacier. It is approached along a forty-mile-long fjord and the approach instructions are that the pilot should turn left at the entrance by the sunken freighter that sticks up in the fjord, or else run out of airspace and crash into the sheer mountains that rise to seven thousand feet at the end of it.

Jenny let Adam descend from altitude towards the fjord, down to two hundred feet above the frozen water. He enjoyed that most of all; the plane seemed like a toy, suspended between the high-rising mountains on each side, hanging in the vast glacial landscape.

They found the sunken ship with its bow pointing upwards and he turned left towards the runway four miles down the fjord.

'Can I land it?' he asked.

'All yours,' she replied, but she kept her hands near the controls. He was good but not yet that good.

The landing was bumpy and they skipped over a small iceberg at the end of the runway where it sloped down to meet the fjord. That annoyed Adam for he was a perfectionist and Jenny smiled. It was time he came down to earth with a bump, she thought, literally.

'Any landing you walk away from is a good one,' she exclaimed as they taxied in to the small terminal. His grunt of annoyance made her chuckle even more.

Billie stretched her legs while Jenny refuelled and Adam bought some food for the next leg in the cafeteria at the rear of the terminal.

Nobody asked to see their passports and they were airborne half an hour later, on their way to Keflavík on the eastern side of Iceland, where they landed seven hours later. It was a quick turnaround; the last leg to Manchester, nearly five hours' flying time, would be exhausting.

They took off in the dark. Adam climbed out of Icelandic airspace and steered westwards towards Scotland, intending to cross the coast at Stornoway. Jenny dozed off and he switched on the autopilot. He had promised her that if anything out of the ordinary happened, any unnecessary flicker on a dial, he would wake her. Billie was fast asleep; it had been a long and boring trip for someone crammed in the back. He had offered her the front seat for the last leg, but she had turned it down. He sensed it was because she could see he enjoyed the flying and there was little she could do. She was a fine person and he knew they related to each other, shared the same sense of humour. But she might still be a hindrance when it came to the rough stuff. He would have to see how he could avoid that.

He was pleased nobody had asked for his passport.

He started to work out the next stage. It was time to clear his mind.

Nordhausen and Albert Goodenache were coming into view over the horizon.

Jardin des Tuileries
Rue de Rivoli
Paris

THE JARDIN DES Tuileries is Paris' garden; sixty-four acres housing a glorious Orangerie, exotic blooms and a mini Arc de Triomphe which was build to celebrate Napoleon's many triumphs. There is also a fairground that houses what must be some of the worst rides in Europe. Modern, brash and cheap, it is an annual event, running from December into January. For all its shoddiness, people flock there, day and night, to spend their francs being whisked around on ghost trains and dodgem cars.

Helmut Kragan had left Dresden immediately after the council meeting and flown to Paris. He booked in to the Inter-Continental Hotel, only a few minutes' walk from the fairground. The desk clerk saw nothing unusual about Kragan; he was just another businessman in a dark suit with a Liberty's all-wool overcoat draped over his shoulders.

The same desk clerk was on duty when Kragan left the hotel two hours later, at nine in the evening. He recognized him and acknowledged Kragan's wave. The German was wearing the coat properly now as would be expected on a night as cold as this.

Kragan turned right outside the hotel entrance and walked towards the Rue de Rivoli. Once he had turned the corner, he took the coat off and slipped it over his arm.

This was no businessman. He wore motor-cyclist's leathers underneath, black and shiny, with calf-length boots to match. He crossed the Rue de Rivoli and entered the fairground.

It was lively as usual, the mishmash of pop music blaring through loudspeakers as he walked among the crowd, mostly young people on the look-out for instant fun and excitement in an otherwise dreary world. Kragan fitted in, a motor-bike boy out for the night. Here and there a fight broke out, girls screeched as someone goosed them, lovers clung together and ignored all that went on around them, pickpockets worked their art furiously and everyone set out to enjoy themselves.

He stayed in the shadows as he passed the House of Mirrors with its queue stretching outside, everyone jostling for position.

Past the dodgem cars, he saw the Dancing Fly. It was in motion, a carousel of two-seater chairs that spun unbelievably fast whilst it bobbed up and down on its rollers. The girls screamed; some gritted their teeth, others stayed cool as if nothing worried them. Kragan grinned. He never understood the fools who paid to frighten themselves to death.

He saw the curly-haired man with the red scar on his left cheek talking to two short-skirted, high-heeled girls, who were no more than sixteen years old. The over-mascara'd make-up and glossy lips couldn't camouflage their age. Young and slim, dressed in blue jeans and denim jacket, the man worked the Dancing Fly. His position in life, although not a great revenue-earner, was obviously supplemented by an endless supply of young girls who found his lifestyle exciting.

Kragan retraced his steps and left the crowds to walk behind the House of Mirrors. When he was sure he hadn't been spotted, he moved in the darkness back towards the Dancing

Fly. The sounds from the rides and the carnival continued, nothing seemed out of place. He felt the gun in his shoulder holster.

The girls were still there, standing where he had seen them earlier. There was no sign of the curly-haired man. Shit. Alarm bells started ringing in his mind. Kragan moved his hand over the butt of his revolver and loosened it in its holster.

'This is a Colt hand-gun, with real lead bullets,' he heard the voice say from behind him. 'It's not a fairground toy. It will kill you when I pull the trigger.'

Kragan felt the hardness of the muzzle in his back, just behind the heart.

'Piss off. I hope that's not your prick you're sticking in my back,' he said, his annoyance obvious. He spun round.

'Not in this weather, Major,' said the curly-haired man. He held a large metal spanner against Kragan's body. 'Fall off in the cold.'

'How the hell . . .?'

'Did I see you? Eyes in the back of my head, sir.'

Kragan nodded in admiration. 'I thought your desire to fuck those two tarts would have kept your attention off me.' He knew Kaas' reputation and sexual capacity well. He knew everything about all his men. 'Anyone else been around?'

'No, sir. Nobody suspicious.'

Kragan believed him. 'We need to talk. Can you get away?'

'Yes, sir.'

'There's a cafeteria restaurant on the Rue de Rivoli. The Atlantic. Be there in five minutes.'

Walther Kaas had been his best man in the Stasi, had fulfilled everything Kragan had ever asked of him. He had found him as a young officer in the Prenzlauer Berg division when he was no more than eighteen, but he already had a considerable appetite for the harsh and cruel police work that the Stasi required. Prenzlauer Berg was one of the most deprived and crime-ridden areas of East Berlin, a haven for the criminals who lived off the poor and an ideal proving ground for the young officer. Kaas' reputation grew as he relentlessly and ruthlessly tracked them down. His brand of police work soon became feared, especially his notorious ability to torture confessions out of even the most innocent.

Kragan had taken Kaas under his wing and transferred him to the Stasi pre-trial detention establishment at Berlin-Hohenschonhausen. There, under the protective umbrella of the Hoeneker regime, Kaas had excelled at the intimidation and torture that was the mainstay of the Stasi method. Pain was something he enjoyed dishing out. He seemed to have no sense of fear, but that had been easy in the days when the Party ruled supreme and there was no opposition. By the end of the Eighties he was the youngest captain in the crack Guards Regiment Feliks Dzerzhinsky. Then the Wall came down and everything changed. With no prospects and a troubled future, Kaas turned to Kragan once again. The older man, himself an outsider in the new world, had already joined the National Socialists at the request of Peter Frick. He admired Kaas' lack of fear, saw it as a formidable weapon in such a cool-thinking operative. Working for the National Socialists had suited Kaas. It was his home, his passport to the world of pain and violence he enjoyed so much. The discipline of a police state was what he had grown up with, what suited his talents best.

Kragan had the coffees waiting for Kaas when he arrived. Both men were dressed in styles that were suitable for the Atlantic. A spacious, cheap self-service place, it was packed with young people on their way home from the fairground.

'Lined them up for later on?' he asked. He hoped he didn't sound jealous.

'No, sir. I didn't know what you wanted to do.'

'No pleasure this trip, Walther. Unfortunately.'

Kaas shrugged. He knew Kragan's hunger for young girls, usually those under the age of fourteen. It didn't mean anything to Kaas, everyone had their own secrets. And Kaas had soon learnt that part of his duties in the criminal division of the Stasi had been to supply the hierarchy with whatever was needed by way of eroticism and perversion. There was always something for someone in the criminal world. 'I read there was a riot in Berlin. At the Olympic Stadium,' he continued.

'Not good. These riots.'

'It said it was a big riot.'

'Bigger than expected.'

'I'm glad to see they can work on their own.' Kaas meant the other storm-troopers.

'It wasn't difficult. Everyone was pleased with your leadership in Hamburg and Neu-Isenburg.'

'Is the main project ready?'

'The plans are in place. We need you back in Dresden. It's time to train your people.'

'How many?'

'Four. Including you.'

'Tight.' He shrugged. 'But enough. I choose the other three?'

'Of course.' Kragan already knew who were Kaas' favourites, who he would choose. It was important that an operation of this magnitude had continuity. Kaas' team would give it that. 'This whole thing will be strictly on a need-to-know basis. That includes your team.'

'When can I tell them?'

'At the last moment. The training will ensure their readiness.'

'How long?'

'A week. Ample time.'

'Do we go back together?'

'No. Fly to Berlin. There's a plane from Charles de Gaulle at nine tomorrow morning. A driver will meet you at Tegel Airport and take you to Dresden. Finish your work tonight. No suspicious movements. I shall probably be back before you.' Kragan took a newspaper out of his overcoat and openly passed it across to Kaas, as friends would when discussing points of interest. 'There's a good article on Berlin in there. Read it. I want you to understand exactly what is expected by the time I see you tomorrow.'

The two men left soon after. Kaas returned to his final night at the fairground and Kragan to the Inter-Continental.

The desk clerk had gone off duty, but had he seen Kragan, he would only have seen another businessman in an expensive coat returning to his hotel after a night out.

London

As THE BRITISH Airways Boeing 757 twin-engined jet touched
down on Runway 27 Left at Heathrow at 8.33 a.m., Adam
concluded that there would probably be someone watching
for him at the shuttle terminal. He decided then to brazen it
out. The last thing they would expect was the obvious, it was
a certain way to catch them flat-footed.

The Immigration officer at Manchester hadn't made anything of it, but Adam knew he recognized the names from
his priority list. As soon as he saw Adam's passport he had
flicked his eyes down at the register under the counter.

He reached over and took Billie's American passport, flicked
through it.

'You two travelling together?' he asked in a thick northern
accent, too nonchalantly for Adam not to notice.

Jenny had already gone through the crew customs, signed
her general declaration and disappeared into a back room to
sort out all the customs formalities on the imported aircraft.
Their farewells had been short. They all had other things on
their mind.

'Yes,' said Adam.

The Immigration man nodded and passed Adam's passport
back. 'Where will you be staying in England, miss?'

'Where will we be staying, darling?' Billie turned to Adam.

'We're going to hire a car and do some touring,' he declared.
'My friend's never been here before. We'll drive until we find
somewhere to stop for the night.'

'Going to be a long day,' said the Immigration man. It was
nearly six-thirty in the morning. 'Why did you come across
on a ferry flight?'

'Cheaper than a scheduled flight.'

The Immigration man was loath to let them go, but the

instructions on the register were clear. DO NOT DETAIN, DO NOT CAUSE SUSPICION. IDENTIFY THEIR PROBABLE DESTINATION. PROCEED WITH CAUTION. REPORT IMMEDIATELY. CONTACT CUSTOMS TO CLEAR WITHOUT SEARCH. He was tired and there was little else he could do without alarming them. He handed Billie back her passport.

'Can't you stamp it?' she asked. 'I get that done everywhere I go.'

'We don't stamp passports,' said the Immigration man huffily as he turned away from the desk and went into the little room behind that served as his office.

Customs had waved them through the green section. Adam was relieved; his brown bag with the weapons had been his only concern. He didn't know that Customs had already been put on notice to clear them through.

Now, as they left the shuttle lounge at Heathrow, mixed in with the commuters and shoppers who had come down for the day, Adam saw the tail. Military type in a camel coat hiding behind a newspaper. Adam chuckled and took Billie's arm and led her straight up to him.

'Looking for us?' he asked cheekily.

'Sorry?' queried the Military. He was out of breath, had obviously been dispatched to Heathrow in a hurry in case Adam turned up there. He had run down the long corridors to the lounge and arrived just as the shuttle passengers were disembarking.

'We're going home. You can pass that on to Control.'

They left the shuttle lounge with the Military confused and still pretending to ignore them. As soon as they had turned the corner, however, he put his paper down and headed for the row of pay phones that lined the wall.

'How did you know he was waiting for us?' asked Billie as they took a taxi into the centre of London.

Adam chuckled. 'They're desk jockeys, not field men. We probably have the best field operatives in the world. But they're in Northern Ireland, places like that. These guys are jokers.'

'We're still a long way from Herr Goodenache.'

'We'll be there soon. Trust me.'

'You keep saying that.'

'And you keep following.'

'Hmm,' she grumbled, then sat back and looked out at the rush-hour traffic crawling into London on the M4.

'Sorry you came?'

'No. Just that . . . not a lot seems to happen. I'm tired, worn to a frazzle, dirty. My body's cramped from spending all that time in the back of the plane. I've probably lost my job, probably a hunted fugitive in my own country. Hell, this is rapidly turning into shit. So much for looking for excitement. Nothing's happened since we left New Orleans.'

'And you think this could be a wild-goose chase?'

'What do you think?' she snapped at him.

'It could be. But I live in a world of half-chances. I probably shouldn't have left New Orleans as I did. But then I've always done what I probably shouldn't. And, in view of what you've told me about the computer and knocking off all those agents, this whole thing is a lot bigger than just guarding Trimmler. At the end of the day we're working for our own people. We've not turned against them, just creating space to work in. If we fuck up, then we go back, hold our hands out and let them smack us. If we're right, then we've served Queen and Country. Sorry, President and Country.'

'Still a helluva long shot.'

'Maybe. But it could end up as the only game in town.'

She had loved the flat from the start and it had cheered her up unexpectedly. She had assumed it would be functional and simple. Now she saw the love that had gone into it, saw it for the home it was, sensed it as only a woman can.

He had shown her to the guest bedroom. 'Get some sleep,' he told her. 'I've one or two things to do. If you do get up later and find an old lady around the house, then—'

'Lily. You told me.'

'You'll like her. Don't forget, you're probably jet lagged on top of everything else.'

'Prop lagged, you mean.'

He laughed. 'Whatever. It's still only four-thirty in the morning in New Orleans. See you later.'

He left her to settle down and went into his study.

He made three calls, the first of which was to Lily.

The second was to a number in Manchester. When a girl's sleepy voice answered, he said, 'As arranged. Shouldn't be late.' Then he put down the phone before the number could be traced. He knew the line was probably bugged by now.

The third call was to Coy, his briefing officer.

'We really are in the shit, aren't we?' came the sarcastic reply.

'Are we?' replied Adam. It was Nintendo time.

'You were ordered to stay and help our friends.'

'Things changed. I decided to take the initiative.'

'You always do. Is the woman with you?'

So the Americans were keeping Coy informed. 'Yes.'

'Why?'

'She wanted a holiday. Never seen England before.'

'Did she come of her own volition?'

Adam ignored the question. 'How much do you know about our friends' difficulties?' He heard the sharp intake of breath.

'Wait,' commanded Coy, then Adam heard him speak to someone else in the room, his voice muffled by the hand over the receiver. 'You need to come in here,' he said at last.

'No. I want some rest. But we need to talk immediately.'

'All right. I'll ring you back in five minutes.'

Adam grinned and put down the phone. They'd be frantically disconnecting the wire tap. The last thing they wanted was for the Americans to know they were about to learn their secrets.

The phone rang nine minutes later. It was Coy. 'This is a free line,' he said. 'Tell me about their difficulties.'

As briefly as possible, Adam told Coy about the computer virus, about the death of the American agents and about Trimmler's conversation with Goodenache. He even told him about Fruit Juice and the manner of Trimmler's death. He never mentioned Nordhausen or the involvement of the Russians, but knew that if he could commit the British Secret Service, it would keep the CIA off his back and give him the time he needed. These security agencies all loved gossip, especially about their Allies.

'In the shape of a swastika?' exclaimed Coy when he had finished. When Adam didn't answer, he continued, 'Gruesome, even for the Yanks. Did the woman tell you this?'

'No,' Adam lied. 'I overheard various conversations between her and other CIA people.'

'Why did she come with you?'

'She knew I was leaving. I forced her.'

'All the way across the Atlantic?' came the disbelieving reply.

'By then I think she'd decided she might as well continue. After all, she's one of their people. Maybe she just wants to find out what's going on.'

'Possible.' Coy paused and Adam waited for him to continue. 'An intriguing tale,' he said at last.

Adam chuckled to himself. He'd bitten. 'I need some sleep,' he said, hoping he could get the time he wanted.

'Yes. It would be better if you didn't mention our conversation to the woman. Say we haven't contacted you yet.'

'I understand.' You're damn right, I understand. Now the tongues would start wagging round MI5, MI6 and the other, smaller Intelligence Agencies. They'd love to see the Yanks dig themselves out of this hole. Keeping the girl out of touch, of her own volition, would add spice to the game. 'By the way, your chap at the shuttle was rather obvious.'

'Did she see him?'

'Yes.'

'Pity. But if you keep your head down, say the flat's being watched, she should accept that. Just play along with her.'

Very bright, thought Adam. She'd really believe that after your goons have already shown themselves. 'A splendid idea,' he said.

'Good. We'll contact you tonight.'

'Tomorrow might be easier. I'm going to get some sleep, then I need to keep her amused for the rest of the day. A call in the evening might warn her something's up.'

'All right. First thing in the morning, then.'

'And could you keep someone watching the front door. I don't want her sneaking out while I'm in bed.' That should impress them.

'Good idea.' They both knew the place was under surveillance already. 'Talk to you tomorrow with your instructions.'

Adam put the phone down and went to the front door. He switched all the door and window alarms on before going to bed and crashing out. But before he did, he made sure the brown holdall was under his bed.

Lily let herself in with her alarm key at six that evening and found Adam in the shower. She left a cup of tea for him on his bedside table and went into the kitchen to prepare the evening meal.

'Is our guest still asleep?' he asked as he walked through into the kitchen in his towelling robe, the cup of tea in his hand.

'Out to the world,' replied Lily. 'What time do you want me to wake her?'

'Give her another hour. She's had no sleep for nearly two days.'

'Coffee or tea?'

'She's American.'

'Coffee, then.'

'Decaffinated.'

'We haven't any.' She smiled as Adam looked up quizzically. 'You always say, only the real thing. What do you think she'd like to eat tonight?'

'Steak and kidney?' he asked.

'Not much time. But all right. I'll manage.'

'Thanks,' he grinned, then leant over and kissed her on the cheek. 'It's good to be home.'

'Your mail's in the study. Mostly bills, from what I can see.'

'Some things never change.'

He put on a cool cotton grey shirt and loose cotton slacks. The leather slip-ons were an old, comfortable pair. When he was satisfied with his appearance, his hair now well gelled back in its customary style, he went to the study and examined his mail. There were the usual circulars, a few invitations to nothing very exciting and a batch of bills. When he had finished, signed a few cheques for Lily to post for the gas, electricity and other essentials, he wandered into the kitchen.

Billie had joined Lily and they had obviously hit it off.

347

Lily was proudly going through her steak and kidney pie recipe and they were both working together and preparing the meal.

'Sleep all right?' he said.

'Didn't I just? Hey, do you eat like this all the time?' replied a fully refreshed Billie.

'When I'm home. Yes.'

'You wouldn't want to move to California, would you?' she asked Lily.

The old lady smiled and shook her head.

'You couldn't afford her,' remarked Adam good-humouredly.

The meal, one hour later, was as good as they expected.

'Penny for them,' said Adam, when they were halfway through the meal and she had said nothing for a while.

'Despair,' she said softly.

'Don't tell Lily. She'll think it's the food.'

She smiled and shook her head. 'Lily's beautiful. And so's her food. No, I was just thinking about . . . being alone. I mean, I've been alone ever since I left Peter. I've lived with guys . . . Gary was just the latest. But, I could've done without them. I just didn't want to be on my own. When you don't have a purpose, you know, it's easy to keep looking for something . . . I don't know.' She paused. 'Something other people can't give you. You see . . . I'm no good at explaining emotions, I never was. Probably why I get so screwed up.'

'Don't stop.'

'For all his faults, for all our shouting and yelling, for all the bad, we reached heights I never knew I could. And I miss him desperately. Old "screwing around, don't let me get old" Peter. Nothing replaces truth and . . . real love. Substitutes never work. However hard you try and make them fit. Maybe we only fall in love once. And everything else is just . . . second best. Guess we can't face our own failures. Or don't want to.' She hung her head.

'When I first met you, I took you for a pleasure anorexic.'

She looked up. 'A what?'

'Pleasure anorexic. A nonc person. No smoking, no alcohol, only eating food that was good for you.'

'Thanks for nothing.'

'Don't get snappy. As I said, that's what I thought when I first met you.'

'And now?'

'You're OK.'

'Do I get a medal for that, or something?'

'Or something.'

She laughed. 'You know,' she said after a while, 'I enjoy . . . I feel the past doesn't matter as much, somehow.'

'What's brought this on?'

'You. And this place.'

'I don't understand.'

'You've learnt to live with loneliness. No. No, that's not true. Not loneliness. You've just learnt to live alone. Most of us can't do that.'

'Learnt that at a young age. It's too all-consuming, loneliness. Becomes an obsession. A demon in your brain. Sort of takes over your imagination. I learnt young to ignore it, built my own values. It's the only way you can cope.'

Afterwards, when Billie had helped clear up and Adam had finished the list of instructions for Lily, they settled down in the living room with a large jug of coffee.

'We haven't any decaf, I'm afraid,' said Adam when Lily brought it through.

'No sweat. Be good to taste real coffee again.' Billie noticed the quick look between Adam and Lily. She smiled. 'I haven't always been a pleasure anorexic, whatever you think.'

'Want a cigarette?' he responded quickly.

'No. Not that ready to jump over the edge yet.'

'Will you be seeing Mr Marcus before you go?' Billie heard the housekeeper ask Adam in the kitchen as he followed her through for a new packet of cigarettes.

She didn't hear his answer.

At ten Lily left and Adam escorted her to the door. Billie could see their closeness when Adam let her out, saw that they cared deeply for each other. She wished she had a Lily. Maybe that's what she would look for when she returned to La Jolla. That's if the lawyers left her anything after they'd picked over the bones.

For more than half an hour Adam took Billie through his plan for the next stage of their self-initiated assignment. She listened without interrupting and was impressed with the way he had thought it through, his plans being laid before they'd even landed at Manchester.

'You can get out now if you want to,' he said, after he had told her about the phone call to Coy. 'My people think you were taken away from New Orleans under threat and that you're now stringing along just to see what I'm up to. That's what they'll tell the CIA.'

'That's not nice. They'll think I blurted everything out. About the computer and the asset base?'

'I said I overheard you and Tucker and also picked things up as I went along. They'll believe that. It's what they'd expect.'

'What the hell? I'm probably unemployed anyway. You think I should drop out?'

'Your decision. It all started out as an adventure. Now it's real. If you want to . . . '

'I won't. Unless you want me to.'

'You're going to be in the way.'

'You don't have to worry about me,' she replied, irritated with him. 'I'll look after myself. Don't smirk, I mean that.'

He laughed. 'I wasn't smirking. But you need some protection.'

'A gun.'

'We'll sort that out later.'

'You're not going to sneak out on me, are you?'

'It had crossed my mind.' He grinned at her.

'You bastard. You would as well. I'm going to have to sleep across the front door so you can't.'

'You're safe. If I did, you'd only tell them where I'd gone.'

'I wouldn't. And please don't go without me.'

'Time to rest up. We start early.'

'I've only just got out of bed.'

'Us secret agents have got to ride above things like jet lag, you know.'

'I'll never get back to sleep.' She looked at him earnestly. 'Are you really tired?'

'No. But I know what's good for me.'

'Meaning?'

The attraction was growing between them. It was something they had both known since New Orleans. Adam realized this was not the time to bring it out in the open. He couldn't afford anything that could blunt his instincts. He stood up. 'Meaning that I'll need all my strength in the next few days. I need the rest.' He wasn't rude, just matter of fact. 'If you can't sleep, watch TV.' He grinned, tried to take the sting out of his words. 'You'll feel at home. Most of our programmes are American.'

He reached out and touched her shoulder, squeezed it and bade her good night. He saw her lift her chin, trying to once again lift the wrinkles. He said nothing, she was beautiful as she was. Then he left her and went to bed.

He was restless and knew it would be difficult to sleep. The smell of her was still in his nostrils, the scent of sex and all that that brings. Damn, he needed a clear mind. He listened for the sound of the television from the lounge. Maybe she'd decided to try and go back to sleep.

She came in five minutes later, just as he had brought himself under control, and quietly slipped into his bed.

He lay still, his back to her, curled up, pretending to be asleep.

'I know you're awake,' she said, snuggling up to him, putting her arm round him, pushing gently against him until she fitted in with his body, becoming one person in the big bed. 'Companionship or sex. It doesn't matter, tough guy. I just wanted to be with you.'

He said nothing, just squeezed her arm to let her know it was all right, that he wanted her to be there as well.

After that, it was easy. What they felt was out in the open and they both knew it could go no further until whatever lay ahead was over.

She nuzzled his ear. 'Beats sleeping across the door.' They slept until 4 a.m. Then the alarm buzzed and they knew it was time to restart their deadly game.

Georgetown
Washington

IT WAS ONE in the morning when the DDA put down the phone and wiped his hands on his pyjamas. The phone call had made him sweat.

'How the hell did they get to England?' the Exec Director had asked him on the phone. It was the first the DDA knew about it. 'Fuck it, you said they were still in New Orleans.'

'We presumed . . .'

'Weren't we watching all the airports and ports?'

'Yes, sir. The DDI had his men there, too.' He quickly tried to shift some of the blame. 'We even had the roads covered. I don't see how . . .'

'Well, they did. All the way back to England. You'd better find out what the fuck's happening. Get on to our embassy there. Get them to ring this number.' The Exec Director gave the DDA a number that he had just received from his bureau chief in London. 'That's British Intelligence. Guy called Coy. You just get on with it and come back to me in the morning.'

The DDA went downstairs to his study and dialled the number in England. It was engaged. While he waited he switched on the television, flicked it on to CNN. There was an item on a big drugs haul in Seattle and then the President's face came up on the screen.

'The President left last night for a series of visits to Europe—' the picture cut to the President boarding Air Force One at Charles De Gaulle Airport – 'which will culminate in a private meeting with the Russian President in Germany. His first port of call will be London where he is to meet with the British Prime Minister. After that, he flies to Paris for a meeting with the French President, then on to Germany for the first historic conference with the heads of all the NATO, European Community and Warsaw Pact countries. This meeting, seen by many as the first step towards a united Europe spanning East and West, is . . .'

The DDA had left the phone on automatic redial and now it was ringing back from London. He picked up the receiver, listened, then introduced himself.

'My name's Coy,' came the answer. 'Our man's done a runner.' He wasn't about to tell the Yank that he'd also been duped, that he'd sat on the information for nearly twenty-four hours.

'Runner?' queried the DDA.

'Yes. Bolted. He got back to his flat and our people spotted him. I spoke to him, on the phone, and he said he would come in this morning. Next thing I know, he'd driven out of there, hell for leather, in a bright red sports car, and headed south. We're trying to trace him now.'

'Was the woman with him?'

'Yes.'

'Did he say why?'

'No,' Coy lied back. 'I would've found that out this morning. I think the best we can do is wait until we find them.'

'I can't understand how you . . .'

'Listen. This was your show. We were there to help. You lost them in the first place. I'll contact your embassy when something turns up. Goodbye.'

The phone went dead in the DDA's hand. He slammed the receiver down.

On the television he saw the President waving at the cameras before the doors on Air Force One closed. He also saw behind the President the smiling face of the DDI.

The bastard had gone with him.

He suddenly felt very alone.

Shit to the British. Shit to them all. They'd destroyed his career and he didn't even know if he'd ever find out why.

It was time to start digging. Go back into the files. He'd salvage it somehow. Dig into everything. Something always turned up.

Dresden *Heide*
Dresden

THEIR FEET CRUNCHED on the brittle undergrowth, leaving sharp footprints where the early morning frost had taken hold. Kragan and another senior *Sturmabteilung* officer, in the standard mustard-brown shirts, dark brown riding breeches and black leather boots, led their leader through the woods. It was an important time for them; they had to prove that they were on target and ready to execute their task successfully.

Frick was proud as he walked between them, his long black leather coat reaching to the ground. Their military insignia excited him. He imagined it as it would be, centred in red and gold on a black flag, high on a standard, waving in the wind over the stadiums where they would hold their rallies, a symbol of a proud and new Germany, the Fatherland in its true glory.

The wooden cabin with its chalet-style sloping roof, some forty metres long and twenty wide, was in the middle of a clearing. It was sheltered from prying eyes by trees, in the very heart of that section of the Dresden *Heide* that Mitzer had purchased for the Party. It was far enough from anywhere to be unnoticed, far enough for the loudest sounds to be muffled and lost to passers-by.

As they approached, storm-troopers stepped out from cover. All had hand-guns holstered at their sides; two of them had machine-guns. It was not a place that unexpected prowlers would ever escape from. Round here, security was tight.

When they saw Frick, whom they had been told to expect, the *Sturmabteilungen* snapped to attention, their arms held out in the traditional Nazi salute.

'Heil, heil.' The salute was repeated, different from the old Nazi one that had been discredited when Germany lost the last war. In their wisdom, the council had decided that to repeat all the slogans, wear the same swastika insignia and copy all the other mannerisms of the old Nazi party would simply create a credibility gap. So things were changed, honed down, made to appear not quite so militaristic. Frick said nothing. He could live with it, until it was time to change and emerge as the Party it really was.

He returned the salute as he passed the guards. He enjoyed their adulation. They had a common cause. It was imperative that they looked up to him, feared him, respected him, loved him.

A *Sturmabteilung* opened the door that led into the cabin and Frick walked through, the others following. It was dark inside. A long narrow corridor ran down the middle of the building with doors leading off it. Each door had a single glass pane in it. This was ostensibly a centre for the teaching of self-defence and disciplined order; in truth, it was a training ground for killing and subversive terrorism. Its sole purpose was the development of the *Sturmabteilungen*.

Frick idled his way along the corridor, looking in through various windows. He saw the storm-troopers practising karate, crowd control, baton practice and their skills with the knife and knuckleduster.

Near the end of the corridor was a fully equipped modern shooting range with ten bays. They didn't keep the weapons or ammunition here, however. They were hidden elsewhere in the Dresden *Heide*, in a safe place. All the equipment here could be explained away; this was no more than a training ground for those interested in self-defence, martial arts and war games. It was, to the outsider, a complete survival centre.

The door of the last room, beyond the range, had no window in it. Kragan excused himself as he pushed past Frick and opened it. His leader and the other officer entered and Kragan closed the door solidly behind them. You could tell it was heavier than normal, probably wooden, clad on a solid steel frame surrounded by high-ratio sound-proofing. The rest of the room was similarly protected. A single electric bulb dangled from the ceiling. In the middle there was a Formica-covered kitchen table on spindly metal legs. Three

355

chairs were pulled up at it. One was empty, the other two occupied by men in civilian clothes. Their hands were tied behind their backs and they were gagged. Behind one of them was a shop-window dummy dressed in a military uniform. Another dummy was placed by the window on one of the walls. Beyond the window there was another wall. In all, there were three other windows in the room, and one further door. It was a room within a room, with windows looking out on to the cabin walls beyond. A third dummy was in a seated position on the fourth chair which was set away from the table.

'Please don't cross the white line,' Kragan warned Frick as he handed him a set of noise excluders. The white line, painted on the floor, ran across the room, no more than three feet from the door and parallel with it. 'We shall be another two or three minutes,' Kragan added nervously; he knew Frick hated being kept waiting.

Frick nodded. It should have all been ready for him.

'The white line,' said the second officer, 'is drawn across to protect you. If you cross it, then you will come into the line of—'

The look of contempt on Frick's face stopped him. 'I know what it's for,' stated Frick coldly.

'Of course, sir.'

Kragan signalled the officer to step back, then moved closer to Frick. 'We've had calls from council members about the Charlottenburg Riots.'

'What did they say?' asked Frick, now partly deflected from the irritation he felt.

'That the reports on television and in the papers support your view. The public is becoming sickened by these pictures of violence and death. It seems you are right – it may well be time for the Party to come out into the open.'

Frick smiled. 'They said that?'

'That was the gist of it.' He didn't add that he had argued Frick's case vigorously, had hammered the points home until they could do little but agree with him.

'Good. And Albert Goodenache?'

'Nothing yet. We know he flew to Frankfurt from New York. He's somewhere in Germany.'

'Find him. He's dangerous, with all that knowledge. Trimmler's death will have terrified him.'

'He could be coming here.'

'Let's hope so.'

The door opened behind them and a junior officer came in. He nodded to Kragan, who turned to Frick. 'We're ready now. If you would put on your sound protector.'

Frick and the others slipped the protectors over their heads and turned towards the table. The single light dimmed to half-strength.

They waited for nearly a minute for something to happen.

Frick was getting restless once again when the place simply exploded into action. A stun grenade was hurled through the window on the left and landed in the middle of the room. It exploded, sound and brilliant light smashing through the room and dulling the senses, smoke gushing out and fogging the scene. The door on the left was blown off its hinges by strategically placed charges that slammed it flat on to the floor.

At the same time a balaclava-masked soldier rolled in through the window where the stun grenade had come from, his Kalishnikov automatic aimed at the dummy that stood by the opposite window. The bullets sliced the dummy in half. A second soldier burst through the door which had been blown open and fired his automatic rifle at the kitchen table, its powerful round of bullets knocking the head off the dummy planted in the chair. Another stun grenade was thrown in and a third soldier hurled himself through the window after it, before it had exploded. As the grenade went off, he opened fire with his semi-automatic hand-gun and shot the dummy in the chair away from the table.

The first two soldiers had now crossed the room and dragged off the men who were tied up to the floor. They cut their bonds. The third soldier covered them, his weapon at the ready for any surprise intruders.

Then the floodlights that were hidden in the roof came on. The soldiers relaxed, laughing, whilst the hostages stood up and joined in the celebrations. The whole thing had taken no more than five seconds.

Frick took off his sound protectors and walked across to

the young man he knew to be the leader. 'Well done,' he congratulated Kaas. 'You have trained your men well.'

Kaas snapped to attention and gave the salute, and the others all followed his example.

'Using your men as hostages,' questioned Frick, 'is that a good thing? You might lose one. We need all our young men, you know.'

'It's the only way . . . to understand the reality of death,' replied Kaas. 'They've got to face it if they're to inflict it.'

'And you move the positions of the dummies and hostages every time?'

'Yes, mein Führer. The whole action must take no more than five seconds. My people have to identify the enemy and act instantly.'

'Good. Excellent. Is this the full complement of men you'll need for our next operation?'

'Yes. Plus Krische, the officer who came in to tell you we were ready.'

Frick turned to Kragan. 'When will this room be ready to represent our next objective?'

'This afternoon,' answered Kragan.

'The most important mission of all,' Frick said to Kaas. 'Your men will not be told the location until they arrive there. This time, security must be absolute. We cannot afford failure. Now, let me meet your men.'

As Kaas introduced his leader to his band of warriors, Kragan finally relaxed. Things had gone well. Charlottenburg had been a glorious success. But it was only a springboard for what was to come. If the public had been sickened by the carnage at the Olympic Stadium, the next spectacle to fill their television screens would be in such spectacular technicolor and DestructaVision that it would make *Rambo* look like a Disney movie.

Normally a cautious man, Kragan felt the glimmer of satisfaction spread within him. He sensed success.

Nothing could stop them now.

European Airspace

ADAM CHUCKLED TO himself as the four-seater Piper Arrow flew at two thousand feet across German airspace.

'What's so funny?' asked Jenny Dale, sitting to his left and piloting the single-engined, low-winged plane in her usual deft manner across the turbulent, cumulus-covered sky.

'Nothing. Just something I was thinking about,' he replied.

'How long?' shouted Billie from the rear, loud enough to be heard over the roar of the two-hundred horsepower engine.

'Twenty minutes,' answered Jenny. 'We're nearly there.'

Adam went back to his private world as the plane bucked across the sky, the unseen hands of the veering winds twisting and turning it as it flew towards Hanover.

That morning he had watched the surveillance team from the living-room window. They were parked across the road, outside the chemists, with a layer of frost covering their Rover Sterling. The team inside the car, three of them, would occasionally turn on the engine and try to warm themselves, but he knew they'd feel the cold after such a freezing night.

'I'm ready,' Billie said as she came out of the bathroom.

'Let's go,' he replied.

He drew the curtain shut. Then he opened the front door so that they could see where they were going, and flicked the bathroom light off. He picked up his brown holdall. Apart from the weapons, he had packed two sweat-shirts, some underwear and his toiletries. This time he really was travelling light.

She followed him out into the hallway, toting her small suitcase.

The red F40 was parked and ready in the underground car-park.

'Wow!' he heard Billie exclaim. 'They yours?'

He nodded. Emma and Steed, side by side. He'd be glad when this was over and he could settle down to enjoy himself again. He knew his service days were finished. After the New Orleans episode and this latest scrape he was about to embark on, Coy and his sort would never have him back.

He stroked the Gullwing as he passed it and then unlocked the Ferrari's passenger door to let Billie in. He slid the holdall between her legs, on the floor pan, then walked round and climbed in to the driver's side.

He started the engine as gently and quietly as possible. It still sounded like an express train in the confines of the small garage. He backed her out of the parking space, then drove towards the automatic garage doors. The remote control was clipped to the sun visor and he pressed the button.

It was the last thing the surveillance team had expected. The driver saw the garage door spring upwards. He hurriedly tried to wind the window down as he couldn't see clearly through the thin layer of frost and condensation, but by the time he'd done so, the red Ferrari had spurted to the top of the ramp, its undipped lights blinding him, swung to the right and roared down the street.

'It's him!' he shrieked to the others as he started the engine. 'It's him! He's doing a fucking runner!'

The engine turned, was slow to fire before it came to life. The driver gunned the accelerator too hard in his anxiety and the car slid sideways, its rear wheels spinning as it tried to grip the tarmac, but only contacted the thin layer of overnight frost. It slid helplessly into the next parked car, slammed into its side.

'Shit!' screamed the driver as he tried to extricate himself from the situation.

'Come on!' yelled the man in the rear seat.

The car eventually pulled away from the kerb and drove after the F40. But it had disappeared at high speed into the early morning darkness.

'They'll radio all the police cars,' said Adam. 'Not to stop us, but to keep an eye on us.'

'Why not stop us?'

'We've done nothing wrong. And they'll want to know where we're going.'

'Then don't speed. Unless you want to be caught.'

He grinned. 'It's all right. I'm taking all the back roads.'

They drove for nearly forty minutes through the empty suburb streets. Past Chiswick and Heathrow Airport, under the M25 and through the villages of Wentworth and Sunningdale, out towards Woking.

They parked where he always did, hidden deep in the shadows.

'Will you be all right here?' he asked.

'I'd rather come.' As she answered, she sensed his nervousness. 'If a cop comes and finds the car, with me in it, I wouldn't know what to do.' They both knew she was lying.

Suddenly he didn't care. There was nothing to hide. He wanted to tell her, had never shared the secret with anyone before, only Lily, and that was a long time ago.

'Come on,' he said and they both left Steed parked there and made their way to the twisted and bent railing that was his door to the family. She shivered as they crossed to the west hill.

She stood back and watched him approach the three headstones, saw him touch them as gently as she had known he would. She heard his low voice as he spoke to them, greeted them after his long absence. When he'd finished, he turned and called out to her, beckoned her over.

Billie picked her way between the graves, stumbled just before she reached him, but he leant forward and easily caught her. She was always surprised by the strength in such a compact body.

'Morbid, eh?' he chided her.

'Don't be stupid,' she snapped back. 'You should know better.'

'Sorry. Not used to letting my defences down, I suppose.'

She touched his cheek. 'Talk to me, tough guy. Like you talk to yourself.'

'Just like that?'

'Just like that.'

'I've already told you about Marcus. And my parents. About how they died.'

'What do you talk about when you come here. I know they're real. In there' – she stroked his forehead – 'they're alive.'

'Yes.'

'Can you feel him now?'

'He never leaves me.'

'What's he saying?'

'Nothing. He is me. No, he's half of me.'

'How?'

'I don't know. I . . . there's feelings inside me that I can't explain. Evil with depression. It comes from nowhere. For no reason.'

'Is it there now?'

'Was. Before we left home. It consumes me. When I'm in danger, when it's all going against me, that's when it's at its strongest. I kill without thinking, so cool I think I must enjoy it. Pain becomes bearable through pleasure. I have no soul in those moments.'

'And you think that's how you really are?'

He nodded. 'I was the best field agent we ever had. That's true, because you always know your own worth. It wasn't because I enjoy killing, not just going out and doing it. Or danger. That's how they saw it. The boys behind the desks. No, it was because I didn't care. Didn't give a shit whether I lived or died.'

'Why?'

'No-one to care for. They were dead, since I was that small.' Adam held his hand down, palm outstretched. 'I just had a go at everything. If I lost, then I got the final reward. I went over to the other side.' He smiled as he said it.

'To join them.'

'Something like that.'

'The death-wish. They saw it in New Orleans.'

'Spooky, that.'

'I've seen you with Lily. With me. Here, with your family. You *do* care.'

'So, what is the blackness that I feel inside? The evil?'

362

It suddenly hit her. 'You think it's Marcus. Him, pushing inside you.'

'No. Not him. Me.'

'Oh no. Not you, tough guy. Not you.' She put her arms round him and held him. 'Not you. Not even Marcus. Just the hurt. Of a little boy. Don't you see? Not any of you.'

'But Marcus is there. I know he's inside me.'

'He is. He always was. But he loves you. Like you love him. But you were still a little boy left on your own. Don't you see? It's just what you were. Lost and hurt and full of pain. Don't you see?'

And he started to cry, there, alone with her in the cemetery, next to those he had loved the most and missed the most.

The police had picked up the red sports car nine miles south of Ashford in Kent. It was doing seventy down a country lane, in a fifty-mile-an-hour zone.

The police car was speeding up to give chase when the co-driver warned his partner to ease off. 'That's the car they were looking for. Report but don't apprehend.'

'But he's over the limit.'

'Stay well behind while I report in.'

By the time they had received instructions to follow and observe, they had lost it in a swirl of speed at one hundred and forty miles an hour.

'They're really going to come after us now,' said Billie pinnned to the seat as it accelerated through the corners.

'By the time they get search teams out we'll be there. You OK?'

'Yes. In a numbed sort of way.' She'd never been driven that fast before, never experienced the sheer exhilaration and heart-stopping fear that merged into one as the F40 powered on the knife edge of its optimum limits. But she trusted him, saw the way he handled it through the bends, fed the power in as it was required, was part of the hurtling machine that he controlled so gently. Like making love, she thought. And then shuddered when she remembered his death-wish.

Just north of Dungeness atomic power station, he slowed through the village of Lydd and followed the road out to the small airport. The F40 swung into the entrance and pulled up outside the terminal. Adam parked the car behind a large yellow Ford Transit van and switched off the engine.

'Let's get going,' he said, turning to Billie.

'I can't!' she gasped. 'Not yet.'

He suddenly realized how much the speed had affected her. He leant over and put his arm round her shoulders. 'Legs shaky?'

'Don't laugh, you bastard.'

'I'm not.' He grinned cheekily back. 'But we've got to go.'

'In a minute, in a minute.'

He kissed her on the forehead, then climbed out of the car and walked round to the other side. He opened her door and held his hand out. 'Come on. We've got to get moving.'

'Shit to you, tough guy,' she answered, then took his hand and scrambled out.

'They really are shaky!' he exclaimed as she wobbled towards him. 'Sorry about that.'

Then he picked up the two bags and led her into the terminal.

Five minutes later they walked through the departure lounge for national and European Community destinations to the Piper Arrow that was parked on the ramp.

Nine minutes later the plane was airborne from the pitted runway. It was a visual flight-plan route, with no destination recorded.

'Where the fuck's he gone now?' Coy's superior asked him later. It had taken them over an hour to find the F40.

'No idea. We've got air traffic on to it. The plane came in from Manchester. The pilot was hired to fly them in a chartered plane.'

'To where?'

'Nobody knows. It's a visual flight. They don't need flight plans if it's out of controlled airspace.'

'Who's the pilot?'

'The same one, a girl, who flew them across the Atlantic.'

'Dear God. It gets deeper by the minute. Anything else?'

'Not yet.'

'We'll keep this away from the Yanks for now. Come back when you've got something.'

Coy put down the phone. There was nothing he could do

anyway. Not until the plane surfaced. And that would take time. It was impossible to contact every air-traffic-control unit in Europe, every airfield, every charter company.

Blast, it had been a long night. He put his feet up on the desk, tilted back the swivel executive chair and went to sleep.

'Thanks,' said Jenny, taking the traveller's cheques from Adam and putting them into her flying jacket. 'Nice to do business with you.'

'Take care when you get back.'

'No problem. As you said, you're not running drugs, or anything like that. It was just another charter.'

'Even so, the Intelligence arm will want to grill you.'

'Tsk, tsk,' she clucked. 'They're not going to torture me, are they? Pull my nails out one by one.'

Adam laughed. 'I doubt it. But they will question you. And remember, when they ask about Billie, say she was edgy, always nervous. Seemed scared of me.'

'Aye, aye, captain.'

'And thanks. Safe journey back.'

Adam went to get the hire car as Billie and Jenny said their goodbyes. Twenty minutes later they were on the Salzgitter Autobahn, heading for Nordhausen, some one hundred and ten kilometres to the south.

KGB Headquarters
Dzerzhinsky Square
Moscow

'YES, DIMITRI DIMITROVITCH,' said Rostov into the phone.

'The Americans are growing more concerned by the minute,' reported Sorge over the receiver. 'They now think the British know more than they're admitting.'

'The British know nothing.'

'They are frightened that we are all working against them.'

'Poppycock.'

'That's what I told them.'

'You must take the heat out of the situation. Just because some of them don't know their arse from their elbow doesn't mean that we're not bringing the whole thing under control.'

'You want me to repeat that?'

Rostov laughed. 'No. But diffuse it. Calm them down.'

'I will do my best.'

There was a considerable pause before Rostov continued. 'We've found Albert Goodenache.'

'Can I inform them?'

'Yes.'

'And tell them where?'

'No. Just that we think we've traced him. That we're following it up.' He'd identified various locations where Goodenache was likely to turn up. He'd even questioned some of the older members of the Lucy Ghosts in private to help trace the fugitive. Nordhausen had been one of these places. And his people there had soon found the scientist.

'I'll pass that on.'

'Good. We will resolve this situation, Dimitri Dimitrovitch. Just keep the Americans calm. This thing is bigger than they realize. I now have some idea of what it's about. But I don't have all the answers. Time is short, but I need all I can get.'

'I will, as they say here, keep them off your back.'

'I know you will. These people have crawled out of the sewers. And that's where we've got to go, if we want to end it.'

The road to Nordhausen
Harz Mountains

THE ROAD FROM Hanover to Nordhausen passed through all that was best in West Germany and all that was worst in the East. The first section is a mixture of three-laned autobahns and twin-laned primary roads. The traffic moves at a fast pace and averaging a speed of over one hundred kilometres an hour is not difficult. The surrounding countryside is fertile, a mixture of productive, well-maintained fields and bulbous forests that spread over the horizon. The towns and villages are prosperous, clean and bustling with enterprise. The people look affluent and busy.

When the four-wheel-drive saloon they had hired, an Audi Quattro, reached the old border that split the villages of Tenterborn and Mackenrode, everything changed. The transformation was sudden. The old wall still stood, stretched across the countryside like a giant fourteen-foot picket fence, disappearing over the horizon on both sides. The road, where the border post had once split it, became narrow, just wide enough for two cars to pass each other. They could see the empty watch-towers to the left and right.

They parked the Audi where the guardhouse had once stood, on a small patch of concreted ground to the side of the road. They walked across the field to where the wall stopped, sliced in its eternal stride by some giant wire cutters.

'I always thought it was solid,' said Billie, coming up to it, reaching out and touching it in awe.

There were two walls, running parallel with each other. The one they stood at was made of heavy chain-link, stretched between towering concrete posts that were spaced fifteen metres apart. The second row, the inner wall, was of the same design. The gap between them, that area which had been mined and

367

covered by machine-guns from the watch-towers, was about forty metres wide. There was little growth there, just patchy, overgrown grass, a desolate, don't-come-here sort of area.

They stayed there for about twenty minutes, walked where once there had been fear and intimidation, tried to imagine it as it had been, wondered who'd died there, whose dreams had been shattered.

'I guess they'll get round to dragging it off to the junk yard,' said Billie, her arm linked through his as they made their way back towards the car.

'They should leave it up. To remind people about the dark side of life.'

It was different now, the countryside more desolate, less machinery in the fields. The roads were potholed and had received little maintenance since 1944. The villages and towns they passed through were shabby where buildings had long since been left to decay. Sleek Mercedes Benz and BMWs intermingled with smoke-belching, rattling Trabants, Wartburgs and Ladas, but it was an environment that lacked the hurly-burly of enterprise.

Then there was Nordhausen - an industrial centre which was an ecological disaster. It was an old town, its wealth based on brewing before the Second World War came along and transformed it into a steel and munitions centre. Since then, under the Communists, Nordhausen remained a metal town, spewing its untreated, black, smelter smoke into the atmosphere and polluting the beautiful countryside that surrounded it. In time, the forest trees in the magnificent Harz Mountains started to thin out as they were poisoned. Gradually the untreated smoke and grime turned Nordhausen into a dirty city, with dirty people, all with little to do except work and drink and then go back to work. The town had suffered from the worst of industrial enterprise and was now the recipient of a major twenty-million-pound clean-up. But it would take many years before Nordhausen became a green town, many years before it could even start to ease back on the pollution it coughed on to its inhabitants and the surrounds in which they existed.

They drove in from the west, on the 243 through Gunzerode, and along the cracked road that led past the IFA Motorenwerk where they once made bicycles and now were being upgraded to motor bikes. It was nearly five in the evening when they finally reached the centre of Nordhausen.

The car rattled along, crossing the myriad narrow gauge loco tracks that ran between the factories lining the route. Three sets of lights later, they came into the town centre, a wide boulevard that sloped up a hill with the shops and offices set back from the pavement. There was the usual panoply of McDonald's and other American fast-food imports mixed with the traditional shops.

'Can we get a hamburger or a pizza?' asked a famished Billie.

'At the hotel. We'll be there soon.' It was a decision he was later to regret.

Adam pulled up and asked directions, and having found out he had come too far, he drove back to the IFA Motorenwerk and turned right. Nine blocks down, in the middle of the mass of square-slabbed, drab yellow-and-green workers' apartments, he turned into Yorckstrasse. The Kurhotel was on the next block, a 1950s five-storey tower of glass and unpainted concrete that had once been the pride of East German architecture.

The receptionist, fat, well-fed and dismissive of all before her, followed in the tradition of her countrymen and spoke little English. It suited Adam not to reply in German and he gesticulated wildly as he tried to make her understand. Eventually, after she had been joined by two others whose grasp of the English language was as poor as hers, they booked in to two rooms.

'Why two rooms?' asked Billie as they waited for the slow-moving lift to ascend to the third floor.

'It's safer.'

'Who for?'

'For both of us. If somebody comes after us, then we've always got cover.'

'Bullshit,' she remarked and punched him in the arm as he grinned.

Their rooms were next to each other and identical: shabby exercises in spartan comfort, designed to keep you out of the room and in the hotel lounge.

'I don't believe these beds,' groaned Billie, throwing her case on hers and seeing a cloud of dust rising from it. It was a single, narrow affair with a wafer-thin mattress that sagged in the middle and was covered by a brown woollen blanket that had probably been there since the hotel was built. She looked round the room, furnished only with a small table, a steel chair with a plastic seat and a chest of drawers with a Formica top. The wardrobe was a hole in the wall with no door and a metal bar stretched across it.

She went next door to Adam who was hanging up his few belongings in his hole in the wall.

'Is this what they call European hospitality?' she asked.

'No. European culture.'

'I can't stay here. It's worse than that place in New Orleans.'

'It's all we've got.'

'Shit!' she swore, sitting on the chair. 'You really know how to treat a girl, tough guy.'

'Listen, this is luxury to some of the places I've dossed down in.'

'Dossed?'

'It means just as it sounds. You can't live much rougher.'

'I don't suppose they have room service?'

'Another filthy capitalist habit.'

'I'm hungry.'

'Then let's eat.'

The food was as bad as they expected. Sausages and sauerkraut with brown bread. It was the traditional fare and they had agreed it might be something worth trying.

'We could've had a pizza in town,' she reminded him. 'I've decided I'm not always going to follow you from now on.'

When they returned to reception there was no-one on duty. Adam quickly crossed to the desk, leant behind it and pulled up the register. He flicked it open and searched through it.

'Look out!' warned Billie, seeing a movement from the room behind.

Adam put the book back and stepped away from the counter as the fat receptionist came out in to reception.

'*Bitte?*'

Adam smiled, shook his head to signify he wanted nothing, took Billie's arm and pushed her towards the lift.

'Well?' she asked once the door had closed on them.

'Floor above us. 416.'

'So you were right.' She felt the tingle of excitement. 'You were right. You were fucking right.' She punched his arm in a show of victory. 'You found him, tough guy. Let's go get him.'

'Not yet. He's out.'

'How'd you know?'

'Key was hanging up in reception.'

'You don't miss much, do you?'

It was 8 p.m. when Adam saw Goodenache coming up Yorckstrasse. He was wearing an overcoat and leant forward to protect himself against the biting wind. He limped just as Adam remembered. He was also weaving and Adam realized that he had been drinking. Goodenache entered the hotel, but Adam didn't leave his post, waiting for almost five minutes to make sure no-one was following. Then he and Billie climbed to the next floor and walked down the corridor to Room 416.

When he was sure that they were alone, Adam knocked on the door.

'*Bitte?*' he heard the scientist ask from inside.

'Police,' he answered.

There was silence for a moment, then he heard the safety-chain being withdrawn and the door opened slightly. He saw Goodenache's face react in surprise as he recognized Adam, saw him start to close the door again. But Adam had his foot against the frame. He pushed hard, too hard for the scientist to resist.

'What do you want?' shouted a frightened Goodenache as the two of them came into the room. 'You have no jurisdiction here.'

'We're here to help, Mr Goodenache,' said Adam, closing the door behind him. 'Nothing else. You could be in danger.' He could smell the drink; it had obviously been a heavy session.

Goodenache watched them, not knowing in his befuddled state what to do.

'Just relax, Mr Goodenache,' Billie said from behind Adam. Maybe a woman wouldn't present such a threat, wouldn't panic the man. Her training in dissemination would be of help now. 'I'm an American. This gentleman is British. We were assigned to protect your friend, Mr Trimmler. We simply want to find out what happened. And to help. If you need it.'

As she spoke she moved past Adam and put her arm on Goodenache's. 'We really are here to help,' she comforted him.

'Who else knows I am here?'

'Nobody. As far as I can be sure.'

'Your people. They will know.'

'Not yet.'

He pulled away from her and sat on the edge of the bed. He couldn't comprehend why they were there. 'How did you find me?'

'The authorities traced you to Frankfurt, sir,' interjected Adam.

'So where are they?'

'Still looking for you.'

'I don't understand. Why are you both here? How did you know . . . ?'

Billie held her hand up to interrupt him. 'My colleague overhead the conversation between you and Mr Trimmler.'

'Which conversation?'

'In your hotel bedroom,' interjected Adam, then continued, lying as he did so, 'My room was next door. It was pure chance, nothing else.'

'You were spying on us?'

'No.'

'Don't insult my intelligence. People don't just hear conversations in hotel rooms.'

'OK. I wanted to hear you. Not spying. Just curiosity. Hell, I was meant to be looking after him and then you both started talking in the room next to mine. So, I listened. The walls were thin, it wasn't difficult. I heard you talk about this hotel. About Nordhausen. When Mr Trimmler was murdered and you vanished, I thought this was where you might head for.'

'So you just followed me? The two of you?'

'The answer to Mr Trimmler's death had to be with you.'

'Why?'

'Because of the Lucy Ghosts.'

Stunned silence. Goodenache was frantically sobering up.

'By now, both the Americans and the Russians will be trying to discover who the Lucy Ghosts are,' Billie took over. 'We've been out of touch for a few days now. They could already have the answers.'

'So why you? I don't understand why you should come alone.'

'Because someone was trying to set me up. As Trimmler's killer,' said Adam.

'Why?'

'I have no idea. This whole thing's a mystery. Nobody knows who's fucking who. I just know I was being set up.'

'You're British?'

'Yes. On special assignment. To guard Trimmler.'

'Why not an American?'

'Because they had a problem with their computer. They wanted somebody who wasn't listed on it.'

'Ah!' Goodenache suddenly smiled, and Adam understood why.

'You knew all about the computer, didn't you?'

'You knew about the virus,' Billie backed him up.

'I know of your problems. Yes,' Goodenache replied.

'Why?' she asked.

'I don't know,' he said, suddenly shutting them out.

'Look, I need to find out what's going on.' Adam changed the subject. 'For my own sake, to clear my name.'

'It's not my problem.'

'Trimmler wasn't mine. But I'm in a hole because I tried to protect him. And he was your friend. You owe me that.'

'I owe nothing.'

'Do you know why he was killed?'

'No.'

'Do you know who by?'

'I've said, I don't know.'

'OK. Then let me tell you.' Adam took out a cigarette and offered one to Goodenache, who took it. When they had both lit up, much to Billie's dismay, he told the scientist about the harrowing experience with Fruit Juice, about the deadly games that were played in New Orleans and culminated with Trimmler's death.

'None of it makes sense,' Goodenache said finally. 'It's unreal.'

'It's real. It happened. You know what they did with his arms. It's real all right.'

'Why is she, an American, with you?'

'Because we're lovers,' stated Billie. 'And I don't want him to take the rap for something he didn't do.'

Goodenache put his head in his hands, exasperated. 'I don't understand. I don't understand.' When he looked up there were tears in his eyes. 'It's awful. That they should kill Heinrich. Like that. With his arms like a . . . What kind of people are they?'

'We were hoping you would tell us.'

'I don't know. Why do you think I came here?'

'In case you were next?'

'I have . . . considered that.'

'If we're to help, we need to know who,' asserted Adam.

'The Israelies. Who else?'

'I don't get it.'

'Because of the Lucy Ghosts. Because it's all coming out. Because they have waited for this moment.'

'Tell us,' said Billie. 'About them.'

'It's a society. From the war. Some of them with . . . things to hide.'

'War criminals,' said Adam.

'No!' snapped Goodenache. 'Some, maybe some. But not all. It was war. We did as we were told.'

'Where are these Germans?' asked Billie, quiet of tone to soothe Goodenache. She looked at Adam angrily. He shrugged and moved away, left it to her.

'Everywhere. In Russia. In America. Africa. Even in Germany. We have been waiting for nearly fifty years.'

'For what?'

'To come back. Why else would we wait? I thought you were smart.' He tapped his forehead as he spoke. 'Now Germany is

374

one, it's finally time to come home. Don't you understand? But we can't. Because the bloody Jews are waiting to take their revenge on us. I was a scientist. There are doctors, nurses, clerks and all types. Many have long since died. Not war criminals. Yes, some of us belonged to the Party. But only so we could do our work. The Lucy Ghost Ring is there to bring us back to Germany.'

'Who runs it?'

'Not one person. Many. Many, since the war ended.'

'Including Grob Mitzer?'

Goodenache nodded. They saw the pain of that memory in his eyes. 'Yes,' he said eventually. 'Grob was the most important. He kept it together all these years, when others lost faith.'

'But he had the knowledge?'

'More. Much more. There's knowledge and there's wisdom. Grob had the wisdom. The rest of us just had knowledge. Who do you think introduced the virus into your computer? His people. That's how brilliant he was.'

'But why?'

'To wipe out our records. To wipe out our pasts. Can you imagine what would have happened if Heinrich and the others had wanted to leave America and come home? How long before they would have been branded as Nazis, with all their war records published in the newspapers? Can you not see the dangers for us? People have no idea of what was really hidden from the public after the war. There were few records kept, and those were transferred on to tape by the Americans years ago. All the sensitive OSS archive was on the computer.'

'And you wiped everything out just to camouflage the truth?'

'It went wrong. The virus could only be triggered off when someone wanted classified information on our files. Not mine, but on those involved in the Paperclip Conspiracy.'

'The what?' asked Adam.

'The Paperclip Conspiracy,' Billie answered him. 'That's what they called the operation. The one bringing the German rocket people out covertly after the war.'

'Not just rocket scientists,' added Goodenache. 'All types of research people. Even some medical people from the concentration camps. There are more in those records than just Von Braun and his few. We had the same problem in Russia. Only it wasn't on a computer. Grob organized that as well. For our safety.'

'What about the deaths of the American and Russian agents?' Billie asked.

'What deaths? What agents?'

Billie realized his answer was genuine. She didn't tell him it was what had triggered off the virus. 'Why come back here? If you're running from the Israelis. Why not Russia? You would've been safe . . . '

'Russians. Philistines. I'm not a Russian. I'm a German. This is my home.' Goodenache rose from the bed and went to the window. 'Do you know why Heinrich and I wanted to come back here?'

Billie shook her head.

'Up there, in the mountains, there are big caves. We were moved here from Peenemünde. To be out of range of your bombs. We built factories in those caves. Factories for rockets. V1s and V2s. How do you think the Russians and Americans got into rocketry? By taking V2s from here, from the mountains, shipping them back and using them for their own experiments. They used all our rockets. We couldn't fire them in 1945 because we ran out of fuel. Because the idiots in Berlin cut off our supply. We could have changed the course of the war. Another six months and we could have changed everything. This is where we worked, with no resources, just our ideas and our hands.' He turned away from the window, came back to the bed and sat down once again. 'We built rockets from nothing. I was twenty-two years old. It is where we were happiest. Then we were sent back to Peenemünde. To tidy up. Burn the documents that could have won the war for us. Only it went wrong and I got caught by the Russians. To save my life, I became a Russian. For forty-five years I was something I wasn't. It's not a crime to want to come back, is it?'

'But why here?'

'Because if I'm going to die, then let me die where I was happiest.' He suddenly yawned. The drink was having its effect.

376

'Where is the society run from?' asked Billie quietly, wanting to move the discussion on, but not wanting to alarm Goodenache. 'Maybe that's where you should have gone.'

'They let us down.'

'Who?'

'The Party.'

She knew immediately who he meant. They were fucking Nazis. But she wanted confirmation. 'The National Socialists?'

'Of course. In Dresden. They let us down. They spent millions trying to get us out, to wipe our records clean, then they go and change their minds. New objectives, they say. And we, the ones who kept the dream alive all these years, made their beloved Party possible, are told to find our own way home.'

'Let's take you back to Dresden. They'll want to know where you are.'

'They couldn't give a damn.'

'Then let's tell them.'

'No.'

'How do I get hold of them?'

'They're in the *Heide*. That was Grob's idea. They'll fail without him.'

'Where's . . . ?'

'Forget them. If they had stuck to the plan instead of . . . ah! forget them.' He yawned again. 'I am tired.'

'The organization. How big . . . ?'

'No more. Not now. Let me sleep. Tomorrow, we'll talk then.'

He lay down on the bed. Adam saw how tired he was; his eyelids were already half-closed as he fought off sleep.

'Come on,' Adam said to Billie. 'We can finish tomorrow. At least we know what's going on.'

Adam didn't think there was any danger to Goodenache, his instincts would have warned him.

They returned to his room. He didn't say much, was simply prepared to listen. He had left the interview to Billie. He knew that Goodenache would respond better to a woman.

'Nazis,' she said, once the door was shut and she couldn't

377

be overheard. 'A bunch of Nazis, all waiting to come back. All waiting for the dust to settle.'

'Could be.'

'Got to be.'

'He's a Russian. They play tricky games.'

'But they're in this with us.'

'So they say.'

'OK. So we don't jump in with both feet. But we're still talking about Nazis. War criminals. Christ, there could be hundreds out there. Maybe more. Have you thought of who could be there? Even if they're dead, to know what happened to them. Wow!'

'You won't find Hitler, you know,' he mocked her.

'Shit to that, tough guy. How do you know? How does anybody know what happened? Except some of these guys. Do you have to?' she snarled at him as he took out a cigarette.

'It's my room.' Damn, he sounded too shirty, but he didn't like the way she could get under his skin. 'I need one, if you don't mind.' He lit his cigarette whilst she watched him.

'How can you do that to your lungs? In your profession?' she said, as he inhaled deeply.

He decided to ignore her comments. 'So let's say they are Nazis. Why kill Trimmler? Why the swastika mark?'

'Could be Israelis.'

'But why take out American and Russian agents?'

'Discount operation. Two for the price of one.'

'Very funny.'

'I don't know. But it's the obvious solution.'

She said nothing for a while. Then, 'There're still a lot of Nazis out there waiting to come back.'

'I agree. But it's got to be more than that. And it has to be stopped.'

'We can find out, but we can't stop it.'

'That's the difference between us. You're trained to get information. I'm trained to use it. No point in the information otherwise. Look, Billie, this whole thing is changing shape. We're getting close to something. I can smell it.'

'So can I. But what's that got to do with us?'

'You won't be able to cope with it. It's not in you. Power

378

and violence go together. It's called the law. Where power is backed by violence. By people like me. Fighting for the good guys. Then you come across this, where the violent have the power. No fucking scruples. And they chop someone's hands off because they think it's OK. That's when I go down to their level. Not pretty. And not for you, Billie.'

'Time for me to get off, eh?'

He nodded.

'I can't just go back. Not without a good reason.'

'You found Goodenache. Just say that's what you set out to do, to stick with me in case I knew something, and that when the mission was accomplished, you brought him home.'

'He's a Russian responsibility.'

'Still linked to Trimmler.'

'You really mean it, don't you?'

'I have to.'

She came towards him; in her eyes he could see the dread of what was to be. Trouble was, he didn't want to lose her either. But duty had to be the priority.

She reached up and stroked his chin. Then she leant forward – they were almost the same height – and caressed his cheek with her lips. He stood still, not daring to move, unable to break away. Damn it, they'd become too close.

'Not tonight, tough guy,' she whispered. 'No more alone.'

She put her arms round him, held the back of his neck and stroked his hair. Then she leant forward and kissed him on the mouth, brushed his lips, stroked them with hers, watched his eyes looking back at her. She knew he was hers and it thrilled her. She kissed him harder.

Incomprehensible, the enormity of it all. Why the two of us? Of all the atoms of the world. In this tacky room. No diamonds, no chandeliers, no party frocks and silk stockings, no glitz, no strains of smooching Sinatra. Just us and a dusty bed.

He put his arms on her waist and pushed her away, held her firm.

'What's wrong?' she asked.

'I'm not used to this.'

'What do you mean?'

'I can fuck. This I've never done before. This is more.'

'Ooh, tough guy. Just let it go. No performance. Just you.'
And she took his hand and led him to the bed.

She tugged at his sweater and he helped her take it off. She smiled. 'It's easier if we just undress ourselves.' Then she went and turned off the light.

'Why?' he asked.

'It's better. Too harsh,' she lied. She didn't tell him she was embarrassed by her forty-one-year-old body, didn't tell him that his youth made her feel old. Breasts squashed with time, overloaded in their fullness, stomach too relaxed with middle age.

He didn't push it. He understood the real reason. He grinned in the darkness. In time, she'd learn to trust him. Then they slipped under the blanket, wrapped into each other, their eyes locked in wonder and anticipation. They moved little, just pressed against each other, felt the excitement of unknown flesh. He loved her skin, the smoothness of her. He'd never felt skin like that, velvet skin, warm and slippery skin that absorbed him into her.

For a moment she felt fat, hated her skin, dreaded him feeling the wrinkles. To her, his body had a firmness she had never felt before. It was a smooth body, not bumpy and muscular like Gary's, or soft like Peter's, just rounded with muscle and firm. Later in the night she would discover the scars, the knife wound across his shoulder-blades where he'd been slashed in a Belfast bar, and the bullet wound above his right knee that had never healed properly, a legacy from when he was on border patrol and one of his own men had panicked and opened fire on him. All she felt now was his firmness as he pressed against her, probed gently into the dandelion fluff of her mound.

It was a desperate moment, full of emotion, urgent.

They were side by side, and she rolled on to her back, arched herself to receive him as she stretched her legs outwards and clasped them round him.

He kept still, wanting them both to crave each other beyond emotion. It was a full two minutes before he pushed firmly into her and felt her envelope him, felt her bury her face in his shoulder, heard her gasp, a little pain, unused to him being there, then the gush of warmth, love and pleasure.

He felt her tears on his shoulder and looked at her, but she was showing pleasure. They groaned, their love expressed in their sounds. Suddenly she'd forgotten the darkness, suddenly she was only twenty-one. They held each other tight, so tight that it took their breath away, zipped together into one being.

'I see stars,' she whispered into his ear, clutching him tightly, her eyes shut, all-seeing in the darkness, understanding earth and time and life and what it is in the moment's joy. 'I see flashes of light. God, I love you.'

It surprised him. No-one had ever said that before. He'd never allowed anyone the opportunity. 'I love you.' Strange words, but suddenly they seemed natural. He had never felt this power of emotion before.

They stayed like that for a long time, sometimes moving, sometimes still, the hardness of him and the warmth and softness of her blended into one. It had to go on for ever. Then, when he could take it no more, when he was on the edge of the precipice, but knew he was ready before her, he pulled back.

He saw the sudden disappointment in her face, the flash of a scowl across her eyes. He smiled. 'It's OK,' he said. And then he kissed the rose petals, wiped the dew from her lips. He felt her soften.

He knelt between her legs now. He wanted to taste her, to taste the heat and wetness. He watched her face before he entered her. He was surprised by her, there was little expectancy, just blankness. She'd turned her head away. He moved his tongue slowly inside her, felt her arch her back again, as if in some form of eager surprise. He had never done that before to anyone, had always found it beyond him. But, with her, it was natural. With her the body was a vessel of love, tenderness and belonging.

Her taste was new to him, and, as he ran his tongue along her, curled it deep into her, it excited him. He washed his face in the perfume that was her love for him. Then he searched out the little hard protruding button that was the energy of her sex, he stabbed at it with his tongue, felt her respond quickly, then urgently.

There was no awkwardness now, no face turned away, just

the joy and exhilaration of love and flying where she hadn't been before.

He felt her lift up to him as they started the final phase of their journey. No violence, no rapid motion, just feeling and tenderness and a pressure that was beyond sex, somewhere on another plane.

When he was once again close to his own explosion, holding back for her to join him, she said, 'Stay.'

He stopped moving, just pushed harder into her, held her with his love and waited for her.

'Stay,' she gasped.

She pulled harder at him, squeezed the very breath from his body.

'Stay.' Once again. The word thrilled him.

'I love you, Billie,' he said, regretted it, didn't want to break her own private intensity, but wanted to say her name.

'I love you,' she replied.

Then he heard that fluttering little gasp, the breath caught in them both, and the gasp was overtaken by a louder excitement in her voice, in her sounds of love. It was joined by another voice; he realized it was his own. The intensity was more than he had ever felt before. All that he had to give her with his mind and body was sucked out of him into her. He lay still, not wanting to break the spell, attempting to work out what was different. Before this, sex had been a temporary relief in a world of melancholy and crisis. It had been forgotten as quickly as it had begun. But this was a homecoming. Only Billie had ever done this for him.

He wrapped his arms round her, in the security of their warmth, smell, taste and foreverness, and they started to fall asleep.

'Good night, Princess.'

'Night, tough guy,' she replied, softly in her half-sleep.

'I love you.'

'I love you, too.'

The homecoming was complete.

'Did you hear that?' he asked her.

'What?' she answered, barely conscious.

'I'll be back,' he said and climbed out of the bed. He slipped on his trousers, sweat-shirt and shoes. There were no more sounds of men running, but his warning bells were ringing.

What, Marcus, what's going on?

'Where're you going?' she demanded, suddenly awake and watching him take the Browning from his holdall.

'Just checking everything's OK. Be back in a minute.'

He slipped out of the door and checked the corridor. It was empty.

He climbed the emergency stairs to the next floor and crossed to Goodenache's door. It was all quiet. He could see the light under the door. They'd switched it off earlier, when they'd left Goodenache. He put his hand on the door handle and tested it. The door was unlocked and he opened it carefully, the Browning cocked and ready in his right hand.

It was a carbon-copy deed, just as terrible as the first time.

A naked Goodenache was sprawled across the bed. The slash of blood across his throat and down his cheek revealed the knife wound he had died from. The blanket was thrown back and the sheet was swamped in blood, thick and red like liver. It was thickest at each side of the chest, where his arms had been.

Adam closed the door. He already knew what had happened to the arms. They were on the other side of the bed, crossed over, shaped like a swastika.

He searched the room, went through Goodenache's suit pockets, his suitcase and briefcase. There was nothing of interest or value, nothing that gave any clue as to why the scientist had been killed.

Five minutes later he returned to his own room. Billie had drifted back to sleep and he shook her awake.

'What's the matter?' she asked.

'We've got to get out of here.'

'Why?' Still sleepy.

'Goodenache's dead.'

'What?' she exclaimed, waking instantly and sitting up. The blanket fell away from her, revealed her nakedness.

'You're beautiful!' Adam leaned down and kissed her left breast.

'Adam!' She covered herself in her forty-one-year-old embarrassment. 'For God's sake!'

He laughed and stood up. He'd forgotten death wasn't part of her everyday vocabulary. 'I'm sorry. Come on. Get dressed.'

'You serious?'

He nodded.

'How?'

'Same way as Trimmler.'

'Oh no!' She looked shattered. Then she swung her legs out of the bed and hurriedly got dressed. Adam packed his few belongings, then went next door and did the same for Billie. When he returned with her case, she was ready and he led her down the hall, through the emergency exit, past the sleeping night porter in his little room and into the car-park.

It had started to snow and the thin white covering reflected the lights of the two police cars as they swept down Yorckstrasse towards the hotel. They didn't need their sirens at this time of the night.

Adam grabbed Billie and hid her behind the Audi, glad that he'd chosen a four-wheel-drive Quattro. He unlocked the car, clicked off the interior light and pushed her across to the passenger seat. He threw the two bags in the back and climbed in, pulling the door shut behind him.

'Down!' he commanded as the first police car pulled up outside the Kurhotel entrance, its lights illuminating the car-park. Two policemen climbed out as the second car arrived, and when the four officers had gathered, they entered the hotel.

'Why don't we just brave it out?' asked Billie.

'They'd never believe us. What with Trimmler in New Orleans and Goodenache here. Would you?' He saw it made her think for a moment, about him. 'Don't be stupid. I was with you.'

She didn't reply and Adam saw she was desperately trying to believe him.

'I didn't. And if I had, I wouldn't have called the police. Come on, love. It's called a frame-up.'

'Means you're stuck with me.'

'I've worked that one out already.'

He switched the engine on and swung the Audi out of the car-park, down Yorckstrasse towards the outskirts of the city. He stayed on the wrong side of the road, followed the tracks recently made by the police cars as they drove through the snow. The last thing he wanted to do was leave a trail for them.

It was two in the morning.

It was a long drive to Dresden.

The snow continued to fall as the Quattro clawed its way eastward towards whatever it was that they were seeking, whatever terrible things were waiting at journey's end.

66 Vauxhall Bridge Road
London

YOU COULD TELL nobody was welcome just by looking at the building. The metal shutters on the windows and behind the doors of the four-storey grey structure were designed to keep out unnecessary callers. There was no-one in reception, but if a stranger entered, he would soon find himself in the company of a gentleman in a blue suit with a friendly smile on his face and a bulge under his coat.

The roof bristled with antennae, of all shapes and sizes, tuned to a variety of radio signals and wavebands. This was a building of secrets, a part of British Military Intelligence, but not linked to Cheltenham's GCHQ, and a place for only the most covert communications.

There had been some concern in the early Eighties, when one of the national dailies, *Today*, moved its headquarters into the next-door building. After the initial flurry which prompted an internal memo warning staff not to fraternize with their neighbours, things soon returned to normal. The newspaper eventually followed others into the Docklands print centres that were fashionable at the time, and 66 Vauxhall Bridge Road returned to its position of anonymity.

As the black chauffeur-driven Jaguar pulled up outside, Coy came into the reception area to wait for his guest. The DDI climbed out of the car and walked into the building, past the smiling man in the blue suit who held the door open for him.

Coy took the American up to a meeting room on the third floor. In the centre of the room on a large mahogany table was a folder secured with the red wax seal of the United States government.

'Would you like me to leave you for a while?' Coy asked.

'No need,' replied the DDI as he took a seat and waved Coy to the opposite side of the table. The DDI pulled the folder to him, snapped the seal and opened it. It had been delivered from the American Embassy for his attention twenty minutes earlier. He wasn't worried about security; the seal ensured that.

Inside the folder were two sheets of faxed paper. He flicked through them, then threw them down on the table. 'Nothing. Not a fucking thing,' he cursed.

'A communication from America?' Coy murmured.

'An admission of failure. That's what you get when you stick the administrators in charge. No offence, Charlie.'

He knew that Coy was an administrator, that he had never been in the field either as a soldier or as an agent. But then Coy was present because he was a high-ranking nobody. The British had obviously decided to wash their hands of the whole affair. Coy was there to assuage the American's ego, to help without being too helpful. What his masters didn't know was that when Coy had worked in Washington for six years as a junior military attaché in the British Embassy, the DDI was one of the young Americans he had befriended. They had both been nobodies then.

'None taken, Norman.' As he spoke he remembered his nickname from the wild days. Stormin' Norman. In those days it reflected his ability in bed. Coy saw the attitude still applied to his old friend.

'Yeah. We got nothing over there. What about you?'

'They confirmed that his arms were cut off. And placed in the shape of a swastika.'

'Jesus. These arseholes are perverted.'

'Or they're trying to tell us something.'

'Come on, Charlie. You've been sitting behind a desk for too long. Course they're trying to tell us something.' He leant forward confidingly. 'Have you spoken to our friend?'

'This morning. Before I came in.'

'From home?'

'Yes.'

'Where was he?'

'In the office.'

'Fucking amazing, you can just ring right through to his office. What did he say?'

'He sends his regards.'

'Come on.'

'He's aware of everything. And is following it up.'

'Good.' He leant back in the chair. 'Nothing further from Germany?'

'No.'

'Take me through what you have. Just in case we got conflicting stories.' He picked up the papers he had discarded and laid them out so that he could check his own reports while Coy spoke to him.

'The police got a phone call saying somebody had been murdered in the Kurhotel.' Coy pulled a report from his pocket and put it down so that he could use it as a reference. 'They arrived ten minutes later. They had no idea who'd been killed. After arguing with the night porter for another ten minutes, they worked their way up floor by floor. Just knocked on doors and waited for people to answer. The night porter used a passkey for those rooms that were empty or where no-one answered. They found Albert Goodenache on the fourth floor. Time was recorded as 2.25 a.m.'

'Anything unusual in the room?'

'No. Well, apart from our man with his arms cut off and placed in the shape of a swastika. They found that rather unusual.'

'You're in a god-damned humorous mood today, Charlie.'

'I'm sorry. This whole affair's got to me. Nothing fits.'

'Everything fits. In the end. Go on.'

'No, there was nothing else unusual. He was naked and his throat had also been cut. I suppose that's because they had

387

to kill him first. You don't chop off a man's arms while he's sitting there watching you.'

'Cut the jokes, Charlie.'

'They called their chief in. He arrived at 3 a.m. In that time they'd sealed off the room and the hotel. Then they checked the belongings. That's when they found out who he was. When their chief of police saw Goodenache's passport, he called the Russian Embassy in Berlin. Some of these people still feel loyal to the Russkies. By then the local press had arrived. We think the night porter called them out, probably to make a few quid. Pounds to you.'

'I know what a few quid means.'

'The local journalist rang Frankfurt. His paper is part of a national chain. They carried it in the late-morning edition. That's how we picked it up.'

'That's how we got it.'

'They questioned all the residents. Nothing suspicious. Apart from one couple who weren't there. Registered as English. Two separate rooms. But only one was used, only one bed slept in.'

The DDI raised his eyebrows. 'We didn't get that.'

'The address they registered doesn't exist. We presumed the names were also false.'

'What about their passports?'

'It's all part of the European Community now. No frontiers, no passports.'

'How'd they settle the bill?'

'Didn't. Just left. Police think it could've been just a dirty night out. That's why we knew about the bed.'

'Then why two rooms?'

'Exactly.'

'No car number? No credit card imprint?'

'This is East Germany. They're not as sophisticated as us. Yet.'

'It was snowing. Car tracks?'

'Nothing.'

'Was it them? What's your gut say, Charlie?'

'I think it was.'

'So do I.'

'I also know about your computer.'

'What do you know?' The DDI was alarmed. There were some things you didn't tell even your friends.

'That it's been infiltrated. I also know what happened in New Orleans. Probably more than you do.' Coy then took the DDI through the report Adam had made to him on the phone. When he finished, the DDI sat back and said nothing for a while, just digested it. Coy watched him; it wasn't a time to interrupt.

'I wondered why they'd taken off together,' the DDI said eventually. 'That's if you believe them.'

'I do. The man is headstrong, but he's no traitor. And I don't believe he killed Goodenache.'

'No motive. Whoever killed Trimmler also did this one. And we . . . ' the DDI stopped. 'Hell, we still don't know who killed Trimmler. Maybe it *was* these two.'

'Lay off, Norm.'

'OK, OK. It wasn't them. So, who was it? And where the hell have they gone now?'

'Short of putting out an all-persons' alert, which would include the police and the Press, there's little else we can do.'

The DDI pursed his lips and pursued his own thoughts. Coy waited for him to finish his deliberations.

'I don't think that's a bad idea,' the DDI said at last.

'My people wouldn't like it. They want it kept low profile.'

'It's not their assets that are getting knocked off. Listen, Charlie, just give me a photo of our boy. I'll do the rest.'

'They won't allow it.'

'They won't know about it. We've got to spark this thing up. They just could be up on what's going on. We have to find them. And pronto. Give me the picture and we'll get it splashed across every newspaper and TV station in Germany. Once they're picked up, I can get someone in there and find out what's happening.'

'Are you going to release the girl's picture?'

'Damn right.'

'I'll think about it.'

'Charlie, you've got—'

'I said, I'll think about it. This thing, about involving our chap in the first place, not your style, at all.'

389

'Didn't know about it. The whole thing was dreamt up by our head of administration.'

'No, it definitely didn't have your imprint.'

'Even so, you sure sent us a lulu.'

'Best man.'

'Crazy man.'

'Unorthodox. With a splendid pedigree. A loner. But the best.'

'One of your Northern Ireland boys?'

'Yes. And experience in the Gulf. Nearly knocked out half the Iraqi command force one time. Missed them by about two hours. But he still went on, left his unit, and took out a couple of generals before getting back to our lines. Very successful for us, there and in the province. Trouble was, he never would listen to orders, rubbed everyone up the wrong way. But he always got the job done. In his own time.'

'What're you getting at, Charlie?'

'That he won't like being beaten. Trimmler's death was a sign of failure for him. He'll have picked up something. And he'll see it through to the end.'

'You got that much faith in him?'

'Yes. Can't stand the little shit, personally. But, given half a chance, he'll sort it out.'

'I hope you're right. Was there anything else?'

'No.'

'That's it then,' said the DDI, starting to return the papers to the folder. 'I've got to get back.'

'Everything on schedule?'

'Yeah. Presidential trips always are.'

Coy rose and walked round the table. 'When do you leave?'

'Air Force One's at Heathrow. We leave at two.'

'What's it like?'

'What?'

'The Presidential crapper. Don't you use it?'

'Shit, Charlie. You English have a real predilection for toilets. You know that? You're all crap happy.'

They both laughed.

'I'd better get going.' The DDI jumped to his feet. 'Hell, this thing's a mess. I got to stick with the President and all

I can think about is those two and what they're up to. One bed slept in, huh? Who the hell do the sonovabitches think they are. Bonnie and fucking Clyde?'

Air Force One lifted off from London Heathrow on schedule at 2.02 p.m., climbed out from Runway 27 Left and turned south on track for Paris.

Once the President had retired to his quarters for the short flight, the DDI opened the envelope he'd been handed when he arrived at the airport. The picture he took out was of Adam Nicholson. He smiled, mentally thanked Charlie, and slipped it back into the envelope.

Time to flush them out.

We're coming to get you, Bonnie and fucking Clyde.

Bellevue Hotel
Köpckestrasse
Dresden

THERE WAS NO need to register in separate rooms this time.

Once Adam had flashed his passport as a European Community resident, the reception clerk at the Bellevue had simply pushed the register card over the desk and asked the Englishman how he was going to settle the account.

'American Express.' Adam signed the register 'Mr and Mrs Nicholson'. The address he gave was a false one in Market Harborough in the Midlands.

At three o'clock that afternoon the four-wheel-drive Audi had disregarded the thickening blizzard and raced away from the threat of Nordhausen towards Leipzig and Dresden. But the westbound Route 80 continued in the tradition of the best East German roads and was difficult to follow in the snowy landscape without the hedgerows and markers that western drivers take for granted. It had slowed them down. At least it was the same for all traffic and Adam was soon convinced that no-one was following him. Throughout the night, throughout the seven hours it took to cover the one hundred and twenty kilometres to Leipzig, they had not passed another vehicle until they joined the rush-hour traffic into the city. They breakfasted, then picked up the autobahn at Leipzig and followed it all the way to Dresden. By now the snow had stopped, and what little had settled, quickly thawed. Characteristically, Adam decided to stay at the best hotel in Dresden. He had felt a hint of satisfaction as he walked through the lobby. It was crowded with businessmen, half of them English-speaking.

Their suite, on the fourth floor, overlooked the Elbe, a similar view to that enjoyed by Grob Mitzer when he had last met Frick on New Year's Day.

'Welcome to civilization,' Adam said as Billie unpacked. 'They've actually got room service here. Want something?'

'Anything. I'm starved.'

He ordered eggs Benedict and a steak sandwich for both of them, then went to the mini bar and poured an Evian water for himself and a diet Coke for Billie.

The room-service waiter appeared with their order twenty minutes later and prepared the table in the sitting room.

'You speak English?' asked Adam from the settee as he watched the waiter. He decided to continue the charade of not speaking German.

'Little,' replied the waiter, laying the table out.

'You live in Dresden?'

'*Ja*. Here. Me, in Dresden.'

'Is nice,' said Adam, lapsing into broken English like foreigners tend to do in a strange land. 'You know the *Heide*?'

'*Was ist?*'

'*Heide*. Place. Dresden.'

'*Ja. In Dresden.*'

'The *Heide*. You know . . . the *Heide*?'

The waiter shrugged and concentrated on his task.

'Dresden,' continued Adam.

'*Ja. In Dresden.* You' – the German pointed at Adam – 'Dresden. Here.'

'I know where I am.'

'Pliz.'

'I know . . . Where is the *Heide*?' He accentuated the last word heavily.

The waiter shrugged, smiled. 'Food. Is goot.' He finished his task, then held out his hand. Adam slipped him a five-mark coin and he left, full of smiles and goodwill.

'Impressed,' said Billie. 'You're very good.'

'Shut up and eat,' he replied, a big grin spreading on his face.

Meanwhile, the waiter went straight to the staff rest area and, using a coin phone, dialled his contact. He was meant to pass on any unusual information. By the time Adam and Billie were drinking their coffees, the contact had interrupted Kragan at a training meeting and told him of the two foreigners in the Bellevue Hotel who were enquiring about the Dresden *Heide*.

'I'm tired.' Billie yawned and stretched. 'We've had no sleep, you know.'

'I know.'

'Your eyes are red.'

'I've been driving a lot.'

'No way you're going to be fresh . . . unless you get some rest.'

'Billie. Will you stop it?'

'No.' She came over and put her arms round him, knelt in front of him and buried her head in his shoulder. He returned the embrace and they relaxed for a while in the comfort and safety of each other.

'This is why I didn't want to bring you,' he said finally.

She leant back and looked up at him. 'You don't mean that.'

'I do. I need to . . . to be myself. Out of touch with people. No emotions. Can't afford them.'

'Too late now, tough guy.'

'I know.' He knew she didn't understand his dilemma. She made him vulnerable. Danger, and the possibility of death, had never worried him before. That's why he had always won. Because he went further than most into that unimaginable world of extreme pain and violence. But now she made him like others. Now he could be hurt, because he didn't want to lose her. He suddenly thought of Marcus. Would he be there when he needed him out there in the unknown? Then he pushed everything from his mind as she touched him between his legs.

'Can't help myself,' she whispered. 'Never felt like this before. Never this alive.'

He knew what she meant.

They hung the DO NOT DISTURB sign on the door.

Billie went into the small shop next to reception while Adam, the brown holdall over his shoulder, asked the concierge for a map of the city and surrounding areas.

'Ah so! A *Falkplan* you need,' said the concierge, reaching behind and taking a map out of the rack behind him with a five Deutschmark price-tag pin on it. 'Bill it to your room, sir?'

'Please,' answered Adam, taking the map with one hand and showing his room number on the key tag with the other. As the concierge filled the bill out on the computer, Adam opened the brightly coloured map and spread it on the counter.

'You are looking for something?' asked the concierge.

'We wanted to visit some sights while we're here.'

'The main tourist visiting is over the river. The Zwinger and the cathedral.'

'I saw them from my window. We'll go across there later.'

'Is very good.'

'A friend of mine was here last year. He said something about the *Heide*. You know that?'

'Dresdener *Heide*. Yes, of course.'

'Where is it?'

'To the north. But it's no good.'

'Show me,' said Adam, pushing the *Falkplan* forward. 'I would like to see it.'

The concierge shrugged, opened the map and pointed at a large open space to the north of the city. 'This is the *Heide*.'

'A park?' queried Adam, bewildered.

'*Ja*. Also where the Russian camp was.'

'Russian . . . Their military base?'

'Their camp. For the soldiers.'

394

'All of it?'

'Much. *Ja.*'

'Thank you.'

'Is not good. Just buildings. For soldiers.'

'Are the Russians still there?'

'No. Gone back to Russia. Now it is empty. To knock down and build something new.'

Adam joined Billie in the small shop in the lobby where she was browsing through some silk scarves.

'Like this?' she asked, holding up a bright yellow-and-black creation.

'Nice. I've found the *Heide*.'

'Good. Where?' She walked towards the counter to purchase the scarf. Adam followed her.

'North part of the city. It's a park. It was a Russian military camp when they were here.'

'Russians?' She stopped as she spoke.

'That's right,' said Adam, taking the scarf from her and handing it to the girl behind the counter. 'On my room, please. Four two six.' He showed the girl his registration card. 'Do you want it wrapped?' he asked Billie.

Behind them a bellboy walked in, a pile of newspapers under his arm. The girl tapped Adam's room number into the computer and waited for it to print out the bill.

Billie shook her head and he took the scarf and handed it to her. 'It's empty now; the Russians aren't there any more.'

'Are we going . . . ?'

'How did you guess?'

The bellboy dumped the papers on the counter, gave the shop girl a big flirtatious smile, winked and left the shop. The computer started to print out the bill as Adam looked at the picture on the front page of the newspaper. It was a three-column shot of Albert Goodenache.

He picked up the folded-over paper, flicked it so he could scan the lower half of the broadsheet. His own face and Billie's stared back at him. He turned the paper over and put it back on the top of the pile.

The girl held out the bill for him. Billie had started to look through the English-speaking magazines on the rack.

'Time to go,' he said as she pulled out Newsweek from the others.

'I want this.'

'Now.' She sensed his urgency and looked towards him. He nodded. She put the magazine back and followed him out of the shop. He didn't wait for her. The Audi Quattro was parked at the far end of the small, packed car-park.

'What's happened?' she asked as she caught him up.

'Our pictures are in the newspapers.'

'Oh no!'

'Our people will have released them. It's the only way the Press could've got them.'

'So everybody's after us?'

'Looks like it.' He unlocked the car and they climbed in, Adam throwing his bag into the back.

'Why don't we contact them? Tell them what we know.'

'What do we know? That's not going to change anything. We have to keep going, Billie. Just keep going and hope something turns up. Unless . . . ' Adam paused.

'Unless I contact them and leave you to go on. Alone.'

He didn't answer, just switched the engine on and backed out of the car space.

'No,' she continued. 'Not now.'

They joined the evening traffic.

'You must promise me . . . that if anything goes wrong, you'll run for cover.'

'Not if you need help.'

'Especially if I need help. If I worry about you, if we're in real danger, I won't be able to protect either of us. I want your promise.'

'OK.'

'Don't lie to me, Billie.'

'I said' – she replied tetchily – 'I said I promised.'

'Good.'

He followed the signs out to the airport to the north. It was a simple route, left on to the Strasse der Einheit, up to the Platz der Einheit, across the vast square and straight up the 97.

But Adam didn't cross the Platz der Einheit, turning left instead into the Friedrich Engels Strasse. He followed it for two blocks, in the inside lane, then suddenly cut across the traffic to the centre, executed a left U-turn and returned to the Platz der Einheit. The traffic he had cut into blared at him for his boorish behaviour.

'I've seen this in the movies,' she joked.

He didn't answer right away but kept his eyes on the rear-view mirror. The headlights of another car swung across the central reservation and followed him down the Friedrich Engels Strasse.

'Bet it doesn't work as well as in real life,' he replied.

She swung round, but only saw the myriad jostling headlights behind them. 'Is somebody following?'

'I think so.'

'They don't let up, do they?'

'Never do.'

'What next, tough guy?'

'Let's tickle them.' As he turned left at the Platz der Einheit and north on to the Otto Buchwitz Strasse he explained what he wanted her to do.

'One hour thirty,' she said, when he finished.

'One hour thirty. To the minute.'

'OK. And if you're not there?'

'Give me no more than five minutes. Then get out of here and go to Berlin. Straight to your people.'

'Five minutes isn't long.'

'It's enough.'

'I love you, Adam.'

He reached over with his free hand, wrapped his fingers round hers and squeezed them. She squeezed back.

Twenty-five minutes later they saw the high blue-concreted wall on the right, the barrier that had kept the secrets of the Red Army from the citizens of Dresden. The traffic slowed to a halt once again. 'Come on,' he said. 'Now.'

He put the handbrake on and waited for her to slip her legs across the centre console, then he lifted himself up so that she could slide under him. He fell into the passenger seat and heard her squeal.

'Sorry,' he said. 'You all right?'

'I'm fine.'

A car honked from behind; the traffic was moving again.

'Where's the handbrake?' she shouted.

'Here.' He released it for her from between the seats. She put the car into gear and edged forward.

'Remember the route. Stay with the traffic,' he reiterated, opening the *Falkplan* for her and putting it above the glove compartment.

'Damn it, Adam. Stop treating me like a kid.'

He laughed. 'You take care. And no more than five minutes.'

'You take ca—'

It was too late. As the traffic slowed, he had thrust the door open and rolled on to the tarmac between the lines of cars.

'Adam,' she shouted after him, but the door had already been pushed shut. 'Damn you, tough guy,' she whispered to herself. She glanced in the rear-view mirror and saw the headlights of the traffic behind her. Which of those lights were following them? She looked into the back, which was when she realized the brown holdall had gone.

A car honked from behind, the traffic had begun to move again.

Adam kept low and dodged between the cars as he ran to the pavement. Once there, he kept close to the wall and walked northwards. There were few pedestrians about and the dimly lit pavement afforded him the cover he needed. He could see the Quattro's tail-lights drawing slowly away from him in stop-start jerky movements. He didn't turn his head to identify the car that was trailing it in case he was recognized. He hoped she'd be all right. Then he switched her out of his mind. He needed Marcus. He needed all the strength he had.

Three hundred metres farther on he neared the double steel gates and the *Sturmabteilungen* who guarded them. He hadn't spotted them standing deep in the shadows. There were two on duty, both in dark brown, ankle-length, leather coats. To the outsider they would be mistaken for smartly uniformed security guards rather than the trained storm-troopers they were. They leant against the gate, not expecting trouble as they joked among themselves.

He kept walking; there was little point in making them suspicious by turning round and retracing his steps. He knew they were watching him, but he ignored them; he was just a worker on his way home. As he drew level with the double gates, they swung open. He heard the whine of electric motors. He slowed to look inside the complex as a black BMW 5 Series swept out and joined the traffic jam going north. Before the gates closed again, Adam had seen the gatehouse and guards on the other side, and the tarmac road that led into the woods behind. He continued up the road until he was well clear of the gate and its watchers.

The wall was topped with rolls of barbed wire and jagged ends of glass stuck into the eight-foot concrete slabs. Every fifty metres there was a television camera scanning the road. It didn't take a great mind to work out that this was some security conscious area.

He looked down the road and decided on his course of action. It was unusual, but worth a shot. The traffic had started to move more freely now and he walked to the bus shelter at the road side, and waited.

It was five minutes before he saw what he wanted.

A single-decker yellow-and-black bus was travelling fast in the inside lane, its headlights dipped and no traffic immediately in front of it. When it was some ten metres away and was obviously not going to stop at the shelter, Adam stepped right into its path. As he did so he frantically waved it into the side.

The driver, travelling at some eighty kilometres per hour, had little alternative but to stand on the brakes and swing the bus hard right. It swerved wildly towards the wall, bounced over the pavement and came to a stop four feet from the concrete wall.

The driver, swearing loudly as his passengers picked themselves up from the floor and out of each other's laps, opened the front door and jumped down to see what had happened to Adam. There was no sign of him. The driver walked round the bus, then checked the road once again. Satisfied that there had been no accident, he cursed loudly to himself and climbed back inside.

Adam watched him from the top of the bus. He had scoured up the ladder at the back and now lay flat on the roof. He heard the hiss of the door closing and knew the driver was checking his passengers, making sure that there was no damage. After some time, he finally started the engine and crunched into reverse gear.

Adam came up into a kneeling position and waited for the bus to start moving. As soon as it lurched backwards, he stood up, ran the length of the bus as fast as he could and jumped over the wall. The bus stopped sharply as the driver heard the footsteps above him and listened. There was no more sound, so he slowly reversed back into the road as the *Sturmabteilungen* from the gate came up to investigate. But there was nothing to see and they soon returned to their posts as the bus continued on its way.

Adam landed in the clearing between the tree line and the wall. He rolled as soon as he hit the soft earth and crashed into the base of a tree. The impact winded him and he lay still, breathing deeply. When he was satisfied that he was all right and that no-one had heard him, he picked up the brown bag and moved into the safety of the trees.

Within a hundred metres he came across the first tank paths, ghost-like trails that appeared to be overgrown now, ever since the Russians had pulled out and taken their exhaust-belching tanks home on low-loader trains. He'd seen similar paths near Farnborough. But when he knelt down and tested the earth with his hands, some of the tracks seemed fresh. There were four-track and wide-wheel indentations. He wondered what sort of vehicles had made them.

He followed the widest of the paths northwards and eventually came to a deserted airfield. There were three hangars on the far side, buildings with curved roofs that extended down to the ground, camouflaged against cameras in the sky. The runway, running east to west, had individual taxiways leading off it from all sides, taxiways to the circular parking bays where Russian helicopters had once parked. He recognized the pattern. He reckoned the guards were in the small building at the easterly end of the runway. Bright lights glimmered inside, and smoke billowed from the chimney.

He found the two armoured personnel carriers that had made the four-track trails, four Jeeps, five cross-country motor bikes and two army trucks in the first hangar.

The second, lit by a single row of fluorescent lights, was stacked with large wooden crates from end to end. He crossed over to the side wall where he could watch the entrance while he opened one of the crates. He prized the sealed top open and found army uniforms, with no insignia marks on them.

A job lot, Marcus. A fucking job lot.

He checked three other boxes before he left. They were the same, full of khaki shirts, khaki socks and khaki singlets. Someone was buying army surplus, enough surplus to dress an army.

He went into the third hangar. Two Jet Ranger helicopters, two twin-engined Piper light planes, one single-engine Cessna four-seater and a six-seater Citation jet. They all had civilian markings and were German registered. He mentally clocked in all the registration letters; it would make tracing the owners easy when he got back to his own people.

He left the hangars and worked his way towards the centre of the *Heide*. He kept to the edge of the tree line and saw nothing until he reached the blocks of apartments that stood in an incongruous group in the forest area. They had obviously been the Russian barracks, with officers and men quartered there. In the centre of the buildings was a square parade ground with a forlorn flagpole. He surveyed it all from the safety of the trees.

Some of the flats housed families, but most seemed occupied by single men. They were identical, skinhead clones with square faces and frightening brutish expressions. *Millwall and England football supporters, Marcus. Hard men. Looking for violence.* Many of them wore uniforms, even at this time of night. Mustard-brown shirts, dark brown breeches, black leather boots. The insignia, a cross with the ends linked up and an eagle's head at the centre, wasn't far from the old Nazi swastika.

It's that bad, Marcus. It's the fucking Nazis all over again.

Keeping under cover, Adam followed a group who were setting off from their barracks. Two hundred metres down the road they came to a big old house standing in its own grounds. Though it was brightly lit, it had a forbidding aspect. Next to it was a modern block which the men headed for.

401

Adam approached as closely as he could. It was a large, tiled canteen and was obviously the main social gathering place for the troops. For that's how Adam saw them now. Troops. Men of war.

Storm-troopers, Marcus. Brown shirts. Fucking Nazis.

Then he thought of Billie and hoped she was safe. Neither of them had expected this. Nothing on this scale. This was an organization of trained killers. Hundreds, maybe even thousands of them. And he knew the effectiveness of small forces. The SAS was one. He knew how every SAS trooper counted as twenty or more ordinary squaddies.

Be safe, Billie. Stay with the traffic. Don't disappear into the darkness where they might come after you. Stay with the traffic. He felt the blackness return, felt its clamminess across his brow as he started to sweat. Only this time it wasn't for him, but for Billie.

Stay with it, Adam. He suddenly felt Marcus very close, felt him taking over. *Stay with it, Adam. For both of you.*

For all three of us, Marcus. For all three.

He checked his watch. He still had forty minutes to run before he met Billie. He was less than five minutes from the road, and he needed another five to get over the wall. He'd seen enough trees close to the boundary to know he could use them to scale up, and his coat would protect him against the barbed wire. Traversing walls like that was part of his standard training. It gave him ample time to check the house.

He watched the canteen building for a while. The men inside, whom Adam had already christened storm-troopers, had a close camaraderie. He watched them joking with each other, sharing in the songs. They'd be a tough bunch to deal with, these skinheads.

Then he circled the building and crossed over to the big house. It was lit up, reminiscent of a Christmas tree. Like the other built-up areas, the sections immediately surrounding it were floodlit. Even here, this distance from the road and behind the protection of the barbed-wire wall, security was of the utmost. The entrance to the house was guarded by three storm-troopers, all with pistols strapped to their waistbelts. One of them was cradling a sub-machine-gun in the crook of his arm.

Heavy-duty skinheads, Marcus. This is where it's at.

He skirted the house to the rear, but guards were also there. Two of them this time, both carrying holstered pistols.

Not now, Marcus. Not the time to show our hand. Get out and report back. Tell them this is where Trimmler's road ends. In a boy's camp for Nazis.

There must be arms here, Marcus. Dig deeper. You've still got twenty minutes.

Three men came out of the rear of the house. Two seemed ordinary storm-troopers, the third was different. He wore a black uniform, black breeches, and a flared jacket. The new National Socialist emblem was emblazoned on his armlets and on the badge on the peaked hat he carried. His blond hair wasn't short cropped like the others, but was curly and fell over his collar. At that distance Adam couldn't see the scar that ran down Kaas' cheek.

They moved away from the house complex down one of the narrower paths. Adam followed them from the security of the trees, watched the senior officer talking as the others listened and followed him. There was a closeness about them borne of familiarity.

This is a team, Marcus. These bozos are different.

There were warning signs now to deter people from going farther. The path led to a log cabin with a chalet-style sloping roof in the middle of a clearing. There was no floodlighting here, only a small fluorescent light over the entrance. It was a most secret place.

The three men entered the chalet led by Curly Top. Adam circled the building. There were no windows he could look in; whatever horrors went on within those wooden walls were kept well secluded from prying eyes.

He decided to investigate, to see if he could gain entry, and crossed the clearing towards the front door. There was sand on the ground, about four inches deep, completely surrounding the building.

No-one challenged him.

Carefully he peeked through the glass window in the door. A long corridor ran down the length of the building with doors leading off on both sides.

*Go or stay? Follow my logic or my nose. Shit, why can't
I keep out of trouble Marcus?*

As he turned the door handle to enter the building he saw a
storm-trooper come out of one of the side rooms. He stepped
back quickly and slipped into the darkness. He crept along the
wall, keeping in the shadows.

He wasn't sure whether the klaxon blared first or the perimeter floodlights snapped on, saturating the clearing with harsh
blinding light. He must have triggered off one of the alarm
beams that ran along the side of the chalet. No wonder they
didn't need lights, the alarm system was warning enough. As
he ran into the trees, he heard the chalet door open and the
shouts of the men coming out. He kept going, didn't stop to
see what his hunters were up to.

'Over here,' shouted one of the *Sturmabteilungen* and the
others, six to start with, but soon joined by more from inside
the building, ran to where he had found the tripped alarm.

'That way. Look,' said one, pointing at Adam's deep footprints in the mixed sand and snow.

The men started to follow when Kaas shouted after them,
'Wait. Get some weapons.' His own revolver was already in
his hand. 'And spread out. Oberleut'nants, take charge of your
groups. Spread out and find him.' The footprints told him it
was only one person. 'And I want him alive. Get going.'

As his men fanned out, Kaas went back into the building and
called the east and west gatehouses on the internal phone. Once
he had warned them, he contacted Kragan in the main house.

Two minutes later, as Kaas joined his men in the forest, the
klaxon alarm sounded at the barracks and canteen buildings.
At the same time, the forest path and road lights were switched
on and lit up vast tracts of the *Heide*.

Adam was under one of the lamps as it burst to life. He
moved deeper into the trees. The distant klaxons told him
the whole camp was being mobilized. He knew they'd be
armed. He dropped the brown bag and took out the Heckler and Koch MP5K sub-machine-gun. He pushed a clip
into it and rammed four more into his jacket pockets. The
Browning was already holstered under his shoulder. He took
out the remaining hand-grenade that Frankie had given him

in New Orleans and slipped that into his inside pocket.

OK, Marcus. Let's give as good as we get. Time to take the initiative.

He changed direction and started to head north. He could hear vehicles moving along the road, dropping storm-troopers off at regular intervals as they started to search the forest. There was a lot of shouting, helping him pinpoint where the search parties were positioned. They had too many people out; there was a good chance that they would trip over each other. Half the number would have been ideal, with the rest ringed around the perimeters.

He worked his way northwards, back the way he had come. They wouldn't be expecting that. Marcus was with him, his second sense acting as well as ever, warning him of any storm-troopers. Very soon he had retraced his steps and was back at the wooden chalet.

He kept clear of the sanded clearing and the alarm beams and bypassed all the inhabited areas. He could hear people shouting in the distance and knew that they had gone chasing off in the opposite direction. But he remained ultra-cautious.

He heard the helicopter winding up when he was only two hundred metres from the airfield. He had reached the open area of the tank trails when the helicopter's lights blazed on and it started to lift into the sky. Adam was trapped in the open and he sprinted towards a deep tank track as the aircraft swung towards him, nose low as it gathered speed. He threw himself, face down, into the two-foot-deep trench and lay still. Within seconds the whole trench lit up. He tightened his grip on the sub-machine-gun, waited for the helicopter to slow and swing towards him. But it passed by, the crew too involved with the early flight of their craft and not expecting to find any intruders this close to the runway. It gathered speed and raced towards the built-up complexes.

When he was certain it was out of range, Adam rose from the trench and made his way towards the hangars, alert to any further helicopters being readied. There was nothing to alarm him, no activity in the building at the end or near the hangars. He presumed those men who had been on duty had all gone in the helicopter to help the others.

The hangar doors on the furthest building had been opened to bring out the helicopter. Checking all was clear, he peered inside. There was little point in going further. The two twin-engined aeroplanes were trapped behind the Citation jet. It had been a fanciful idea, flying out of there, and he laughed at his own foolishness. Jenny Dale's lessons would have to be used another day.

He quickly ran over to the first hangar. The big door was still shut. He eased himself in through the side door. No-one there. He surveyed the Jeeps. The keys were in them.

He went to the side door and checked outside; still no obvious movement.

He re-entered the hangar and searched for the switch to slide the double doors open electrically. He found it on the far side, punched the red button and watched the big metal doors start to move.

He climbed into a Jeep and turned the key. The vehicle was slow to start, coughing with a metallic grind as the fuel refused to fire. He cursed, pumped the accelerator, hoping not to flood the engine, and turned her over again. The Jeep fired up and he slipped it into gear, released the clutch and edged it forward. The doors had opened wide as he reached them.

'*Achtung! Wie gehts?*' shouted a voice from the darkness. Adam looked up and saw a storm-trooper running towards him, waving his hand. When he realized that Adam was not one of his colleagues, he stopped and reached for the revolver in his belted holster.

At fifteen metres distance, he was no match for the Browning. The 9mm slug cut through his neck before he had unholstered his pistol.

Shit, Marcus. Now it starts. Now it fucking starts.

Adam felt the blackness race through him as he saw the storm-trooper fall. He switched on the lights and drove down the tank paths towards the front gate. They wouldn't expect him to be in a vehicle.

The blackness was still with him – the depression of a life taken. *Why the fuck am I here, Marcus? Why am I always in the shit?*

Hope you're OK, Billie. Five minutes. No more. Please do as I told you.

He saw the first group of storm-troopers in the forest to his left. They were moving towards the perimeter wall. One of the men waved in his direction and he waved back, kept his head down and hurtled on down the track.

The helicopter was now working an area to the left, near the chalet, its strong searchlight playing through the trees. A group broke cover in front of him, but his headlights were on full beam and blinded them, protected him as he drove past. One of the men tried to jump on board, but couldn't make it as the Jeep was travelling too fast. Adam heard him curse and the others laugh at his misfortune.

The track he had chosen turned into the forest. He would rather have stayed in the open, where they weren't searching for him, but he had to return to the gatehouse. It was his best way out.

He had to slow down, there were too many men crossing the road in the forest in front of him. They had torches, heavy weapons slung over their shoulders. But somehow he got through. Nobody shone a torch at him, nobody recognized the stranger in their midst.

His headlights picked out Curly Top in the black uniform. He stood in the middle of the road, his arm outstretched in a signal for the Jeep to stop.

Bastard's tired of walking, Marcus. Can't stop.

Adam slowed to a crawl, as if stopping for him. The bright headlights confused Curly Top, who now held his hands up to shield his eyes. He waved to Adam to turn off the lights.

Adam grinned, his blackness gone as danger touched him.

He gunned the engine when he only had a few metres to go, felt the Jeep claw at the hard ground and hurtle forward.

Curly Top dived out of the way, grabbing for his revolver as Adam drove past.

Go, Marcus. Go. Go.

He was clear before the storm-troopers could react. They may have been well trained, but they weren't match fit. Before the first shots rang out, Adam had turned the shallow bend and was shielded by the safety of the trees.

He drove for his life, knew that Curly Top would be screaming into the radio he carried over his shoulder, screaming for his storm-troopers to find and stop the Jeep. He decided not to abandon it, not to go on foot. He'd be at the gatehouse within two minutes. Maybe he could just crash his way through.

He saw the searchlight before he heard the helicopter. The roar of the Jeep's high-revving engine had drowned the turbine's sound.

He swung left to right, back again, careered across the road, in and out of the trees. In front and to each side, people were shooting at him, but they all missed. He unswung the machine-gun and sprayed the bullets into the trees, sending his hunters scattering for cover. He heard the machine-gun fire from the helicopter, but it was difficult for the pilot to manoeuvre in such a tight space, even more difficult for the machine-gunner to take aim. The bullets from the helicopter were wild and causing more trouble to its own troops than to Adam.

As he raced and bumped down the track, the helicopter suddenly lifted and flew forward, leaving him on his own.

He's heading for the gatehouse, Marcus. He's going to wait for us.

He pushed the accelerator to the floor and hurtled flat out down the track, more off the ground than on it. When he rounded the final bend, he saw the helicopter hovering in the middle of the road, no more than five feet off the ground and some twenty metres from the gates.

The gates were closed.

There were a few guards scattered to the side of the road, all armed, no more than six or seven as far as Adam could make out. Curly Top hadn't had enough time to get more people to the gatehouse.

Adam saw the machine-gunner hanging out of the open door of the Jet Ranger. He didn't wait, just aimed his Heckler and Koch MP5K at the helicopter, one-handed, and opened fire. He saw the machine-gunner panic, and open fire blindly at the Jeep. He smashed the windscreen with one bullet and Adam felt a sliver of glass cut into his cheek, but he did little other damage.

Adam kept firing in short bursts and drove straight at the helicopter.

The pilot, realizing that the Jeep was going to ram him,

applied the cyclic and tried to lift clear. But the front of the vehicle caught the undercarriage and sent the helicopter shuddering sideways. The pilot, frantically trying to avoid disaster, felt his craft tilt and knew the big rotors were going to hit the gatehouse before they actually did. The rotors slashed through the roof of the building, as if through a doll's house. The Jet Ranger arced upwards, a big prehistoric pterodactyl lurching blindly in its death throes. Then it crashed to the ground and died, no explosions, no flames reaching to the sky. It simply flipped over and died in nothingness.

Adam had slammed the Jeep to a stop before the helicopter was on its back. He took the grenade from his pocket, unleased the pin and threw it at the base of the double gates.

Nobody was shooting, they were all watching the helicopter in its death throes.

He swung round and drove away from the gate. He saw some of the storm-troopers turn their attention to him and he sprayed them with his MP5K.

German bullets for German flesh, Marcus.

Then the grenade exploded, tore the doors apart some two metres, enough for a man to get through, but not the Jeep. He wrenched the wheel round and rammed the gate, the bullets now ripping into the air around him. The Jeep slammed into the gates some more, but still not enough to drive through.

Adam was thrown forward, up and over the shattered windscreen and on to the bonnet. He kept rolling, still hanging on to his weapons, and fell over the front of the Jeep and on to the pavement outside. Somebody was yelling and the bullets suddenly stopped. As Adam looked back through the split in the gates, he saw Curly Top, saw the evil hatred in his eyes.

Keep going. Just because they've stopped shooting it doesn't mean they're not going to come after you.

He turned and started to run down the road, southwards, into Dresden.

The Audi Quattro honked from across the road. 'Here. Over here!' Billie shouted through the open window.

Shit, Marcus. She shouldn't be here.

There was little traffic on the road and he ran across to her, ran round to the passenger side and jumped in.

'I said no more than five minutes,' he shouted.

The words hurt her. 'But you needed me. Look at your face.'

He'd forgotten the glass that cut his cheek. 'It's OK. I said five minutes.'

'But you needed—'

'Five means five. If it was more, then I was in trouble. Shit, I didn't want you back. Let's go. Where's your tail?'

'I lost him,' she said proudly.

'Come on, get going.'

'Where?'

'Just go. Come on.'

She pulled away. As she moved away from the pavement, a black BMW slowed down and drew abreast of them. Adam remembered the BMW that had pulled out of the complex when he walked past earlier. She hadn't lost her tail, they'd had two following her.

Before Adam could react with his weapons, the passenger in the BMW, a young blond skinhead, set light to a glass bottle half-filled with petrol with a piece of rag stuffed in the top, and hurled the Molotov cocktail through Billie's open window into the Quattro.

The bottle shattered in the back of the car, the petrol saturating and sticking to the upholstery. As the fumes spread, they were ignited by the flaming rag and exploded. Some of the petrol stuck to the back of Billie's hair and caught fire.

She was already screaming, desperately trying to steer the car away from the BMW, where the youth was attempting to light another Molotov cocktail. Adam leant over and wrapped his arm round the back of her head, protected her from the flames and blocked out any further damage to her. With his other arm he wrenched the wheel to the right, forced the Audi on to the pavement and against the wall. The car jerked to a sharp stop. The engine was still screaming.

'Take your foot off the accelerator!' Adam shouted. 'Come on, come on. Get out.'

He leant over and pushed the door open, shoved her out as the engine died. The BMW had come to a stop and the boy was climbing out, his Molotov cocktail now lit and ready.

With the flames engulfing the roof of the Audi, Adam lay across the two front seats, aimed the machine-gun and shot the bomber dead. The skinhead fell backwards into the BMW and the bomb exploded in the car, spewing its liquid of flaming death.

Adam crawled out of the Audi, grabbed Billie and ran with her before the petrol tanks exploded.

The BMW went first, its roof torn open by the flames and blast as if by a giant unseen can opener. The Audi Quattro blew its doors and windows out twelve seconds later.

As Adam dragged Billie to her feet, he saw Curly Top in front of him. He wasn't alone. They were surrounded by storm-troopers.

He went for the machine-gun, but someone kicked him hard in the back of the head. He resisted the pain, tried to bring the weapon to bear.

Another sharp blow hit him between his shoulder-blades.

No pain, Marcus. Kill the pain.

He willed himself forward and upwards.

Another blow on the side of the head. Then another.

The bastards were kicking him like a fucking dog. He twisted to shield himself, tried to pull himself round and use that big machine-gun he had carried for so long.

But they didn't let up, kept at him. In the stomach, the shoulders, more kicks to the head.

He managed to keep the pain at bay, but only because, unconscious, he was forced to let himself go. Just before he passed out he heard Billie screaming his name.

Adam. Adam.

Help her, Marcus. Help her till I come back.

CIA HQ
Langley

'YOU'RE ABSOLUTELY CERTAIN about this?'

'Yes, sir.'

The DDA sat back and waited for the Exec Director to continue. The news he had just imparted had had the effect he had expected. His superior was baffled, unsure of the validity and import of what he had just been told.

'How the hell did you find out?' the Exec Director asked suspiciously. There was bad blood between the two men, something he had himself nurtured. Divide and rule had always been his style.

'I decided to run a check on all personnel involved in this matter.'

'All personnel?' questioned the Exec Director.

'Up to the level of Deputy Directors.' There was no way the DDA was going to run a check on his superior.

'Why?'

'This thing's taken so many damn twists and turns . . . that I just believe we should question every angle. I also ran a check on my own records, I should add. There could've been something there, someone I'd met in the past that might open another door.'

'Wasn't your door you opened,' cut back the Exec Director sharply.

'I can only report what we found. We just threw all the names into a big data base and sat back to see what the computer threw up.'

The Exec Director rose from his desk and crossed to the window, stared out on the cold, snow-filled landscape that filtered down to Langley. He didn't speak for nearly a minute; the DDA sat quietly, knowing this was not the time to interrupt his thoughts.

'Was a time when we played these games and enjoyed it. We knew who our fucking enemies were,' reminisced the Exec Director. 'Now we're all on the same side. Trouble is' – he went on, coming back to his desk – 'you don't know whose side you're on, including your own. I tell you, pork and beef just don't mix on the same plate.' He sat down. 'How close were they?'

'The Englishman or the Russian?'

'All three.'

'They just all happened to be in Washington at the same time. Guess they mixed in the same diplomatic circles, got to know each other. That's not unusual. Even in the cloak-and-dagger community. A good source of information.'

'They ever communicate now?'

The DDA shrugged. 'A few letters, cards. Nothing unusual. The DDI's met Coy a couple of times. As would be expected. They worked closely during Desert Storm. This visit to Coy in London was logged as gathering information on Nicholson.'

'Did he discover anything?'

'We've had no report, sir.'

'I can live with Coy. But the Russian worries me. Shit, Rostov's the number two in the KGB. They say he's going to be the next Director.'

'They were friends a long time ago. Rostov was only a military attaché . . . '

'Fuck the title. He was a spy. They all were.'

'Our people knew that. They still had friendships. There's nothing to suggest any different.'

'I hope not.' The Exec Director paused for a good twenty seconds before continuing: 'Did they share any women, anything like that?'

'No. Nothing along those lines.'

'Happened in England. That scandal in the Sixties. War Minister, John Profumo. He was porking this hooker who was also in bed with a Russian spy.'

'Ivanov.'

'That's the guy. Brought the whole damn Government down. These things happen.'

'I don't think that's the case here. They just went out for dinner, that sort of thing.'

'Chase it, anyway. I'd hate it to rebound from another direction.'

The DDA knew he meant from above. The Exec Director was no different from the rest of them. They all spent time covering their asses. 'I'll keep an eye on it, sir.'

'The German police come up with anything on Bonnie and Clyde?'

'Not a smell.'

'I guess we got Nicholson's picture from the Brits?'

'If we did, then no-one's admitting it. They've been on to us. Want to know if we released it.'

'How the hell would we . . . ? Coy. Is that where it came from?'

'You'll have to ask the DDI.'

'That'll have to wait. His first responsibility's looking after this Berlin trip. Let's just hope the German cops get hold of Nicholson and the girl before they cause any more trouble. Shit, I'd like to know what the hell they're up to. I really would.'

So would the rest of us, reflected the DDA. So would the rest of us.

The Main House
Dresdener *Heide*
Dresden

THE PAIN BROUGHT him out of his unconsciousness. It was a sharp pain, on his left side and below his ribs. It wasn't long before that pain merged with the others that covered his body.

Adam lay still, his eyes closed, not wanting to alert whoever was in the room. He listened intently, heard nothing immediate, only the muffled sound of a radio or television from another room.

He opened his eyes slightly. Curly Top sat watching him from a chair, a mischievous grin on his face.

'Welcome to Dresden,' he said in English, the accent heavy but clear. When Adam didn't respond, he scraped the chair back and stood up. 'I know you can hear me. I can either kick you hard or you can open your eyes and save the hurt. It's up to you.' As he spoke he moved menacingly forward.

No point, Marcus. I need the strength for later. Adam opened his eyes and looked up at Curly Top.

'Good. We understand each other. We're both professionals,' stated Kaas.

Adam didn't reply; he was more concerned about working out where he was being held. His hands were behind his back and he felt the sharp metallic bite of the handcuffs on his wrists. His feet were unshackled; he still had his shoes on.

The room was of medium size, a bare room, probably an attic. The snow-clad tops of the trees outside the window confirmed that. Where the hell was Billie? He suddenly realized she could have died, that something awful could have taken place after he passed out.

Kaas turned and walked to the door, pulled it open and shouted in German: 'Get Kragan.'

Adam lay still as Kaas came back and sat in the chair once again. Where was Billie?

Kaas stretched his right foot out and prodded Adam's thigh with it, grinning as he did so. Adam jerked his leg back as the pain seared up his muscles. They must have kicked him very hard for it to be so tender.

'So, Englishman. Mr Nicholson. Adam Nicholson. You are a famous person now.' As he spoke, Kaas pulled a newspaper from his jacket pocket and held up its front page for Adam to see. He looked at his own face staring back, with Billie's face next to it. The headline in German screamed, SEARCH FOR MURDER SUSPECTS.

'Where is she?' Adam asked Curly Top.

'Your girlfriend? In good hands.' The German grinned as he put the paper back in his pocket. 'You like being famous, Mr Adam Nicholson? Your photograph is also on television.

All this . . . such a famous person, and no-one to ask for your autograph. Because no-one will ever find you.'

As Curly Top laughed, Adam saw the door open and Kragan enter. Curly Top stood up as his superior came into the room.

'Has he said anything?' asked Kragan in German.

'Only wanted to know where the girl was.'

'What did you say?'

'That she was in good hands.'

'Don't tell him any more. Let the bastard worry.'

'He's hurting a lot. We softened him up nicely. Make things easier when we go to work on him.'

'Good.' Kragan knelt down in front of Adam and looked at him as a butcher would appraise a cut of meat. 'We know you speak German, Mr Nicholson,' he said, still in German.

Adam didn't respond, just stared warily at Kragan.

'As Walther said, the girl is in good hands. Our young men's hands. She will be enjoyed by them. No doubt she will also enjoy herself with the best of our manhood.' Kragan continued in German, but saw no change in the Englishman, no sign of recognition, no flicker of anxiety. He stood up and turned to Kaas. 'I don't know. Maybe he understands, maybe he doesn't. But it'll take more than a few bruises to soften him up. I want five storm-troopers to give that girl the time of her life. And I mean all together. When he sees her, I want him to know they've fucked her in every hole she's got. Everywhere. His bruises aren't going to hurt him, make sure the ones on her will.'

'OK.' Kaas left the room.

Adam kept his silence and cursed his helplessness. If he allowed them to know he understood German, it would have made little difference. They just wanted to break him and would use any means available. *Get the hands free, Marcus. Sit it out until I've got my hands free. Oh, Billie, I must have been crazy to let you come with me.*

'Where is she?' Adam heard himself ask Kragan.

'Mrs Wood? That's no matter,' Kragan answered in English. 'Who else knows you are here?'

'What're you talking about? Why should . . . ?' He stopped

and gritted his teeth as Kragan lashed out at him, punching him sharply in the ribs.

'You know what I'm talking about,' Kragan shouted. 'Who else knows?'

'I said, I . . .'

Kragan smacked him again, this time open-palmed across his cheek. Then he jabbed him in the ribs again. Three more times, harder and more furious with each blow. Then Kragan kicked him in the stomach and, as Adam doubled forward, he kneed him in the cheek, sending him sprawling backwards, banging his head against the wall. Before he could recover, Kragan punched him sharply, twice, in the ribs again. The pain seared through Adam, almost sending him into unconsciousness once again.

'Who else knows?' repeated Kragan coolly.

'I don't . . . shit, I don't know . . .'

'The pain you feel now is nothing to what the others will do. Why are you here? We know you were in America together. That the Americans called you in to protect our friend Heinrich Trimmler. Do you know who killed him? Hey?'

'I don't know.'

'Did you kill him? Is that why you ran away? With the girl?' He waited for Adam to answer, but nothing was forthcoming. He jabbed the Englishman twice in the ribs again, watched him fight to control the pain, watched his victim's eyes drift back into focus. 'Why come after Albert Goodenache? Why did he die?'

'I don't know.'

'The newspaper says you are a British soldier. That the girl is an American agent. That you were in Nordhausen when poor Albert was killed. Why?'

Come on, Marcus. If it's not these chaps, then who? Who's fucking responsible for all that's been going on?

'Where's the girl?' he asked again.

'Who else knows?' Then the repeated jabs to Adam's ribs. The question followed once again as the pain subsided. 'Who else knows?'

Behind Kragan, Adam saw Kaas come back into the room. He realized he hadn't been anywhere, that it had been a trick they played on him to see if he spoke German. So she was all right. He had to believe that. He couldn't afford to believe otherwise.

'Where's the girl?'

Kragan swung round in disgust. 'I didn't tell you to come back,' he barked at Kaas in German.

'You won't get anywhere like that,' replied Kaas. 'This boy's been in the wars. He's no soft—'

'Then *you* find out what's going on. I don't care how. Just get it done.'

Kragan stormed out of the small room as Kaas crossed over to Adam.

'He doesn't understand, Mr Nicholson.' He chuckled. 'It takes more than a few bruises, and a few kicks, to make people like us talk, eh?'

Adam didn't respond. He saw the psychotic in Curly Top, saw the arrogance of the bully paraded before him. *We're in for a rough time, Marcus. This guy doesn't do it for anything but fun.*

Kaas leant forward and dragged Adam to his feet as he yelled for the guards to come in and help him. Adam didn't struggle; no point in wasting energy when all he'd get for his efforts would be a clip round the ear. He had to wait, keep patient, until a time for action presented itself. There was always such an instance. The key was in recognizing it, not letting the moment pass.

'Our men will soon get the truth out of him,' reported Kragan.

'You've had long enough,' Frick retorted sharply, the anxiety in his voice obvious. 'We have to find out what these people are up to. I don't want any more time being wasted on this shit. There *is* no more time. We need to prepare ourselves. Our moment is here.'

They were in the big room on the second floor that served as Frick's office. It had once been the master bedroom and looked out on the woods to the east. Frick stared at the winter scene, the snow now falling heavily.

'We won't let this matter slow us down,' said Kragan, moving closer to Frick. 'But we need to find out what—'

'I know what we need to find out. Just get it done.'

'It is being done, but—'

'You asked why they are here?'

'Yes.'

'And they said nothing at all?'

'Not yet.'

'Why would they kill Trimmler? And Goodenache?'

'If they did.'

'You don't think they did?' Frick turned back to face his lieutenant, surprised by the answer.

'I don't know. I just can't see why.'

'Then why come here? To Dresden. Here, into the *Heide*. Unless to trap us. By the authorities. Or the Americans.'

'Their pictures were spread all over the news bulletins. Pictures that could only have come from the Americans or the British,' Kragan answered warily. Frick hated being contradicted and often flew into a rage when put in such a position.

This time Frick was thoughtful. 'Then the Russians. To embarrass the Americans. And to force us out into the open.'

'It's very possible, Führer.'

'What happens in the next few days is critical to our success. Nothing must get in the way.'

'Nothing will, Führer.'

'Are there any changes in Berlin?' asked Frick, suddenly changing tack.

'Buhle says not.'

'I hope he keeps his mouth shut.'

'He's a newspaper man. He's used to secrets.' Kragan didn't add that he had never trusted the newspaper proprietor who sat on the council. It was not that he wasn't loyal to the cause, but because he appeared to enjoy his own sense of importance too much.

'He's also used to leaks,' stated Frick. 'But he's all we've got at the moment.'

'If there are any changes, I'm sure we'll find out in time. I think it's unlikely. These things are planned and rehearsed well ahead of schedule.'

'As long as no-one suspects. Just find out what the Englishman and his woman know. They could hold the key that saves us.'

Her fear had turned to anxiety, then to boredom and now to anger. Billie had been roughly bundled by a group of storm-troopers away from the burning car and into the Dresden *Heide*. She remembered screaming, remembered one of the storm-troopers punching her in the face to stop her. As they dragged her away from the flaming Audi, she had turned and seen Adam lying on the road, shielding himself. She had shouted out to them, 'Don't hurt him! Don't hurt him!', but it was lost in the general mêlée and then she was punched once again, this time harder and more painfully. She felt her top lip swell up as she tasted blood, and she said nothing more. She could only think of Adam and pray he would be all right.

They'd thrown her into a Jeep and driven her into the *Heide*, through the woods, to a large wooden building hidden in the trees. They manhandled her out of the vehicle and through the front doors, down the corridor and into the small, windowless and empty room that had become her home for the last nine hours.

Nobody had visited her. Her only companion was the bright light that was set high in the wall and was shielded behind a thick glass cover with bars. There was no furniture in the room, just wooden-slatted walls and a wooden-blocked floor. It was uncomfortable, but the wood kept it from being cold.

When the fear eased, she had banged on the locked wooden door, but there had been no response, apart from the laughter of the guards who were stationed on the other side.

She sat in a corner facing the door, her lip now hurting badly. She tried to imagine what Adam would expect her to do, how he would want her to handle herself. She worked hard at it, at bringing herself under control, at pushing the fear back.

'Not easy for a middle-aged broad like me,' she joked to herself. Then she examined what she could of her singed hair, licked her cut lip better and tried to smooth her broken nails. At least she'd be half-presentable if they, whoever they were, came for her. If only Peter could see her now. And Gary? No doubt busy proving himself to his latest admirer. Damn you both. Damn you all. You don't matter any more. Then she cried for Adam, cried because she was suddenly frightened he was dead, cried for the loss of something she had only just found.

Then she finally controlled herself. Hardened herself. Framed her own mind in Adam's will and learnt to sit patiently and wait for whatever happened next.

Nine hours after she'd been bundled into the room, they unceremoniously dumped Adam in with her. The door was quickly opened and shut, and suddenly he was there with her.

His hair was matted to his scalp. His shirt had been ripped from his body and there were deep cuts across his back and under his arms. There were minute burn marks on his hands and on his shoulders. His trousers were still on, but the zip had been torn open, and there were few parts of his body that were not covered in bruises.

'Hi, Princess,' he said softly, his eyes warm through the puffiness of his swollen lids.

'Hi, tough guy.' She didn't know what else to say, she was horrified by what they had done to him.

He smiled. Then he passed out.

She rushed over to him, gathered him in her arms and held him to her. After some time, she lay him down on his back and checked his body. She found nothing broken and his breathing was regular. Then she licked his face, washed away some of the dirt and blood that spread across it, cooled the swelling round his eyes and cheeks. It seemed the natural thing to do. With her tongue she tried to wash off the blood that covered him. It seemed to work; her saliva and dampness helped his body fight the damage.

She did that for half an hour and he only came round for a short time. She didn't catch what he said – his words too soft and indistinct – but his half-grin told her it had smutty connotations. God knows what he thought in his dream world as he watched her licking his body.

The second time he came round, he suddenly pulled himself up into a sitting position. She could see him trying to concentrate, trying to control his mind and body, trying to focus. She moved away, left him in the corner of the room and stayed where he could see her clearly.

'No danger,' she said.

'Where are we?' He spoke painfully and slowly.

'Somewhere in their camp.' She cursed herself for stating the obvious, wished she had taken more note of where they had brought her. 'I'm sorry. I don't . . . ' She stopped, her inadequacy confused with her compassion for him. He looked so vulnerable, so damaged.

'I'm all right.' He understood her feelings and tried to reassure her. 'Have you been here all the time?'

'Yes.'

'And nothing happened?'

'Nothing. They just stuck me in here. I've seen no-one.'

He nodded, relieved that they had left her alone although he knew this business had only just started.

'What have they done to you?' she asked, now unable to hide her concern any longer, the tears starting to flow.

'Hey. Come on. Take it easy.' He moved towards her, his hands held out.

'No,' she blurted out, not wanting him to move, not wanting him to hurt himself. 'No. Keep still.'

'Really, I'm OK.' He tried to reassure her, but the pain was obvious. He slumped back into the corner.

They said nothing for a while; she controlling her emotions while he gathered his strength.

'What sort of building is this?' he asked eventually.

'How do you mean?'

'Is it in a big complex?'

'No. It's in the trees.'

'Brick or wooden?'

'Wooden.'

'Like a big Swiss chalet?'

'Yes.'

'I know it.' He didn't tell her that they had brought him here unconscious after torturing him in the main building. He didn't tell her how they had beaten him with plastic tubes filled with sand so that he would hurt and bruise without breaking his bones. Or how they had inflicted cuts with a small sharp knife, then sprinkled salt into the wounds and kicked him round the room so he had to twist sharply and feel the pain of the salt crystals in the raw open flesh. They had hosed him down after that, then poured urine over him. The next time he awoke, they blistered the back of his hands with cigarette burns, but this time, mercifully, he had passed out within ten minutes and didn't regain his senses for nearly two hours. Then they beat him with the pipes once again, but when they realized that he had managed to keep his secrets from them, that this small Englishman was not for talking, they turned on him in their fury and kicked and beat him until they feared they had killed him. Finally Kaas ordered his torturers to stop and they dragged Adam down to the wooden chalet and threw him in with Billie. Maybe that would soften the Englishman up, or give Kaas the opportunity to break the woman. It had been Frick's order that the girl should not be tortured. But now things were bound to change, once he found out that the Englishman hadn't been broken.

'They need to know why we are here,' Adam said. 'They seem as confused as we are. They don't seem to have any idea about who's behind these killings.'

'Do you believe them?'

'Got to. Why go through all this if they already have the answers? No, they need to keep us alive. Until they get their answers, anyway.'

'I won't be able to stand up to them like you, Adam.' She couldn't hide the fear that raged within her.

'It may not come to that.'

'If they couldn't extract anything out of you, then they're . . .'

'Don't let it get to you, Billie. All we've got to think about is how to get out of here.'

'Adam! How do you think . . . ?'

'It's not my intention to stay cooped up in here, waiting for them to go on with their little games.'

She started to laugh.

'What's so funny?' he asked, hoping that her mood didn't suddenly break into hysteria.

But she continued, her laughter growing until her body started to shake with the force of it. He didn't react, just watched her with deep concern. After a while she brought herself under control.

'You're priceless,' she said.

'Why?'

'Because you're sitting there, all beat up, in a real mess, can't even stand up, let alone walk, and all you can talk about is getting out of here. You're some tough guy, my love.'

'We'll be out of here.' There was a certainty in his tone that surprised her. She felt his strength reach out to her. Damn it, if he believed it, then why shouldn't she?

He moved towards her and cupped her face in his hands. Then he kissed her softly; they took the warmth of living from each other.

'They singed your hair,' he said.

'I thought you'd like it short.'

'Are you sure they didn't do anything?'

'No. They never touched me.'

'So, why's your lip cut?'

'Because I shouted at them. One of them slugged me to shut me up.'

'Big mouth.'

'Always was my problem.'

He held her for a while and they said nothing. Time was short and they needed each other's strength.

'Was Marcus with you?' she asked suddenly.

'You both were.' He didn't tell her how difficult it had been to withstand the pain they inflicted on him. He didn't tell her that he had been so worried about her that it had been hard to concentrate on sharing the hurt with Marcus, on blocking out the punishment they put him through.

Half an hour later the door clanged open and Kaas entered. He laughed when he saw them huddled together. But he was angry, having just been hauled over the coals by Kragan and Frick for not getting the Englishman to talk. He'd asked if he could work on the girl, but Frick had refused. If that ever got out, he'd have to worry about his public image. Kaas had said nothing, had just wondered what they would say about his public image if they ever discovered the extent of the terrorist acts he had unleashed in the last few months. The trouble with all these guys is that they had become too aware of their public image after Saddam Hussein's little escapade into Kuwait and

424

the atrocious acts his troops had performed. That was the difference between Kragan and Frick. Kragan would simply have done what was necessary. He would have found out what these two were up to by now.

'Pretty little lovebirds.' Kaas signalled two of the *Sturmab-teilungen* into the room. They moved past Kaas and grabbed Adam, wrenching him away from Billie. She screamed, but it had little effect, just added to the confusion that reigned in the room. Adam struggled, but he was too weak and the storm-troopers tore his trousers off, leaving him stark naked. Then they held him down, flat on his back, as another *Sturmabteilung* poured a bucket of salt over the Englishman. It stuck to Adam's body, burnt into the jigsaw of cuts that had been carved into his skin. Adam screamed, loud and violent, in his attempt to absorb the pain. The two storm-troopers who pinned him down now rubbed the salt all over his body, massaging it into his skin, tearing the cuts wider as they did so.

Billie hurled herself at them, tried to push them away from Adam, but the storm-trooper with the bucket hit her across the head with it, sent her sprawling backwards across the room. He then knelt down, took out his small, sharp penknife and cut into the fleshy area between Adam's toes. He picked up what salt was left in the bucket and rubbed it between them.

Then the guards were gone.

Billie crawled over to Adam, who was still yelling loudly, and knelt next to him, waiting for him to bring himself under control. It was five minutes before he stopped yelling, before he started to absorb the terrible pain that burnt through his flesh. Then she started to lick him again, slowly and deliber-ately, trying to absorb the salt from his wounds. She stemmed the flow of tears that came, knowing they would sting his body. With considerable difficulty, she tore a piece of cloth from her blouse and wetted it with her spittle. Slowly she worked on Adam's body. It would be a long task.

Vnukovo–2 Airport
Moscow

THE DIRECTOR WATCHED the President's Illyuishin Yakovlev YAK-40 tri-jet lift into the clear winter sky and turn westward for its flight to Berlin.

The arrangements had gone well. As Moscow's VIP airport, Vnukovo-2, was easy to police, security was not difficult here, but the Director was always nervous where his leader's safety was involved.

'I never like it when he's out of our jurisdiction,' he said, turning to Rostov.

'We've taken all the precautions we can.'

'Even so. There are too many hotheads running around these days. Too many people with old scores to settle. I never like it when any of our people go back into the old territories.'

'When I get back to the office, I'll double check all the arrangements.'

'It won't do any harm.'

They walked together down the corridor towards the exit, joining the small army of officials and *apparatchiks* who had come to see the President off and gain brownie points for so doing.

'Why do you think the Americans and British released the pictures of their agents to the media?'

'I don't know.'

The Director laughed. 'And you wouldn't tell me if you did.'

'I don't think they mean us any harm.'

'Who? The Americans or the two runners?'

'Any of them.'

'I hope you're right. These are historic times. Also nervous times. It wouldn't take much to shake everything up again.'

Rostov didn't answer. He already knew how delicate the balance of peace was, how slender the thread of hope. One bullet, one bomb in the right place, and the world could easily plunge back into its gloomy shadows of mistrust and attrition.

Dresdener *Heide*
Dresden

SHE CRADLED HIM to sleep in her lap. Her mouth was dry with the salt.

He'd stirred once as she licked him, came erect within seconds. She'd looked up at him and he'd grinned. So she'd quietly squeezed the love out of him with her hands and her mouth, wanting to help him take his mind off the hurt, wanting to be close to him. After that he'd slept and she'd continued her ministrations until her mouth was too dry, her saliva spent.

She watched him as he slept, so vulnerable as he tossed and turned. It was impossible to believe that this powerless and battered body could stand so much pain. Finally she'd dozed off.

He woke her nearly two hours later, softly so as not to alarm her.

'OK?' he asked.

She came awake quickly, trying to work out where she was. She was pleased to see him, but her expression turned to dismay when she recalled their predicament. She sat up suddenly, her mouth foul-tasting and dry.

'It's OK. Take it easy,' he comforted her.

She saw he had put his trousers back on and remembered why her mouth was so dry. She pulled herself upright, her tiredness rapidly evaporating.

'I'm fine,' she said. 'What're you up to?'

He grinned. 'Getting us out of here. But you're going to be miserable.'

'Why?'

'Because I needed your bracelet.'

She looked down at her hand and realized her gold Cartier Double C bracelet was missing. She looked up and saw that

Adam was holding it out to her. But it wasn't curved for her wrist any longer, but straight. The big C on the end had bent so it now formed a sharp arrowhead. She regretted its loss for a moment; it had been her favourite piece, a gift from Peter and happier days.

'That won't get us very far,' she said.

'This might.' He pulled a sliver of wood from inside his trouser leg, sharp and pointed and over eight inches long.

She was amazed; from nowhere he had produced two weapons. 'Where'd you get that from?' she asked.

He pointed at the wall next to the door, and she saw that he had prised it loose from one of the wooden slats, carved it out from the wall. 'With the help of your bracelet.'

'Mr Cartier will be most impressed. What next?'

'Wait for them.'

'Just like that?'

'Of course. There are other ways of waiting.'

'Like what?'

'I had a funny dream last night,' he grinned as he spoke, 'that you were doing more than just licking the salt off my body.'

She shook her head, then started to laugh. He was incorrigible.

'Why've they left us alone so long?' she asked.

'To soften us up. It's an old trick. If they've got time, they can leave people alone for days.'

'But they haven't got time with us. Not if they really don't know why we're here.'

'I realize that. They'll come at us harder this time.'

'I doubt if I can take it. I mean, the things they did to you. I don't know . . . ' She lapsed into silence.

He squeezed her reassuringly. She hadn't been trained for this; it wasn't part of her brief. He remembered the Gulf, the nightmares that the Iraqi soldiers had inflicted on the Kuwaiti women. He'd been sent in undercover before the American and Coalition troops had taken Kuwait City. He remembered one woman, hiding herself in shame in her own home, raped, her nipples bitten off, branded with a red-hot poker with the initial S across her thigh. She'd begged him to kill her, but he'd covered her with a blanket and stayed in the house with her while he waited for the Allied troops to take the city. Two of the soldiers had returned, no doubt for more pleasure at her expense. He'd killed them, slowly, with a knife. They lay, bleeding to death with gags in their mouths, with him and the woman watching. It had taken three hours for them to die. Three painful and tortuous hours. Then, when they were dead, she'd suddenly grabbed his knife and plunged it into herself. She'd looked up at him as she lay dying. And smiled. Damn woman, after days of not speaking, she had said thank you before she passed away. The Coalition troops had taken the city the next day.

'We'll be out of here before they touch you,' he said. 'Just remember, when I say run, or jump, or whatever, you just do it. Don't question it. Just do it.'

The *Sturmabteilungen* came for them an hour later.

They were both taken this time, bundled out of the small room into a larger one which led on to the corridor that Adam remembered. The corridor was bare, wooden-walled with only light switches and Halon gas fire-extinguisher levers. There was nothing he could use as a weapon, nothing to turn on his escort. He tried to keep between the five storm-troopers and Billie, tried to protect her from the roughness, but the salt between his toes rubbed into his flesh and made walking difficult and painful. One of the *Sturmabteilungen*, frustrated at the slow pace, stamped his heavy boot on Adam's bare feet, forcing him to cry out as he tried to hobble along faster.

The door at the end of the corridor was open. From it came the sound of a machine-gun firing, followed by the single pops of a silenced revolver. Adam and Billie were led into the room, a firing range that spread some forty metres. Kaas cradled the machine-gun; another storm-trooper was firing at a target with the revolver. He stopped as the couple came in.

Kaas walked across the range and signalled the *Sturma-bteilungen* to follow him with the prisoners. They entered the room at the far end, the room with no windows and reinforced walls. Two guards stood by it, fully armed.

The room had been changed since Frick and Kragan had watched the last exercise. There were now rows of seats, banked upwards in four levels, that ran in a semicircle around the left half of the room. In the middle there were two lecterns, a long table and six chairs. The banked rows had tailor's dummies seated in them, all dressed in suits, all blankly staring forward as if waiting to be conjured alive. Other tailor's dummies stood, in police uniform, at the free-standing doors that had been placed at the top of the banked sections. It was like a stage set, with actors frozen for ever, waiting to burst forth and speak their lines.

'Put them in their places,' ordered Kaas.

He watched as Adam and Billie were manhandled towards the lecterns and placed behind them. They found themselves facing the room, as if they were the speakers and the dummies the audience.

'Enjoy the game,' said Kaas, and signalled his men to leave the room.

Fuck you, Curly Top. Adam knew what was coming next. After all, this whole thing had started with the SAS. 'Keep still,' he hissed at Billie.

The lights went down, the whole scene was in semi-darkness.

'Whatever happens, keep absolutely still.'

'What's going to happen?' she asked as Kaas closed the door behind him.

'Nothing. As long as you keep absolutely still.'

'But . . .'

'Think about something. Anything that takes your mind off where we are.'

'What . . . ?'

'Think thirsty, Billie. Think about how much you want a drink. And don't think about anything else.' He hoped she'd do as he told her. He also hoped they weren't going to go further than he expected, that one of them wasn't a real target. If they were, then he didn't want Billie to see the danger that could end her life.

Nothing happened, there was just silence and her nervous breathing.

'Why sh . . . ?' She broke the silence.

'Think thirsty. Nothing else.'

Listen out, Marcus. Listen out for the bastards.

It was nearly another full minute before he heard the shuffling from behind the seats on the right.

They're not that good, Marcus. Bloody amateurs. Which is what makes this thing so dangerous.

'Think thirsty. Shut your eyes and ignore everything,' he whispered urgently to Billie. 'For God's sake, don't move. Whatever happens.'

The shuffling continued, spread out now, from behind the centre and left-hand seats.

I hope they know what they're doing, Marcus. I hope they know that they're only trying to scare us.

The stun grenade exploded from the left, ripping brilliant light and deafening sound into the chamber.

'Do as I said,' Adam shouted across to Billie. In the brightness he saw the shock on her face, but was relieved to see that she had her eyes tightly closed, her head angled downwards.

There was a second grenade from the right and, as it exploded, four men burst through the doors at the top of the stands, their Heckler and Koch HK54 sub-machine-guns aimed and blazing at their intended targets. This time the targets were three dummies on the right-hand seats and two on the left. The third targets were the two dummies at the table immediately behind the lecterns.

One of the attackers rushed at the lecterns and opened fire at short range on the two targets, the blast of repeating gunfire deafening. Adam, accepting finally that they were not the targets, looked back at Billie. Her eyes were still clamped shut, her lips moving fast as if in silent prayer. Bless you, darling. We'll be all right. *Think ahead, Marcus, think about how we're going to get out of here. This little performance is for show. Nothing else.*

He watched the gunman turn his HK54 on to the dummies and blast them to smithereens. Then the gunman threw something at Adam, something sharp that stuck into his flesh just above his heart. Before Adam could react, a final stun grenade went off, blinding him with its nearness.

When Adam opened his eyes, the gunmen had gone, the stage was empty except for the wafts of drifting smoke and

431

the disinterest of the lifeless dummies in this terrible rehearsal for death.

'OK,' he said to Billie. 'It's all right now. It's all right.'

She opened her eyes and looked around. That's when she screamed. 'You're bleeding.'

He looked down at his chest. The gunman had thrown a dart at him, with some sort of plastic sac attached to it, filled with red liquid. It had spread across his chest. 'I'm all right. It's only red ink.' He pulled the small dart from his chest as he replied and held it up to her, showed her it was harmless.'

'Why? What's going on?'

'Softening tactics. To scare you.'

'They did that.'

'Take it for what it was. Just to scare you.'

'I love you.'

'I love you, too.' He heard the main door open and the overhead light snapped on. 'Believe it, we're going to get out. When I say jump, jump.'

Before she could answer, Kaas had entered with three of his men, weapons pointed at them.

'Cool, eh, Englishman?' sneered Kaas as he reached the couple. 'Our tricks don't impress you.'

'Like your toys, do yo—'

Kaas lashed out, hitting Adam on the chest and sending him sprawling backwards against the table. 'I talk. Not you,' he shrieked. He signalled his men to grab Adam and pull him to his feet. When they had done as he ordered, he stood before Adam, his gun at his victim's throat, his voice shaking with rage. 'You've only lasted this long because of them. They won't let me go further. But even they will get impatient. All this here' – he waved his revolver round the room – 'is only a rehearsal. They'll get impatient because they need the answers before this game becomes real. Then I'll do things my way. But . . . ' he shrugged, 'we have to leave today. So, we must learn to speak faster. Eh. The Tiergarten won't wait for ever?' He jabbed the gun barrel into Adam's stomach, forcing him to double forward in pain. 'Bring him next door. Both of them. Let's beat the crap out of them.'

Kaas swung round and went up the banking, followed by the others who dragged Adam and Billie along.

When they got to the door, Adam stumbled and fell. As his two manhandlers tripped and tried to grab him again, Adam pulled the sliver of long wood from his trouser leg and drove it up into the heart of the first storm-trooper, killing him instantly. The wood snapped and the trooper staggered backwards and fell against Kaas, forcing him to the ground. Before any of the other storm-troopers could react, Adam had chopped Billie's escort to the ground and kicked a third with his outstep, breaking the guard's shin bone as he did. Then he grabbed her and pushed her through the door. As the others were reaching for their weapons, slow to react in their confusion, and Kaas was trying to lift himself out from under the storm-trooper, Adam pulled the lever of the Halon fire extinguisher.

The Halon gas, a bromotrifluoromethane, superpressurized to 360 PSI at 70°F with dry nitrogen gas, exploded out of the canisters that were fitted in the ceiling and instantly sucked out all the oxygen from the air. As Adam raced through the door and closed it behind him, he saw those left in the room gasping for breath. Shutting the door, he flicked the latch and locked them into the airlessness he had created. It wouldn't kill them, but it would certainly slow them down.

There was no-one in the firing range; Kaas had cleared the area while he went about his awful business. Adam couldn't see any weapons lying around, so he took Billie's arm and pulled her towards the exit door. He opened it carefully, but two armed *Sturmabteilungen* were standing there. They swung round, surprised at seeing him, and drew their sub-machine-guns level. He slammed the door before they could fire and bolted it. Then he led Billie back into the room. There was a small basin on the side wall, and Billie broke from him, rushed over to it and frantically started to drink from the tap.

'Don't drink too much, or you'll be sick,' he shouted at her, and pulled her away from the tap.

'I never thought water could be so—' she gasped.

'Come on,' he interrupted. 'Let's get out of here.'

From his left, someone opened fire with a sub-machine-gun

433

in an attempt to blast through the thick wooden door. So Curly Top, or one of his men, was still alive. From the right, as if in stereo, another gun chattered as the two guards at the entrance to the range also tried to smash their way through.

'What the hell did you do in there?' she asked as she followed him down to the sandbagged area.

'Put their fires out.'

'What?'

'Save it for later.'

He led her to the end of the range where the targets were lined up. There were no windows behind them, no obvious means of escape.

'Up there,' she said, pointing at the ceiling.

It was a trap door, a workman's entry into the roof.

Adam turned and ran to the other end of the range, grabbed one of the wooden chairs lined up there, and placed it under the trap door. He stood on it, and looked into the darkness of the roof tresses. Then he stepped down, signalled Billie on to the chair and helped her climb into the roof.

The door on the left burst open as he pulled himself up into the dark void. He heard the bullets thud into the woodwork of the ceiling as he closed the trap door and bolted it shut. The men underneath were firing into the ceiling, but the wood was too thick. Adam looked down the roof area. It was wide, an enormous football field of sloping roof and supporting tresses. He moved away, running on the boards towards a light at the far end. Billie followed him.

The light came from a skylight with a ledge below it. Adam opened it and looked out. It was a murky day, foggy and cold. Below him, standing at the side of the building, was a *Sturmabteilung*, who had crept off duty from the front door to have a quiet smoke. The gunshots hadn't concerned him; it wasn't unusual from the area of the firing range.

As Adam came out on to the ledge, the alarm bells shrilled, warning all storm-troopers that something had gone wrong. The *Sturmabteilung* quickly ground his cigarette in the sand, slipped his HK54 sub-machine gun off his shoulder and turned quickly to take up his position at the front door. It was too late. Adam had dropped on to him from the ledge. As the trooper staggered to get up, Adam drove the Cartier bracelet into his neck, through his voice box, severing the artery.

'Jump!' Adam shouted. More nervous about the automatic fire behind her than the height before her, Billie jumped without question. He caught her, softened her fall.

Then he took the HK54 from the dead guard, slipped off his boots and put them on himself, grabbed his topcoat and led Billie into the trees. This time he triggered off the alarm that surrounded the chalet, but he wasn't worried. It would be lost in the sound of the main klaxon that was already blaring through the camp.

'What's that?' asked Frick.

'I'll find out,' replied Kragan, picking up the phone on Frick's desk.

Frick turned back to Karl Schiller, the newest member of the council who had replaced Mitzer. The banker was stunned with what Frick had just told him. He knew they were on a dangerous course, but had never expected anything so drastic.

'Only you and Klaus Buhle know of our plans. And those who will fulfil our aims. A small team, specially trained by Kragan. Six in all. Nobody else will ever know.'

'What part do you wish me to play?' asked Schiller nervously. He wasn't being told because Frick liked him.

'When it is over, there will be chaos. Everyone will blame everyone else. The business community will be nervous, will not know which way to turn. They all think highly of you. You must divert attention away from us. Spread the blame. Spread the fear. And then point towards a new order, towards our party, towards the past that will help make Germany great again. Convince them that we are the unity of the future. That will be your part.'

Schiller was relieved. 'Did you know I was invited to the ceremony?' he asked.

'Yes. I hope you accepted.'

'Yes.'

'Good. That will help. To have been there. To describe it to your colleagues. It is a moment you will never forget, Karl. Even when your estates are returned to you from

435

the hands of the Jews.' Frick never let the pressure off. He knew greed was the banker's greatest motive. 'Even then, you will remember you were there when the course of history was changed in our favour.'

'Do you think they will listen to me?'

'Of course. They are good businessmen. Germany always comes first. Didn't Thyssen build arms factories for Saddam Hussein even though they had already signed an agreement not to do business with Israel? But they still did. And how many others helped in the manufacture and supply of chemical warfare plants? At the end of the day we must look after our own interests. We have always done that. That's why we have such greatness as a nation.'

Kragan slammed the phone down, his fury obvious.

'What's wrong?' asked Frick.

'They've escaped.' It was the last thing Kragan wanted to say, here, in front of Frick.

'The Englishman?'

'Yes. But they're in the compound. We'll find them quickly enough.'

He steeled himself for the torrent of abuse and vilification that followed, the usual harangue that Frick let loose when things went wrong. It lasted a full five minutes. Schiller was shocked, never having seen Frick in this manner. When it eventually died down, when Frick had expended himself, Kragan spoke.

'We'll find them. They can't be far.'

'They must not affect our plans.'

'They won't, Führer. They have no idea of what we're doing. And it's too late now. Our men leave today.'

'Kill them!' shrieked Frick. 'Kill them and then we won't have to worry about them. Give that order now.'

French Airspace

THE PRESIDENTIAL BOEING 747, Air Force One, had settled into its cruise when the DDI was told there was a call for him on the High Frequency set.

He went forward into the cockpit and the engineer vacated his seat so that the DDI could take the call.

'It's London, sir,' said the engineer handing over his headset.

The DDI nodded and put the headset on.

'Yes,' he said into the microphone.

'It's Charlie,' came Coy's scratchy voice over the HF receiver.

'Hi,' the DDI replied. He kept his voice low so the two pilots and the engineer couldn't hear. He wasn't worried about the conversation being overheard; he knew the HF system wasn't being recorded. But they would be overheard by the operator who had connected them through the international SELCAL network.

'Just wanted to confirm that everything's all right.'

'Great.' He knew that Coy had been speaking to their friend. Arrangements were obviously going ahead as planned.

'Anne' – that was Coy's wife's name – 'wanted me to thank you for the family pictures. But she thought some were missing from the folder.' So they still hadn't found the two agents.

'Sorry, I thought they were all there.'

'She gave me a real earful for not checking them with you.' Coy was letting the DDI know that he was under fire for releasing the picture of Adam. 'We made up, anyway. I said it won't happen again.'

The DDI laughed at Coy's pretend joke. 'Women, they're the same the world over,' he cracked back. 'Any idea where your kids are going on holiday?'

'Not yet.' Coy's answer told him that they had no idea where

Adam and Billie had got to, or what their reason for running was.

'Used the crapper yet?' added Coy.

'No comment.'

'Have a good trip.'

'So long.'

The DDI took off the headset and handed it over to the engineer, then went back to his seat, past the rows of media hounds.

What the hell were the two of them up to? Why had they run? Were they going to turn out to be the jokers in the pack, the wild cards that changed the game?

As he stared out of the window, Air Force One crossed into German airspace on its flight from Paris to the new capital of Germany, Berlin.

Dresdener *Heide*
Dresden

'Shoes are too big.'

'So, find a cobbler.'

'Got no change to pay him with.' Adam riposted back as he led her through the trees. He was heading towards the main complex; it wasn't where they would expect him to go.

'I'm sure you'll find something, tough guy.'

He stopped suddenly and pulled her down into the undergrowth.

'Kind'a sudden, isn't it?' she whispered in his ear.

He shook his head in mock amusement as a group of storm-troopers went past, at double march, towards the chalet. When Adam was satisfied they were clear, he rose and, with Billie following, moved towards the complex.

The fog helped; the visibility was down to twenty metres. The sun wasn't going to burn it off; it was too cold and there was too much cloud cover overhead. The damp from the bushes and moisture in the air helped cleanse the rest of the salt from his wounds. It was a cooling sensation and it was a welcome relief from the pain he had endured through the night. When they reached the complex, they found it was packed with storm-troopers being marshalled into search-parties. He realized he would need time, there was no way they would get out now.

'Come on,' he said, taking her hand. 'Change of plan.'

He worked his way round the complex and headed north, towards the hangars.

It took twenty minutes, twenty minutes of ducking and diving through the undergrowth and round the searching groups before he reached the building he had targeted.

It was the second of the hangars, and Adam, after ensuring that no-one saw them, let himself in through the side door.

'What's this?' asked Billie, looking round the building that was stacked with large wooden crates.

'Our safe house.' He walked deep into the hangar until he found a crate that was big enough for them both. With his gun butt, he levered the top off to reveal army jackets.

'Come the revolution,' she said behind him.

Adam then opened a second crate; this one was also packed with jackets. He swung round and emptied most of the contents from the first crate into the second, packed them down tight and then sealed it up again. He repeated the deed twice more until he had created enough space in the first crate for the two of them. In the third crate he had uncovered army trousers and he picked a pair that were his size. He tried a few more of the smaller cases until he found some khaki shirts, and he also chose one of those.

There was a commotion outside and he slammed the smaller box shut, then signalled Billie to climb into the first of the crates he had opened.

'In there?'

'In!' he commanded.

She climbed in and he followed, slipping the top over them as the door at the end opened and a group of *Sturmabteilungen* entered to search the hangar.

It took five minutes; the searchers were not as diligent as they should have been. In time Adam and Billie were left on their own. After another ten minutes, when Adam had checked that they hadn't left a guard, he settled back into the crate.

'I like this,' she said, snuggling up to him in the cramped area. 'What a way to spend our honeymoon.'

'I know. I really take you to the best places.' He winced in some pain as she squeezed against him, but he said nothing. He wanted her to relax, knew that she was frightened and was trying to lift herself out of her fear.

'How long do we stay here?'

'Until it's dark.'

'That's the rest of the day.'

'Till four. Unless we get a chance before then.'

'Any ideas on how we pass the time?'

'I'm sure we'll think of something.'

She heard him chuckle in the darkness.

'Shouldn't we be thinking about how we get out of here?' he said.

'You know us older women. Once we find something we want . . . ' she trailed off seductively as she spoke. 'Especially if we're going to spend the next eight or nine hours stuck in a small, confined space like this. How's the pain?'

'It'll hold out. You?'

'God knows. Terrified. But pleased to be with you, even if it's in a shoebox. Wondering what's next.'

'I don't hurt that much. If you're very careful.'

'I'll be careful,' she hushed softly into his ear, just before she started to nibble at his lobe. 'Is that careful enough?' she asked after a while, when her hand had brushed his hardness.

He grinned at her in the darkness, then turned his head and kissed her, softly, brushing her petal lips, probing her mouth gently with his tongue.

It was difficult, but no different to two youngsters in the rear seat of a Mini Minor, green-painted names splashed across the windscreen. Adam and Billie. Teenagers for ever, love in the teeth of death.

They undressed slowly, Adam slower than Billie because of

the cuts on his body. She helped him off with his coat and shirt, her top and bra already beside her.

She kissed him. 'Want some help with the shoes?' she purred at him.

'Shoes stay on,' he whispered.

'You can't . . .'

'I can. If we get interrupted, I don't want to be caught—'

'With your pants down,' she giggled.

'Are you taking this seriously or not?'

'Of course I am. We're in a box, with no room to move, in the dark, in a freezing cold hangar, with guys out there trying to kill us, we've been tortured and we're trying to make love with our boots on. And I presume that is your penis pressed against me, not one of your guns. Of course I'm taking it seriously, tough guy.'

'Good. Just wanted to make sure.' He laughed, then took her hand and let her stroke his hardness. 'I also want you to know that I'm serious.'

'So I see. Hey, you've got no zipper. Buttons. I never did it with buttons before.'

'Can you manage?'

'Oh, yeah. I'll get in even if I have to dynamite my way in.'

'Don't. Brings tears to my eyes.' He slipped his hand down and helped her pull her slacks down.

'Tough guys don't cry.'

When they were both ready, half-clothed, he started to pull her on to him. It was near impossible in the confined space, but they managed. She lay on top of him, her legs slightly parted and, as she kissed him, he entered her. Then all that mattered was that they were together.

In the dark she didn't worry about her body, about the sags and marks that creased her skin. In the dark she was for ever, a youthful eternity that was hers to share and give. To her, in the shadows, she was as she expected he would want her. But he never needed the darkness to know that she was perfection.

They moved very little, just felt each other in the dark, allowed their senses to do their loving. She started to moan and he put his hand over her mouth to quieten her. And they made

441

love like that, hardly moving, sensing everything, until they allowed their exhaustion to send them into a shallow sleep.

Billie woke suddenly, her left arm wrapped round his shoulder. She shuddered as she moved it, the pain shooting through it as she tried to slide her arm from under him.

'Pins and needles,' he said.

'Ow,' she complained as the pain refused to go away.

'Keep moving it around. It's the only way.'

'I know, I know.' She did as he told her, but the pain took nearly a full minute before it started to subside. 'What now?' she asked, still pumping her arm up and down.

'Get dressed.'

'Funny.' She smiled as she arranged her clothing, felt him adjust his. 'How long to go?' she asked eventually.

'Six hours.'

'You didn't sleep, did you, tough guy?'

'No.'

'We can't sit here for six hours.'

'Sat in worst places for longer.' He sensed her brooding and knew that the tension of doing nothing was getting to her. She was beginning to appreciate what a fun-fair duck in a shooting gallery felt like. 'Whatever they're up to, Curly Top said they were leaving today.' It was time to get her grey matter working, switch her thinking away from the trepidation that was churning her stomach.

'Curly Top?'

'Blondie. The chap who enjoyed his work so much.'

'Kaas.'

'That's his name?'

'That's what one of them called him.'

'I missed it.'

'At least I'm good for something. Don't you think they're going to get here and search this place?'

'Probably.'

'So, why are we staying here till dark?'

'Because they'd find us quicker somewhere else.'

'Whatever it is they're planning, it's obviously very important.'

'Curly Top said the Tiergarten wouldn't wait for ever.'

'When?'

'Just before we got away.'

'That's in Berlin.'

'I've heard the name. What is it?'

'A park. Like Central Park. In the middle of Berlin. It doesn't take much to work out that's where they're going.'

They got no further than that, even though Adam made Billie run over what she knew about the Tiergarten. It wasn't much, just that it was a big park and that it had been bombed heavily during the war. She remembered a story that all the trees had been cut down by the Berliners for fuel after the war and that it ran up to where the Wall had cut across the city. She recalled that a vast Japanese Embassy had stood there and that Hitler had held his biggest rallies in the park. The Victory Column is positioned in the middle which was partly built with cannon barrels used during the Franco-Prussian War. 'Erected in 1873, if I remember correctly,' she recalled. Then she laughed. 'That's really interesting stuff, isn't it? Some way of getting us out of here.'

The muffled banging in the distance alerted them.

He pulled her to him, then reached down and moved the HK54 into a position where he could use it quickly.

The banging continued, still at a distance. Occasionally, someone would shout, but the words were lost through the thickness of the crate.

'What if they . . . ?' she asked, alarmed as the sounds got closer.

'It's random. They won't have time to search every box. We'll be OK.' He comforted her. But the HK54 next to him was armed and ready.

The searchers missed them, left them safe in their bolt hole. Then the sounds were gone. The hangar returned to silence.

Twenty minutes later, Adam eased himself out of their tight shelter. There was no-one in the hangar and he worked his way carefully towards the door through which they had entered, dodging behind the crates for cover in case anyone suddenly entered the building. When he reached the door, he listened for any movement outside before turning the handle and opening it slightly.

It was a busy scene.

The runway area was guarded by armed *Sturmabteilungen*. The two Jet Ranger helicopters had been pulled out of the far hangar and sat parked next to the Citation jet, one of the twin-engined Pipers and the single-engined Cessna. A fuel bowser had just finished refuelling the second helicopter and was now backing away from the row of aircraft as two Jeeps and a black Mercedes came up the road from the main complex and stopped at the ramp, next to the parked aircraft.

Curly Top sat in the first Jeep and he swung out and walked back to the black Mercedes. His colleagues in the Jeeps, five of them, followed and lined up next to him, as a guard of honour for the passengers in the car. Adam noted that they were all out of the uniforms; that they wore civilian suits and overcoats.

Curly Top leant forward and opened the rear door of their Mercedes.

Adam recognized the first man who came out. It was Curly Top's superior, the bastard who'd kicked him round the room before they'd taken him off to be tortured. He saw the men salute him, then turn and wait for the next passenger.

Adam didn't know this one, but sensed he was important, that he was the man. The storm-troopers round the perimeter area snapped to attention, the guard of honour saluted in the old Nazi style. The Führer, as Adam dubbed him, returned the salute and walked towards the helicopters. The others fell in step behind him. When they reached the aircraft, the Führer turned to his men as they formed a semicircle round him.

They were over sixty metres from where Adam watched through the small gap in the door, too far to be overheard. But he could tell it was important, that the listeners hung on the Führer's every word. When the speech was over, he stepped forward and shook the hand of each member of the guard of honour.

The Jet Rangers started to turn their rotors as the final words were spoken. Then Curly Top and two of the men climbed into one helicopter, the other three into the second.

As the helicopters wound up their throttle, then lifted into the air, tilted to their left and swept away towards the north, the Führer and his deputy crossed over to the Citation jet and clambered in.

444

Four minutes later the small jet lifted off the runway and also turned to the north.

'No point hanging round here,' Adam said to Billie when he had returned to their hideaway. 'They've moved the pitch.'

'And the whole damn football team. Coaches and all,' replied Billie, after he had told her what happened.

'Time to move on.'

'What about, wait until it's dark?'

'Somebody changed the rules.'

'How do we get out of here?'

He grinned. 'Just leave it to the birds.'

The runway perimeter was deserted when they got to the entrance. He led her out of the hangar and towards the line of planes, keeping under the protection of the hangar walls. They could hear the roar of motor engines in the distance and the occasional shout, but no-one approached as they made their way to the ramp.

'You're putting me on,' she said, holding back as he took her arm and led her towards the aircraft.

'I've had lessons.'

'Lesson.'

'That was with two engines. This bird's only got one. Piece of cake.'

'I love you, Adam,' she said, digging her heels in and stopping him. 'But I'd like us to have a chance at living our lives. I don't think this is a good idea.'

'It's the only idea. As I said before, you've got to trust me.'

'Damn you, tough guy. This isn't a game.' She instantly regretted her words. 'You really take this "till death us do part" stuff seriously.'

'Come on,' he reassured her, knowing the fear had returned now she was out in the open. 'It's the easiest way out of here.'

He opened the door of the single-engined Cessna, a Skyhawk 172. He searched the panel and saw the key inserted in the starter switch. It looked similar to the Seneca he had flown with Jenny. Only this time there was only one throttle and one mixture control instead of the two that had confronted him on the twin. 'Come on,' he urged her, stepping back and helping her into the right-hand seat. Then he climbed into the left-hand one and pulled the door shut.

He knew time was against him. If the engine didn't start immediately, the sound would alert any storm-troopers in the vicinity. He tried to remember what Jenny Dale had taught him.

Battery. He hit the master switch and saw the instruments come to life. The fuel gauge read low, but enough to fly them out of here.

Magnetoes. He found the switch and turned them on.

Starter. Turn the key and bring the engine to life. He looked out of the window to check there were no storm-troopers near by. Satisfied that they were safe for the moment, he leant forward and turned on the key.

Grunch, grunch. Metal on metal. The engine turned but nothing happened. He looked across at Billie, but she was busily scanning the area for any intruders. Grunch, grunch, grunch. He turned it again, but the engine still refused to start.

Shit, Marcus. It's got to start. What have I forgotten?

'There's someone coming,' warned Billie, pointing to the south.

He looked up and saw two *Sturmabteilungen* about two hundred metres away. They were walking slowly towards the hangars, unaware of what was happening in the small plane.

Grunch, grunch.

'They're coming . . . ' The alarm was building in her voice.

Grunch, grunch.

What is it, Marcus? What . . . ?

'They're looking over this way,' she shouted.

The fuel. There's no bloody fuel. Of course the thing wouldn't start. He leant forward and pushed the mixture lever forward, then pushed the throttle to its idle position. Just as he remembered Jenny doing.

It fired as soon as he turned the key, burst into life as it caught the precious vapour and sparked the first explosion that moved the first cylinder.

'They've seen us,' she warned again.

'We're on our way,' he shouted back at her over the roar of the engine. He pushed the throttle forward, but the plane shuddered where it stood, refusing to move.

The brake. Kick it off. He looked down, found the small lever to his left, and twisted it free. The plane finally rolled forward.

He looked up and saw the two *Sturmabteilungen* frantically signalling to unseen colleagues. One of them was shouting into a hand-held radio transceiver.

He pulled the power back and pushed on the brakes. He was taxiing too fast. Then he steered the small aircraft as he had Jenny's Seneca, by the pedals which were linked to the front wheel.

He looked up as he reached the runway and saw that many more *Sturmabteilungen* had arrived. They were in general confusion, but some of them were running towards the aircraft.

He lined the Skyhawk up with the centreline and pushed the throttle towards the firewall. The engine surged to full power and the plane started to roll forward. In the distance he heard the rat-a-tat-tat of an automatic being fired. He heard Billie cursing and yelling at him, but he ignored it, concentrated on the task in hand.

He looked at the airspeed indicator and saw they were thundering along at over sixty knots. He wasn't sure what speed the small aircraft would fly at, so he waited while the speed increased and the runway threshold got nearer.

Rat-a-tat-tat. The firing was closer, only this time it was more than one gun.

Time to go, Marcus.

He pulled the yoke back and the nose lifted, held itself for a moment, then started to climb as the plane staggered into the air. He heard something crash into the side of the plane, heard Billie scream.

Attitude. He had to concentrate. That's what Jenny had said. Hold your attitude otherwise you'll flip her on to her back. He eased the yoke forward and held it as the Skyhawk climbed out over the trees, over the blue concrete wall that the Russians had built and now surrounded the *Heide*.

He looked for the altimeter. Five hundred feet. Then a

thousand. He was over the city now, over the houses and squat buildings of Dresden. The engine was starting to scream. He sensed there was too much throttle and he eased it back until it sounded right. Then he found the compass. He was heading south.

He started a gentle turn, remembering what she had taught him, remembering to watch the horizon and hold his attitude to it. The small Skyhawk settled into its level cruise. The compass told him they were heading north.

Billie said nothing. She left him alone to concentrate on his flight. She searched the cabin compartments until she found a map. She opened it, saw it was a topographic map showing the roads and rivers and towns as you would see them from the air. She found Dresden, flattened the map on her knees and tried to identify the countryside below them.

Berlin lay to the north and she knew there was more to come. She felt a pride in him. He'd said to trust him.

She heard him laugh.

'What's so funny?' she asked.

'I once told someone that if I had a wife, I'd get her to travel in planes with two children.'

'What?'

As he concentrated on his task, he told her of the young mother who'd flown with him on the jumbo from London to San Diego, to the place where he'd first met Billie.

'Sounds good,' she smiled when he'd finished. 'Get this thing down in one piece and we'll make it come true.' She suddenly hoped he wouldn't be disappointed if they found she was too old to have children.

'We'll make it,' he said. 'Piece of cake, this flying.'

Well done, tough guy. You done well. If only Peter could see her now. If only . . . ? She sighed.

All that was an eternity ago.

BOOK FIVE

Flames from the Past

Soviet War Memorial
Tiergarten
Berlin

THE DDI LEANT against the fender of the black Chevrolet
Impala and watched Hilsman and Gerbhart walk towards
him. Behind them was the curved Soviet War Memorial, still
guarded by Russian soldiers, on the Strasse des 17 Juni. The
Western Allies had allowed the Soviet Union to build it in
what was West Berlin, near the Brandenburg Gate, in 1946.
Constructed of marble taken from Hitler's headquarters, the
Reichskanzlei, it is flanked by two Second World War Russian
tanks.

'Did you know those two tanks were the first to enter
Berlin during the war?' shouted the ruddy-faced Hilsman.
'Some history, huh? If they'd been ours, they would have
been in Disneyworld by now.'

The DDI nodded. He didn't like Hilsman. He would have
preferred to have had his own Berlin Station Chief along. It
was easier to trust your own. But then he didn't like anyone
in the Secret Service. Their sole responsibility was protecting
the President. And they always acted as if that responsibility
gave them rights over every other service. The Secret Service
had earned that duty in 1894 when they detected a conspiracy
to assassinate President Grover Cleveland.

Gerbhart, the Berlin police inspector following Hilsman,
ignored the comment. He hated these bastards coming over
here and rubbing their noses in it. The war was long over
and Hitler was just a bad memory. If he had his way, he'd
tear down all these fucking monuments in his city.

'They stop here for fifteen minutes,' Hilsman went on. 'It's
a private ceremony. No public, just the Press.' He turned to
Gerbhart and pointed to a small group of trees on the opposite

451

side of the road. 'You need extra cover there. It's the sort of place a sniper could take cover. You got that?'

The policeman nodded and wrote in his notebook. He'd make sure nobody could move here when the two most powerful men in the world came to visit the memorial. Gerbhart had other problems. His Intelligence people had already told him there were going to be riots. Not here, but where they could get the most publicity. That's where the danger lay. Until then he'd just nod, take notes and make sure he covered his back. Just in case.

'OK,' said the DDI, opening the car door and getting in. 'Next stop for the grand finale.'

Hilsman followed him as Gerbhart climbed into the front seat and signalled the police driver to take them to the next location.

'Any more angles on your two runners?' asked Hilsman.

'No.' The DDI didn't want to discuss the matter further.

'Wouldn't have happened in our set-up. Shit, they could be up to anything. Even coming here.'

'There's no link between them and the President's visit.'

'Not a chance we can take.'

'Meaning?'

'Shoot to kill.'

'No way.'

'The only way. If they turn up here. Then they're up to no good.' Hilsman leant forward and spoke to Gerbhart. 'Those pictures in the paper. We need copies circulated to all your men. Identify and arrest. If they resist, don't take any chances.'

The DDI shook his head and looked out of the window. He saw the Brandenburg Gate in the distance. He remembered when the Wall had cut across it, remembered the now-defunct Checkpoint Charlie where he had personally supervised the exchange of agents between the Agency and the Russians. For all their horrors, they had been good days. Days of purpose. A good day's work done.

The Mercedes turned the corner and crossed the Square of the Republic. At the end of it stood their destination.

The vast grey building that was the Reichstag came into view.

Autobahn E6

THE LYCOMING ENGINE'S one hundred and sixty horses spluttered, coughed and died at three thousand feet.

'Damn!' muttered Adam under his breath as he tried to control the small Cessna as it wallowed in the sky, its airspeed bleeding off, its propellor suddenly still, useless and standing to attention. He pushed the yoke forward, forced the nose down and the little plane picked up speed again as it started its earthbound glide. 'See anywhere we can land?' he shouted.

'There's a freeway over there.' Billie pointed to her right and Adam saw the thin ribbon of tarmac that ran through the forest.

He swung the plane to the right and aimed the nose towards the autobahn. They descended towards the treetops, the roar of the engine now replaced by the hiss of the wind as they cut through the air.

'Brace yourself,' he said. 'It's tight.'

'You'll do it, tough guy.'

He wished he had the faith in himself that she had. He kept the nose down, lowered sufficiently to give them enough speed so that their descent wouldn't be too sharp. They seemed to hang for ever, suspended in the stillness of the rushing air, floating for ever until everything blurred into a final rush as the snow-pointed tops of the trees crashed into the fuselage and wheels under them, tearing at them, trying to pull them into the forest.

But the small Cessna broke the clawing hold and it slithered downward through the trees, its weight and momentum smashing through the branches as it fell through the tree line and towards the autobahn below. It hit the ground so hard that it felt as if the undercarriage would smash through the bottom of the fuselage and kill them.

But she held. Just settled into silence as a few branches and the falling snow enveloped them. Then there was nothing. Just their harsh breathing.

He tried to turn the handle of his door, but it was jammed. He knew they had to get out, in case the damn thing exploded. He twisted and leant over Billie, slammed at her door. It opened. 'Go!' he ordered. 'Go now! Move!'

She didn't need to be told, just went through the door and the snow and debris round her. She turned and looked back, saw he was behind her. He still carried the gun, loosely in his left hand, and she marvelled at his ability to let nothing interfere with his purpose. She kept running.

Then she heard him laughing. She swung round again and saw that he had stopped.

'Come on!' she shouted. 'Don't stop! Run!'

'It can't blow up. The fucking thing ran out of fuel.'

Then she started to laugh.

At that moment, the plane exploded, a great slash of a fireball erupted up into the trees, then vanished just as suddenly, leaving a deafening in their ears.

Billie had thrown herself to the ground and she looked to where Adam still stood. The bastard was still grinning.

'Just shows you how wrong you can be, eh?'

He held out his hand and helped her up, brushed off the snow that was caked to her. Then he put his arms around her.

A Trabant driver had seen the explosion and he pulled off the autobahn and down the gentle incline towards them. It was the only vehicle on that strip of road; the bad weather had kept most drivers at home or in their offices.

'What happened?' the driver shouted as he clambered out. A young man in his middle twenties, he wore a cheap, but new, brown shirt submerged by a wide garish flower-patterned tie. The suit was of a style long since gone; early Armani in its baggy shape. Over his shoulder he carried a portable phone in a plastic case, slung as one would a shoulder holster. 'What happened?' he repeated. 'Are you all right?'

Adam turned to face Armani Man and led Billie towards the car. 'We're fine,' he returned. 'Everything's OK.'

'What the hell happened?'

'Plane ran out of fuel. Couldn't make the road to land.' Adam walked Billie past the young man who gaped at the flaming wreck. 'Fucking fantastic.'

'We need to get out of here,' yelled Adam as he got to the little yellow car. 'Can you take us?'

'What about the police?' Armani Man asked as he caught them up.

'What about them?'

'Shouldn't we tell . . . ?' He stopped suddenly as he took in Adam's dishevelled appearance. 'You're a mess. You in the Army?'

'We have to get to Berlin.' Adam ignored the questions.

'You've a foreign accent.'

'British.'

'You on the run?'

'Look, just take us to Berlin.' Adam was impatient, wanted to get moving before any further traffic came upon them. 'We'll make it worth your while.'

Armani Man thought for a moment, then grinned. 'My mother always told me I'd get into trouble. Come on.'

Billie climbed into the back of the car, a two-door 501S. Adam and Armani Man sat in the front and the young German started up, fiddled with the strange little gear lever that disappeared into the dashboard, and wheeled the car back on to the main road.

'I'm Bernard,' he said as they headed north. 'You're lucky. I was going to Berlin anyway. Pissed off with the south. No bloody work. No bloody nothing. The price of Reunification. All everyone wants is a free fucking ride.'

'Thanks, anyway. I'm Adam. That's Billie.'

He looked backwards and acknowledged Billie who nodded back at him. 'You speak good German. For a foreigner. Why you on the run?'

'Not from the police. From people out to harm us.'

'I could've called the police.'

'No point complicating things. We'll sort it out in Berlin.'

'You look like shit.'

'I feel like shit.'

Bernard laughed. 'I don't suppose you've got any money.'

'Not on me. But I meant it when I said I'd make it worth your while.'

'That's the fucking trouble. No-one's got any money when you need it.'

The Trabant trundled towards Berlin, fifty kilometres to the north. Bernard talked as he drove, told them of his life in Cottbus, the town he had lived in all his life and was now leaving. It was a dreary story; a tale that was commonplace a million times over in modern Germany. After the hope came the despair. The search for jobs and a better future became a shuffling migration for millions in the East, and a bitter resentment for those in the West who saw their own future threatened, their own prosperity reduced. Bernard, after trying to earn a living dealing in anything he could buy and sell, had learnt the first harsh lesson of any would-be entrepreneur. If you want to sell something, you've got to have someone who wants to buy it. The simple law of supply and demand. And in Cottbus, like most towns in East Germany, money was for surviving, not for luxuries. Bernard's line of toiletries, including soft tissue paper for the bathroom, was considered by most a luxury.

'Three years. That's how long I stuck it out,' he rambled as the car sped north at sixty kilometres an hour, smoke belching out from its exhaust stack. 'Three years and all I've got to show for it is nothing. Just a bill from the company for all the stuff they supplied me with. If they want it back, they'll have to come and get it. It's all stacked up in my front room.'

'Why?' asked Billie.

'I had to go on ordering, didn't I?' He laughed. 'Otherwise they'd have stopped sending me the stuff. Perfumes, toilet papers, toilet brushes, toothbrushes. You name it, I got it. They thought I was selling a fortune. I thought if I kept ordering, built up my stock, then when things got better, I'd just go out and sell it all.'

'You should've stuck it out. Things always change.'

'Not when the wessie bailiffs arrive.'

'Wessie?'

'West Germans. We're Ossies. Reunification, my arse.'

'So, you ran?'

'Too right. You should've seen them. Big buggers. Nearly as big as the bill they wanted me to pay. I wasn't going to hang around and argue with them. Slammed the door in their face, jumped the back wall and headed for Berlin. Fuck Cottbus. Fuck them all.'

'You don't have a cigarette, do you?'

'Don't smoke. Used to. Can't afford them.'

'Doesn't this thing go any faster?' asked Adam, ignoring Billie's smug expression.

'Not unless you want to blow up. A Zwickau special. That's where they make them. They say the policy was to make them slow. That way they kept the crime figures down. Nobody could get away from the police.'

'So that's why you didn't call the police.'

'Everybody's on the run. That's Germany. Keep moving and maybe you'll make it. You can see why they went for Hitler, can't you?'

'No,' snapped Adam.

'All you see is what he did to the Jews. And the war. That wasn't good. But before that, then he was great. He gave Germany a pride. Filled people's bellies. Something to look forward to. Instead of the despair that people like my grandparents had. Then he went too far. Now, with all these riots, with all our troubles, we could do with someone like him.'

Adam said nothing; an argument would serve no purpose at this stage.

Half an hour later they drove into the outskirts of Berlin.

The streets were clear of snow and slush melted on the pavements. A few pedestrians slithered along as dusk turned to dark and the street lights built in brightness.

'Where do you want to be dropped?' asked Bernard.

'The Tiergarten. Do you know it?'

'Never been here before. Not even when they pulled the Wall down. But there's got to be a sign. That's where the Reichstag is. In the Tiergarten. It's where your people are going.'

'Who?'

'The President. The American President. And the Russkie.

They're here for the big ceremony at the Reichstag. With the whole Bundestag. A proper parliament for Germany. The first time since the place was burnt down. They say it was Hitler's people, you know. Crazy. Why would he burn it down? They arrested a Communist in the end. Blame Hitler for everything. Even . . . '

'What ceremony?' interjected Adam.

'Some trade treaty between Europe, America and Russia. The first step in a world market. That's what the papers say. Big, big deal. Can't be that good. Not with the Russians in it. They'll fuck it up like they fucked up the rest of us.'

'When is this ceremony?'

'Tomorrow sometime. Every bigwig in the world's going to be there.'

'That's it.' Adam turned and directed his remark in English to Billie. 'Got to be.'

'It's too big now,' replied Billie. 'We've got to pass it on.'

'Can't just walk up to the police. Not with Goodenache's murder around our necks. It'd take too long,' responded Adam.

'I thought you said the police weren't after you.' Bernard was suddenly concerned. They realized he understood English.

'Nothing we did,' Adam reassured him. He turned back to Billie. 'Go through the embassies. That's the only way. Contact our Intelligence people.' He pointed to the portable that was still slung round Bernard's neck. 'Let me use the phone.'

'Doesn't work.' Bernard shrugged. 'I stole it.'

'You're a bigger crook than . . . '

'If I'm going to be a businessman, then I need to look like one. At least I didn't murder anyone.'

'Neither did we. Look, we need to find where the British or American Embassies ar—'

A police siren cut across Adam as the green BMW it was attached to swung behind them, its blue light and flashing headlights insisting they pull over.

'Christ!' swore Adam.

'Maybe I should tell you. The car's also hot,' shrugged Bernard as he pulled into the kerb. 'Fucking bailiffs.'

The police car stopped in front of them. Adam turned and gave Billie a warning glance as two policemen climbed out and came towards them. Adam noticed one of them had unfastened his holster button; they weren't expecting trouble but they were prepared for it.

One of the policemen signalled Bernard out of the car.

'Stay put,' Adam told Billie as Bernard opened his door and clambered out.

'Licence!' demanded the policeman.

Bernard took out his driver's licence and handed it over.

'Where've you come from?' asked the second officer as his colleague examined the document.

'Leipzig,' lied Bernard.

'This isn't the Leipzig road.'

'Via Dresden. To see some friends.'

'Let's see your insurance and registration documents,' said the first policeman as he handed back the licence.

'I left them at home.'

'The law requires you carry them with you.'

'My mistake.'

'The rules are for your own good. You Ossies should understand that.'

'I'm sorry.'

'It is your car, isn't it?' As the first officer spoke, his colleague walked round to the passenger door and looked into the car. Adam and Billie smiled back.

'Of course.'

'What do you lot do?' asked the second officer across the top of the Trabant.

'I'm a salesman.'

'And your friends?'

Bernard paused. Maybe they didn't know the car was stolen. Maybe it had just been a routine check. Maybe the condition of his passengers had alerted the policemen. 'Friends. I picked them up in Dresden.'

The pause had been too long. The second policeman, now suspicious, leant down and opened the passenger door. 'Would you mind getting out. I'd like to run a check on the car.' Adam knew that was only a ploy. The check was on them.

'You stay here,' said the first policeman to Bernard. 'I'm going to radio in and run a computer check on the car,' he shouted across at his colleague as Adam and Billie stood on the pavement.

'Where're you from?' the first officer asked Adam.

'Dresden.' Adam saw the suspicion build in the policeman's eyes as he looked him over. *Christ, Marcus, I must look terrible. Unshaven, in army fatigues, ill-fitting boots. He probably thinks I'm a deserter.*

'You in the Army?' The policeman suddenly wondered if Adam really was a deserter.

'No.'

'You always dress like that?'

'It's cheap.'

'You're not German?'

'No. British. We're wandering around Europe.'

'Let's see your passport.'

'Not here. In Dresden.'

'Have you got yours?' he turned to Billie.

'No. It's with his.'

The policeman suddenly remembered his morning briefing. He cursed himself for not remembering, cursed his tiredness because he was about to go off duty. These were the two. The ones they'd been told to watch out for. He looked towards his partner and saw he was leaning inside the BMW, talking on the radio. He decided to wait for him. The Englishman could be dangerous. He smirked, felt smug, saw the door of promotion opening. 'All right,' he said. 'You don't need passports if you're community members. But you should always carry some identity. For your own good.'

'Fine,' smiled Adam. He knew he'd been recognized. 'Won't happen again.' Out of the corner of his eye he saw the first officer scramble out of the BMW, noted the sudden urgency in his movement.

'Hey,' he heard him shout across to Bernard. 'Did you say that car's yours?'

'Yes,' replied an anxious Bernard.

'Our computer says the car was stolen in Cottbus this morning.'

'Can't be.'

'Shit,' warned the officer next to Adam as he realized that

460

things were starting to go wrong. He reached for his revolver, but was too late. Adam had swung behind him, pinned his arms to his side and lifted out the revolver into his own hand. He stood behind the policeman and pointed the barrel straight at his temple.

'If you value your partner's life, don't draw your weapon,' he warned the other officer.

There was no hesitation. The policeman stopped where he was, his hands now held high. Behind him, on the pavement, a woman screamed and what few passers-by there were panicked away from the scene. One woman, her plastic shopping bag in her hand, stayed frozen to the spot under a lamppost near the BMW. She was too frightened to run away.

'Nothing to do with me,' shouted Bernard, turning and running down the street. 'Crazy people. I only gave them a lift.'

'Step away from the car,' ordered Adam, pushing his hostage in front of him, edging towards the BMW. 'Are the keys in?'

The policeman, with his hands still held high, moved away from the car. 'Yes,' he replied.

'Billie, get into the driver's seat. Start her up.'

Billie stepped out from behind him and walked quickly to the car. As she got to the open door, the second policeman suddenly flung himself at her, pulling her down into the road, drawing his pistol as he did. Adam fired at him, but, unused to the German police issue, Glock 17, 9mm and not wanting to hit Billie, he missed. His hostage started to struggle and Adam rammed the gun hard under his chin. The officer stopped battling as his partner dragged Billie towards the protection of the front of the car, his drawn gun now held at her body.

Bloody stand-off, Marcus.

'Let my partner go,' the policeman shouted. 'You can't win.'

Adam knew they wouldn't shoot Billie. It wasn't how they were trained. He pushed his hostage towards the open door, shielding himself from the other. Then he leant in and, with his free hand, turned the ignition key. 'Let her go,' he shouted to the second officer. 'I know you won't shoot her. But I'll kill this bastard. That's for sure.'

'Tell them,' argued Billie. 'Get them to call the embassy.'

'It won't work.'

'Please, Adam. It's the only way.'

'Can't take the chance. Let her go.' He pushed the gun harder into his hostage's chin. 'I've nothing to lose.' To reinforce his point, he swung the gun away and fired a shot towards the woman under the lamppost. He aimed to miss, but the policeman didn't know that. The shot ricocheted off the lamppost, harmlessly away from the sobbing woman who had shut her eyes and was praying to her God. 'I told you I've got nothing to lose.'

The policeman hesitated, then threw his gun away and stood up. Adam pushed his hostage away from the car. 'Hurry, Billie. Come on. Get in.'

But the policeman hadn't given in. As Adam closed his door, he leapt across the bonnet and dragged Billie down to the pavement, away from the car. A police siren blasted near by and Adam knew she was beyond help. His only hope lay in doing what he had always done. Resolve the problem himself. He knew she wouldn't be harmed, that once the CIA had her under their wing she would return to America. He had to go on. Then, when this was all concluded, he would seek her out.

He crunched the gear into first and pulled away. As he careered down the road he saw the policeman who had been his hostage pick up the revolver that his partner had thrown down and open fire. But he was too far away, his increasing speed carrying him to safety.

The last vision he had was of Billie screaming, her face turned towards him, the policeman still dragging her away.

I love you, Billie.

Look after her, Marcus.

Whatever happens, look after us both.

**Embassy of the United States of America
Neustädtische Kirchstrasse 4–5
1080 Berlin**

'THEY'VE PICKED UP the girl.'

'Who?'

'Berlin police.'

Hilsman looked pleased with himself, as if he had personally apprehended her. The message had been telephoned through by Gerbhart at police headquarters and the Secret Service man had taken great pleasure in letting the DDI know that he was the senior contact for the police.

'We want her here,' said the DDI.

'Not so easy.'

'Why not? She's our operative.'

'There's been too much fucking publicity. That's why. There was some shooting. That crazy Englishman. Blasting off at a crowd. The Press want to know what's going on. So do the cops.'

'We've got to talk to her.'

'When the dust's settled.'

'That could be too late.'

'Give it a couple of hours. Then we'll go down to the cop shop.'

'I don't want any German flatfoot listening in. This material's classified.'

'That's the only way they'll play ball.'

'Then pull some fucking strings.'

'We're doing what we can,' Hilsman replied huffily.

'It's not enough.'

'Look, you guys have screwed up. This whole mess is yours. The Germans are going to stick to their guns.'

'I don't want any cops there when I see her.'

'Why? What's going on here that I don't know about?'

'That's Agency business. If you want answers, you get clearance.'

'What's so special about this girl? What the hell does she know?'

The DDI said nothing. That was something that concerned him too. What the hell was going on? What the hell did the girl know?

He found out four hours later.

More than he thought, less than he feared.

The police had run a pretty thorough interrogation before they rang the embassy and told him, courtesy of Hilsman, to come over to the police station. They arrived one hour after midnight and were let in through the back door, as instructed. They waited in an ante-room for another twenty minutes before Gerbhart came in.

'I'm sorry to keep you so long,' he apologized insincerely, pulling up a chair to join them. 'But the Press . . . like dogs with a bone. They've gone now. Deadlines are past.'

'What's she said?' asked the DDI.

'Very little. Except that she wasn't involved in the murder at Nordhausen. And neither, according to her, was the Englishman.'

'Nothing else?'

'That she works for you and will only report to you.'

'Five hours to find that out. Christ, you could've called us earlier.'

Gerbhart had been under pressure from his superiors to hand the whole thing over to the Americans. He stood out against them; it went against the grain not to know what was going on. Bloody hell, it was his patch. 'It was difficult, what with the Press and everything.' He'd have persevered if his boss hadn't finally succumbed to pressure and ordered him to call the Americans. 'They found the Goodenache body and panicked. They knew him from America and he'd promised to show them the old rocket sites in the mountains. From the war. That's why they were there. They took off for Dresden.

464

While they were there, they saw their pictures in the paper. They left the hotel they were staying in – we checked that out – she's telling the truth – and decided to come to Berlin. She says they got mugged on the way. By some crazy Ossies.'

'Ossies?' asked Hilsman.

'East Germans. They were robbed and locked up in a house. She doesn't know where. They escaped and got a lift up here. They were heading for the American and British Embassies. What they didn't know, if she's telling the truth, is that it was a stolen car. That's why they were stopped by a police car.'

'That it?' came in the DDI.

'We have a full transcript for you to read.'

'Later. I want to see her now.'

'Certainly. I'll come in with—'

'Alone. As you were instructed.'

Gerbhart shrugged, then stood up. The DDI followed his example, Hilsman stayed where he was. His instructions were also specific. This was CIA territory.

'You're in big trouble,' the DDI said to Billie, after he showed her his credentials in the interrogation room. 'You look a mess.'

'I want something to eat,' she insisted.

'Later.'

'Now, damn it. I haven't eaten for nearly two days. You want me to starve to death in front of you?'

'Why didn't you ask the cops?'

'I did. Strong silent types. Easy to intimidate a woman.'

'OK, OK.' He went to the door and called for Gerbhart. When they'd arranged for some sandwiches, he closed the door again and searched the room for a listening device. Satisfied that it was clean, he pulled up a chair and sat across the table from Billie. 'Now tell me what happened. All the way from New Orleans.'

The only interruption was fifteen minutes later when a policeman knocked on the door and brought in some stale, curled-up-at-the-edges, cheese sandwiches and a flask of coffee. Billie was too hungry to notice and devoured the plateful that was in front of her. The DDI poured two cups from the flask and waited for her to finish. She continued her report over the coffee. The DDI never spoke, just registered what she said and made the occasional note so he could take her back over it at the end. It was nearly an hour before he spoke.

'You trust the Englishman?' was his first question.

'Yes,' she answered. Billie hadn't told him of their personal relationship, nor did she intend to. She didn't know the DDI already had a police report that her bed hadn't been slept in in Nordhausen. 'Why?'

'Don't you find it strange? I mean, just taking off like that. In New Orleans, after this guy, Fruit Juice. Then all the way over here.'

'No. Not when you know the man.'

'You don't know you weren't set up.'

'I wasn't.'

'Why are you so sure?'

'Because I am.'

'Anything personal between you two?'

'No.' She answered too quickly.

He decided to leave it. 'And you think they're going to try something tomorrow. At the Reichstag.'

'It all points to that.'

'Maybe. Do you think he's gone there?'

'Knowing him – yes.'

'OK. Let's go through it again. But this time we stop for questions.'

It took another hour before they were finished. Then the DDI left her, found Gerbhart and arranged for an hotel room, with police guards, for Billie. 'She says she wants some clothes,' he added.

'What sort of clothes?' asked the police chief.

'I don't know. Jeans, anything. Just clean clothes.'

He returned to Billie. 'You're staying at an hotel tonight.'

'I want to go to the Reichstag tomorrow,' she said.

'We'll see. The police haven't finished with you yet.'

'Do I tell them any more?'

'Nothing. You say it like you already did. And I don't want anyone else to know what you told me. I mean anyone. As far as you're concerned, this is just between us. Understand?'

'Yes.'

'Good.' He knew she'd follow his instructions. The last thing he wanted was anything that might change his plans.

Hilsman was still waiting for him when he returned to the ante-room. 'What she say?' he asked.

'Just what she told the police,' the DDI said. He then went on to tell Hilsman the truth about New Orleans and their flight to Europe. He never mentioned the Reichstag.

'What about the Englishman?'

'What about him? He'll probably show at the British Embassy.'

'He's armed.'

'Who said?'

'Gerbhart. They found the police car. Two revolvers in the trunk were missing. One of the cops is a marksman at a shooting club. He was going there after he came off duty.'

'I didn't know that.'

'His off-duty clothes were also missing.'

'Where'd they find . . . ?'

'Western end of the Tiergarten. The cops actually waved him through a security barrier. Parked about a mile from the Reichstag. With those clothes, it's going to be easy for him to become just another face in the crowd. If he shows up tomorrow.'

'Then we arrest him. Unless he pulls his weapons . . . Hell, we can't take that chance. I guess we'll just have to take him out.'

Square of the Republic
Tiergarten
Berlin

THE CROWD HAD been building since the early morning and, with only two hours to go, nearly a quarter of a million people filled the square. The crowd barriers had been positioned overnight and all around the square, police vehicles, including

467

riot-control vans, lined the side-roads. There had been a sudden snowfall overnight and the early morning street cleaners had wheeled out their snow ploughs and swept the four-centimetre-deep covering into deeper piles around the perimeter.

The square, a vast open area, ran up towards the elevated Reichstag. At its centre was a gargantuan arch supported by six stone pillars that reached the full height of the building. The carved legend '*DEM DEUTSCHEN VOLKE*' was a symbol for one people. The building had four great towers in each corner, representing the original states that had become one nation: Wurtenburg, Bayern, Sachsen and Prussia.

But the symbolism of the building, this badge of unity for the commentators and the television cameras, was not appreciated by many of the crowd who had gathered there. As with any large gathering, there were many different factions, many opposing viewpoints.

It was something Adam was aware of as he mixed with the crowd, moving steadily forward under cover of the jostling mass towards the front of the square. Most of the people were there for a day out, to touch history in their beloved Berlin. Mixing among them were the rabble-rousers and activists peddling their own brand of politics and reform. Some were quite harmless; the Greens and others who wanted to save the earth with their peaceful meandering agendas. But others, under the banners of reaction and revolution, were there to make their own brutal point in the name of whatever cause they believed was their right. He smelt the trouble brewing and knew the water cannons and riot batons would be in use before the day was finished.

Welcome to democracy, Marcus. See the freedom that they would bring, and destroy in the name of their own brand of freedom.

He kept his head bowed, knowing there would be plain-clothes police and other security people mixing with the crowds. The army fatigues had been replaced by the clothes he had found in the police car. He smiled as he remembered the sandwiches and hot flask of tea that had been rammed into the pockets of the thick leather jacket he now wore.

They'd been most welcome, as had the two revolvers that nestled under his trouser belt.

He had followed the signs to the Tiergarten, driving at breakneck speed, and he was lucky no patrol car had picked him up. A police barrier had been set up near the Tiergarten, but they waved him through. He realized that they were part of the security to seal off the area for tomorrow's ceremony. When he had come to the open parkland, he had driven off the road and parked among some trees. After forcing the boot open and finding his spoils, he had changed his clothing quickly and headed east, jogging through the sparse trees. His body was hurting, the cuts Kaas and his people had inflicted on him were very tender now. But he kept going and within twenty minutes he saw the Reichstag building. The snow had started by then and the whole scene, with the bright lights that emblazoned the building, was just like a Christmas card. He grinned when he saw it. *Still a fucking romantic, Marcus.* The square in front of the Reichstag was bright with the falling snow and he had kept in the trees, not wanting to be seen in the whiteness of it all. A high moon and a cloudless sky didn't help. In the distance he saw the police cars and the men working as they prepared the crowd barriers and the gantries for the television cameras.

The tree line had led him towards the enormous rounded sculpture of Henry Moore's Butterfly. He stopped and marvelled at it, its smoothness and size more impressive than the pictures he remembered of it. Behind the sculpture, across a small lake, was the House of Cultures of the World, an ugly 1957 building that had a curved dome, curved like a top lip with yellowed slats that ran down to the entrance. It was like a big mouth, permanently opened to reveal yellowed teeth. He wasn't to know, but to Berliners, the building was known as 'the smile in stone of Jimmy Carter'.

He had seen the tall obelisk through the trees, rising over sixty metres in the air. He crossed over towards it. It was a square building, some eight metres from corner to corner. The sign told him it was the 'GLOCKEN TURM', a bell-tower with sixty-two bells that had been given to the people of Berlin by the Mercedes Benz Motor Car Company. He grinned as he looked up at the tower. *Berlin's Big Benz, Marcus.* He laughed at his own joke, then wished Billie had been there to share it. She'd have enjoyed that.

It hadn't taken long to climb the large struts to the top. Apart from the pain in his body, the only cause for concern had been the surprise of the bells chiming. It had taken nearly five minutes for his hearing to return to normal. Once at the top, he had broken into the engineer's room, closed the door and settled down to enjoy the meal that had been prepared for the policeman. Finally, cold but no longer hungry, he had dropped off to sleep, his only companion being the hourly ringing of the bells. Midnight had been the worst.

Just before daylight, he had looked out of the small window at the square and the Reichstag. From there he worked out his plan of action. He had searched through the policeman's clothes and found his wallet and his police marksman's identity card. Fortunately there was no picture and he was pleased with his discovery.

At eight o'clock when the crowds had started to build, he had skimmed down the struts of the Big Benz and joined the mass. A few noticed him, but no-one was alarmed. They were all trying to get a good vantage point.

Adam finally stopped three deep from the front line. The police stood by the barriers, and beyond them, on the wide steps of the Reichstag, the podium waited for the leaders of the world to clasp their hands in friendship.

He stayed where he was, shielded by a big man who carried a child straddled on his shoulders for a better view. He saw the limousines arrive, one by one, depositing members of the Bundestag, the ministers, the diplomatic envoys, the honoured guests.

Christ, Marcus, there's going to be more of them inside than out here.

That was when he saw Kaas.

Among a group of reporters and cameramen waiting on the steps.

The bastards are inside. Whatever they're up to, it's going to be inside.

470

Then he remembered the room in the chalet, the benches laid out on the rostrum, the two lecterns he and Billie had been forced to stand at.

They were going to kill the President.

No, Marcus. They're going to kill both Presidents. And anyone else they can get.

Grand Hotel
Friedrichstrasse
Berlin

DESPITE HOW TIRED she was, Billie had found it impossible to sleep once she had climbed into the soft-mattressed bed. She could only think of Adam, of the danger he was in. And how much she missed him.

She eventually went and sat by the window and watched the dawn break over the housetops. Then she rang room service and ordered some coffee and a full English breakfast.

At nine o'clock there was a knock on the door. It was the DDI.

'See you've eaten,' he said, looking at the remains of her breakfast. 'Sleep all right?'

'No.'

'Can't blame you.'

'Have you found Adam?'

He shook his head. 'They found the car. Your friend was heading for the Reichstag.'

'If that's where the trouble is . . . that's where he'll go.'

'You could be wrong about him.'

'How?'

The DDI considered for a moment before he spoke. 'Ever hear of the Reichstag fire?'

'Yes. In the Thirties. Burnt down by a Communist.'

'Two Communists. 27 February 1933. Dimitrow and Torgler.

Sounds like an ice-skating team.' He saw she didn't appreciate the joke. 'That's what the Nazis claimed. They were found "Not Guilty" by the Supreme Court. Then they got a Dutchman, crazy guy, called Marinus van der Lubbe. He was found guilty and condemned to death. That judgement was overturned in 1982. The case is still officially open. The real theory is that Hitler's boys did it. They came into the Reichstag through an underground tunnel connected to the Air Ministry. Hermann Goering's Air Ministry. They just torched the place down. Then they accused the Reds. Their aim was to create chaos, then come in as the only party to lead Germany. They succeeded. On 28 February 1933 they introduced an emergency decree that gave them total control over the political system of this country. They even introduced the death penalty for a whole range of offences.'

'I see the connection. But what's that got to do with Adam?'

'These Nazis of yours . . . from Dresden. They're probably up to the same crazy scheme. We've checked the place out. It's definitely a training camp. Only it's registered as an executive survival course. We've got them in the States. Doesn't mean you're not right.'

'But Adam . . . '

'Could just be in on it.'

'Why torture him? If he's one of them?'

'All I'm saying is that nothing in life is what it seems. He could be working for someone else.'

'But the Nazis . . . if they're up to something you've got to stop them.'

'That's under control. We know where they are. But he's the joker in the deck. He could switch-hit on us and all our preparations would be blown. Then there really would be chaos.'

They said nothing for a while. It was Billie who spoke finally. 'Not Adam. Not him.'

'I hope you're right. Helluva chance for us to take, isn't it?'

'I don't know where he is.'

The DDI saw he wasn't going to get any further. 'I've agreed with the police that you stay here. You're still officially under their jurisdiction. They've got their men positioned

outside. Remember what I told you. Don't tell them any
more than they know already. OK?'

She nodded.

The DDI left her alone.

She thought he was going to the Reichstag.

He returned to the embassy building. There was no way he
was going to the Reichstag today.

Plenary Chamber
Reichstag
Berlin

FRICK AND SCHILLER looked down on the half-empty Plenary
Chamber from a public viewing gallery that ran the length of
the hall. It was filling slowly as members of the Bundestag took
their places. The President's podium and the two lecterns in
front of it were empty except for a sound technician who
was checking the microphones.

'Not long now,' said Schiller. It was he who had used his
influence and arranged an invitation for Frick and Kragan. He
knew Frick wanted to be there when history was made. He
knew Frick saw it as part of his destiny.

'We shall rebuild. This is the natural home for government,'
stated Frick. 'The natural home,' he repeated.

Kragan came along the gallery towards them.

'Ready?' asked Frick.

'As planned,' replied Kragan.

'Good. Time to take our seats.'

Square of the Republic
Tiergarten
Berlin

KAAS HAD ENTERED the Reichstag with the other reporters when Adam made his move.

An unruly group of agitators had moved up in the crowd, their banner declaring that they were members of the New Communist Peace Movement. Their antics were anything but peaceful as they pushed through, trampling a path to the front where they could be recognized easily by the television cameras.

Adam saw an undercover policeman infiltrate the group, his handcuffs ready to slip on to the leader. Adam came up behind him as the others in the New Communist Peace Movement turned their attention to him. Realizing he was about to be attacked by the others, the policeman now shouted for help as he reached into his back pocket for a revolver. But he was knocked down before he could pull it and the group set about kicking him on the ground. Those innocents in the crowd who were caught in the violence started to scream and scramble backwards to protect themselves.

Adam snatched the cuffs from the fallen policeman's hand, then turned on the attacking mob. Those nearest him were no match for his martial skills and as they backed away from his vicious attack, the policeman rose to his feet. Uniformed police were now pushing their way through the crowd to bring the situation under control.

'That one!' shouted the policeman who had been attacked. 'He's the leader. He's the one.'

Adam moved towards the youth who had been singled out, a tall thin man in his early thirties wearing jeans and a duffle coat. The man turned to run, but Adam was on him, easily knocking him to the ground.

'I got him,' he shouted as he handcuffed Duffle Coat and dragged him to his feet. 'I got the bastard.' He pushed his prisoner forward, towards the Reichstag. As they moved through the crowd, he fished the marksman's ID card from his pocket and flashed it to the uniformed guards on the crowd barriers. Behind him came the policeman who had initiated the arrest and he also flashed his ID.

The guards opened the barrier and let them through. Adam pulled the prisoner towards the police vans parked at the side of the Reichstag, just under the west tower.

'He's your collar,' said Adam, pushing the prisoner towards the other policeman. 'I'll catch up with your report later.'

'Thanks. For saving me from a beating.'

'Getting rough out there, isn't it?'

'Yeah. And it's going to get worse.'

The policeman hauled the prisoner towards an internment van as Adam walked away, down the ramp that led under the great steps at the front of the building. He crossed behind the police personnel buses that were parked there and looked into them as he walked down. He saw what he was looking for in the third bus and he climbed aboard. There was a pile of police topcoats on a seat. He tried on three of them before one fitted, then he left the bus and went down the ramp and under the door that led into the Reichstag. The armed policeman on duty nodded at him as he flashed his ID and he entered the door.

He was in the Reichstag.

As he entered he heard the roar of the crowd. The procession of limousines that carried the leaders of the European community, the Presidents of the United States and Russia had arrived.

Time's running out, Marcus. Things are coming to an end.

He quickened his pace as he reached the end of the corridor and climbed the wide stairs that led into the heart of the building.

Nobody challenged him; the excitement outside consumed everyone's attention.

Grand Hotel
Friedrichstrasse
Berlin

SHE STOOD AT the window, looking down at the traffic jam below.

The ceremony at the Reichstag had bottlenecked the rest of the city; diversions and frayed tempers had become the norm for the day.

Nobody had contacted her. She'd tried to leave the room, but the guards had stopped her. So she'd turned to what she was best at, what she was trained to do. She disseminated information, broke down the facts as she knew them.

It still didn't make sense. Except for one thing. It hadn't taken her long to realize the DDI had lied to her. The information she had given him had not been passed on. It wasn't the way the Agency worked. They were paranoid about information. By now, there should have been a team of de-briefers working with her; interrogating; probing; tricking; getting to the bottom of it. But there'd been no-one. Which meant they had their own plans; that they'd known what was going on all the time, ever since New Orleans.

The horrible alternative was that the DDI was working alone. Trouble was, she didn't know for which side.

She stared out of the window, could see the crowds in the distance in the expanse of space that was the Tiergarten. She couldn't see the Reichstag, only the Brandenburg Gate.

Be safe, Adam. Watch them. They're going to come at you from every side.

Then she knelt by the window and closed her eyes and tried to see him in her mind. She tried to communicate with him, to give him strength and warning. Finally, she started to pray, called upon a God she had long since ignored and forgotten. God wasn't the Californian way.

Behind her, the television screens showed the world leaders on the steps of the Reichstag, waving at the crowds as they climbed the great steps. When they had gone under the arch and through the entrance, the camera cut to the mass in the square. There was a sudden movement near the front and a tussle broke out between a group of policemen and some youths. Then it spread, more violent and more purposeful as it turned into a mob. A policeman collapsed, his face cut open by a flying brick. His colleagues pulled him to safety, and in their concern for him, lost their ground as the mob advanced.

Suddenly there was rioting.

The camera cut to the front of the building, to the great arch.

DEM DEUTSCHEN VOLKE.
For the German People.

Plenary Chamber
Reichstag
Berlin

THE PLENARY CHAMBER was full; all the members of the Bundestag had taken their positions. They stood in anticipation of the German President leading in his honoured guests.

The chamber was surrounded by four glass walls, a vast room within a room that was the Great Hall of the Reichstag. Two levels of viewing galleries ran round the chamber and looked down on this modern House of Parliament. These galleries were lined with chairs for guests to watch the ceremonies.

Adam stood at the top of the stairs that had led up from the lower level. He scanned the chamber, looking for Kaas or hoping to identify one of the others who had been in the chalet in Dresden. He saw no-one he recognized, so he moved along the wall, searching for the journalists' group that Kaas had been with. He soon identified the undercover security men scattered round the building. He decided to keep his distance from them. He knew most of them would have his photograph. As he moved he recalled the little charade they had played on him and Billie. There had been four of them, four armed gunmen bursting into the room with the lecterns and the banked seating, four of them playing their savage game of destruction.

He looked into the Plenary Chamber and saw the two lecterns, now empty in front of the President's chair and the raised dais where the clerks of the Parliament sat. The lecterns looked out on the banked chairs where the members sat on three sides of the hall.

This is where the two Presidents would speak.

If the rehearsal in Dresden was accurate, the attack would come when they were both at the lecterns.

Adam frantically tried to recall where the four attackers had come from. Kaas, he'd come from the left. He searched there, but there was no group of journalists. He looked up to the first gallery level. Apart from the excited guests there was only one television camera looking down on the chamber.

Two of the others had come from the right, close to each other. He turned his attention to that part of the hall. Once again there was no-one he recognized. The third had kept his distance, had fired from the back of the hall. He crossed the hall behind a line of anxious officials and climbed the stairs that led to the first level. As he did so, he looked out on the scene at the front of the Reichstag. He recognized the leaders coming into the hall, the Presidents of the United States and Russia as well as the British Prime Minister. The party had stopped there, shaking hands with ministers and other dignitaries. That would take some time. Adam guessed it would be at least ten minutes before they came to the lecterns. Behind them, out in the square, he could see a fight going on between the police and a group of protesters. More police were joining in and trying to bring it under control.

'Where are you going?' asked the uniformed policeman at the entrance to the stairs.

'There's a riot started outside,' he replied. 'I've been told to double check no troublemakers have slipped in upstairs.'

The policeman nodded and let him pass.

The stairway led on to the first-floor gallery. Behind the gallery there was a walled corridor with doors that led to offices and storage areas. The corridor was empty and Adam crossed it to the far side of the gallery. He opened the door carefully and looked out. The people in front of him were craning over the balcony, looking down on the chamber and trying to catch a glimpse of the welcoming ceremonies going on below them.

One of the two Russian security men saw the gap in the door and nudged his partner. They were some twenty metres away and they pushed their way through the small crowd towards Adam. The sudden movement attracted his eye and he quickly let the door close and ran down the corridor, trying each door as he did. The fourth one along was unlocked, a small broom cupboard, and he slid into it. As he did so, he tripped over something on the floor, but caught his balance and quickly closed the door behind him. Then he felt for the lock in the darkness, found a bolt and turned it. He stepped back and waited for the searchers.

The security men tried each door in the corridor, looked through the keyholes and worked their way down. They rattled the door of the cupboard, then moved past. Adam heard them talking in Russian. One of the men laughed. From their tone he gathered that it wasn't an incident they were taking that seriously, but one they had to investigate. A minute after silence had returned, and knowing he was short on time, he ran his hand along the wall, feeling for a light switch.

When he found it, he eased it on so as to avoid the click of the switch being heard.

The *Sturmabteilung* lay slumped in the corner, his right leg folded under his left, his head slumped sideways and down. Adam didn't need to see the red hole in the side of his head to know the man was already dead. He still clutched a revolver in his death grip.

Adam knew he was a storm-trooper, had recognized him immediately as one of Kaas' *Sturmabteilungen*, brought here to wreak destruction on the politicians of the world. Except someone else had wreaked destruction on him.

Adam searched through his pockets and found a press pass for the Frankfurt *Daily News*. He recalled that Kaas had also been with a team of journalists. So that's how they got in. There was nothing else, no further ID, no tags on the clothes. Kaas' men had come in prepared for the worst.

Three left. Including Kaas. Unless one of the others had come to the same fate.

No time to work out why. *Got to keep moving, Marcus. Ducking and diving. It's the only way out of trouble.*

He listened at the door, and when satisfied no-one was there, he softly unlocked it and let himself back into the corridor.

There were cheers now from the chamber. The leaders had entered and were getting the applause of the Bundestag members and the collected guests. Adam went to the end of the corridor and opened the door at the eastern end. Nobody saw him as he slipped on to the viewing gallery. The small crowd was leaning over the balcony, clapping and cheering with those below. Adam stood on tiptoe and looked down. The members of the Bundestag were standing and cheering the two Presidents. In their midst, leading them towards the podium and the two lecterns, was the President of the Bundestag and the German Chancellor. The other leaders of the European nations had moved forward and now stood on the podium behind the two lecterns.

Adam stepped back and looked round the gallery. There was nothing unusual there. He turned to go back into the corridor and take the stairs to the second floor. One of the guests at the far end pulled back from the balcony and turned towards him. He recognized Kragan at the same time that the Nazi saw him.

So the big boys were here. Adam didn't wait, just entered the corridor and climbed up to the second floor. Kragan would have to come after him; Adam knew the real danger came from Curly Top and his men. Except one of them was dead.

The scene on the second-floor gallery was a repeat of that of the floor below. He walked behind the crowds, moving fast, checking things out. Nothing unusual, nothing to alarm him. It was too high up anyway. He looked down on the scene again. The two Presidents were climbing the steps to their individual lecterns. The Bundestag members were in their seats, as were those on the first floor. Up here, this high up, the guests didn't return to their seats. They stayed at the balcony; it was the only way they could watch the ceremony.

Adam heard the President of the Bundestag start to speak, to ask for quiet, to introduce the two most powerful men in the world.

'It is a time of peace,' he said as he opened his introduction. 'A time when people are beginning to come together. When the people of Germany pulled the Wall down with their own hands, they unleashed on the world a glimpse of the future. But the future has to be fought for. It has to be won. Our Germany, this one Germany, can be the symbol of that future. A vision of hope risen from the ashes of the bombs. Sworn enemies, bitter enemies, reaching out to each other as friends. That is our legacy. Our duty. And those gathered in this room will rise to that task.'

Like hell, thought Adam as he looked over the edge, trying to see where the destruction would come from. Wipe this lot out and it's back to the barricades.

The President of the United States walked the final steps to his lectern; the Russian leader keeping abreast of him to his left. When they had reached their lecterns, the Russian President sat in the red-leather chair next to his whilst the American leader stood.

Cameras popped, the applause started again and the President of the Bundestag, smiling as a parent with unruly children, waved the gathering quiet once again.

'Two men of destiny,' he continued. 'First, the President of the United States of America.'

The cheers started again, and finally, nearly two minutes later, the American leader started to speak.

Adam had to get down, had to find where they would come from. He left the gallery and went down the stairs at the back, two at a time. If the rehearsal room was anything to go by, it had to be on the ground floor, had to be as it was set up at the chalet.

He hit the bottom floor when he heard the first shot. It was distant, through the closed door, but he knew where it had been aimed. Two more shots rang out before he could open the door and enter the Great Hall.

It was pandemonium. Screams, panic, people trampling everywhere. A policeman, his automatic drawn, was shouting at him, ordering him to help control the crowd. Adam ignored him and looked round the chamber. The shots had stopped. The Presidents were safe, both on the ground with security men on top of them, shielding them from the attackers. One of the officials lay dead behind them, his mouth open in permanent surprise.

Adam looked up and saw a red flag hanging from the top balcony, fluttering its red hammer and sickle at the assembly. As he looked down, he saw Kaas, his face half-hidden behind the long lens press camera he had been operating on the first floor. Adam sprinted back to the door and climbed the stairs.

As he came out on the corridor he saw one of the storm-troopers at the other end, a gun in his hand. A shot whistled by him as he drew his own automatic and rolled on to the floor, firing as he did so. His second shot knocked the *Sturmabteilung* down, slicing his face in half.

Still two left, Marcus. Who killed the first one?

He came to his feet quickly and moved down the corridor. He couldn't hear any more shooting, just the distant shouts and panic. Then the door opened at the end and the crowd rushed in, stampeded down the corridor as they fled in terror. Adam stepped back, fought to keep his balance against the rushing tide. Then he saw what had terrified them. The last of the *Sturmabteilungen* appeared at the door, his gun waving in his hand. But he wasn't firing, just fighting to keep on his feet, swaying out of balance. Adam lifted his gun, which further panicked the crowd, and he was knocked down. Then they were past him.

Adam raised his gun again, but never pulled the trigger. The *Sturmabteilung* suddenly burst forward, as if some giant hand had slammed into his back, and crashed on to the floor. He was dead before he hit it.

Then he felt the cold steel barrel against his temple.

'Drop it,' he heard Kragan say. The bastard had been among the fleeing crowd and then had come up behind Adam. And he was suddenly frightened. For the first time in his life the rush of fear coursed through his body. *No, Marcus. Not now.* And he saw his reason for living. Billie, Billie's sweet face before his eyes.

Kaas came in with two others, rushing through the door where the storm-trooper had just been killed. He'd seen the smaller one before. It was Frick, their leader. The other he didn't recognize. Kaas turned and quickly shut the door into the corridor, locked it with a key he carried.

Adam felt Kragan's gun ease the pressure on his temple.

'We've got to get out of here now,' shouted the one he didn't know.

'Schiller, control yourself!' screamed Frick. He turned to Kaas. 'You failed. They're all alive.'

Kaas ignored him and came level with Adam. Kaas grinned at him, then shook his head. He pulled his gun from his shoulder holster and lifted it slowly, pointing it at Adam's head. 'Goodbye, Englishman.'

Then he turned his hand and shot Kragan dead, just blew his face away.

Frick was screaming behind him as Kaas turned and the next bullet buried itself in his skull. Before his head had exploded with the impact, Schiller was shot in the back of his neck as he turned and tried to run away.

Then there were no more booms, no more noise, just the resonance of quiet returning. Someone started to hammer on the locked door. As Kaas turned, he saw Adam lift his gun towards him. 'Don't be stupid,' he said. 'Just go home, Englishman. And next time, don't play in someone else's game.'

Adam pulled himself to his feet as Kaas threw his gun down and walked to open the door. Adam was on his feet when the door was opened and the young policeman burst through.

'Everything's OK, it's—' Kaas started to explain.

'He's armed!' The policeman panicked, raising his HK54 sub-machine-gun towards Adam.

'No!' screamed Kaas, trying to knock the policeman's weapon away.

But the bullets exploded from the barrel, triggered by the policeman's jumpy finger; they sliced through Adam's waist, punctured him, threw him backwards with their impact.

'No!' yelled Kaas once more.

Marcus. Billie. Please, Marcus. Not now. I want to live. I want Billie. Not now, Marcus. There's got to be something more.

Then the shooting stopped and the corridor was silent once again for the second time in two minutes.

The face that Kaas saw looking back at him was still alive, a permanent question formed on Adam's lips as he tried to comprehend what had happened. It was always the same when those who didn't fear death finally died. The coming of death was real, yet so unexpected that it was beyond realization.

Kaas knelt down next to Adam and held his hand under the Englishman's head, tried to ease the pain of death with a look of warmth and understanding. He heard Adam speak, but couldn't make it out. He leant forward, tried to hear the words. But they were less than a whisper, blurred in the last few gasped breaths. He saw blackness of death sweep over as Adam was lost for ever. Kaas laid the Englishman's head gently on the floor and closed Adam's eyelids. He then took off his own coat and laid it over his head.

Pandemonium broke behind him as others burst into the small corridor.

He squeezed Adam's hand.

He hoped, one day, someone would do that to him, if he was ever to die in such an awful place.

A warrior deserved better.

Then he slid Adam's hand under the coat, got up and walked away.

They took Adam away in a black plastic body bag.

The stretcher squealed in protest down the corridor as the paramedics wheeled him away.

She saw the body bag being carried down the steps of the Reichstag.

She didn't know it was him.

484

She had waited for two hours watching the television, watching the scenes at the Reichstag. Then the DDI came and told her what had happened. She remembered the body bag and wondered if it had been him.

Then he told her the rest, and when he had finished, reminded her that she was still an operative in the CIA and that what she now knew was for her ears only.

'They're closing down your section in California. No point any more,' the DDI finished. 'But we're transferring you. More responsibility.'

She didn't reply. Somehow, her job didn't seem that important any longer.

The next day, Billie Wood flew home to California and the divorce lawyers who were waiting for her.

No mention was made on her record of her flight with the Englishman from New Orleans to Berlin.

That, as the DDI reminded her, was classified information.

The Church of Maria Regina Martyrum
Heckerdamm
Berlin

THE CROWDS HAD long since drifted away. The traffic jams were everyday jams, going nowhere, clearing up as quickly and as mysteriously as they had started.

Berlin, long used to the abnormal, had quickly returned to normal.

The Director felt uncomfortable as he entered the modern, rectangular church. He'd never trusted religion, always felt that a man's destiny lay in his own hands. That, after all, was the core of his Communist beliefs. He smiled to himself. He'd almost meant Communist religion.

Rostov was kneeling at the end of a long line of pews, his head bowed in prayer. The Director crossed the stone floor

485

and slid into the seat next to him. He leant back and waited for his Deputy to finish. As he did so, he looked round the simple, undecorated church. A concrete memorial, not at all pretty, not what he expected. They sat in the lower church; to the front and above them was the church proper, with the whole of the chancel wall covered with a fresco of an apocalyptic vision by Georg Meistermann.

Most of the worshippers and tourists were in the upper church; back here it was quiet, a place of peace.

Rostov finished his prayers, sat up and turned to his superior.

'I thought it wiser that we meet here, rather than at the embassy,' he said.

'I enjoyed the walk,' smiled the Director. 'The last time I was here we had that bloody great wall up. Always was a mistake. Nobody understood that we weren't just keeping their *shpion* out, we were keeping ours locked in. It made espionage very difficult. No, it was strange. To just walk in to West Berlin. No guards, nothing. Very strange.'

'This church was built in 1960.'

'Very symbolic.' He suddenly recalled where he had been when the Wall went up. It was like people always remembered where they were when Kennedy was assassinated.

'It was built in memory of those who were killed by Hitler when he came to power in 1933, and to the rest of the German dead up to 1945.'

'Even more symbolic.'

'This church is Roman Catholic. A place of confession.'

'Am I to be your priest?'

'A priest is bound by his vows never to disclose what he learns in the confessional.'

'Do they pass judgement?'

'If they do, they keep it to themselves.'

The Director laughed. 'Then I'll be a good priest. Too curious, my mother always said. I've always loved the intrigue.'

'You said I was to deal with it in my own way. That I stood alone.'

'It goes with the responsibility.' He didn't need to add that he himself had often stood alone, had risked all to carry out the unsaid orders of his superiors.

Rostov sighed deeply as he collected himself. Finally, with his head now facing the front, he started. 'When I was on the Washington Desk, a long time ago, I decided to understand my enemy. So I went out to the social functions, and, in time, got to know people who worked for Western Intelligence. Two of them, one American and one British, became good friends. We never crossed the lines of loyalty, but we often shared our hopes, our visions. Usually over a bottle of Scotch, or vodka or Jack Daniels.' He smiled. 'Even our drinking habits were of a partisan nature.'

'I, to my shame, have always preferred their beer to ours,' the old man said lightly.

Rostov picked up his story. 'I learnt a lot in those years. Because I understood them, it was easier to take them on when I came back to Moscow.'

'You stayed friends since?'

'The odd letter. The occasional Christmas card. That is, until this thing broke. I couldn't see what the Americans, or the British, could gain by attacking our sleeper agents. They're foolhardy, but they don't go out looking for trouble. Not their way.'

'When did you find out who it was?'

'When I interrogated Ivana Volkov.'

'The cypher clerk.'

'Yes. After the war she remained in Germany. Never wanted to come home. She fell in love with a German, a soldier. Worse, a Nazi. To save him from deportation, she managed to destroy his records. It was easy. She spoke German and she was in charge of the files. They lived together for years before he died of cancer. That's when she decided to return. But her ties had been forged. He, in his time, had been a high-ranking Nazi, I think at one of the concentration camps. She refused to say anything about that. But, like many of them in East Germany, he kept the Hitler dream alive. One of his closest friends was Grob Mitzer, the industrialist. Through her, and her occasional visits to Moscow, Mitzer and her lover kept their links with those over here, with the Lucy Ghosts. After all, they were after the same thing. To get back home and make Germany one again.'

'Who ordered her to burn the files?'

'Probably someone in Dresden. She wouldn't say. It doesn't matter. What does matter is that she was working for them, not for us.'

The Director didn't ask what had happened to the woman. It would have been a harsh sentence; treason had never been dealt with lightly in Russia.

'With the troubles going on in Germany,' continued Rostov, 'there's suddenly a real possibility that a strong, nationalistic political party could emerge once again. We knew there were neo-Nazi groups, but nothing as organized as this. So I went through our records, tried to find whose loyalty we could count on. I picked a young Stasi officer who had a tremendous reputation and had always kept in touch with us after Reunification. His name was Kaas. Luckily for us, the Nazi group he was involved with thought highly of him. It was he who told me of the reign of terror they were unleashing, he who told me of their plans.'

'Who killed our agent in Goose Bay? And the Americans'? I presume it had something to do with their German backgrounds.'

'Frick's people in Dresden. They decided to leave the Lucy Ghosts where they were, in hiding. They wanted to create chaos without being linked to supporters who had Nazi records. Some of the Lucy Ghosts were impatient. They saw the Unification of Germany as their chance. They were old, they weren't prepared to wait. So they were taken out. Even before he became leader.'

'Kushmann?'

'Assassinated. So that Frick would come to power. It went wrong. They hired an amateur. Someone who'd been in Angola. I think he was also meant to take out Trimmler, and possibly even Mitzer. We'll never know now. And, with regard to our agents, Frick's men never knew they were part of our organizations.'

The Director paused for a moment before asking the question that Rostov knew could spell his doom. 'And you told the Americans everything?'

'Old friendships are useful,' he answered eventually.

'Who in the CIA knew?'

'The Deputy Director of Intelligence. He may have told his Executive Director.'

'Or he may be telling him now?'

'Or he may be telling him now.' The point wasn't lost on Rostov. 'As with the British.'

'So the three of you, old friends, decided to resolve it yourself.'

'As I was asked to. By you.'

'Anyone else?'

'My assistant. And an operative in New Orleans. A cripple. But he had no idea of the scale of things.' He didn't add that Frankie Mistletoe was a double agent, one of the few still left in America. Rostov trusted the Americans up to a point, but always believed in keeping his options open.

'Why not simply pass the information on? Once you had it.' The Director knew the answer before he asked the question. That's why he had commissioned Rostov in the first place.

'Because once the authorities became involved, they would have made me pull back. They might have arrested one or two Nazis, but the organization would have simply gone underground.' He paused before he continued. His words were chilling. 'We took the decision to wipe out the organization. To kill their leaders. To leave them headless. Drastic measures were the only solution to bury this thing once and for all.'

'So you let them go on with their plans, let them enter the Reichstag before you acted. A most dangerous and risky move.'

'We didn't think so.'

'We?'

Rostov shrugged. 'Kaas was trusted by them and the best we had. He always had it under control. They never expected him to take them out. One by one.'

'Where is he now?'

'In Moscow. He wants to live there. And work for us.'

'A most dangerous move.' The old man repeated. 'But successful.' It was his way of giving praise.

'In the next few days, when the police have finished in Dresden, from leads and information we have supplied anonymously, the whole plot will become public knowledge.

489

Nazis setting out to destroy world leaders and take control of Germany. Just as Hitler did in 1933. It will horrify people. They won't come back.'

'They always come back. Eventually.'

'Not for a long time. It may also force the police to bring the other terrorist groups under control. It's the chance that peace needs.'

'Ever the philosopher. Ever the Christian.' The Director sat still, saying nothing for some considerable time. He watched a woman take a candle and light it, place it with the other candles. He wondered who she was praying for, who she was remembering. 'Why?' he asked finally. 'It's not up to us to make such decisions. It's up to our masters.'

'The politicians abdicated their responsibility during the Gulf War.'

'How?'

'Because they didn't destroy Saddam Hussein when they had the opportunity.'

'The Soviet Union supported him.'

'But we wanted him dead. And because he lived, because the politicians pulled us back, he turned on his own people and killed them, the Kurds and others, in their millions. While we were patting each other on the back, he was destroying a nation. The SAS or Special Forces should have taken him out.'

'Dangerous words.'

'We never learn from our mistakes. Churchill was right to bomb Dresden, to try and force Hitler into submission. But then, in the name of humanity, the Allies backed down. And Hitler fought on. How many hundreds of thousands of Russians did we lose then?'

'We don't make the decisions.'

'But we police them.'

The Director shrugged. In his heart he agreed with Rostov, but he could never voice that publicly. 'I want you to swear me, in this House of your God, that you will never step outside the bounds of your responsibility again.'

'Someone has to clear the dirt. Someone has to go on fighting.'

The Director sat back, sat stone still and watched people going forward to pray. 'The deaths of Trimmler and Goodenache. Very gruesome,' he said eventually.

'Not as we planned it. Not with Trimmler. Our man in New Orleans . . . '

'The taxi driver?'

'The taxi driver. He arranged the death. Cutting off the arms was purely a symbolic gesture by those he paid to accomplish the deed. They were local voodoo men. Apparently, the arms were not placed in the form of a swastika, but in the shape of an inverted cross.'

'And Goodenache?'

'That was deliberate. We knew our enemies by then.'

'Hmm.' He paused for some considerable time before he spoke again. 'You're not Robin Hood. Never cross the line. That's anarchy. Otherwise we become the masters, instead of the servants. Do I have your word?'

'Yes.'

'In this House of God?'

'In this House of God.'

'Good. Was the Englishman and his woman part of your plan?'

'No. That was cavalier action by the man. The woman simply followed him.'

'His death was unnecessary.'

'It was inevitable. My friend tells me he had the death-wish. If he hadn't died now, then he would have got himself killed somewhere else. He was of that type. An early and violent death, I am informed, was always his destiny.'

Woking Cemetery
Surrey

SHE FOUND THE four gravestones on the side of the hill, exactly where the gatekeeper had told her they would be. They looked different in the daylight, more real than when Adam had brought her here in the darkness.

You could tell one of the graves was fresh.

She carried four small posies, a mixture of simple flowers, forget-me-nots and daffodils. She knelt down and placed one each where his parents lay. Then she crossed to the third grave and stood for a while before it.

MARCUS JAMES NICHOLSON. AGED NINE. BELOVED SON OF HENRY AND MARGARET AND BELOVED BROTHER OF ADAM. Underneath, much smaller in its print was the inscription, THE GODS LOVE THOSE WHO DIE YOUNG.

'Hallo, Marcus,' she said, the sob already in her throat. 'L . . .look after him. Please. He always needed you. Tell him he's not all bad.' After some time, she knelt once again and put the third posy on his grave.

Then she turned to the fourth.

It was why she had come, yet it took a long time before she had the courage to take the few steps that led her to him.

ADAM JEREMY NICHOLSON. AGED THIRTY-TWO. BELOVED SON OF HENRY AND MARGARET AND BELOVED BROTHER OF MARCUS. There was no further inscription underneath. It was as she and Lily thought he would want it.

She knelt down and placed the last posy on his grave. She stayed kneeling, looking hard at the headstone, still not believing he was really dead, trying to force some spirit to speak to her.

Nothing. Just her loneliness and her want.

'Lily's OK,' she said. 'I tried to get her to come back

to California, but she said no. I'll keep in touch with her, make sure she's not too alone.'

But who'll do that for me? Now that you've gone.

'I've paid for her house and anything else she needs. Out of the money.' She felt the tears dampen her cheeks. He'd left the will on his dressing table in the flat, addressed to his solicitor, when they'd shared that first night of love together.

'Don't laugh at me,' she cried. 'I can't help missing you. I'd rather have you than the money.'

Another mourner from the next row of graves left his wife and came over to her as she sobbed.

'You all right, miss?' asked the concerned visitor.

She nodded, tried to stop her tears. But she couldn't.

'We lost our boy,' the man went on. 'Only sixteen. You're not alone, you know. It happens to everyone. We all have our own grief.'

She stood up, and he held out a supporting hand for her as she stumbled.

She looked up at him; he had a kind face.

'And always will, I suppose,' he said wistfully. 'Well, I better get back to my missus.'

'Thank you,' she said.

She knew then that she would always love Adam. He would always be inside her. Such a short time together, such a long time to go.

'Bye, tough guy.'

She knew she'd be back.

She turned and walked slowly down the hill.